W9-CAU-642

HEROIC WOMEN OF FAITH

SHIPWRECK

Brenda Wilbee

HARVEST HOUSE PUBLISHERS
Eugene, Oregon 97402

Scripture quotations are from the King James Version of the Bible.

SHIPWRECK!

Copyright © 1991 by Harvest House Publishers
Eugene, Oregon 97402

Library of Congress Cataloging-in-Publication Data

Wilbee, Brenda.
        Shipwreck! / Brenda Wilbee.
            (Heroic women of faith series ; bk.1)
        ISBN 0-89081-858-4
            1. Wooldridge, Emily—Fiction. 2 Shipwrecks—Cape Horn—
Staten Island—History—Fiction. 3. Staten Island (Argentina/
Cape Horn)—History—Fiction.
I. Title. II. Series.
PS3573.I3877S48   1991
813'.54——dc20   91-10768
                                                                        CIP

Printed in the United States of America.

First Hardcover Edition for Family Bookshelf: 1992

*To Russ Karns,
sailor and friend!*

Acknowledgments

My biggest thanks go to RUSS KARNS, not only for giving me Emily's journal, and thus the story, but more for his expertise in the life of the sea and seafaring vessels. A man who can build his own sailboat is not always a man who can wade through the tangled riffraff of a first draft, but such a man is Russ Karns. Everything from the sounding of the ship bells to dialogue to the structure of the brigantine itself, Russ reviewed and redid. To him I owe a great debt.

I also owe a hearty thanks to my mother, BETTY WILBEE, not just for hauling scores of seafaring books back and forth between my front stoop and the library, but for her takeover of the mundane in my life, such as buying the yogurt my kids like and taking back Blake's shorts that I bought too small. To anyone but a single mom trying to make a living writing stories this might sound trite, but thanks, Mum.

A big thank-you goes to my neighbor, CHARLIE WATSON, surrogate mum to my kids, and always handy for a cup of flour, spare eggs, ketchup, and popcorn.

I thank my daughter, HEATHER KENT, for her consistent and brilliant editing advice. It was she who threw out my first three chapters and told me I must, simply must, switch from first person to third because, "Mom! Nothing's happening stuck up inside her head!"

ROY CARLISLE of Page Mill Press must be thanked not just for teaching me the dynamics of the male mind, but for laughing at my naivete, and for helping me develop the psychological dimensions of my men, 1870 sailors of the sea.

I thank twice ALAN BASHAM. Once for stripping my plot to three archetypal motifs that I might have a hinge upon which to swing my "men." Then twice for flattery. Nay, thrice, for reminding me I always come through.

I thank my friend MOLLY GLASS, author of the Highland Series, for translating my Scotsman's English into brogue.

I owe everything to LAURA KALPAKIAN, and perhaps Harvest House for hiring her, for she has become my very own editing specialist. Swift and unerring in her ability, she rescued this book from the drink, "drowning as it was," as she says, "in the trivia of minutia." Tut, tut, but true.

And finally I thank EILEEN MASON, Vice President of Editorial at Harvest House for going the second and third mile. Oh, that everyone should have someone like Eileen who believes, without doubt, in them!

Foreword

Christmas 1988, a drizzly wet night, my neighbor Russ Karns knocked on the door. He held in his hands two bright boxes for my sons, and a library book for me. Phillip and Blake were delighted to receive so fancy a package from their adopted grandfather, shiny red and green with snowmen and glass balls. And I? Coming from Russ I knew my gift had to be extraordinary.

"I came across this story, Brenda," he told me. "I couldn't put it down. It's a woman's journal of a shipwreck in 1870, and I thought you might like to read it before I take it back to the library."

"Yes, I think so," I said, and while winter rain turned to snow I sailed back in time 120 years, to the very end of the world and to the edge ... emotionally, physically, and spiritually. I too could not put the book down.

Into the wee hours of the morning I sat, turning page after page while outside the wind whistled and inside the fire winked out, and when I came at last to the end, the hush of winter's night wrapping my house, I knew I had another book I just *had* to write—the courageous story of one Emily Wooldridge.

I wanted to write her story in novel form, to translate narrative into scene, not just because it's such a terrific story and warrants a wider audience, but because there are so many of us who live shipwrecked lives, cast upon barren shores and left, we think, to die. But like Emily, in the resolve to live we discover, when push comes to shove, an unknown strength within. Against all odds we triumph. Our shattered faith is restored, our enemies subdued. Loved ones die but loved ones survive, and through it all we learn and grow and suffer and win. And by reading the true story of Emily Wooldridge, we read the inner story of ourselves.

Mrs. Wooldridge's original journal passed into the hands of her doctor before she died in the early 1920's. He in turn passed it into the hands of another of his patients, Laurence Irving. Mr. Irving published it with MacMillan in 1953, and it was this edited and illustrated version that passed into the hands of my neighbor who gave it to me for a Christmas gift: *The Wreck of the Maid of Athens*.

And so by writing *Shipwreck!* I hope to pass the story on yet again, putting into your hands what Russ gave to me, and let you feel the biting wind, the raging fire, the storm-tossed waves, and grief so great you fear your sanity. For in the end we learn that God lives not in the air and earth and fire, in the great tragedies that surround. We learn instead that God lives in the after, in the broken pieces of our lives.

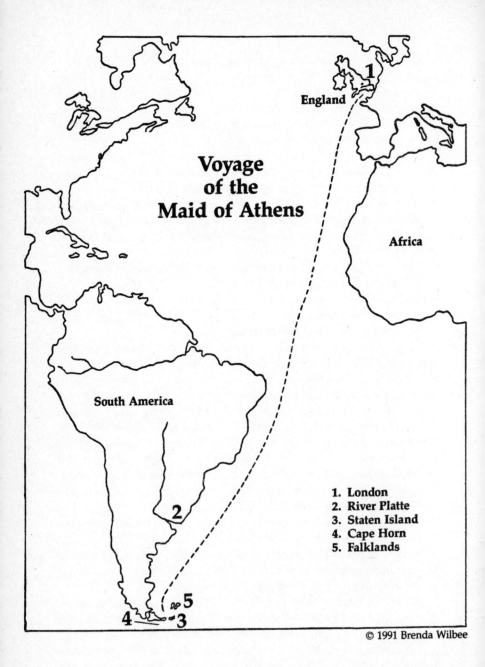

Voyage
of the
Maid of Athens

England

Africa

South America

1. London
2. River Platte
3. Staten Island
4. Cape Horn
5. Falklands

© 1991 Brenda Wilbee

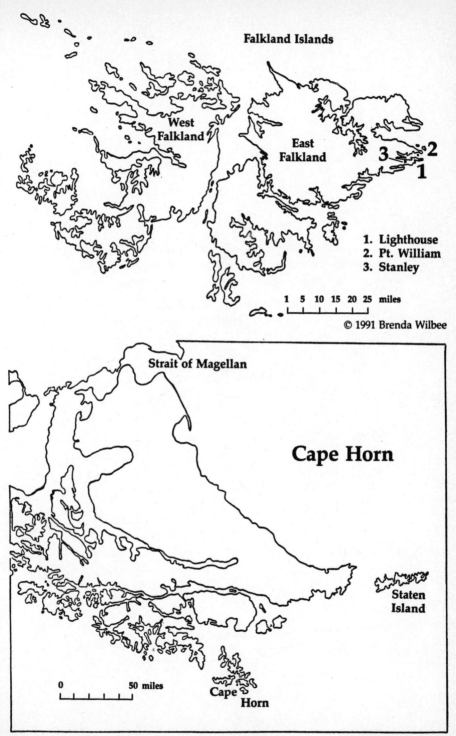

Falkland Islands

West
Falkland

East
Falkland

3 2
1

1. Lighthouse
2. Pt. William
3. Stanley

1 5 10 15 20 25 miles

© 1991 Brenda Wilbee

Strait of Magellan

Cape Horn

Staten
Island

0   50 miles

Cape
Horn

© 1991 Brenda Wilbee

I have so many friends, all of whom want me to tell them some of my wonderful adventures. I am going to try and please them. . . .

Emily Wooldridge
The Wreck of the Maid of Athens

Part 1

Up Anchors, A-Hoy!

1

A life in the ocean wave!
A home on the rolling deep—

—Byron Proctor

Emily Wooldridge stood beside her husband on the deck of their brigantine, the *Maid of Athens*, shivering in the evening dampness of a London fog. She watched in disbelief as their crew was hauled aboard, slung like cargo over the shoulder of a brawny rigger and dumped unceremoniously down into the forecastle at the bow of the ship. They were drunk, every last one of them, and all unconscious. "There, that be the last of 'em," said the rigger cheerfully. "A bit too much to swallow, I see, but they'll be fine once they come to. I deliver good crews, Captain, sir."

Captain Richard Gurney Wooldridge nodded grimly. "And did they sign on knowingly, willingly . . . soberly?"

The rigger ignored the Captain's sarcasm. "They come with experience, every last one of 'em. So see here, here's the Set of Articles, legally signed according to Port law. Ye sign 'ere, Captain, sir."

With a tight lip and low eyes, Richard Gurney Wooldridge began to study the papers thrust at him, bracing them over a knee. "One's missing," he said just as two more men lurched up the gangplank, one scruffy-necked and singing a sea chantey, the other clean-shaven and tidy and doing his best to pull the drunk along.

11

"Ah!" exclaimed the rigger. "Here comes the shipping master now, with your man. If you'll just finish your signature we can settle the advance."

But Captain Wooldridge put away his pen, slapped the document against his thigh, and marched across the main deck to the gangway. "Name and rank?" he demanded of the scruffy man, voice deep.

"John Harris," said the sailor, sobering instantly. "Seaman, Captain, sir!"

"Fall in and explain yourself!"

A slightly built man with cheeks dappled by a sparse blond beard, the man had an insolent, surly air about him. He wore the usual uniform: white duck trousers tight about the hips and hanging long and loose at his feet; a bulky checked shirt; dark, navy jacket with gold buttons, unsnapped; black tarpaulin hat worn on the back of his head. His boots were encrusted with London's mud. One boot he thrust forward; he brought the other up to match. Thud, thud, echoing thumps against the deck. "My apologies, sir! The boarding house, sir, put something, I think, in the rum. At least it feels like it," he added, grinning boldly, lips twisting to the left cheek to reveal good teeth, and pressing his temples between thumb and middle finger. "It'll not happen again, sir. *Hic.*" Suddenly he leaped backward, astonished. "A woman?" He crashed into the shipping master. "I ain't shipping out with no bloody woman! No, sir, I ain't a king's fool—"

"That's enough!" said Richard Wooldridge. "Another word and you'll be swabbing the decks—"

"Now, now," wheedled Mr. Lowry, the shipping master, "sailors will be sailors—you know how it goes. They do have their superstitions. You've signed the Articles? No?"

"No," said the Captain dryly, and because the sun was going down he moved to where the light from the galley allowed him to read. "So you've delivered the six. *Bosun:*

Lawrence Jay. *Seamen:* John Harris, George Hayward, David Lawson, William Oates. *Ordinary Seaman:* James Fielding." Suddenly he stiffened. "The two months' advance payable to *you?*" he queried, lifting the papers closer to the light. "Lowry and Sons Shipping? I thought payable to the men's families. That was the deal we struck, was it not?"

"Yes, well, it was," admitted Mr. Lowry, "but there's been a slight problem." He clicked his heels together when the Captain turned about-face and started for the poop deck astern the ship. "They've run up a bill," he explained, hopping after the Captain and plunging down the companionway stairs in his shadow, "at some of the boarding houses, and . . ."

The Captain entered the dining saloon. "Save your breath. You and the boarding houses run a well-greased ring, preying on weak men just in from sea, pockets full of pay. Sit down, Mr. Lowry. You send out your sharks, like that rigger on deck, to entice the land-starved men into the nearest boarding house for drinks and cards. Flies in a web. Oh, yes, I know how it works. But I had hoped, since I'd specifically asked that the advance of two months' wages be sent directly to their families, that you would do so—on your word. But no, you and your thugs saw to it, as always, that the families will see nary a farthing, for you must, I swear, fleece them all!"

"Nonsense!" said Lowry, squaring his chest.

The Captain began circling the table, hands behind his back, jiggling the papers. He was a young man, 35, and powerfully built; tall, with shoulders that rivaled Hercules. His head, large and well-formed, topped his shoulders with all the authority of a man who knows himself well, and what he is fully capable of. Yet he was a gentle man too, the gentleness betrayed in the lines of his handsome face, particularly about the mouth. There was a softness to the bottom lip, a small tremble, a quivering before he spoke. But only a fool misinterpreted that gentleness for weakness. "Emily!" he said, startled to see his wife at the door. Then, blue eyes soft with pleasure to see her, he said, "Come in."

"Shall I light a lamp, Captain?"

"Please. I hadn't noticed it was so dark."

The lamp, flickering at first and then holding, illuminated the large, wood-paneled room, a room which served as both dining saloon and chartroom, and which was cluttered with instruments of all sorts. There was the clock, the barometer, and a large skylight with a compass beneath. In one corner hung a bird cage. Behind it a whaling harpoon. Books—for the Captain and his wife were an intellectual couple—sat tipped back into fenced shelving and filled the entire lower length of one bulkhead. China, either being packed or unpacked, littered a sideboard. Emily took a seat. The Captain stopped pacing.

"What is going to happen, Mr. Lowry, in the morning when my crew wakes to find themselves at sea, *indentured*—for that is what this is, *indentured* for nigh onto two years—with no memory whatsoever of having signed any of these contracts? These signatures are not those of anyone possessing full faculties." He tossed the papers, all of them, onto the table.

"They've signed a legal document. You only need show them. But supposing you're right, supposing there *is* trouble—why, you need only point out the law, sir. The law. Oh, they might grumble a bit at first, but soon they'll consider themselves lucky enough, take it all by and large, as part of their destiny. Now the hour is late. Lowry and Sons agreed to furnish you a crew, and a crew you have. And I believe you wish to sail within the hour?"

Angrily the Captain scrawled the date and his name, *Richard Gurney Wooldridge, Capt. Maid of Athens*, across the bottom of the Set of Articles and tossed them once again onto the table.

Mr. Lowry gathered up his sheaf of documents, and the bank note which the Captain handed over. "A word of caution," he said with a small nod to Emily. "Best not let them know she sails with you. A woman brings bad luck on a voyage."

"I know nothing of the sort."

"I spoke not for you. I spoke for those drunken wretches in your hold." He tucked away the money. "I mean, of course, those fine seamen in your forecastle." He patted his breast pocket and was gone.

2

"Get out of my way!" Emily's sister stood on the lip of the gangplank amidships. Moonbeam and lamplight outlined the bulk of her shoulders, the red of her cape. *"Get out of my way, I say! Or I'll give you the boot!"*

Emily in the saloon below gave a gasp of delight. "It be Catherine, Captain!" she cried with a smile, and leaped to her feet. Skirts gathered in haste, she hastened up the companionway stairs and arrived onto the poop deck just in time to see her sister punch past the drunken John Harris with her umbrella and leap down onto the main deck.

John Harris fell back. *"Two* women?" he hissed, sucking his breath and howling in pain.

Catherine and Emily paid no heed, the man invisible to them in light of their ecstasy to see one another. It had been the Captain's idea for Catherine to board the ship and accompany them for the night while a tug hauled their brigantine down the Thames and out to sea; and Emily, anxious to assure herself that her sister really had come and was not just an apparition out of the fog, hurried too fast and nearly tumbled off the poop ladder.

She regained her footing, dodged the rattails, and threw herself into her sister's damp embrace. "Aye, but Catherine, you've come! You've really come! I be so worried you scorn me at the last! That you not come after all to bid me Godspeed!"

"Scorn you now?" said Catherine with a laugh, a jovial sound. She gave Emily a happy kiss. "Because you be taking it into your head to follow your husband to sea? Instead of staying at home where proper folk—"

"Don't start!" warned Emily with a glorious smile, for it was an old argument. "I be going. And that be that."

She was a pretty woman: small, petite, with pale blonde hair worn back off her face, ringlets carefully curled with the iron and clustered atop her head—as was fashionable for the day—and held firmly in place by the teeth of two handsome, whalebone combs. Wind had tugged loose the shorter hairs about her face and they lay in wispy curls around her eyes. And despite her 29 years, this served to give her the appearance of a waif, to be looked after. "Aye," sighed Catherine, seeing it, "You do be going, and that be that." Suddenly she laughed, never long melancholy. "But I do have all night to prevail upon your better sense!"

"Hello, Catherine," said the Captain.

"Hello, Richard!"

"Can we," he asked, teasing her, "cast off now?"

"Don't be a bore, Richard. I couldn't help being late, really." She rolled her eyes. "Pippin be sick again and threw up in the parlor, Effie spilled the pee pot—"

"Yo ho! Captain, sir!" A voice from the rigging.

"Yo Yates!" hollered up the Captain, chuckling, to where Mr. Yates, his First Mate and right-hand man, was double-checking all the sails and seeing to it they were bent correctly to their yards, ready to unfurl. An immense man, burly and bluff, Mr. Yates was the brawn of the ship—and the Captain's assurance that no matter the wretchedness of his untried sailors passed out in the "foc'sle," they indeed would be taught.

"Aye!" called down Yates with a full Cockney accent. "Will the new lydy be goin' with us then, Ol' Man?"

"No, I'll spare you this one, Yates! The Missus' sister will be getting off in the morning! At Gravesend! Before we set sail!"

"A pity!" shouted back the First Mate, full of good humor and doffing his cap.

A sudden thrash of water, an abrupt toot, and a tiny paddlewheel tug churned up alongside the ship, getting ready to tow them downriver. The First Mate, hearing it, hurtled down the mast. The Captain shouted for Harris.

"Yes, sir!"

"Stow your duds in the foc'sle! Get Steward in the galley to give you a pannikin of coffee! Make it two! Then report to Mr. Yates, First Mate, for duty! The *Maid of Athens* is casting off!"

"Oh, Emily," exclaimed Catherine, taking hold of her hood with both hands and spinning, chin up, to see the network of taut rigging and the tall, slim spars tapering and towering out of the white deck into the dusk. "You be right, she be beautiful! She be a *glorious* ship at that!"

"Let me," Emily said, pleased that Catherine approved at least this, "take you below to the Captain's quarters and show you my cabin."

The *Maid of Athens*, a brigantine, had two masts, fore and main, a raised poop deck and foredeck, and a lower main deck between with waist-high bulwarks. It was across this lower main deck that the two sisters trod carefully, heading aft for the stern and the Captain's quarters beneath the poop. "Watch out for the lines and ropes," Emily warned, for the November night was quite dark by now, everything distorted and laced with elongated shadows. Catherine tripped once, while skirting the longboat lashed to the deck, then nearly walked into the mainstay, one of the ropes that held the mainmast secure. "Plummy!" she muttered. "I'd hang myself inside a week." Nearby chickens cackled, their pens not yet taken to the poop and secured. "Boo!" said Catherine to the startled banty hen. Then both women gave a sharp cry. John Harris emerged from the dark.

"Better a mishap at launching," he snarled, menacingly large in the shadows, "than sail with a woman."

"He can't *really* believe that nonsense about women and bad luck," said Catherine, hastening after Emily, "can he?"

"You be asking me? What would I know of a seaman's creed?" Emily scaled the ladder onto the poop and headed for the companion hatch. "This be my first voyage, remember? Anyway, he be the best of the bunch. The others be all passed out in the foc'sle!"

"Do be serious!" Catherine gathered up her skirts, cape flying, to hurry after Emily down the stairs, stepping lightly over a foot-high sill below and into a room dark as pitch. "I say, be serious!"

"I am. Perfectly. They be all as drunk as skunks."

"And it be ten months at sea with the like? And back again? How will you abide it? Emily," she whined, "why must you do this?"

A scratch, then flame, and the contours of a large cabin winked into view. Oak and teak, polished brass, skylights overhead all tarry with night. Emily lit the wick of a lamp and the shadows fell back. "Well, what do you think?" she asked, swirling, skirts flaring and rubbing the bedpost, a corner of the footlocker, the washstand. Her smile was sweet with pleasure and pride. "Be it not 'home sweet home'?"

It was a tidy room, arranged with a woman's careful touch. The full-size bed, mounted on an iron bedstead, boasted a rose and blue rug. An oak chest of drawers smelled of lemon oil. The toilet glass was not the size a man would use. A long, low locker with a horsehair mattress and an embroidered pillow sat directly beneath the larger of the two skylights.

"See?" said Emily. "I have Mama's pitcher and bowl, and her marble washing stand."

"You little minx! You stole my crayon drawings!"

"Only your best. Oh, Catherine, don't be cross! I had to have something to remind me of you. And you have such a fine hand. And the pictures cheer the bulkhead so."

"That they do," and suddenly they were both laughing at Catherine's conceit. "But who did these? The watercolors? Aren't they lovely! Dover is it? I'd recognize the hamlet anywhere. Narrow, crooked little town. Look, here be the chalk cliffs, and the stormy beach."

"The Captain's brother painted it—just before leaving for America."

"Ah, yes, their Uncle Jeremy's estate. So Richard's brother is off, is he, investing his legacy in steel, in the United States of America? While Richard resigns his commission in the Royal Navy to spend his half of the fortune on a merchant ship?"

"It be the Captain's dream since a boy."

"Emily, nine years you be married. Must you still call him Captain? My, my . . . and what be this?" She peered through a narrow door. "Your very own sitting room? And what lovely chairs! Not at all the frame sort you find on ships!" Whereupon she threw herself into one of the two easy chairs and was about to say more when they both heard the Captain's voice.

Emily hastily sat opposite her older sister, chestnut eyes round in sudden anxiety and doubt. "He be giving orders, Catherine, to cast off from the bollards!"

"You can still change your mind! One word and—"

"No!"

It seemed Catherine would say something. But she held her counsel and instead asked, "Do you wish to go on deck and watch?"

"No. What be there to see of London? And at this time of night?"

"Tut, tut," mocked Catherine. " *'When a man be tired of London he be tired of life; for there is in London all that life can afford.'* "

"I hate Dr. Johnson! Must you quote the pompous man?"

"Oh, bless me! I nearly forgot! I have a wee gift for you, a going-away present."

"But you already gave me a gift—the china."

"Pshaw! That was for the ship." Catherine unbuttoned her red cape and rummaged around in the wide pocket of an apron she wore over a gray, linsey-woolen dress. "Here, here we are!" And she handed Emily a small, leatherbound book, the pages all gilded in gold. Her eyes, a matching chestnut set to Emily's, danced in the lamplight as she quoted, " *'It be the best of times, it be the worst of times . . .'* "

"Dickens! Oh, Catherine, you shouldn't have! You've bought me *A Tale of Two Cities,* and such a lovely edition! Now here," she said, "is a man who can write!" And she kissed the book, a favorite of her favorites, and pressed the prize to her chest, laughing with delight. " *'Aye, it be the age of wisdom—'* "

" *'—it be the age of foolishness—'* "

" *'—it be the epoch of belief—'* "

" *'—it be the epoch of incredulity—'* "

They were giggling and had to bury their noses in their skirts lest they be heard from the deck. Suddenly Emily jabbed her thumb to the ceiling and whispered, still clutching her book, "Better a mishap at launching! For the love of St. Mike, have you ever heard such nonsense? *Oh great epoch of incredulity!*" In a flash she was on her feet, strutting about the cabin. "Yo ho!" she cried, thumping her chest with the book. "Better to sail on a Friday"—she spun suddenly to face Catherine, nose to nose—*"than sail with a woman!"*

"Emily, do sit down. What if there be something after all to the old superstition?"

"Don't scare me like that! And take off your cape or you'll be roasting to death!"

Catherine tossed the cape onto the locker. "Handy thing," she said, eyeing the locker while Emily sat down. "Don't let the natives of South Africa be walking off with it."

"South America."

"South Africa, South America, I can never remember." She settled into the easy chair, resting her head comfortably against the stuffed back and eyeing Emily down her nose. "What cargo, then, is Richard carrying to South America? Or did you tell me that too and I forgot?"

"Baby bottles."

"Baby bottles? Surely you jest."

"Eau de cologne?"

"Nay . . . what would cannibals want with perfume?"

"Same thing as camphor, I suspect. And boilers. And white lead." She started to count on her fingers, trying to remember all the Captain had told her. "Cement. Wool. Coal." It *was* the best of times, truly. A journey halfway round the world, to Chili and Peru and Ecuador. The very names left her dizzy with enchantment. And to think—she be not left this time at home, to worry and fret, to walk her widow's walk in search of the horizon, waiting, ever waiting for the return of her husband, Lieutenant-Commander Wooldridge of the British Royal Navy, gone from her side two, three years at a time. Ah, but it be the worst of times as well: She be having to say goodbye to Catherine. A terrible thing, to love a sister almost as much as one loved a husband.

"Come. Sit before the mirror." Catherine pulled out the dressing stool. "I shall brush your hair. We have lots of time."

Emily sat carefully before the glass, eyes not on her own face, but Catherine's, watching to see how her dear sister's tongue darted in concentration, how her dear eyes laughed. Catherine, so very like their father. Small-boned they be, delicate features, Catherine with freckled skin so thin it looked almost translucent. A sparrow in spring. And she? Like their mother before them. Shapely, buxom, and narrow-waisted, with pretty ankles and a sure walk. Peacocks, mama had said. "Ouch!"

"The price you pay for such lovely hair! Do you ever see the like? So fine, so soft. It be no wonder Richard be taking you with him!" Catherine brushed upward, over and over, pulling loose the ringlets and loosening the curl. The long golden strands caught the soft light and Emily, watching, found herself relaxing as the night grew late.

"Taking chances, isn't he?" said Catherine, seeing the object of Emily's quick, sleepy glance. "Thought the chronometer too valuable to be left out like that. What if it slips, Emily? What if it falls off Mama's marble in a lurch, and breaks? How will Richard navigate you back home again?"

"You worry too much."

"You can hardly peek over the stern, squint at the sun, and say, why, Captain, we must be at the corner of Blackfriar and Fleet—there be St. Paul's Cathedral. No, no, Emily," and she shook the brush at their reflection. "Break your chronometer and you might as well throw out your map."

She had to laugh. "I'll tell him to put it away if it makes you feel better."

"Aye." A final sweep, a quick twist, and Catherine had her hair back in place atop her head and spilling down in loose curls. There was a knock on the door.

"Yes?"

"Captain be wantin' to know, Missus, if ye will 'ave a cup 'a tay?"

"Is that you, Johnny?"

"Aye, Missus."

The door swung open and a small boy no more than eight or nine stepped inside, tea tray clutched tightly in his hands and a parakeet perched on his hair. "Johnny," said Emily, "meet my sister, Catherine Wainwright. Catherine? This be Johnny, the orphan I told you about. The Captain picked him up in a pub, last week."

"You have a bird on your head, Johnny," said Catherine.

"That where 'e got to now? I thank ye, ma'am. Be'olden I am. I be lookin' everywhere for 'im, I 'ave." And a round, wide smile opened his face.

"Next time rub your head and pat your stomach. You'll find him quick enough. Is he your bird?"

"Oh, no, Missus. He be Steward's. I 'ave nothin' b'long to just me."

Emily took the tray. "What of your boots, Johnny?"

"Oh! But that dinna count, I dinna think!"

The moment the door was closed the two women grinned. "He looked so silly, Emily. Tea in his hands, bird on his head!"

"And the Captain *bought* him those new boots just yesterday!"

At the approach of dawn and the long, reminiscent hours of the night gone, the two sisters stood subdued and tired at the poop rail at the stern of the ship. Despite coat and cape pulled close to the chin, they both shivered in the chilly dampness, and for a time it was all so dark they could only see the white water hissing alongside the hull.

"Please, why must you go?" Catherine asked again, leaning over the rail. "Tell me one more time why you persist in exposing yourself to such foul men as those that flock the sea—and risk the ruin of your sensibilities."

There was only one answer. "I love him. As Ruth and Naomi I suppose."

"Aye, I love my husband too, but I'd never follow him to sea."

"Perhaps because you have Pippin and Effie as well?" Emily lay a hand upon her sister's arm. The sky had turned gray. All along the Thames bank lights flickered on. "It's been nine years since I married the Captain. In all that time there has never been a child."

Catherine nodded.

"We are all we have, Catherine. Without each other . . ."

"But men be beasts," persisted Catherine stubbornly, "when they go to sea. It be not fitting for decent women to keep their company."

"They be the company the Captain keeps."

"The Captain," said Catherine slowly, looking to find the full light of dawn. "I wish to God he never came into money, that—"

"Catherine! Stop! Surely you don't argue his luck!"

"Luck?"

"God's providence, then."

"You credit God with this *foolishness*! There be nothing *lucky* about this, or *divine*! It be nothing but a foolish venture—" her voice cracked, "full of risk and danger and—"

Emily took her sister in her arms and held her close and let her cry her great wrenching sobs. So this was what her sister feared. Catherine was afraid not of the sailors, but that she might not come back. T'was the same great grief that had nearly worn her own heart out, and which now pressed so heavy in her sister's mind. "Oh, my poor dear sister," she whispered. There was no comfort to give.

Suddenly, from the bow. *"Gravesend sighted!"*

They both wept, holding fast to each other. The smell of her sister's skin? She would remember it long, until God should bring them together again.

"Godspeed!" Catherine called, and Emily wondered if her heart might break after all as the longboat that had come to take her sister from her rowed away in strong and steady strokes toward the Gravesend harbor and docks. But her husband's arm, slipped round her waist, was a comfort indeed as she watched her sister take her leave amidst the dawn of the last day of November, 1869. She waved until the fog thickened and hid her from sight.

"Harris!" hollered Mr. Yates, First Mate. "Hoist the jib! Fill away the foresail and board the main tack!"

"Aye, aye, sir!"

A sea gull cut through the air, fluttering to the stern of the brigantine to perch atop the poop rail stanchion, wings open and squawking. The Captain pulled Emily close. "Darling," he whispered, and took her face in both his hands. Tenderly he rubbed his thumbs over the soft peach of her clear skin, for he saw loneliness in the chestnut depths of her eyes. Fifty yards away the tugboat that had hauled them out to sea cast off, releasing the hawser, the long cable that had joined tug to ship. "Don't be sad. Catherine's gone, I know, but this day we begin, Emily. You and me."

When he was happy his eyes equaled a summer sky, and Emily, sister forgotten in the pure light of summer blue, reached up to kiss his strong, full mouth. "I love you, Richard."

"And I you." He sighed with content. Suddenly he dropped his hands to her waist, and with a chuckle, lifted her off her feet. Chin in quick, hands to his shoulders, around she spun, round and round until at last, dizzy, she felt the poop again beneath her feet. A quick twist, back against his chest, beat of his heart through slicker and coat, and she tipped her head to a shoulder so his could fall in beside her own. Together, cheek to cheek and breathing hard, they watched the tug turn back up the Thames, the light come full in the sky. Soft rain fell all around. "You and me," he whispered, happy, against her bonnet.

"Aye, you and me," she murmured, content, wondering that God could be so good to give so much.

3

He that will learn to pray,
let him go to sea.

—Randle Gotgrove, 1611

First Mate Yates and George Allan (George Allan on land, Steward on sea) shared the tiny mate's cabin behind the Captain's quarters and across the narrow aisle from the dining saloon. A lesser man than Yates might have balked at the notion of sharing a berth with a mere cleaner of pots and pans and haberdasher of hardtack and ship's gruel. But not Yates. Born and bred before the mast, he had no use for rank and file; he looked always beyond the outward appearance to the inner worth of a man. And Steward? Here was a man of sterling worth.

Their quarters reflected not their contrast of rank, as one might expect, but more to the point, their personal natures. On Yates' side of the shared space all that adorned the bulkhead was a swinging crucifix, austere in its singleness, polishing a streak to the sway of the ship where Christ's feet rubbed raw the cherrywood. His sea chest, however—closed only because the bounce of the vessel closed it—was crammed with everything that could be crammed: sheath knife, pocket knife, monkey coat, oilslicker, tarpaulin, sea boots, woolen mufflers, a shaggy watchcoat, two hats, red long johns, and assorted shirts. Sandwiched and scissored between the lid and trunk and advertising his hurried state of affairs were wrinkled garments both clean and dirty: a checkered shirtsleeve, a smelly stocking, a holey pair of drawers. Way in the bottom of the chest, hidden amidst other garments of various sorts, were two daguerreotypes, one of his sainted mother, another of a plain woman without smile.

Steward's side of the cabin was quite the reverse: the *bulkheads* were crammed. Brass hooks displayed in tidy order clothes hung to dry, shirts and shoes all swinging rhythmically, softly, like wind in a poplar, back and forth with every roll of the sea. A bookcase, bolted to the cherrywood between a green coat and yellow slicker, held books with dark spines of blue and brown, with darker letters of black spelling such names as Voltaire, Rousseau, Kierkegaard, and Elizabeth Barrett Browning. A closer look revealed an Old Testament in Hebrew, a tattered volume, and a Greek New Testament. Marked in fountain pen was a passage in Ephesians with *kephale* circled, with a notation that read: *no metaphor of leadership in Gk "head." Strictly Eng. Gained pop. Sir Frances B. Cf. rape/S.F.B. trans "dominion" Genesis.* A well-worn volume, shoved beneath his feather pillow, was the biography of Dr. Johnson. And amidst the neat profusion of books and clothes, and tacked beneath a lamp so that light could bring her back to life, was a daguerreotype of his dead wife, a locket of her pale blonde hair sealed behind the glass.

Opposing rank, opposing natures—such difference might well have hindered friendship between these two. Mutual devotion to Richard Gurney Wooldridge, however, brought forth the opposite. Friends—indeed, companions—Yates and Steward would together serve their Captain on this virgin voyage of his *Maid of Athens*.

Clearly their Captain was the brain behind the venture, the integrating intelligence in back of the purchase, negotiations, contracts, and finance. But if the Captain represented the brains, Yates would be the brawn to see it through. Strong, forceful, pivotal, orders would issue through him, sails furled and unfurled at his command, repairs and maintenance his directive. He and the Captain, brain and brawn undivided, would command the ship in partnership—yet not without Steward. For Steward, the steward and cook, was the very soul of the ship, and without him the Captain would never think to sail, not even as Lieutenant-Commander of the Royal British Navy in command of a whole fleet of good men.

And so this first morning out, this last day of November, 1869, tug paddling upriver in the rain and they drifting down, Steward was dressed in his yellow oil-slicker and a handknit toque, bedarned and ragged, and was squatted low on his haunches beside the windlass near the port hawse, one of the two small holes either side and just aft the bow's nose, ready to pull in the tow rope that yet dragged the sea. Nostrils. This was how he saw the small oval hawse holes. And the hawser? The four-inch tarred tow rope? Nothing more than a stout cord of hardened slime that passed through the "nose."

Normally the tug supplied the hawser and pulled her in, but the Captain was an independent man and had his own way of doing things. Which was fine, since they could pull in the rope just as well, but the air was biting and his hands ached, and this was not his job. He was Steward and Cook. He should be burning his thumbs on the stove. *Stupid, drunken cretins!* he thought, resentful of the seamen still sprawled unconscious in the foc'sle below. Yates approached and Steward pulled to his feet, tugging off his toque long enough to run a hand through a thinning thatch of scrub red hair atop his head and then down over his wrinkled face. "The two of us," he said, putting his toque back on with both hands, jamming it down round his reddened ears, "got a job on our hands if we expect to pull the hawser in ourselves. Best kiss the sleeping beauties down under and put them to the harness."

"Ye fergot to count me!" piped the orphan lad, all but lost in his oilskin and swinging off the knighthead, one of the two timbers that supported the bowsprit. He pointed a muddy finger to Yates. "And me muscle, I 'spect, be as good as 'is."

Yates smiled from the corner of his mouth, an indulgent gesture of goodwill. "Aye, very well then, matey. We'll give 'er a dash go-round and see 'ow ye do! If ye can't cut the muster we'll wake the old boys. 'Ang to, old boy, and 'eave 'o!"

The windlass was a huge, backbreaking, unyielding, and thoroughly despairing arrangement of a drum, round which the hawser cable, wet and cold and coming through the hawse, wrapped round a full turn before rattling around and down and into the spurring pipe, where it dropped coil by coil into the chainlocker below deck and fore of the foc'sle. The beastly contraption was made to work by laying hold of wooden bars inserted into an archaic mess of gears and applying brute force, around and around.

"Ready now?" Yates hollered good-naturedly, feet braced, massive back bent to the work. "*There's a fire in the hold, fire down below . . .*" Their voices, the two men's and the boy's, to the tune of the old chantey, squeaked her in slow but sure, three feet in, one foot out, three feet in. Sweat mixed with the rain on their faces and dripped into their eyes. "*There's a fire in the main hold, the cap'n didn't know, There's a fire—*"

"Yo! Captain!" John Harris stood at the helm, in the far stern of the ship, swinging the wheel—to port, to starboard. "Trouble on the poop, sir!"

Emily, in the saloon at the foot of the companionway, where she had gone to admire her sister's gift of china (pretty but absolutely impractical), heard the commotion, and without wasting a moment slid into her coat and returned to the wheel, where her husband, white-faced and tense, barked brisk questions.

"How does she steer?"

"She gripes, sir!"

"Did you notice anything amiss during the night? While we followed in the tug's wake?"

"No, sir!"

The Captain's blue eyes traveled the foremast to the topsail and foresail, the only sails yet set, searching for the trouble even as he took the wheel himself. Suddenly he cried for Yates in the bow to rouse the drunken crew. Quickly he ordered Harris to the windlass to help reel in the hawse before the ship ran over it. "We're rudderless!" he shouted to Emily, abandoning the helm and vaulting off the poop, racing Harris the full length of the ship to the bow. Harris scaled the foredeck. Steward, alone with the boy, made him room at the windlass. The Captain ducked into the forecastle below, where Yates, bellowing and belting about with a belaying pin, yanked first one, then another of the five unconscious sailors onto their feet.

"Up, up!" he bellowed, head bent low and kicking ribs, shins, and skulls. "Up or I be feedin' yer carcass to the sharks! Up and man the win'lass 'efer we go down. UP! UP! Fall in!" He grabbed a bucket of water and gave it a heave. One sailor was up and roaring, water spraying off jacket and sleeve and chin. Another bucket, another cry. "Up, I sye! 'Aul in the 'awser! UP! UP!"

Out of the foc'sle and onto the head he drove the groggy, stumbling sailors, then up and down the foredeck he himself went, bellowing, cracking the slackers where he could with the belaying pin to get them in motion. *There's a fire in the foretop, fire in the main!*" he thundered. *"To me weigh, heigh, heigh, ho!"* The men, stunned and stupid with surprise, fell to under the ringing blows and drive of familiar work and song. *"Fire in the win'lass and fire in the chain!* Faster! FASTER!" Now Yates joined, every ounce of his strength with every ounce of theirs on the bars, brute perspiring force and hammering, hollow hearts, for now they saw the danger themselves. But the heavy shackles which marked the tens of fathoms of rope wouldn't come in, and Yates was back with the belaying pin. *"There's a fire down below!"* he bawled, driving one, driving two, driving three. *"There's fire in the forepeak, fire down below—"* The shackles inched in. He flung again his giant frame, in despair now, upon the sweat-stained wood, too exhausted to even cry out the chantey, or to summon the crew to greater and still greater effort. But they held to, damp wind blowing first in their faces then whipping against the backs of their necks, danger driving them on, round and round and up and down, heaving, pulling, faces wet with sweat, wet with rain, faces red with pain.

"Aye!" screamed Steward at last. "She's in!" They all fell back with a gasp, hands burning, hearts thudding, ears and heads ringing, stinging behind their eyes, but still the ship listed, dangerously so. A command from the Captain and Steward and Yates quickened, manning the clew garnets and braces to pull out the plug of wind in the foresail.

Even then Emily had no moment for relief. One of the sailors roused, and with the others, marched cross deck in the drizzling rain to the poop, where the Captain had returned to attend the broken rudder. "Ye shanghaied us is what you done," he growled. Tall, straight, with a chest like an oak barrel, he presented a stark, harsh face, a leering snarl.

The Captain stiffened under the assault he had known would come. Privately he cursed Lowry, who had indeed shanghaied them. Publicly he declared, "You signed a contract. You owe me two months' wages, with the remainder payable when we come dockside."

"But I ain't workin' if he's the boss!" growled someone miserably from behind, holding his head and jerking a thumb back at Yates.

"It was a knock upside the head or a watery grave." But there was no time for further words. The brigantine wallowed. The Captain ordered her worked over to the lee side of the Thames Mouth, where they could lay anchor and get help.

The men complied, reluctantly enough, soaking wet and blinking from headaches made worse by their brutal awakening. By some luck they reached the bank. Soundings were ordered. Yates collared the closest man available and gave him the task, but when the man hollered out the deep fathoms, mumbled from beneath a heavy black mustache, Yates looked to the Captain, mystified. "There ain't no such depth as that out 'ere, sir. It be a 'ole lot shallower 'an wot he be lettin' on, Ol' Man."

Silent communication passed between Captain and Mate, and Yates, nodding in agreement, ordered a new sounding taken. In it came, with mud and sand, and abruptly he dismissed the mustached blackguard. "Weigh an—CHOR!" he yelled, but the six seamen, the five plus Harris (who had thrown in his lot with them), refused to make the sails fast. The voyage, they declared, was ended. They were "dockside."

"We demand to be put to the bloody shore," said the man with the mustache. "We ain't stayin' on. Think we're bloody fools as to head out to sea with somethin' wrong with the bleedin' rudder, *and a bleedin' woman to boot?*"

"Name and rank!" the Captain ordered.

"Lawrence Jay, Bosun."

So, thought the Captain grimly, this is the man I've hired to oversee the rigging, *and* the sailors to work the riggings. A sorry lot—but best dealt with now. "The rudder," he said with cool terseness, "*and* the lady, have nothing to do with your demands. That much, you cheat, is clear. You, Lawrence Jay, see a fast way to beat the advance note and get the best of the boarding house keepers. But it's *me* you owe the two months' wages, not the boarding houses, and if you, Lawrence Jay, after two months want to be put ashore I will be more than happy to throw you off ship. Do I," he said, "make myself clear?"

In the silence Lawrence Jay's gaze moved over the men.

"Good. Now that we understand each other, ready the small boat for going ashore. You and Yates will row into Gravesend for a diver. Yates?" He turned on his heel.

But he was no further than the mainmast and Yates no further than reaching for the knots that lashed the small boat to the deck when Jay, with a signal to the others, rushed the deck in close formation, armed with handspikes and whatever else they could lay their hands on.

"Richard!" screamed Emily from the galley.

He whirled. "Halt!" The sound was so cutting that the men stopped midstep, arms stiff, eyes sharp, as if frozen.

"Mr. Yates! Put Jay in the chains!"

Yates reached for the irons hanging from a mast but Jay lunged, and with a flash of silver in the morning's cold light, he forced Yates backward, up against the rail at the break of the hook, knife winking and slicing. Emily reared back into Steward's arms. Yates bellowed and Jay jumped aside, dodging the blow. Steward, shoving Emily aside, dashed to Yates' aid and together they took him down, Yates snapping on the irons, Steward kicking the knife aside so that it spun, winking, blinking, clattering across the deck, sliding to a stop right at Emily's feet, where she stood numbed and struck stupid by the lightning speed of events too brutal to absorb as real.

The Captain motioned for Steward to hoist the flag for mutiny. "The Bosun's two months' wages be hanged. Life's too short to court his kind. Let the Navy take Mr. Jay ashore."

"The others?" Steward asked, running up the flag.

"They seem to have lost their mettle, now that their leader's in irons. Best let them cool their heels a bit and carry on."

Yates ordered the five up to the windlass on the foc'sle head, where he had them searched and chained, and a muster call made for all knives.

"What!" cried Harris. "You're taking our knives? But you can't do that! They're part of our proper gear! How're we going to splice a line or cut a buntline stop? *How're we going to cut our bread?*"

"The Captain an' me," said Yates, undisturbed, when at last all five knives were collected, "be good mates to work fer. Fair. Reas'nable. We run a clean, tight ship. We pull no rank. But get a knife pokin' our 'earts an' our patience wears a might thin. So to keep our tempers cool and yer souls out 'a 'ell, Jack, I'm goin' to strike off the points. Johnny," he ordered the orphan, "run get the 'ammer and chisel from the galley, lad."

The sailors let up a roar, a fearsome cry, and Emily, pulling back from the galley door to let the boy through, watched her husband move past without recognition and mount the foc'sle head.

"From now on," he said, standing before his crew in the rain and speaking quietly, "possession of a pointed knife will be regarded as a declaration of war against the government of this ship. Mr. Yates!"

One by one and in front of them all, Yates struck off the points. Wee triangles of blade jumped like fleas, only to be buried, lost, in the cracks of the deck. He handed the blunted knives back just as Captain Merrymore of the *Victoria* came alongside in response to the flag, a scrubby little man with a frown on his face and with an irritated gruffness in his stance.

Jay, in double irons, was hustled aboard his clipper, and Captain Merrymore, recognizing a former Navy colleague, warned Richard, "They'll run you up the mast if you don't show them who's boss, Wooldridge."

He fixed a beady eye on the five seamen chained ankle to ankle on the foc'sle head of the foredeck and added, "Looks like you've done just that. Now Bully Hayes, should he run afoul you," he snorted sarcastically, "might deserve your pity." Suddenly he laughed. "But these men? Throw the lot of 'em into the foc'sle, turn the key, and keep 'em on bread and water. Without," he finished, disembarking, "too much bread."

"Who be Bully Hayes?" Emily asked Steward.

"An old pirate, turned blackbird with the passage of the Queensland Act in '65. Hunts South Sea natives, then sells 'em down under as slaves. A profitable business, but the Navy'll put a stop to him soon enough."

The clipper moved on, and Yates, after a quick consultation with the Captain, lowered the small boat, shinnied down the davit rope, picked up the oars, and made for Gravesend to hire a diver to tend the rudder—and a new Bosun.

The Captain, seeing him go and quelling the foreboding that rode in his stomach, went to loosen the chains of his men. Churlish they were, yes, but almost embarrassed too. Too much to drink, shanghaied, their lives in peril, they hadn't meant to go so far. He strode their line, their furtive eyes watching as he paced the length and back. Let them measure me, he thought with grim satisfaction. Let them measure the fiber of which I'm made. At last he said, "Put up your duds in the foc'sle. Find your bunks and then go down for breakfast."

They blinked stupidly at him. "I'm not Captain Merrymore," he told them, "to starve my men. I am Captain Wooldridge, and you'd better learn what that means." He left them to their own wits. "Ring the bell," he told Steward on his way past, "or they'll be brewing up another pot of trouble, I warrant."

When the last chair at the dining table was pulled up, and when silent, sullen stares were cast round about the table, this time measuring each other—and Emily at the end—he leaned forward from behind his Captain's chair, placed both his hands firmly on the smooth oak, and spoke quietly and cautiously, welcoming them aboard the *Maid of Athens*, and then spelled carefully the two watches. "Harris, you and Hayward and Lawson—port. Fielding, Oates, and the boy—starboard. No," he said, quelling any objection over the boy. "Johnny may be no larger than a spritsail sheet knot, but he's strong enough to knock down an ox and he's a monkey in the riggings. You'll work 12 hours a day, men, four hours on, four hours off. Pretty straightforward and standard. I'll run through it once, though, so there's no question. Starboard takes the first watch, the night watch, beginning at eight P.M. Port relieves at midnight, the middle watch relieves at four in the morning, the morning watch relieves at eight. You know how it goes. Forenoon watch is eight to noon, the noon watch noon to four. The dog-watch rotates, four to six, six to eight, so you can alternate the hours of day you're on duty. When the new Bosun arrives, he'll oversee the starboard watch. Mr. Yates, First Mate, has the port. You'll obey him without question. The First Mate and I, you'll find, are undivided."

He glanced down the very long table to Emily.

"My wife, Missus Wooldridge," he said in way of introduction, proud and pleased to see her soft smile and brave, circling eyes. She met the scoundrels without a flinch, cool as a cucumber, although he knew she had to be afraid. This was not how they'd planned to set sail. Harris burped. "I will hear no nonsense," he went on quickly, "about women aboard ship bringing bad luck." He kept Harris deliberately in his range of vision. "Nor will I entertain mumblings about mishaps at launching. If there's been any bad luck, if there's been a mishap, count it your own foolishness. Running up debts, allowing yourself to be snared by too much to drink. But enough," he said, and bowed his head to give thanks for their food.

"May Your sustaining grace, Lord God, go before us this day and in the days to come. We plead Your watchcare, we ask Your guidance and quick hand with the rudder. And now for what we're about to receive may we truly be thankful. Amen."

"Captain?"

"Name and rank."

"Oates, sur. William Oates. Seaman." A small man with black eyes, a thick nose, and wearing a rather smart-looking tam-o'-shanter of dark green plaid. When he spoke it was with the thick brogue of a Scot and the rumble of a man no longer young.

"Yes, Oates."

"Why the breakfast, sur? Shude it no' be breed an' watter? An' no' at the Captain's table either?" he asked, very confused. "The foc'sle wid do fine wi' al the usual kid and kettle."

"Have you never read the New Testament, Oates?"

"Aye. When a was a wean at me mither's knee, sur."

"Read it again, this time with a man's eyes, and see if you have to ask why."

⚓

It was as if a new crew had boarded the *Maid of Athens* by the time Yates returned with a diver and a new Bosun. The five seamen were singing chanteys and spinning yarns, bantering and arm wrestling, all drinking Steward's tea and milling beneath the foc'sle awning to keep out of the rain. "Meet Robert Sargent," he told the five, eye on the Captain and slinging the new Bosun's pack down into the foc'sle. An even half-dozen now, to bunk in the forecastle, a tiny, triangular-shaped cubby at the bow below the foredeck. "Missus?" he said. "Our new Bosun, Mr. Robert Sargent."

A remote man. He flattered her with an empty smile. Emily dropped her chin politely to thank him, but stiffened, gooseflesh crawling on her throat. A red flash of malice, it seemed, darted from black eyes; but when she looked again, unsure, he was as remote as before, eyes veiled like a curtain drawn upon dusk.

Two hours later the lower pintle, broken off at the rudder, was replaced without going into harbor or drydock, an answer to prayer and one the Captain had not really expected. They would set sail after all, and the new man bawled out the hoarse Bosun call of *"A-a-ll ha-aands! UP ANCHOR, A-HOY!"* Unintelligible orders, fired rapidly, were quickly discharged. Boots thumped the deck. Cries came from aloft, alow, the whole a discordant symphony of odd cries and odder actions, and Emily, standing in the galley door, out of way, watched with a pitch of excitement in her heart as up went the sails and round flew the yards. The brigantine was on her way, Bosun Sargent at her helm and scudding before the wind.

Out of the mouth of the Thames, round and down the shoreline of North Foreland they sailed, into the Straits of Dover. The moment they entered the English Channel, the sun, setting in the west, broke through and the wind picked up. The very first real waves ran up under her prow. "She's a real ship after all!" exclaimed the Captain, setting his left hand in the crook of his right elbow in a way that was all his own.

"That she is!" cried Emily. "You've done it, Captain! Just as you said!" Two hundred thirty tons with a length of 92 feet, a beam of 21, depth 15, the *Maid of Athens* flew with the wind, square-rigged sails billowing from her foremast, fore-and-aft snapping and cracking from her main, sun rays spilling from clouds and sky and over her bow. Emily slid her fingers beneath the roped triceps of her husband's upper arm and they strolled down the lee side of the deck. The sun could be nothing but a sign from God, and she found, walking alongside her dear husband and hearing the starboard watch "blowing the

man down," that her spirits had lifted—soared, even—
in the damp, chilly wind that belonged only to England.

"It be nary a task," she said gaily, "to unload our cargo
halfway round the world and be on our way home again!"

"What? You want to go home? Already?" He stopped
and faced her. "Emily. If you want to go back, I will take
you at once! I will! And I won't blame you. It was a
devilish start."

That it was, and just the memory of it stopped her
blood cold. But would God have given them their heart's
desire—their own ship and good men like Yates and
Steward—only to let them be undone by weak men such
as these that sluiced the masts and scrubbed the decks
and took their trick at the wheel? She thought not.

"Do you want to go home?" the Captain asked again.

"Never!"

They stood facing one another, smiling, with the wind
in their hair and snapping at their clothes. "Emily, my
love, we shall, despite the rakish beginning, have ourselves a merry wee trip! That I shall swear to, sweet
Emily!" and he was hugging her to make her laugh.

She *did* laugh. But then she caught sight of the bowsprit, lit by the low sun, and shivered. The figurehead of
the *Maid of Athens*, carved in oak, smiled broadly, her face
to the horizon, the unknown.

4

If a boy wants to go to sea, let him, for if you don't, he will be a stranger at your table.

—Jan deHartog
A Sailor's Life

The brigantine was not yet out of the Channel when Emily decided she had better find a place in Steward's pantry to put the china—before it broke. The set was lovely, fine bone and all ivory and pretty and soft, with fragile fuchsia blossoms, everything pink and white and lichen green. Handpainted from Germany, laurel leaves imprinted on the bottom of each cup and saucer, the set was far too lovely to use on a voyage. But Emily was determined. Each cup of tea would remind her of dear Catherine. And so with resolve she dragged the wooden crates out of the saloon and into the hallway.

Steward's pantry was long and narrow, tucked between the ship's starboard sheer and the mate's cabin. Here in the pantry he did most of his food preparation, the flour and much of the foodstuffs being stored in narrow cupboards along the paneled bulkhead to the fore and backed into the hold. The cooking, though, and the cleaning of dishes, he did in the galley on deck, a small house built amidships, tucked snug up against the water tank and mainmast—for in the galley was stove and sink. There too was tea set to seep all day. There was the rum dished out at dogwatch. There the men gathered for swapping yarns at eight bells and for begging a pannikin of grog should the winds blow high, or to warm their backsides by the crackling stove.

"Steward?"

Three portholes let daylight into the pantry. Steward was nowhere to be seen. She glanced about once. Wooden spoons and sharp knives swung off tenpenny nails. Mixing bowls tipped crooked on high fenced shelves. Another glance and she pulled open a bottom cupboard. Perfect. Kneeling, with her russet gown and heavy cotton layers of petticoat pulled aside, she pushed to the back of the cupboard what ironstone was there and started laying in the china, plates first.

She could hear the pleasant banter of the men on deck, their voices muffled and indistinct, and she thought of their first morning—goodness, just three days ago? How, she wondered for the hundredth time, had the Captain earned their respect so quickly, when they had all been so wicked and frightening? Perhaps Yates was correct when he'd said men respected those who could beat them at their own game. *She* preferred to think Providence played a role.

"Shoo!" she scolded, flapping at Polly-wants-a-cracker. "You be a silly nuisance." Steward's parakeet ignored her and perched on the flounce and ruffle of her shoulder, squawking and pecking at her ear. "Go on with you! *Johnny!*" she called, seeing him pass.

"Yes'm?"

"Be a good man and help me put up these empty boxes." Eleven sat on the floor and in the way.

"But Mister Yates, 'e 'ave me sweep the deck!"

"Come back down then when you hear the ship's next bell! And where be your boots, lad?"

"Under me 'ammock!" But he was off before she could scold further, bare feet flying.

She would put the empty crates, she decided, into the lazaret, the long, low storage space that opened off her own cabin. And so with three boxes stacked high in her arms, she maneuvered back into the narrow hall: dining saloon to her left; the pantry, mate's cabin, companion-way, and at last her own quarters to the right.

Four more trips saw all 11 boxes of various sizes piled about her cabin. The lazaret door, beside the bureau, was heavy and unhinged. But with just the right wiggle the whole piece careened forward into her knees, and she set aside the plank and peered inside, sniffing the locked-up air, the pine tar, the rancid tallow ... the bilge water. Ugh! Blinking, she could see shadowy crates and sacks and tins in the dim, dusty light. To her ears came the stark creaking of the ship's innards, woodwork and fittings all groaning in a thousand keys. Where be the boy? Had the half-hour bell yet sounded? Would she have to do this herself?

The first two boxes slid in easily enough. The third managed to snag and she scrambled across the top, ducking, catching her bustle. "Plummy ..." A tug and she was free. She was just hauling a fifth box to a black corner, sneezing and crouching to keep from smacking her head atop the roof, when she heard a low whine. She froze. Don't be silly, she told herself, there be a dozen ways for a ship to whine in her ribs. But another cry and she leaped to the hall, taking the stairs two at a time, short hairs racing up her neck.

She was about to cry for the Captain, but sight of the men, one at the helm, another in the rigging, reminded her quick enough that she couldn't be bothering him with such trivial matters; he had a ship to run. "Oates! have you seen Johnny?"

The dapper Scot put down the sennit he was plaiting. "Aye, bit he wiz here a wee while ago! Sweepin' mud from one end o' the deck to the other!"

She found him asleep in the longboat, parakeet perched on his only shirt button. She gave him a jab; he sat up with a start and Polly-wants-a-cracker flew off with a shriek. "The ship bell?" he said, startled, guilt rising behind his eyes with apprehension, "'it already be rung?"

"Johnny, there be something in the lazaret. Come see what it be."

"Neh! It be a ghost!"

"Don't be daft. There be no such things as ghosts. Don't you believe the Good Book? It says there be no ghosts, for they have all gone to heaven or hell."

"The good book?" His eyes went round with doubt.

"The Bible."

"Never 'eard of it."

"Well, never mind," she said, and gave him a poke in the back, marching him astern. She was going to have to teach the boy his catechism on Sundays, this was clear, but for now there was the matter in the lazaret.

Once inside they crouched, waiting just inside the opening to allow their eyes time to adjust to the darkness. "Over there," she whispered.

They crept forward, hand in hand. The noise came again. "Why! That be a dog!" exclaimed the boy, darting forward and scrambling lickety-split over a crate. "Ma'am! 'E's stuck! 'E's got 'is paw stuck in a box!"

Weak with relief, she managed to reshift the heavy bundles and crates, back against the boards, heels braced against a rib joist. The dog, apparently trapped when the hold had been loaded, was pinned beneath a slipped box. "Oh, you poor thing," she whispered.

"Aye, bit he's no' a he, he's a she!" diagnosed Oates the moment they got "her," an emaciated and very weak black lab, on deck and all had gathered round. "Och, bit she's got a brokin hind leg the poor thing."

Steward was called to set the leg and bind it, and all through the afternoon in the galley by the stove, and as the ship bowled along the Cornwall coast out toward the Atlantic Sea, the empty crates and lazaret forgotten, Emily and the orphan, when he could, took turns spooning a thick gruel that Steward had made of rice and duff pudding down the dog's throat. "What are we," she asked the orphan, "going to call our stowaway?"

"Stowaway," he answered, kissing the mutt again. "Can she sleep with me?"

The sailors put up a row; the foc'sle was crowded enough.

"But only 'alf 'a ye sleep at one time! She can trade 'ammocks at the change o' watch, me think!"

"They could hardly argue with that," Emily told the Captain that night. She sat in bed, arms clasped about her knees and feeling warm in her flannel nightie. The Captain stood by the chest of drawers, one arm propped on top. He was breathing hard, having just finished putting away the rest of the china boxes and setting the lazaret door. "And who trades hammocks with me?" he teased, rubbing his thumb across the corner of his mouth and looking at her sideways. "When I leave on watch?"

"You don't leave on watch, *Captain*," she said, hiding a smile.

The very next breath he was in bed, rolling her over in his arms and throwing up the covers.

"Take off your boots, Richard! *Richard!*" she squealed, kissing him, hugging him, laughing hard and happy, happy to have him all to herself, the long day over. "Richard! Take off your boots first!"

Yates thumped the bulkhead behind them.

"Hush now," she whispered, "you be embarrassing me."

⚓

The *Maid* cleared the Channel late on Saturday, the fourth day of December, 1869, and the Eddystone Light on the cliffs of Plymouth dipped below the winter horizon astern. England winked out.

The Captain stood at the taffrail in the very stern of his ship and watched her go.

"Aye, but it be good to feel again the 'ive 'a the say," said Yates, coming up beside him.

"Aye, and it's good to feel the air, cold, apart from the land." A shriek wove the air, and in the warp Richard took the heave in his legs, feeling the rise and fall of the *Maid* beneath his feet, ever responsive to the caress of the sea. Waves gently lapped her hull, and rose up soft to kiss her sheer. Ah, but the kiss of the sea could easily be the kiss of Judas, he knew, a cold welcome before betrayal. Soon enough these same waves would fume and fuss, and roar around the sweet cutwater at the bow, sweeping angrily astern, where the deep bottom would cleave them in two. Ah, what was he doing by bringing Emily into such treachery?

"She be a plucky woman, Ol' Man," said Yates, reading his thoughts. "And we be prepared, come wot may."

Ever since they'd met, some six months before at a shipping office, they had taken an instant liking to one another. The Cockney mate had been brought up before the mast, serving time on lime juicers and worse, and was remarkably unhardened by the cruelty he'd seen and known. He'd come out knowing how to hold a man in line; he also knew how to be fair. More than that, he understood the Captain's aversion to the misuse of power. They made a fitting pair. And the last five days had more than proved the Captain's suspicion that Yates was a godsend. Strong, commanding, keenly intelligent, he'd been able to transform the crew of coarse, foul men into a finely tuned team, able to reef, set, and bend sails in record time. More than that, to enjoy it. And so together the two men, Mate and Captain, stood in the cry of the wind.

"Eight bells, and all is well."

Together they stood in the soft echo of the words passed between change of hands at the helm. Eight bells, and all *was* well.

The brigantine lifted over the long rollers like a great horse loosed upon the plains, and the Seamen were quick to give her rein and let her run to Yates' call. The route was laid to conform to the path of the prevailing winds, and the *Maid*, ever responsive, clipped along unfettered into the open sea.

5

*Oh, the wonder of the trade wind! All day we sailed, and all
night, and the next day, and the next, day after day, the wind
always astern and blowing steadily and strong.*

—Humphrey Van Weyden
The Sea Wolf, Jack London

So this is my husband's world, thought Emily. She
stood as one entranced. Not a flat world, well-ordered
and tidily arranged as was hers, but moving and surging, an undulating sea where massive waves rose before
and behind and all around like so many swirling hills
of deep green blue. First at the stern, then the bow,
dropping and rising wherever they pleased with nary a
warning. The rail beneath her hands rose and fell to meet
sky and sea, and she clung fast. To port, to starboard,
tipping and tilting, the little ship sliding about the frothy
unrest like an insignificant bobble of flotsam. *The seas,*
sang an old Psalm in her mind and all around, *have lifted
up, O Lord, the seas have lifted up their voice.* This was her
husband's world, singing its song, and here she was in
it, within sight and sound of him, dreams come true.

A delight he was to see, Richard Gurney Wooldridge,
and in all their years of marriage his perfect beauty had
never waned but waxed. Fair bronzed skin, sun-bleached
hair that hung in heavy curls, eyes a pretty light blue and
crinkled from facing thousands and thousands of miles
of wind and sun, chin thrust forward and square with

determination, body tall and strong. Like no other, he was a sailor, born one—the call coming from the other side of the moon. Nothing could have been done but seek that call, and long ago Emily had given up the notion of keeping him home with her. To call him from the sea would have been to call him from life. She had begun instead to pray for the day she might explore the darkness of the moon, and move into his watery world.

Her prayer had been answered the day his uncle had died. A benevolent legacy and here she was—here they were—dreams come true and more: She had not expected to love the sea.

The sea, the sea, the deep blue sea. Cessation of time, endless liberty. No beginning, no end, everything now. Today. *Today*.

To occupy herself (for she was not one to sit idle, mind wasting without thought) she'd brought her books, a few in her cabin and the rest in the saloon, as well as some wool to card and spin. She was wanting to knit the Captain a sweater, since his old fishernet hung so gracelessly upon his body. And so when she wasn't acquainting herself with the ship—prowling the deck, either peering into the various lockers or poking her nose into every nook and cranny, or dizzily watching the men clamber the riggings, swinging high on the yards as they bowled along—she was on deck in the thin sunlight with books and wool, bundled against the wind. Tucked into a lawn chair amidships, where she could keep an eye on her dear husband with a mere glance of the eye, she read and carded and spun, more content than she dreamed possible. Was this all she wanted of life? To be a part of those who lived and breathed upon so frail a contrivance as a tiny ship, made only of wood and cloth and afloat a ruling sea, adrift a wind that reigned? Aye, for now, and her fingers flew, cold, yet also soft from the lanolin of her wool.

A week they ran thus, sailing into the nights and into the days, prevailing winds always astern and blowing steadily and strong, putting 250 miles between each dawn. Staying out of the way as much as possible while the men worked, she watched, fascinated, not only by the workings of the ship, the pulling and hauling of sheets and tackle, but by the men themselves as they pitted their strengths against each other and measured their weaknesses—working a system between them.

She kept her distance, watching carefully from behind her spindle and knitting needles. Their readiness to quarrel, to put up their fists, forced a wary reserve. But their quick resolutions, fight done and winner declared, invited envy as well. So different from women. Women smiled even while seething on the inside when wronged. Was it not better, she wondered, to air the difference, as did the men? Get it out in the open? Not that blackening another's eye was any solution. But it certainly cleared the air. Certainly, too, it defined the order of respect.

Yates the men obeyed instantly, without fuss. To Steward they nodded greetings each change in the watch, indebted for the generosity of his galley and grog. But amongst themselves they maneuvered their attachments and resentments.

It took Emily some time to sort out who was who, plus how they related to one another. Within a fortnight, though, she knew not only the various personalities (and some of the quirks), but the varying alliances and silent boundaries as well. Increasingly she understood a masculine world so few women are privy to.

The new Bosun kept to himself, as if bored. He barked his necessary orders, then withdrew into silence, whittling, ever whittling while pacing the decks, black eyes on sails and wind—and on his knife.

Hayward, built like an oak barrel, was a handsome man. Easy goes, easy does, he did as little work as possible. Rheumatism, he complained. The others refused the complaints, and his whining became part of the ship.

Fielding, the only Ordinary Seaman of the six, was just 16 and slow to learn the ropes. He appeared dimwitted—unlike Lawson, a young man in his early twenties who boasted a halo of golden locks and whose pretty face held a sly cast: Wide-spaced eyes reflected a whole den of fox's tricks.

Oates, the Scot, was the eldest of the crew, 45, a spritely man and the most dependable. The only man with a family, the Captain's concern for the welfare of women and children left in England was relieved: Oates was not irresponsible.

And John Harris? The sailor who'd come stumbling aboard singing "Blow the Man Down"? Every mishap, every blunder, every piece of ill luck aboard the ship he blamed on Emily, jocular and jolly but nonetheless deliberate in his delivery.

These then were the foremast hands, six in all, and thus the first days passed, wind holding, drawing every sail except the jibs. And so they swept along at ten, twelve, and eleven knots as they settled in amongst themselves.

Each morning the watch coming off duty "turned to" at six bells, seven A.M. They washed, scrubbed, and swabbed the decks. They ate their breakfast with the new watch at half-past, then went to bed at eight. At eight bells the real work began, for a ship, like a lady's watch, was always in need of repair. Studding-sail gear had to be roved, and running rigging overhauled, replaced, and repaired. All the ropes and yards—frayed and chafed and worn thin—had to have "chafing gear" put on. There was always the standing rigging to tend; it inevitably hung slack. And the seizings and coverings had to be taken off, tackles got up, rigging bowsed, seizings and covering replaced—this job endless, for when one rope was stayed, another slackened. Old "junk" was brought out of the hold: Spun-yarn, marline, and seizing-stuff was all made on board. The spun-yarn winch, a masculine version of a wheel and spindle, could then be heard, spinning new rope. If this wasn't enough, there were the ceaseless tasks of tarring, greasing, oiling, painting, scraping, and scrubbing—all in addition to the steering, reefing, bracing, and making and setting sail. Through it all the men jostled, defying and defining, and Emily, watching, and listening, grew more comfortable with their ways as they fell into predictable routine.

On Sunday the twelfth day of December she collared the boy and started him on the Ten Commandments—a tough task. He was negligent and inattentive—not only of the Word, but of his tasks as well. He kept forgetting to clean the foc'sle spittoons and the sailors' pannikins. He constantly had to be reminded to dump the stoke ashes over the *lee* rail and to polish *all* the brass—the doorknobs, the hinges, the binnacle post at the helm that housed the compass, and the ship's bell. His interest lay instead in the sailors, in being just like them, and he spent hours trying to imitate their speech, their mannerisms, their gait. And if the sailors were uninterested in reciting the Ten Commandments? "Thou shalt not" were but stones in his mouth. He wished only to spit them out and be done.

Emily had better luck with hymns. He had a yen for music, an ear for parts, and when he had mastered "Amazing Grace" they sang it often, his voice and hers adrift on the wind. "Do you know who wrote that song, Johnny?"

"Someone wrote it?"

"Why, yes. The words didn't just come into their own, now did they? Someone had to make them up and put them together."

"I niver did think on that 'afore now."

"Well, a sailor wrote that song. A very bad and wicked sailor, too."

"Did his ghost go to 'ell then?"

"No. Listen." And she sang for him the words again.

"I be lost! But the Cap'ain, 'e find me! I ain't be blind, though. I see out 'a me eyes like any bloke whut's got a mum."

All the sailors had once been to church, had once learned their catechism, forgotten now. But aloft and alow they listened, memory stirring. And when she sang, whether chanteys or hymns, they were ready to join—ready to join in too when the ship's Sabbath bell rang in the first half of the dogwatch and the Captain gathered them all on the poop to read from the Gospels and to lead in prayers, a common custom.

Sargent, the Bosun, was the only one to object. "It never hurts," insisted the Captain without apology, "to hear of Christ's parables. Thinking men," he added, "never mind."

And so the days passed peacefully enough, growing warmer as they neared the equator, stretching long and longer as if the sun were hesitant to go down on a world so well-ordered, predictable, and masculinely measured.

Evenings saw a respite from their measured work. Tar buckets put away, marline and spun yarn dropped back into the hold, Yates and Sargent, instructed by the Captain, eased up on their orders, and song filled the air, more so as they drew near the Line and the nights fell short. This was Emily's favorite time, and she sat with the Captain at the taffrail, warm at his side and drowsy, while from the foc'sle head, from the helm, from aloft and alow came the words of "Tail Out Men and Give Us Boney," "Boney Was a Warrior," old chanties set adrift to see the reluctant sun sink. Eight bells and the watch turned round. New voices came on deck: "Ranzo," "Blow the Man Down," and "Nearer My God to Thee," chanteys and hymns to welcome the first constellations of both hemispheres. And when the sun at last winked out, Emily and the Captain would go below to talk over the day, to lie in a bed rocked by the sea, and to fall asleep content.

They crossed the equator early the morning of January the sixth, between longitude 20' and 30' E. "Bull's-eye!" cried Yates, winking at Emily and grinning at the crew, quadrant in hand and the day's blazing sun in his marble blue eyes to make them shine. "All 'ands on deck! An' a 'oop an' a 'oller fer the Ol' Man!" he cried. Hats flew. Harris stood on his head, Lawson imitating. Johnny tried. But then the wind stopped, like someone had just run out of air.

All day they sat on the Line becalmed, no wind at all, not even a whisper. Emily came out of the companion hatch to catch a breath. Harris was at the helm, shirt undone and hanging loose. "Better a hatch left open than sail with a woman," he reminded her, sullen eyes on the empty sails.

"There be other ships on the Line," she retorted, but Harris only mopped his brow and stared straight ahead.

Day after day, heat instead of wind. Emily put away her woolens and brought out her lawn cotton. The men unbuttoned their shirts and tried to stay out of each other's way, tempers bubbling. Still they sat on the mirrored sea until the water, filmed in oil, gurgled with a sorry sigh round the cutwater and stern.

The heat stuck in the throat; lungs couldn't suck it in. Minutes became as hours and time weighed so heavy that the men carried it in their shuffle, in the stoop of their shoulders, in the quickness of their fists and their flash of eye. Time suspended, reality took wings. Wait! A puff of wind, a breath of life! The sails fill, the yards groan, the ship creaks again! No! The breeze falls off, the sails hang limp, the ship settles and motion ceases once again, and silence presses them one more time to the shining sea like a fly in a treacle, and they badger each other unmercifully in the web of inactivity.

Midweek they still hadn't moved. Six days and no wind, not even a ripple to ease the blistering heat and cool the tempers. More ships than ever clustered the Line, a dozen if the eyes were to be trusted. Yates, beside himself to find chores to keep the men busy and out of trouble, paced the decks, growling at both man and beast. The masts had been slushed, greased down by the fat skimmed off the "salt horse," the salted beef that was the mainstay of their diet. The decks had been holy-stoned until they squeaked, the riggings checked, tarred, and tightened, sails mended, seams sewn. All that was left was to plait sennit and make thrum mats in the shade of the foc'sle awning.

"Let them take out the small boat and gam," said the Captain finally, "since we're not going anywhere. Two at a time!" he yelled when one and all made a dash. "Bail fast and you won't drown!" He and Yates stood chuckling at their unhindered haste.

Now there was laughter instead of irritated mutterings, and the second dogwatch became, instead of listless complaints, a time to show off what they'd traded other crews of other ships for—and to barter the prizes amongst themselves. A new deck of cards for a Dutch plug of tobacco. An Italian pipe for a useless set of tom-toms.

Nine days becalmed and Yates asked if Emily would like to take a turn in the boat.

"Nay," she said, backing away. "I've seen the water swirl up the thwarts, Mr. Yates."

"But it'll do ye good," he urged, cheeks blistered and peeling from the sun. "Ye must be wary 'a our faces. It can be no more excitin' 'an stirrin' the porridge."

"But she doesn't stir the porridge," said Steward, coming out the galley, wiping his hands on the burlap sack tied round his waist, a greasy and tattered apron.

He squinted suddenly down deck to where the men on watch had gathered. "What's this? Yo, Yates. I think our fair-haired boy is about to go over the side!"

"That I am!" Lawson of the golden locks declared, flinging off his socks and hopping about the hot deck with bare feet. "I've had it! It's so bloody hot my liver is 'bout boiled!"

"Wot do ye know of yer liver, matey?" Yates hollered, angling after him. "Let's 'ave a pint 'a sense 'ere, boy."

Lawson tossed off his cap for an answer, letting it rim and collapse onto a sail locker. He ran a man's hand through his thatch of curls, spit over the rail, and started undoing his buttons.

"Someone give the bloke a bucket over the 'ead!" said Yates, collaring him. "And cool 'im down a bit."

But Lawson slid out of his shirt before anyone could act and Yates, left standing with the shirt in his hands, tossed it atop the cap.

"Dearie me," said Fielding slowly, the seemingly dim-witted 16-year-old. "I heard a tale 'bout a chap whut jumped side and got himself eat by a shark. Womp, chomp, half his body gone."

"You lie, Jack," hissed Lawson, furious, peeling off his pants now.

"No," protested Fielding, thinking it all through very carefully. "God's truth. They brung up the shark, sliced him open, and there the bloke be, in bits and pieces. Half 'a Jack anyways. A bloody sight."

"Bloody indeed," said Lawson. He stood naked, skin whiter than the empty sails. Emily looked away. "There's no sharks around here! No there ain't, Steward!" he argued, shaking his fist at the cook.

They were all leaned over the rail, including the Captain, watching Lawson. A few vigorous strokes, churning through the water, and he turned his back, laughing at them all. "Come on in!" he called, kicking, splashing, ducking back his head to douse his halo. "Harris, you fine chap, come on!" Emily put her arm through the Captain's, conscious of the muscles tightening in his jaw, the worry behind his eyes. "The water's great!" Lawson hollered. "Come on, Hayward, you bloody chicken! Take off your boots and—" Emily saw the shark first, a black triangle of fin cleaving the surface. She couldn't speak, throat squeezed so tight she couldn't even breathe. It was Hayward who screamed "Shark! Shark!"

Lawson's face went white. He somersaulted, knifing back toward them, the shark zooming in from the side, mouth scissored with teeth visible through the water's surface and refracting sun. Before any of them could move, an exploding howl broke beside them, a flash of iron shot past, and the brute shot up dead over Lawson, jaws clamped shut and falling lifeless onto the water, 20 feet long—the saloon harpoon skewered through its head.

Lawson came up the Jacob's ladder and was onto the deck like a flying fish. Johnny wailed, moaning, peering through eyes covered with spread fingers, and when Emily looked out a dozen monsters were upon the first. Nothing but blood, staining the water in swirls of crimson, remained ten seconds later . . . and the sinking harpoon without line.

Yates stood at the rail, chin trembling, face as white as death. "Don't ever," he said, "do that again, matey."

6

My first meeting with this resourceful ruffian, whose name and deeds fill the Pacific even now, was in 1873. At that time he was posing as a missionary to save his oft condemned neck.

—Joshua Slocum
Capt. Joshua Slocum

The sun melted slowly that day, dripping finally into the sea to the west and puddling the ocean surface with her golden wax. Watches alternated, but the men slept fitfully in the stifling evening heat of the foc'sle, air stale and stagnant with pipe smoke and body sweat. At the approach of dusk a silent longboat pulled up beside the *Maid of Athens* and a tall figure hollered up the hull "Praise be to God!" while motioning simultaneously to his crew to throw up a dozen ropes. Up they came, coiling all along the starboard rail and down, men climbing quickly, and before the crew on the *Maid* could rally themselves, a dozen men had leaped aboard.

Amazingly tattooed, belted with knives, beards knotted like bushes, and hooks for hands, they nevertheless paled in comparison to their leader. He was well past middle age, whiskers gray, blue eyes sharp daggers amidst fleshy wrinkles on either side of a long, bony Roman nose, all his face folded and creased, and nearly black with the stain of years and years of sun and wind and rain, making the eyes all the more sharp. He stood stripped to the waist, baked brown, abdomen muscles tight, the skin of his chest and arms nearly bursting under pronounced, hard muscle made shiny with sweat. Six feet, three inches, he bristled with dignity and authority.

Stowaway pulled to her feet, growling low and hackles up. "Stand by," hissed Yates to the Captain and Emily. "I know the bloke. He be Bully Hayes. We best go along—for the moment."

"Yes, praise be to God," said Richard slowly. What, he wondered, was Bully Hayes doing in the Atlantic? *And what was he up to?* He wished Emily were not on deck, but perhaps no place was safe. Already Bully's men, swarthy and tattooed, were overrunning the decks, trading oranges for boots and pipes and miscellaneous truck. He returned his attention to the pirate in front of him. "To what do we owe the honor of this visit?"

"My own copy of the Holy Scriptures has been worn out by much use, and if you would be so kind—" The pirate snorted and spit. "My poor natives, of whom I serve as missionary, are without spiritual nourishment for want of reading the Word."

"They carry coal," whispered one of Bully's crew to the man's cheek.

"A Bible and perhaps a little coal—for the Lord's work, of course."

"Coal ye ask fer!" said Yates suddenly, angrily stepping into Bully's line of vision. "Wait a few years and you'll 'ave more than enough coal, blisterin' 'ot, too, and the Devil 'isself be the stoker! I know who you be, ye old goat!"

"Remember, mate, the good book warns, Judge not that ye be not judged!"

"So you admit who ye be!"

"Who am I?"

"You rip! Ye know full well who ye be! We met under cloudier skies. There be no use to deny it."

"Emily," said the Captain, not taking his eye off the pirate of such ill fame, "go fetch Bully Hayes our Bible so we can bid the man adieu. Yates, go with her."

"Bloody blackguard." They entered the Captain's quarters. "Joseph, Mary, and—"

"Don't swear, Yates."

"I ain't swearing, Missus. It be a rusty sailor's pryer. A Bible? Now don't that take the king's crown. Wot's 'e really want?"

Emily pulled her Bible from the high shelf of books. They must get the man off the ship, quickly. Before night fell. Give him what he asked for, play the game, and be done.

Her eyes fell on *A Tale of Two Cities* tucked into the tipped shelving. The two volumes looked exactly alike. Dare she? She knew what happened in the end anyway. Sydney Carton, as always, each time she read the story, died in stead for Charles Darnay. He never reconsidered, he always did—as Christ for us. But how, she thought, could she give up Catherine's gift? Yet it was Dickens, or their only Bible . . .

Quickly she traded.

"You don't suppose, do you, Yates, that he might be sincere? That he really be converted?"

"Missus, don't you go and get soft. 'E be the scoundrel I sye 'e be, and ye better know 'e be plyin' the convert only to save 'is ugly neck. The black ship 'a 'is be a missionary barque. Killed all the missionaries to get it, too—afer stringing the men up by their thumbs near on fer nine hours and violating all the ladies right in front of 'em, them not seeing a thing, a' course, fer the pain behind their eyes and a tearin' through their limbs. And now he be usin' their ship—and the London Missionary Society flag—to sail into 'arbors all through the South Seas. Easy pickin's. Natives know the flag—and the *Leonora*," he said, as they turned to leave. "They flock on board, praising God. All 'e 'as to do is 'old a few pryers, then fer a benediction clap on the 'atches and sail straightway fer the sugar and cotton plantations in Australia, where 'e can sell the whole congregation—"

"Yates, I shall be sick if you go on."

She stood in the hatch, pale, her lovely dark eyes pleading.

"I only wanted ye to know, Mrs. Wooldridge. So ye don't be makin' the mistake of believin' 'is lies."

Bully Hayes bowed when they approached, a flamboyant sweep with his hat dusting the deck. "Praise be, the dear lady has brought what I search for! The Holy Book of God! Thank you, woman." Too late she saw the words. *A TALE OF TWO CITIES* as bold as you please, embossed in gold right on the front cover! How could she have been so stupid?

"Nice. Very pretty. *THE KING ... JAMES BIBLE*," he said, holding out the cover to read, smiling, two gold teeth sparkling in the sunset. "Are you sure you want to give up so fine an edition?" He couldn't read! *He couldn't read!* What a low-down scoundrel, she thought while assuring him, yes, yes, he most certainly could have it.

"Now you have your Bible," said the Captain. "So summon your men and get off my ship."

"We have not," said Bully tersely, hand to his firearm, "finished discussing the coal."

"We have," said the Captain. "And put away your pistol. There are too many ships about to risk the noose, my friend. One cry and you'll be hanging from this very yardarm before dark." His eyes pointed to the foresail yard above.

A whistle from Bully, abrupt and shrill, and immediately tattooed ruffians appeared from every hatch— burdened by sacks of goods ferreted from every corner of the ship: flour, sugar, coffee, tea, sea biscuits, honey, yams.

"Nay!" thundered the Captain, hand flying to his knife, the knife twinkling in the last of day's light as he leaped toward the pirate and pressed the blade to his grimy throat. He grabbed the man's arm, twisting it up behind his back. "Emily, step behind Yates. Oates, take Bully's gun from his belt and throw it over."

"This is not," wheezed Bully, "the way a Christian behaves."

"No? And stealing a man blind is? Drop what you carry!" he commanded Bully's crew. "And get off my ship! GET OFF! Or your Captain will be arguing with God through a slit gullet!" He drew back on his hand, ever so lightly. Blood bubbled along Bully's throat.

"Do as he says," croaked Bully. The crew quickly disappeared over the rail.

"Be gone from me!" shouted Richard, and he flung the pirate to the bulwark. "No, wait, here is your Bible. You dropped it when I jumped you."

"Bible?" sneered Bully. "I've a dozen Bibles. And I'll get another dozen next week if the captain is not as shrewd as you."

After the crew from the *Leonora* left, the Captain stood alone, pensive, brooding, leaning on the bulwarks and staring out to the flat, wide, idle sea, the book in his hands. Emily came to stand silently beside him, hands flat on the mahogany, fingers straight.

"This is *A Tale of Two Cities*," he said at last, "your book from Catherine. It's not our Bible."

"I couldn't give him our only Bible."

"Did you think a man like Bully Hayes need not read of God's love?"

"He can't read, Richard. He wouldn't have known the difference."

"More's the pity. But Emily, don't you think Bully Hayes needs to read of God's love?"

"I think," she said slowly, "it would have been casting pearls before swine."

He suddenly chuckled and patted her hand. "Aye, you're right, my lovely Emily. You're always right."

"Would you have killed him?"

"Aye." He straightened slowly, still patting her hand. "I wonder," he said with a winsome sigh, "that God should spare us from ourselves. Come, let's walk the deck, darling, and then go down to bed."

7

These pomperos, later to become notorious among Cape Horn sailors, carried the fragrant perfume of the pampas grass, but blew with malicious suddenness.

—Felix Risenberg
Cape Horn

Wind crossed the water in a sweet ripple about half past eight the next morning. Yates, hunched over his breakfast in the saloon, felt the sweetness in the sway of the ship, and he swallowed the rest of his tea in one scalding gulp. "Eh!" he bellowed, sucking quick to cool his tongue, throwing serviette and biscuit onto the plate even while shoving back his chair. "All 'ands on deck! We be settin' the bloomin' sails! Ye too, matey!" he said to the orphan with a wild grin that put the starch into Johnny's legs.

Stowaway lumbered up the stairs ahead of them, tail wagging, barking to beat the band. The sailors in the foc'sle, having just tumbled into their hammocks and nodded off, roused with a shout. The orphan hitched his pants and shinnied up the rattails, the web of ropes that accessed the sails, and began releasing the gaskets, the canvas straps that reefed the sails to their yards.

Hayward, rheumatism forgotten, sprinted round to the lee capstan, where the halyards, the ropes used to raise the sails, were held by belaying pins on the mainmast. With a primal cry he threw the coiled-up buntlines and downhauls onto the deck so the lines would be clear for setting the sail. "Yo!" he hollered.

Fielding, thin-chested and all arms and legs, jabbed a wooden bar into one of the numerous brackets around the top hub of the lee capstan, a cylindrical winch that looked like an ugly gnome with dark, hollow eyes. He waited by his post, sniffing the wind, waiting for first the call from Johnny aloft, then Yates below, before tramping round and round, turning the capstan that would uncoil the buntlines at Hayward's feet and unravel the downhauls.

Aloft, Lawson, Harris, and Oates eased out on the footropes. Aft, Steward took the cook's position at the foresheet, the line which held the lower corner of the foresail.

Further aft, Sargent took the wheel from the Captain.

"Just look at 'em 'ussle," said Yates to the Captain when he joined him at the break in the poop. "An' just feel the wind, Ol' Man! 'Ay—*waaard*! Stand by to lye aloft!"

The boat rolled gently in the waiting, ropes and blocks comfortably creaking.

"Yo!" at last shouted Johnny, aloft and out of the way, "everything clear!"

"Aye, aye! Stand by an' 'ang back!" said Yates as he leaped to Fielding's side, led the halyard end to the capstan, inserted a second bar into the hub, nodded to the youth, and then together and with a cry heaved into it. "*A Yankee ship come down the river*," he sang, exultant, everyone joining in—from aloft, from capstan, from deck and helm, "*Blow, boys, blow!*" Round the capstan squeaked, a quarter turn, a half. One full turn and on. "*He luffs her up till her tops'ls shiver; Blow, my bully boys, blow! Yankee ship, she's a Yankee clipper—*" The capstan picked up speed, circling once, circling twice; the sails unfurled, one inch, two inches, three inches, four. Five in the riggings scrambled along the yards to ease out the sails, letting the canvas take wind and belly out. Emily, carrying a tray of the breakfast dishes up from the saloon, chantey in her ear, was just setting the dishes into the galley sink when the ship took her first real gust.

"Whoa," she whistled, throwing her weight onto one leg and bracing herself with a grin. They were on their way! *"This Yankee ship she's bound to China!"* she sang along. *"Blow, boys, blow!"* The hand pump next to the sink, with a direct line into a copper water well built into the hold below, gurgled under her hard hand; faster, faster, choked, and then sucked. A pot, quick. Keep her pumping. Pot full and over to the stove, still burning. Steward breezed in. *"Blow, my bully boys, blow,"* he sang, tossing his toque to a hook where it caught, swung, and hung. "We're on our way, Missus! Here, let me do that. Ye ain't supposed to sully your pretty hands with a man's work. Out of my galley and get on with your fancywork. Go on now."

Sails unfurled, yards swung round, they were on their way, blow high, blow low, till the *Maid* fairly danced like a mite on the ocean waves, making it a job to sit down, forward and on.

"I'll help carry the dishes," said Emily, as restive and energized as any of the men, "back down to the pantry when you get them washed."

"You can keep me company. If," he added, stoking the stove and giving his bread a punch, "you have the mind."

So she brought up her knitting, and Polly-wants-a-cracker. "She needed air." Steward whistled. Polly fluttered off her shoulder to his, and Emily laughed.

The wind turned brisk before the day passed, and with the topsail set out to windward, they bowled along like the blazes. A bracing wind, vibrant, it whipped up the blood and set fingers and toes atingle.

A week later the sea took on a deeper hue as they crossed the 40th latitude. The men buttoned their jackets, and battened down their hats. Emily unpacked her woolens. The first albatross of the Southern Hemisphere flew out of heaven's breath and Emily fell back, quite unprepared for the beauty. Fourteen feet from wingtip to wingtip, and the graceful bird wheeled, soaring and soaring, the very poetry of effortless motion.

"Boo!" shouted Harris, coming up behind and scaring the daylights of her. "Just watch, woman. There flies the soul of a lost sailor."

"Don't be silly. It be a bird, Harris, plain and simple."

"Maybe, but ask yourself this, Missus. Where does it sleep? What does it eat? I tell you, that albatross is the soul of a drowned man."

Another ten days they ran before the wind, the sea high beam and full. At times the sea sloshed over the deck and out the scuppers, long drainage ditches along the deck edge. Everything wet, nothing dry. But no one cared—they were moving, clipping along under full press of sail, closer and closer to the Horn. Each day, precisely at noon, Yates and the Captain pulled out the quadrant and recorded their rapid progress latitude by longitude into the ship's log. Wednesday, January 26, they came into the crosswinds blowing off the River Platte of Argentina, and Yates, for the first time in nearly a fortnight, ordered the topsail shortened, a safeguard against the sudden squalls of the higher Southern latitudes. While it was being done Charles Darnay married Lucie Mannette on page 186, and Emily, drowsy, dropped *A Tale of Two Cities* to her lap to idly gaze astern.

What was there, she wondered, about the sea that made the things of home seem so remote? Stowaway, broken leg mended and lazy, lay asleep on the poop nearby. The crew bustled out and about, the day blustery and bright on the hard blue sea. Emily, the sounds all ahum in her ears, sat content and happy to be exactly where she was, mesmerized for some curious reason by the long furrow or wake they were leaving behind. Suddenly she sat up with a start.

A great rack of clouds was building itself up with amazing speed. A dozen albatrosses, spinning round and round the ship, suddenly spread their wings, pinwheeled, and then scudded before the wind at breakneck speed and disappeared.

"Captain?" she called even as Stowaway raised her head to turn her face into the wind. A growl rattled low in her throat.

"I don't like the looks of that," he said, coming to stand quietly beside her. Together they watched the clouds billow and foam and then rip open with spilling sunlight, all yellow and tainted gold in the gap. The waves took on queer, unusual shapes, the sea turned a drab metallic tinge. The air turned cold, the waves gurgled against the smooth sides of the ship in seductive softness, and the little brigantine moved uneasily, as if she knew danger stalked. Stowaway lumbered to her feet and began to pace the poop, whining, looking at them all with imploring eyes.

Oates popped out the companion hatch. "The barometer's fa'in' fast, sur!"

The Captain looked up against the darkening sky. Overhead the sails had fallen limp. Suddenly they filled, snapping wildly, only to fall flat again. A sinister change had come over the ship, and then on the sweet scent of pampas grass the Captain leaped to his feet. "Yates! *Pompero!* All hands to your post!"

In a moment there was the frenzied activity of frightened, purposed men. The main and aft hatches were battened down, the galley fire put out.

"*All ha-ands on deck!*" roared Yates. "Sargent, take the helm!" and he chased Lawson aloft to help reef the shortened topsail.

"Help on the topsail!" shouted Sargent to Fielding, taking the wheel. "Lay aloft!" Up, up the gangly youth climbed to meet the other two. Up, up, and up, gaining the yards and edging out on the footropes where he clung swinging in the gale, the three of them tossed about on the spar by the stiff, billowing canvas. They hugged the yards, fingers on the iron jackstay, grasping the gaskets. One broke loose and Lawson swore: The belly of the sail was loose!

Cold bodies forgotten, fingernails broken and bleeding, they fought to smother the bulge of canvas. It had broken nearly clean of its bottom leach and was standing out horizontally from the yard, snapping with whiplash cracks. "Now!" screamed Yates even as the wind cut hands and face. "Together!" The new turns held. Lawson's fair hair streamed in the wind. The boat rocked on her beam and Fielding, scared, edged out the yardarm to finish the job. The brace had slacked and the heavy, jerking spar bounced and swung low, pointing down into the white seething water, a boiling bed of bubbling foam. Job done, he started back, slowly, horrified, into the safer slings of the yard, and Emily, watching the terrified youth, book in her belt and holding fast to the taffrail, let out a low breath, her own heart beating in fear in the fury of the driving wind.

The wind howled against the reefed sails. Sargent, at the helm, fought to keep the ship as near into the wind as possible, running before the storm. Heavy combers reared ahead and behind, crests blew off and spit spindrift, rearing again to break in a rage across the rolling decks. One last look and Emily scuttled for the safety of her cabin, Stowaway quick behind. The dog whined to be put up on the bed, where she burrowed, whimpering, nose under the pillows. Emily lay, queasy, upon the locker with the horsehair mattress, under the large skylight, the ship rolling heavily in the symphony of violence. She could hear the cymbals of the waves crash overhead, the wail of a high-pitched violin in the wind, the deep rattle and vibration of a bass.

"What's our position?" *Yates.*

"I can't get a reading!" *The Captain.* "The sun—"

The skylight burst, water poured through broken glass, and Emily flew with a smack against the bulkhead, deluged and gasping and drenched to the skin. Her workbox went over. Scissors and knitting needles flew. The locker door snapped open. Out rolled tins of meat, everything bobbing and sinking in a foot of water. What had happened? She looked around, stunned. Everything tumbled about, afloat—charts, chairs, pillows, books. Papers, more broken glass. The chronometer? No, tucked safe in its box, anchored to keep Catherine happy, thank goodness. She was still rubbing her head in agony when the cry came, *"Man overboard!"*

She tripped, wool skirts tangling about her ankles. She tried a few more steps, but no. She was imprisoned by the layers of stretched heavy, wet wool. Quickly she seized the scissors off her bed and started cutting away the weight.

"Two men overboard!"

Oh, Richard, *Richard!* She ripped through the layers, shears snip-snipping, tangling, snipping again, and once free, stockinged legs exposed below the ragged hem, she sloshed through the water, rushing, tripping, driven up the stairs by the force of her dread. *"RICH-A-A-A-RD!"*

He met her at the hatch. "Go below!"

"Oh, Richard!" she sobbed, clinging to him. "Thank God you be safe!"

"Go back! Get down!"

"Who! Who be lost?"

"Fielding and Yates!"

"NO!" She scrambled past him. *Yates, oh Yates!* Her husband caught her, and she plowed into his wet arms, seeing now the terrible gap in the starboard poop rail—stanchion ripped right out and gone.

The Captain held her tight. "Fielding fell off the yard! Yates went right through the rail. Head slammed the stanchion!"

She pushed her forehead into his chest and ground it into the harsh rubber of his slicker. "No," she moaned, "please, dear God, no..." But Yates was gone, only blood and bits of his skull left, splattering the deck.

"Please, Emily, go below..."

The ship, plowing and plunging on, nearly tipped her off her feet as she blindly headed for the companionway.

"*Emily!* Look out!"

A hill of water, towering higher than the main mast, was rushing to meet them, and she only had time to see her husband fling himself at the helm and to throw herself at the binnacle post before they were tossed to the crest of the wave. The ship heeled, tipping so quickly that the world spun upside down. The sting of salt, head against the post, hanging so tight her shoulders ripped in their sockets. When the water rushed back and she could see again, the Captain was still there, turning the wheel. Harris was lying along the yard desperately trying to gain control of the foresail on the foremast. The poop and foc'sle head were just small islands, a mad river of seawater rushing between to flood the main deck.

"Fielding!" someone cried. "I see 'im!"

"Emily!" thundered the Captain again. "*GO BELOW!*"

The ship was listing, the whole poop sloping like a mountain cabin's roof, water running off and carrying everything loose with it. She slithered and slipped and finally clambered on all fours back to the hatch, grabbing onto cleats where she could, skirting the henhouses lashed to the deck, her teeth chattering. The hens cackled, spitting water from their lungs. A sudden jolt threw her flat, and down came her teeth on her tongue. Hot tears stung. But then she was at the hatch, sitting, huddled over her knees on the first stair, too breathless, too cold, too bruised to move.

"Down helm!" Richard roared. *They were going back?* "Weather the main braces! Back the mainyards, and let fly the clews of the foresail!" They *were* going back! For

Fielding, if he lived, if any of them lived. The ship bounced—to bow, to stern. She grabbed hold of the rail. Another wave, and water swirled across deck, sucking about her waist and down the stairs. The cold drove her to her feet and she stumbled, step by step, stair by stair, chilled to the bone, into her cabin below.

Winded, panting, shivering, back to the door. The creaking and grinding, snapping, thudding—oh, the awful clattering and groaning, the moaning, a cacophony more frightening below than up on top. She slapped her hands over her ears but could not, of course, shut out the din and clamor above. Heart in her throat, pounding; pounding in her head. Stowaway yelped from where she'd been thrown, pawing to get back on the bed. Emily tried to lift the dog, but couldn't. Too wet, too heavy and slippery. She tried again, and nearly collapsed when she succeeded.

Slowly she realized the water was going down, rushing through to the bilge below where the men, later, would pump it out. *Yates?* She whirled, for she'd heard his tread outside. But no, of course not. She lit a lamp with a trembling hand. Everything in the bottom two drawers of the chest was soaked through. She heard him again, this time in his cabin, behind the bulkhead, tying on his boots. No, no, he was not there. She knew the truth certain enough, yet in a curious way her mind refused to believe. Perhaps this is a nightmare. I'll wake up, pinch myself, see? No, she be awake and Yates be dead, and water puddled the floor and everything stank of salt and oil.

The narrow aisle outside her cabin was still awash, water gurgling and running off. In the pantry pickles had fallen on dough that was rising. The dishes still jumped. Cheese rolled on the floor, first this way, then that.

"Ready the small boat!" Richard's voice shot down the

companionway, and ship tacked, he stood back against the course. It had been a dangerous thing to do. He wondered at himself. The seas could easily have swept end to end, the wind could have snapped the sails back to uproot the rigging. And for what? How was he to find anyone in this hell? Only a miracle could bring him to the spot. And now it had begun to rain, a drizzle right out of the Antarctic, bringing ice and hail. But he had to try, didn't he? He had to trust the chance. He could not, if he had any power at all, leave a man behind.

Oates took charge of the boat, laying out the orders in his thick brogue. Efficient, speedy, not a command too many, not one raised shout. Oarlocks, oars, coiled rope, blankets. Quick words and the boat was supplied, and swung over the ship's side, ready to be lowered at a moment's notice. Steward, shaking his head and muttering, leaped the bouncing gap between ship and boat. He took the bow. Oates followed, taking the stern, hanging onto his tam. Sargent and Johnny stood by, and Richard, at the helm with Lawson, watched the syncopated teamwork in gratitude, his eyes quick, though, to keep sweeping the murk ahead. Harris, aloft, broke the tension. "I see him! I see him! Fielding two points to port!" He could *see* through such muck and rain?

"Stand by to lower the boat!" Richard hollered, both hands cupped to his mouth. "Oates! Be careful not to let her stove in against the hull when you go down! When we roll your side down, and the sea skims your bottom, let the tackle rip! If you don't, you'll be dragged on our upswing, and be tipped right out. Stand by! One!" he shouted, watching the tilt of the deck. "Two! Three . . . *Now!*"

The little boat rode free, smacking the sea with a bounce. Oates and Steward, fore and aft, flung the tackle-blocks from their hooks, then pushed off and were away before the side of the ship rolled back up.

They gaped at one another, swallowing. Nothing but moving walls of foam-soaked green, and pouring rain. Steward took hold of a huge steering oar and stood aft, bracing knee to gunwale as they slid into a trough. "Where is he?" he bawled above the roar.

"I dinna ken! Canna see a bloody thing!" The boat flung them high onto a crest, up, up, up until Oates thought they might take to the air, and still nothing could he see but a third, a fourth wall of sea. Down they skidded, reeling.

"Canna even see the ship noo!" the Scot hollered, fighting panic.

Steward said nothing but glanced hard into the storm when they rose, one more time, high on the waves. He heard the Captain's voice, and turned. Yes! Oil from the old wake! He set in his oar, Oates rowing from the rear, riding the waves back along the way they had come, dropping into the swale, riding high again. They dare not go far from the ship, *but had they already gone too far?* It had happened before, at sea.

Rain came down in droves. Steward's eyes burned, his hands throbbed, fingers needles of pain. Was the youth still alive? His head told him no, not this long in the sea.

"Oates! You bloody old Scot, you! I see him! Four boat lengths away! Straight ahead, Jack! Row!"

Oates threw himself at the oars, rowing furiously, the miracle of it all fueling his flagging strength as he yanked back the sea. They brought the boy up over the stern lest in the struggle they all capsize—after prying loose his frozen hands off the oar he clutched. He was hardly conscious, but he breathed and the two men joyously flung about him the blankets they'd brought and lit for home.

The Captain could not believe they'd done it. "I thank you," he stammered, quickly loosening the noose that Oates had slipped around the young man's chest and under his arms so they could haul him up the bobbing hull of the ship. "The sea," he said, cradling Fielding in his arms and quickly carrying him into the galley, "does not always have the last word."

8

Night came on with more wind and gloom and weeping rain, the pompero settling into a dead monotony of punishment. Yates' absence became a piercing pain. The lookout did not walk the foc'sle head in any attempt to keep warm, but stood huddled beneath the jib lamp. Aft, when hands changed at the helm, the course was whispered softly and in gentle tones. In the foc'sle nobody slept, nobody ate. The sailors off duty sat, dipping hardtack into tea but not eating.

Down in the mate's cabin where Fielding lay fevered and delirious in Yates' bunk, Emily endlessly chaffed the heat back into his thrashing limbs. Why Yates? she asked with everyone else. Death came to those at home, in quiet rooms, curtains drawn, friends and family gathered to say goodbye. Death came to the worn and aged and those made weary by life and ready to let it go. But to a vigorous man? Full of strength and life? To *Yates*? The question floated behind all their eyes, anchored in the storm of their minds. *Why? Why?* And all through the long night the figurehead of the *Maid* smiled on, as if nothing at all had happened.

By morning the pompero blew out. The sun came out. Everything dripped: the riggings, the sails, clothes and caps. Sargent, as Bosun, ordered the old sails unbent, folded, and stored away. New sails of thick canvas, better able to handle the Southern latitude storms, were bent on the yards. He ordered the sea-tossed deck holystoned, and the men, sandstone strapped to their feet, vigorously scraped down the deckboards as if to wash from their minds the tragedy.

"A capful of wind," said Steward, taking hot tea down to Emily and the Captain, where they sat with Fielding still thrashing in his sleep.

"Wait till we get to the Horn," said the Captain wearily. "We haven't seen anything yet."

A little before one o'clock he ordered the mainyard backed, the Union Jack hung aft at halfmast. Tradition dictated the ritual of a funeral. Sargent he instructed to toll the ship bell, a melancholy, moving sound, and together and one by one the men traipsed aft to the break in the poop, their faces ashen and troubled, their eyes shadowed. The ship pitched in her stop. Water sloshed, swirling around the main deck, sometimes lapping at the rusty bulwarks before gurgling through the scuppers. No longer did the wind howl; it moaned instead—an eerie, strange sound in the riggings that thrummed raw nerves. Bareheaded and silent, the crew clustered before the Captain, rolling slightly with the ship. How strange they each looked—Steward with a whitened face, Lawson with his golden curls combed, the boy with his little eyes red-rimmed.

Richard didn't know what to do or say; tradition did not include an empty funeral bier. Where was tradition when naked truth smote you between the eyes, and you stood before a vacant grave? For Yates was gone, as irretrievably as yesterday, and all the loneliness and uncertainty and unanswered questions rose up to crush his throat, striking him dumb. His men waited. He must say something. He held the answers, their eyes said. But there were no answers. There never were, he realized. He coughed, he cleared his throat. His heart forged words—poor words, but a beginning—for his tongue.

"We aren't men," he said, "trained in philosophy or theology that we should take comfort in theory and abstract thought. Nor are we old that we might ferret out and understand truth in tragedy. We're young." Emily, he noticed, stood with lips tight, dark circles sharp beneath her eyes. His men stood stooped, shoulders slumped, hats respectively removed and quiet in their hands: Hayward, Harris, Oates, Sargent, Johnny, Steward, Lawson. Only Fielding was missing... and Yates. He began again. "We're sailors. We don't make theory of life, we live it; yet one of us is dead. We feel bitter and disillusioned—as if life doesn't end in death." Feeble words took shape, molding thought. "Perhaps we've been going about our days with notions of forever, when to live is really to die. Why *should* we feel shocked? Why *do* we stand stunned? Why do we cry against God? And yes, we are all crying against God. But is it God who smites us down? When death comes to us all? I don't know. Unless it's because we've been caught off guard, unprepared. But is this God's fault," he asked, "or ours?"

The wind picked up in the riggings. Gray murk and storm rack clouded the sky. "We have," he said, seeing at least one answer now, "been living careless lives, day to day, week to week, intent upon the little things. Lawson cheating at cards—yes, we all know you cheat. Johnny shirking his responsibility because he thinks he won't get caught. Hayward," he galloped on, "exaggerating his rheumatism. All of us snared by pettiness and selfishness, missing the life we claim to live. No, we are not preachers or philosophers, nor are we wise old men. We are sailors, and yet for all that we do not know how to live. May God teach us all how to live."

The Bible whispered in his hands. The words of Christ

beckoned. Christ had died young too—brutally and suddenly and without reason. Richard, as Captain, turned the Bible in his hands.

"*I am the resurrection and the life,*" he read, opening to the familiar passage. "*He that believeth in me, though he were dead, yet shall he live.... And whosoever liveth and believeth in me shall never die. Believest,*" he asked, of them, of himself, "*thou this?*"

Emily began the hymn, quickly harmonized by the boy. Richard joined and they all sang "Nearer My God to Thee." When the song was done he took from his pocket Yates' crucifix. "And now," he said, "in the name of the Father, the Son, and the Holy Ghost, we commend your soul, John Yates, to the tender hand of God who saves us all. Amen."

The sea took the crucifix as it had taken the man—one moment with them, the next moment gone.

⚓

"The men sing hymns," Emily whispered to Richard when they lay in bed at last, the long day gone.

"Men will always sing hymns when someone dies."

She kissed the arm that held her. She worried, for and with him.

"There is none I can leave in charge of the deck," he said at last, "with Yates gone."

"What of Oates?"

"He's a good man, but the others won't obey him."

"And Sargent?"

He snorted, amending himself quickly. "I ought not snort, but there's something I don't like of the man."

"He seems quiet enough."

"I suppose you're right."

She rolled over, sliding into his arms. His belt buckle rubbed the skin on her spine, and she knew this was the way it would be until reaching Chile. As long as there was none he could leave in charge, he would not be able to undress and go to bed properly.

"I'm sorry, darling," he whispered.

"*Amazing grace...*" The orphan's clear soprano voice sifted down the companionway, coupled with the more resonant bass of the older men. The Captain's breathing grew deep and Emily knew he slept, trusting her to wake him should anything sound amiss.

Yates... the ship heeling over... the wall of sea... scraps tossing and turning in her mind. *Back to Yates, back to Yates. Dead. Washed overboard and into eternity.*

The men's voices subsided. She started up, the ship heeling. No, only memory turning again. The ship rocked gently, all at peace, all at peace, and she grew calm and serene in the gentle breathing of her husband. A kind Providence surely watched over them all.

But then like the roll of the sea, towering, towering, the chilling thought hit: *What will I do if something should ever to happen to my dear Richard?*

9

Although I wear gloves, my hands turn blue...even while sleeping I now wear long underwear, wool pants, four shirts, two pairs of socks, and watch cap, and I am still cold....

—Webb Chiles
Storm Passage

Eleven minus one, and without the help of Fielding, for he yet pitched and tossed in Yates' bed, they neared Cape Horn and the Magellan Strait, clipping along in a wind that grew more bitter and more fierce the further south they flew. On clear nights the Southern Cross warned to come no further, yet into the face of the cross they flew. The cold increased. Whales spouted, albatross screeched and wheeled. The men turned cold and blue, and out of the southeast came a shouting wind, abrupt and capricious. It demanded all their time, their vigilance, their strength. If they had missed Yates before, they missed him now all the more with every hour of lost sleep, every minute aloft. Sleep, warmth, and time on their hands became a thing of the past, dimly remembered and deeply yearned.

The main deck rarely saw air, awash always with the surging sea. Waves, driven by the same wind that batted the sails and tore at the riggings, climbed the bulwarks with a sweeping roar only to swirl about deck before draining, gurgling and choking out the scuppers and back from whence they came—but not before another wave, driven by the same wind, slapped the same bulwarks, leaped the same deck, swirled the same and drained the same.

The men pulled on long underwear, wool pants, flannel shirts and two pairs of socks, all wet; they laced up wet boots and bundled into wet pea-jackets, buttoning them to wet chins. They donned wet slickers and faced their watches wet and wretched. Emily wrapped a scarf around the orphan's neck and tucked it down his slicker, but still he was wet the moment Sargent rang eight bells. Wet, they made fast the sails; wet, they set them again. Wet, they brought down ripped-up and blown-out sails; wet, they repaired and replaced the shredded canvas; wet, they rotated watches. Wet they worked, ate, and slept until the battle to get through the Horn became an obsession, driving all else from their minds.

Driven, silent, they carried out their tasks mechanically. Yet there was a difference among them too. There was little laughter or song, but there was something else—more subtle, more secret. There was more kindness, a more gentle exchange of words, hands more willing to help. Subtle, secret—like Lawson lending his cap and Harris dumping Johnny's ash. And when Fielding made his debut, rising from bed a fortnight later, it was Hayward with his rheumatism who kept a sharp lookout for the youth, ready to spring to his aid; he'd been left so weak that he was unable to perform even the simplest task without collapse.

In this blossoming kindness Emily found refuge in the galley each evening during the dogwatch, for it was here that the men gathered, and in Yates' death she no longer felt a stranger to their ways. Men were not so different from women after all. "Well, Yates is gone now," one would say. "God won't be hard," another would respond, "upon the poor chap." A warm stove, baking bread, Stowaway in the way and whining for a rub behind the ears—everything sane, everything fine. They all came to feel the sanity, to smell the security, to refill their grog and tea, to gain the assurance they needed. "His cruise was up, he was a good mate." Nods all round and Steward would pour another cup.

"Steward," said Emily one morning, eyeing Polly-wants-a-cracker and the four banty hens who'd survived the storm, bird and fowl perched together atop the roost Steward had strung over the stove so they could dry out. "I hope their droppings don't find their way into the soup."

"You'll never know, will you, Missus?" He laughed, his first since Yates' death, when she made a face.

An attachment had grown between these two. In the days after the storm had passed, the ship ever pressing south in the icy winds, the others ever facing the foaming, choppy seas, she and Steward had faced the galley stove, propped on their stools, thrown against the bulkheads with each toss of the ship, peeling potatoes and baking bread, boiling rice, keeping the tea hot.

Today the hour was early. Steward had just put on the morning's coffee and a pot of tea and was mixing the bread dough. On the stove eggs boiled and oatmeal thickened in pleasing bubbles and smells. Through the narrow galley window dawn had just broken to illuminate a gray sky with grayer seas, high gray waves tossed with frothy combers of a lighter gray.

"Steward?" Emily asked. "Why do men fight?"

Steward's eyes lifted lazily in response to Emily's question, yet underneath the movement was disguised curiosity.

"Last night Lawson and Hayward—"

"Ah, yes, the marmalade," and he perched himself atop a high stool, putting the wooden bread bowl between his knees. "I didn't set out enough, and Lawson—"

"—took what was left before Hayward could—"

"—get his share. And afterward they got into an altercation."

"Yes."

"It takes so little," he said thoughtfully, pensively, squeezing slowly the dough between his fingers, "to bring out the brute in a man. Particularly a man at sea. Have you ever thought, Missus," he asked, looking up, wrinkled face creased and crossed with thin light from the window, "what the world would be like without Eve?"

"Eve of the Old Testament?" she asked in surprise, teacup hesitant at her lips. "Eve of the Garden of Eden?"

"The same."

She had to think on it a minute. "Men would say, I suppose, that without Eve there would be no sin."

"This is where men commit their first sin. Do you want to hear this?" he asked suddenly. "A bit early in the morning . . ."

"Yes," she said, intrigued, "I think I do."

"In Genesis, what is the account of creation?" But he waited not for an answer. Squeezing the flour and lard between his hands, he began what was clearly a summary of deep study and well-thought ideas, beginning with a quote, apparently from memory, from Genesis. "'Let us,'" he said, "'us,' plural, 'make man,' and in Hebrew man, 'adam,' is androgenous, without gender. A closer translation would be 'Let us make humankind in our own image. Male and female created he them.' It is the male and female together which mirrors the image of God and reflects the creativity of the godhead." He paused, she poured herself another cup of tea.

"In Genesis chapter 2," he went on, kneading his dough, "we find how he made male and female. We also," he punched his dough, "find explanation for the relationship between male and female. 'It is not good that 'adam should be alone; I will make an help meet for him.' And here, Mrs. Wooldridge, men commit a second sin. They reduce female to servant, yet this is not what help meet means at all."

The cook pulled himself straight, punching and pulling on his dough: punching and pulling, punching and pulling. "Help meet," he went on, "*ezer* in Hebrew, does not mean to help from a position of subservience. *Ezer* means to help from a position of power, as a mother her child. The way you help the boy," he added, and she nodded, beginning to see what he was saying. "A woman helps a man not because she is weak or inferior or less capable, or because she's been told to, but because she is strong—"

"How do you know that *ezer* means—?"

"To help from a position of power? Because the same word used in Genesis to describe women is used 17 out of 21 times in the Old Testament to describe God. God is the helpmeet of Israel, bringing salvation and protection to his people. He did not do this from the limited corner of subservience. Did He?" he asked gently.

"Steward, I didn't know you were a man of letters. Where did you learn all this?"

He shrugged. "There is much you don't know of me, ma'am. Shall I go on? Are you bored?"

"Ney, I not be bored. I have never heard this before."

"The way I see it—" he tore off a lump of dough and began shaping it in his hands, "—it's the male and female together, strength and gentleness if you will—not master and servant—that makes us the image of God."

"But we started talking about marmalade, Steward! And Harris and Lawson. How did we get—"

"—onto this sticky subject?" He stood to put the bread by the stove where it might rise, and to stoke the fire, wincing at the stiffness in his knees. He sniffed the oatmeal and poured himself a cup of coffee, grimaced and threw it back into the pot with a splash. "You asked why men fight. Why Lawson stole all the jam and why Harris got so upset and why they came to blows over the whole affair. Hand me the loaf pans, no, cupboard to your right. Thank you, Missus. Forget all my blathering. What it all boils down to is this. Put a bunch of men at sea and their masculinity, the brute in them, becomes over-developed. Men grind against each other at sea, there is so little to remind them of their gentler side. And in their grinding they lose what women bring—so they fight, and squabble. The spiritual and healing aspects of their natures become dwarfed. Why, in some cases I have even seen it completely atrophied."

"Bully Hayes?" she asked.

"Aye, good thinking, Missus. Oops! There goes eight bells! The men will be wanting their breakfast."

A grunt and a groan, the veins in his neck thickened while he lifted the heavy porridge pot off the stove. "Oh, and Missus?" He stood in the door, pot swinging in his fist and knees loose against the lurch of the ship. "Have you heard the shipboard saying, *'Good quarrel, better friends'*?" He angled out, deck rocking, pot swinging. "Don't be surprised to find, Missus, that Harris and Lawson are tight mates from now on!"

⚓

"I think it's a mistake," said Sargent down in the saloon, daring the Captain with a stiff lip. The Captain gave him a cold stare and the Bosun added a reluctant *"sir"* to his dissent.

The two men had Maurey's Wind Charts spread all over the table. The Captain was exhausted, desperate for sleep, desperate for relief from the unrelenting responsibility now that Yates was gone. The desperation was made worse by Sargent, suddenly a thorn without Yates and for some reason ever challenging the Captain's authority in sneaky, subtle ways. It took every ounce of Richard's failing energy to nip the petty insurrections in the bud. "The winds are too capricious this time of year," he said. "We wasted a fortnight on the Line. And if we run aground? I'll not subject the crew to the treacherous natives. I, for one, am not satisfied that the last of the cannibals have died out—or been converted. No, my decision stands, Sargent. We're going to bypass Magellan Strait and sail instead down and around Tierra del Fuego, *around* the Horn."

Several considerations had forced him to this decision: multiple strands of thought and feeling, worry too, and concerns, not the least of which was a distrust of himself to pilot the *Maid* through the intricate passage without sleep. But put the men to the Horn? Good sailors, each of them, there was no reason to doubt their ability to manage the sails and to beat the fury of the wind.

"The Horn is the end of the world," insisted Sargent with a belligerent upswing of the chin. "Sir."

"The Strait of Lemaire," Richard snapped, eyes blazing, "not Magellan Strait! We'll angle in toward the Horn, skirt just inside the Falkland Islands here." His pencil, the flat of it, swept the 500 miles east of the Magellan Mouth and down through the Strait of Lemaire. "We'll bypass Staten Island to the southeast, which *truly* is," he said, hammering his pencil on the spot and looking Sargent straight in the eye, "the end of the world."

"We'll never make it around. We'll shipwreck, sir. Just like the *Patmos* under Captain Nichols, sir."

Richard caught quick enough the double meaning behind the Bosun's words. Nichols had taken his wife—on a honeymoon voyage—and had floundered off the Horn.

"Mr. Sargent, do as you're bid. Set the course." And he strode from the room, sick with doubt. *Had he made a mistake?*

10

Is Envy then such a monster?

—Herman Melville
Billy Budd

There is a sin none admit. Many an arraigned mortal has plead guilty to nefarious sins of weakness and depravity that he might gain mercy and mitigated sentence, but none dare confess this. Has ever there been in a court of law defense made in the name of envy? Or is envy a sin so universally pickled in shame that one might rather admit to all measure of hideous crime to avoid its truth? Would a man rather swing from his gallows, insanity his excuse, than declare to all others he lived a life in covetous discontent? Robert Sargent, Bosun, was such a man.

From cradle on, nothing he ever did was good enough to merit the tender attention of his mother; she kept the softer parts of herself for Jacob, the eldest of two sons by ten months. His father too found his endeavors for recognition insignificant, unworthy of laud, while Jacob, prone to laziness and default, his only merit being first born, was praised and rewarded without restraint. Robert Sargent withdrew to hide behind veiled eyes his inferiority, an innocent defense; but as time went on, envy sprouted and rooted so deep in his soul that his pain became his poison.

Such toxic envy rode in his eye, although he did well to keep it hidden, veiled in practiced retreat. But when he found himself aboard the *Maid* his jealousy knew no bounds, for here he was in service to a man who had everything that should have been his: a rich legacy and a sleek ship of his own, to say nothing of a woman who ever sat by his side, paraded on his deck, took to his bed. That a man should have so much, so easily, stuck in his craw, and daily he chafed at the reminder of his own deprivation and lack of birthright, now a prisoner at sea from what he had hoped to escape on land.

For a time he just chafed, living behind his eyes, coolly calculating how he might secure what he'd decided was his; for this is the elemental evil of envy: Unloved you hate, denied you usurp. And that the Captain was good? It only intensified the passion. No desire to admit the evil within, yet comprehending the good without, his nature could find no recourse but to recoil upon itself and act out the inevitable part to be played. And so when Yates, First Mate, died, the resultant contact with the Captain let Robert Sargent, Bosun, scratch freely the chafing of his envious discontent.

And thus, mid-February and nearing the end of the world, Sargent found his first real chance to claw.

Emily, in her room and lingering over her tea, feet propped on the horsehair mattress of her footlocker, was running through her mind what she might do with the afternoon. The boy's clothing, what little he had, needed attention. The wind and rain had all but turned them to rags. Perhaps, and here was a thought, she could take in some of Yates' clothes and remake them? His blue flannel shirt would do for starters. Mind made up and eager to begin, she rummaged through her sewing box for a measuring tape and finding it, she went in search of the boy. She had not far to go: Voices rumbled out the saloon.

"Run along, boy! I ain't done, you runt!"

"But I needs to 'ave yer plate, 'arris! Or Steward be 'avin' me 'ide now!"

"Then let the bloke have your hide," bawled Sargent. "Do you see the pudding still on my plate? *Don't take the teapot!*"

"Johnny," interjected Emily, stepping into the room and nodding briefly to both Harris and Sargent, the only two besides the boy still present. "Leave off the plates for now and give me your back. Now hold still." Submissively he stood, although he squirmed, shifty on his bare feet, while she measured first the length of his back and then the width of his shoulders, and finally his arms. "There you be and I thank you kind sir," she said with a smile and giving him a pat. "Off with you now. No, take up the turret with you. Tell Steward I'll bring the rest for a wash when the men are done." To the men, whispering back and forth across the table in hushed and furtive tones, she said, "I'll give you five minutes. When I come back with my sewing I want the table clear."

"Listen to the bloody woman," scoffed Sargent to Harris loud enough so she could hear. "Who is she to tell a man what to do?"

Harris giggled like a girl. Both men giggled, and she backed toward the door. What had gotten into them? To be so surly?

"I suppose it was you," said Sargent, addressing her suddenly, "to tell the Captain to take Lemaire and not Magellan?" She took another step back, even as he stood and tossed aside his chair to cut round behind to block the door.

Better to ignore them than respond. She started gathering the dishes onto a tray. Harris grabbed a cup right out of her hand. "Strait of Lemaire is the end of the world, woman. And you know what that means, woman?" He slapped the cup onto the tray. "Of course you do, we all know. Beyond here there be dragons," and he feigned to breathe fire in her face. "Only the Captain don't care.

'Cause he don't have to face the danger, and he don't have to set the sails, do he?"

She piled plates onto the tray, silverware, another cup, fingers trembling.

"It was you who talked him into it," insisted Sargent from the door. "You bloody woman, you told him you were scared of the bloody cannibals! Now we all have to risk the bloody Horn!"

She whirled, tray gripped tight in her hands. How dare he! "No one tells my husband anything! *He* is the Captain of this ship!"

"I don't suppose *you* might have a go at him? Get him to change his mind, eh?" She blushed, for Sargent's eyes held hidden meaning. "Turn on that womanly charm of yours? Get him to reconsider?" His eyes moved down her body and she dropped the tray. Catherine's teapot shattered, lid bouncing and rolling.

"LAND A-HOY! LAND A-HOY!"

The surging cry came again, ringing down the stairs. Sargent spun and plunged through the door, Harris after him. Emily, blinking and hardly able to comprehend, wrenched herself from the broken china and the sharp fragments of Sargent's mean words, and tore up the stairs in his wake.

"LAND A-HOY! LAND A-HOY!"

Oates, eyeglass fastened to his eye, spun in circles on the foredeck. "Aye! Tis land a starboard!"

The Captain took the glass and for a long time studied the highland, chewing his lip. "Let's have a look at those charts, Oates. Here, boy, have a look-see," and he handed the glass to Johnny.

He didn't even notice the mess in the saloon, the shattered teapot, the soggy biscuits and scattered spoons. "Emily!" he cried, looking up from charts spread atop the clutter of uncleared dishes and scattered bread-crumbs. Still he didn't notice, even though she was on her knees, tears in her eyes, china shards in her hands. "It's Patagonia, darling!"

For a moment she forgot her grief. Land with a name? Land where people lived, year in and year out, getting up in the morning, going to bed at night, free to come, free to go? Suddenly she missed the land, and there came over her a quick and vicious pang of homesickness. "Do you know what this means?" he asked her. "Means we're almost to Tierra del Fuego, the Horn! Oates," and his attention was back to business at hand, "we'll reef the sails and set sail for the Strait of Lemaire in the morning—with full daylight on our side. I'll have Sargent give the orders."

⚓

So this be the Horn, thought Emily, retreating to her cabin. For all the reputation she bore, the sea was *not* capricious. And the air was clear. How did men fear this?

She took her sewing to bed, rug and blankets about her shoulders, pillows at her back, and all afternoon while the *Maid* bobbed about like a cork on the heavy Antarctic sea, masts nearly naked in shortened sail, loose lines clattering against their spars, below deck creaking, squeaking, a wooden complaint against forced idleness, she worked on the boy's shirt. She worked on the shirt and thought of Sargent and Harris—their surliness, their insolence. But ripping out seams, making patterns, stitching new seams, boat bobbing, the work served to quiet her mind until at last the unpleasant episode diminished to much less than it was, for this is the way a woman's mind often works: It is hard to accuse another of deliberate malice.

Reasons for behavior are at length explained, dismissed, and eventually forgiven with undeserved understanding. No one is *deliberately* mean, a woman's mind can argue, because if they were? The world would then be unsafe. Very unsafe. And so, in her mind, Sargent and Harris did not intend to be coarse. Nor did they mean to frighten her. Certainly they hadn't purposed in their hearts that she drop the tray and break her teapot. Nay, they just be anxious, she decided, worried about the Horn, which be more than understandable because hadn't one of them already been swept from the decks? *But what of Sargent's eyes?* a voice nagged.

She switched to her knitting, and had just picked it up, the last sleeve to her husband's sweater, when he stuck in his head.

"First dogwatch," he said with a grin. "How are you?"

She held up the piece for him to see.

His eyes danced.

"Come sit with me," she urged, and threw back the covers to make him room. "Do you have time?"

"I do," he said and kicked off his boots. "The men are idle, relishing the rest I expect." He was right. Down in the foc'sle they played cards, and smoked. Harris and Lawson played checkers, and smoked. A few read, eyes squinted in their low, swinging light, and smoked. A glance at their own lamp and Emily knew the Captain meant for her to turn it down.

"My knitting, you've knocked it onto the floor. I don't want the needles..."

He made her forget the knitting. Perhaps she made him forget the men in the foc'sle. Perhaps, for he fell asleep in peaceful exhaustion the moment she pulled the rumpled quilts up round them, and in the flickering, late afternoon shadows she lay content. A long time it had been, all at peace, all at rest, everything predictable, quiet. And if the episode in the saloon had substantially diminished in her mind, it quite vanished now, for in her husband's dear arms there could be nothing or no one to fear. She twisted to see his face, a face that had, when she'd first seen it, turned her inside out for the beauty.

He lay on his back, one arm about her, the other flung up on the pillow. Gently she touched her cheek to his. Slowly his hands came up, and he held her head the way she loved and turned her in his arms, never letting go of her head until it was she, not he, who lay upon the pillows, until it was he, not she, who gazed down.

"I love you, sweet Emily," he whispered. "Have I told you lately, darling?"

"Every hour, every day." She smiled, inviting him to smile with her. His eyes—how could they, she wondered, still be so blue in this light?

"Aye, but I must be off," he said with a sigh, kissing her nose.

"Nay. Just lie with me, talk with me. They know where to find you."

"And what, then," he asked, turning to his side, touching her face, "shall we talk of?"

She thought of Sargent and Harris and her broken teapot, but told him instead of her strange conversation with Steward. "Did you know he had such peculiar ideas?"

"At times we speak of them, yes."

"And what of you?"

"What *of* me?"

"What do you think?"

For an answer he pulled her into his arms. " '*To man woman is as the earth was to legendary her son; he has but to fall down and kiss her breast and he is strong again.*' "

"Michelet?"

"Is that what it is?"

"Aye."

"I need only look at you, or even *think* of you, and I am strong again. Yes, perhaps Steward is right," he whispered thoughtfully, fingers sliding over her skin so that goosebumps raced. "A woman does bring strength to a man—if a man will let her." He took her face in his hands, a slow, teasing smile in his eyes. "I am a lucky chap. Steward *is* right." He kissed her on the lips. "For I have a woman who draws out the best in me." He kissed her again, chuckling, feeling happy to have her, to hold her, to know he was loved. "Aye, but now I really must push off, my darling. The crew—"

She reached for him but he slid free to sit on the edge of the bed. "You be still so tired, darling."

He didn't argue. Rather, he pulled the chronometer out of the box. Half past . . . *five*? She peered closer before he put it back in its box. *Half past five? An hour had already passed?* The ship's bell sounded, a single ring.

"My but it's cold," he said, shivering, coming alive. He thrust his legs, one at a time, into his pants, slid his arms into his shirt, fingers fumbling. "Stockings?" he asked.

She couldn't find them.

"The covers," he suggested.

They started to laugh, for they'd been caught between the bulkhead and blankets.

"Let me help you with your boots," she pleaded, struck with an urgency to be helpful.

"No. I'll worry about my boots. Looks like you need to worry about your knitting."

"My knitting!" And she was upon the discarded project in a fury, for *both* needles had come loose. "How did this happen?" she wailed just as Stowaway whined, backing behind the locker, tail tucked between her legs. "Oh, Stowaway. You've torn out the stitches, they be all awry! I shall have to rip the whole thing out and begin again! And I be almost done!"

"There, Emily, she's only a dog." He plucked the bundle of torn yarn from her hands, flung it all upon the bed, and kissed her soundly. "You'll be knowing how to fix it, I dare say."

Supper was a meager affair—pease soup again, with hardtack and honey. Night fell, brutally cold. The men sat huddled about the saloon table, and when Steward shooed them out they took their tea and another helping of duff pudding to eat in the foc'sle. Richard fell asleep, exhausted, on the horsehair mattress in the cabin, beneath the patched skylight.

I don't know why I bother with this, Emily thought, *in bed this time and nightie on*, trying to mend the mess done to the sweater. She must have dozed, for next thing she knew Harris was tumbling down the stairs. "On deck quick, sir!"

She hardly had time to wonder what might be amiss when Richard's voice shot down the hatch. "Steward! A lantern! Quick!"

She sat with a bolt at the sound and to her horror found smoke in the air. Nightie off, shivering. Petticoat first, she told herself, now her dress, fingers making a dreadful mess of things. She seized her stockings, her boots.

"*Fire! Fire!*" Johnny hurtled through the door. "*FIRE!*"

"On deck with you, lad! Don't be coming down!"

Off like a shot, vaulting the stairs.

Another petticoat. Another pair of stockings . . . but one look at her booted feet, there wasn't time for extra socks. She jammed the stockings into her pocket. Oh, what shall I save? and she spun, hand to her head. The ship's papers! In their tin box! Only it was too full to shut. Out of the cabin she flew, saw a piece of string tying a chair to the saloon door handle, took it off, bound the box. "Sargent!" she called as he hurtled out the mate's cabin, laden with blankets. She piled on the tin box. "What is it? What's happening?"

"A fire! In the forehold! Spontaneous combustion in the coal below!"

She was back in her cabin, no memory of getting there, staring at the bureau. Warm clothes! she thought. The bottom drawer stuck. Please, God . . . open it came; yes, her red woolen jacket! She started to cough, the smoke thick in her throat, her lungs.

Steward tore past, getting out biscuits from the pantry, tins of meat, a ham, cheese, half a bag of flour. The other men, up and down the stairs, collided with each other without words, to invade her room for stores and goods in the lazaret: tins of bully beef, honey, bags of pease.

"Get the boats ready!" came the cry, *Richard's voice!* "Prepare to abandon ship!"

She made for the door, gulping for air. Their ship, their brigantine, everything they'd worked for . . . Up the stairs, gagging, choking, blinded by the burn in her eyes, Stowaway lumbering best she could at her heels, but a howl and a yelp and she went over backward, dead, suffocated before Emily could collect her wits.

Steward pulled Emily up, fresh air shivering into her lungs, wind and sea diluting the reek of smoke. Her mind cleared and she collapsed, suddenly weak, onto a hen coop. Their ship was afire!

11

Fires on the long haul down to the south and off the Horn have been aplenty, mostly the burning of coal cargoes by spontaneous combustion when carrying the combustible through the tropics into the cold air of the Cape.

—Felix Risenberg
Cape Horn

A ball of glowing carbon under the coal spread rapidly through the packed forehold below and Harris and Lawson, tumbling out the hatch just aft of the foc'sle, gave frantic report. The Captain's eyes swept the black sea, the meager boats, Emily, his crew. Again his eyes scanned the sea. He had given the order to abandon ship, yes, but they would never survive out there. They would freeze if they didn't drown.

This was no way to think. He forced his eyes from the sea. *If they could stop the spread of the fire . . . if they could get the flames contained at the bow . . .* "Sargent! Set sail! Your watch aloft and at the helm! We're setting sail for Staten Island!"

"But, sir!"

"Give your orders, Sargent!"

"We'll never make it!"

"Give your orders," he said between clenched teeth, "or I throw you to sea! *Steward!* Salvage what you can! We'll need it all! Harris, the rest of you! Form a water brigade! We fight as long as we can!"

"But we'll burn to death!" cried one.

"No! We'll drown!"

"We are not going to jump like rats!" Richard bellowed. "Every mile we gain is money in the bank! Steady on and make it snappy!"

"But, sir!"

"Burn *or* drown!" he thundered. "We'll not go down without a fight!"

"Hoist the jib!" screamed Sargent, furious, sprinting sideways to the capstan. "Fill away the foresail and board the main tack!"

Fielding raced past, boots hitting the deck. He leaped for the foremast and up. The orphan, barefoot, darted up the rattails after him. Lawson and Sargent, buntlines and downhauls thrown to the deck, stomped the deck, waiting at the capstan. Emily watched in numb horror, hardly aware of her shivering, although she trembled violently—from head to foot—with both fear and bite of the icy, Antarctic wind. Sargent be right, he be right, she thought—they would never make it. Staten Island be too far. She'd seen the charts. But the Captain be right, too. Every mile between here and land gave them another mile of life.

"All clear!" screamed Johnny, swinging from the yards.

Way high Fielding slithered and slipped, bellying out on the very top foresail yard he had fallen from the month before. Quickly he loosened the gasket. "All clear!"

"Now!" screamed Sargent. "Heave ho!" He and Lawson threw themselves at the capstan. *"There's a fire in fore hold, fire—"*

"For the love 'a St. Mike!" bawled Lawson, "sing another chantey, Jack!"

"Haul away the bowlin'! The packet ship's a-rollin'!"

"Haul away, haul away, haul away, Joel!" Lawson cried with him, bending with a grind. Up the sails cranked, snapping, cracking, catching the wind, and popping

with a snap, bellying out white against the night. The *Maid* took the wind and plunged into the blackness.

Moonlight and starlight lit her deck, a thin silver glow, eery iridescence punctuated by the swinging lamplight. Lanterns, a half dozen hastily brought up and tied to the riggings, bounced in the rolling plunge, dropping their swinging light in flickering arcs. Giant shadows, spiked by the light, leaped the deck like giant spiders in panic.

"Yo! Hayward, wake up!" Richard passed off to Hayward, Hayward passed off to Harris, Harris to the fore-hatch, dropping the water, hissing, into the hold. Smoke billowed up in great, gusty black clouds. Richard to Hayward, Hayward to Harris, Harris to the hold. Sweat ran off their cheeks, dripped off their jaws and chins. White fog rushed in gusty bursts from their bloodless lips.

"Steward!" Emily caught the cook, about to descend the companionway. "Can they put out the fire?"

"No! The whole forehold is aflame! We can only hold off the inevitable!"

"But it's night! We can't see! We'll run aground, we—"

"That's why I'm going down! To get the compass, the sextant—"

"Steward!" she screamed when he plunged down the stairs, the unmerciful truth exploding behind her eyes. The ship was gone, truly gone, everything in flames... Which meant, oh dear Jesus, but she couldn't pray. "Steward! My rug!" But he was gone, lost in the smoke. Stowaway! Polly-wants-a-cracker! *Where be the bird?* No, she couldn't think of them, she had to think of Richard, the ship. What to do, what to... *Think!* she commanded, fingers to her temple, hating herself for being so help-less.

Her eye fell on several boxes of matches, just sitting atop a coop beside her. She pocketed two of the boxes. "Oates!" The Scot stood at the helm, face narrowed in concentration. "*Oates!* Put these in your parka!"

"Och?" He saw the matches. "Aye, do what ye will!" and he held out the large kangaroo pocket in the chest of his oil slicker.

"It's no good!" the Captain shouted from the fore-hatch. Dense smoke rushed from the hold. "Shut down the hatch! Drive holes through the deck instead! We'll keep her watered that way!" But no sooner were the holes driven than snakes of orange and black hissed up from the fiery inferno below.

"Cover the holes with canvas!" shouted the Captain, stomping wildly, once, twice, again and again at the snakes of fire and smoke hissing up and lapping his boots. "Keep the water going down through the canvas! We have to soak that coal! Emily!" he called when he caught sight of her. "Old Man," bellowed Harris, diverting his attention. "Have you seen the maul?"

There was nothing for her to do but retreat behind the wheel and to keep out of way. Abandoned and helpless and wretched with misery, she sat apart, shivering, watching. Oh dear God, she whimpered, sick with dread. How would they do this? How? They could not run for closer land, Patagonia or Tierra del Fuego, for there the natives would . . . Oh God, she moaned, pressing her face into her knees.

"Your rug, Missus."

"Oh, Steward," she wept, looking up at his dear, lined face and taking the warm, dry rug he offered. "Thank you."

"You wrap up snug, stay out of harm's way. No, Missus, don't cry. You'll discourage the Captain and we need him right now."

"*Oates!*" The Captain, face blackened by the smoke, leaped onto the poop. "We need the instruments still below!" He slid behind the helm to take the wheel with bloodied hands. Already Oates was at the companion hatch. "Bring up the charts! The Epitome and parallel rulers!"

"Aye, aye! Bit steer oos straight, Auld Man!"

"Emily?"

She twisted to see him, his blistered, black face shadowed by night.

"If we can sail her into Staten Island we might save the ship and cargo yet!"

"No, Richard. It's too hopeless."

"Emily! It's not hopeless! We'll do it yet! We'll outrun the fire. You'll see. We've got the longboat and the small boat! Steward is loading them now with everything he can!"

"Oh, Richard. Will we make it?"

"Aye, sweet Emily. By God's grace."

"But we shall lose so much."

"We shall not lose each other."

Oates fell out the companionway, rulers and barometer, instruments of other sorts clattering to the deck, charts and books, and Emily's sewing box and knitting. "Bulkheads," he gagged, tearing at his eyes, "be blisterin' doon there, Auld Man."

"Did you get the chronometer?"

"Och naw! A'll go back..."

"No! I won't risk your hide. Close the companion hatch! Hayward? Find a way to get water down there. Drive holes through the poop if you must!"

"But we have no more canvas to cover the holes!"

"In the sail locker!" Steward raced for the foc'sle head. "Yards of it!"

Emily, quite dumbfounded that Oates should have thought of her, gratefully gathered her things, her yarn and needles, her precious sewing box. "Thank you," she whispered to him.

"Aye." He stood wheezing at the wheel.

All night the men worked, holding back the flames by a constant stream of water pouring, bucket by bucket, through the canvas-covered holes gouged into the deckboards even while letting out what sail they dare to keep them hurtling through the black combers into God's dark night. Round the clock they labored—dashing flames, loading boats, reading stars, watching the compass, trimming sails, working, working, racing time while night turned round and wee hours wore on. All night Emily watched them wear themselves out; men on deck, men at the helm, men aloft, men below, men driving themselves beyond exhaustion.

"Please," she cried, "please may I do something!" But she could not keep up the frenetic pace at the brigade, nor could she hold the helm in the high seas. Helplessly she sat by, huddled beneath her rug on the poop, thoughts spiraling, spiraling into gloom until at last she felt herself give way to a feeling of dark despair. They *would* burn or be drowned. And if drowned, they would be battered by angry waves and washed ashore a foreign shore. For how could they escape?

12

The next day we saw Staten Island . . . a forbidding, cold kind of place it was. The mountains seemed snow-covered . . . the sea and clouds lay heavily over their grim peaks . . . so gloomy and dull, and mournfully forbidding that one did not care to look upon the land too much.

—Alan Villiers
By Way of the Cape

Emily woke with a start. The moon had gone. A low, gray dawn broke the horizon. Still the men worked, toiling, so exhausted they tripped over themselves and each other. But nary an unkind word, everyone quick with apology. When next she looked to the east, the sun rode the rim of the world. Suddenly it burst forth, ablaze on the horizon, and then exploded upward to vault the sea. The men paused to see what cast the golden beams and Emily, rising stiffly to her feet, pointed beyond them, behind them, to the southeast and cloudbank. They turned, pivoting, silent. Steward broke the silence.

"Hip-hip-hurrah!" he bellowed in a sudden, wild, and exultant shout. For straight ahead and poking up through clouds were the high, distant mountains of Staten Island. The Captain—unbelievably—had brought them through the night. *"For he's a jolly good fellow, for he's a jolly good fellow . . ."*

"Nay," said the Captain, chin trembling in a shaky smile. "God has brought us through. But if we honor His care, we must mind how we go from here and keep up the good work. We've a long way to go and the fire still burns. Hayward, your turn at the pump."

Emily crept from her freezing rug, muscles and joints painfully stiff, shuddering in the full icy blast of the morning wind, and eased across the poop and off the ladder. She was startled to find the main deck blistering hot beneath her boots. Gingerly, and wretchedly cold, she started for the galley.

The men stumbled in and out of the galley, pumping water up the copper water well, burning themselves by the boiling heat of it. A system had evolved among them, each man rotating what needed to be done lest he bruise one set of muscles beyond endurance. Pump to bucket to bucket to bucket to quadrant, to helm to lookout to sails.

"Lawson," she asked, shivering from her spar in the corner, his turn at the pump, "what are we going to do about the hens?"

"Hens?" he asked, surprised.

"Aye, the hens on the poop. We could take them with us..."

"Johnny!" he shouted, head swiveling out the door. "Wring them chickens' necks! Throw 'em in the long-boat!"

"I dinna wanna *kill* 'em, Lawson!"

"You'll wanna well enough where we're going—now git!" cried the yellow-curled man. He took hold of the boy's coat collar before he could say "Jack Sprat" and off the boy darted, hopping like a rabbit over the hot deck. "Someone wrap canvas around the kid's feet! Yeah, yeah," Lawson muttered when Harris threw him a bucket to fill. "Hold your horses, mate. One thing at a time. Missus? Where's the boy's boots?"

"Emily?"

The Captain stood at the door, holding her blue woolen dress with the high collar.

"My wool dress!" she cried, hardly able to reach for it, she was that cold. "However did you get—"

"Steward volunteered to go after it, you looked so miserable. He found the Bible too, a little worse for the wear."

Wet, wrinkled, half the Old Testament missing. "Tell him—Oh, Steward!" she said, for there he was himself, ruddy-eyed and blinking back the sting of lingering smoke. "You shouldn't have gone down. It be too risky, it be hardly worth—"

"Will you thank me or scold me? I'll take the thanks and be glad of it. Captain, here's Oates. He figured a way to get through the skylight. Put down the pump hook, snared some bedding for the Missus, and got your chronometer, too, Old Man."

Emily pulled the blue wool dress on over her amber gown, glad of the warmth, and wrapped herself in the bedding, thick with smoke. She must have dozed in the smoky warmth, for when she woke, her neck was kinked and the sun was high.

She stood at the galley door, hardly able to believe they were still under sail. It had been hours since the fire broke out, yet here they were, still racing for land. Why had the fire, crackling just beneath the deck, not erupted? Keeping to the bulwarks, not daring to cross the deck, she edged out to the bow to better see the approach of the dark, irregular band of land, Staten Island, that danced and drew nearer on the port horizon.

The nearer they drew, however, the more forbidding the island appeared, and she swallowed down her mounting fright. High bleak mountains clad in snow met her eyes, mountains rising straight off the sea, skirted by thick stands of windswept trees with wild, white cliffs moving in and out of vision—lonesome ghosts of white hovering to greet them.

But the island, forbidding though it be, was preferable to the ship, and if she turned around she knew this truth certain enough. Smoke leaked through every crack and through every crevice, snaking up through the canvas-covered holes, blistering the deck despite all efforts to keep it washed with the slosh of water tossed from bucket after bucket. Smoke billowed from the closed doors of the companionway, the fore and aft hatches, the skylights, at times billowing up so thick it suffocated the men at the helm and they had to stagger back to the mended taffrail for air. The smoke, wherever it came through, left a thick black greasy fluid, reeking with stink and searing nostrils, trachea, and lungs. How is it, she wondered afresh, that they did not collapse into the burning hold? *Did God lay out His staying hand?*

The men were not thinking clearly, crippled by hunger and lack of sleep. They kept colliding into each other, tripping over the stays. "Perhaps we should try to eat something," she told them, defending herself when they met her suggestion with hollow eyes. "You haven't eaten for hours. Not since last night and it must be past noon."

"I'll find some bread," said Steward. "And open a bottle of gin."

When the bread was found he cut fresh slices for everyone. But Emily, when offered a piece, found she couldn't eat. "No," she said, "I can't swallow anything."

"Please." He coaxed her with a cup of water. The Captain tried to get her to drink the gin. She managed a wee swallow. "No more, it turns my stomach."

"Do you suppose, Old Man," Steward asked, eyeing Emily and the others, and then the bottled casks of water they'd lined along the port railing, "we better empty those heavy casks? The deck, I'm afraid, will give way under the weight. She treads thin."

The Captain, chewing his bread, empty gin bottle in his hand, squinted to the frozen white mountains ahead. He eyeballed the sails and sniffed the wind, then eyed the smoking, blistered deck before nodding slowly, as if a great pain had lodged in the back of his neck. "Empty the harness casks as well." His voice was weary and full of defeat. "Leave the meat on the deck, throw the casks over. Anybody have a pencil, a bill?"

The men felt about in their pockets, slapping chests, turning out pant pockets.

"My sewing basket!" Emily leaped up, glad to feel useful for once.

He wrote quickly, paper to his knee and tongue pressed between his teeth, face shadowed by beard and blackened skin. He read it out loud while solemn glances circled. "February 16, 1870, the *Maid of Athens* on fire, Captain, wife and eight men running for Staten Island, for God's sake come and help us."

He put the bill in the bottle, plugged in the glass stopper, tied it round with string, and then with a groan threw the bottle overboard. An albatross circled, winged in for a nab, but flew away disinterested.

"It's Yates' ghost," whispered Harris to Emily. "We're gone."

⚓

His feet itched, sweltering inside hot boots, the deck now so hot that pitch was stuck to the soles of his boots. But they could not find a hospitable port of entry, and to Richard, eyeglass trained on Staten Island just ahead, watching anxiously as land passed by—a rocky bay, a shallow inlet, a sharp, jagged cliff riddled with petrels, a narrow beach—it seemed the island stood a contradictory solution to their terrible dilemma. Land, the charts said, with water and without natives, yet land battered by high waves, seashores pulverized by murderous and unrelenting rollers, a land burdened by a barrier reef of jagged granite rock that could kill in a dash. Impossible, he thought, inching the eyeglass back and forth. Impossible. They would never survive the rollers. And those rocks? For a moment he lowered the eyeglass, eyes sliding to the sun. Midafternoon. How long had they held back the flames? Twenty hours? Well then, they'd already conquered the impossible.

"YO!"

"Aye! Hayward! What do you see?" He turned to catch a glimpse of Hayward high in the reefed topsail of the foremast.

"Bay with a sandy beach in sight, sir! Rocks going out on both sides! Just like you ordered, sir!"

"Sargent!" he hollered aft. "Bring her into the wind!" God, he thought, courage returning, had not abandoned them yet.

Sargent swung the wheel. All hands leaped to their posts. "Watch the lulls!" he ordered. "Ease her over the combers! Johnny! Throw out the lead and take a sounding!"

Hayward shimmied down the mast hands-over-feet like a monkey in a zoo. He jumped, exultant. "Yo! We'll put to, righto!" he cried even as the thin deck boards splintered and gave way. Lawson shot out an arm, saving him from plunging over backward through the hole he'd punched. Crackling flames shot up in the fresh draft of air. They all rocked backward, Hayward stumbling over himself.

"It be the dragon!" Harris breathed. "Water, quick! Johnny! Water! Water!" Flames shot up, blue and white, licking the deck seams.

"The galley door!" Richard bellowed at a run. "Tear it loose and throw it over the hole!"

"Johnny!" Harris cried. "Keep the drink goin' down the monster's throat!"

"But me feet, they be—"

"Forget your bloody feet!" he screamed, and leaped after the Captain.

"Throw your weight into it!" bellowed Richard. "One, two, THREE!" But Harris bounced off the galley door. "Let me try!" A running start and a leap, crashing the left side in, brass hinges snapping. The Captain rolled, colliding into the oven. Harris and Fielding were upon him, yanking the door out from underneath.

"Fielding!" shouted Harris. "Lay it flat! No, no! Flat! Now push from your side!"

"I got the bottom!" The Captain threw himself, hands and knees, onto the hot deck, placing the heels of his hands against the bottom of the door, and together the three men, Fielding glassy eyed and stumbling, pushed the heavy narrow slab of a door across the heaving deck and over the gaping hole, leaping back when the thing was done.

"Lower the longboat," said Richard, and he squeezed his eyes shut before looking up again, blinking twice. "We can't last much longer. Steward, Harris, and you, Lawson, you three in the longboat."

"But—" protested Steward.

The Captain cut him off. "Listen to me. We'll make it off this ship alive—"

"But I think," Steward insisted respectfully, "we should take the Missus with us."

"No!" she declared. "I go with the Captain!"

"Captain! Make her come with us!"

"No! I stay with my husband!"

"Get the longboat down and launched!" ordered the Captain.

Steward, sucking air and throwing one last glance at Emily, sprinted gingerly across the smoking deck to loosen the knots that held the longboat and the block and tackle. The boat swung over and down, out of sight. Emily watched, unable to move. *The deck opened, flames at her boots, licking now the hem of her skirts. . . .* Steward vaulted the railing and disappeared, and she was roused from her terror enough to spring to the rail. Lawson and Harris clambered over and jumped, Lawson first, then Harris, dropping down the ship's hull with windmill arms, landing clumsily amidst the plunder—the rug, the charts, the instruments, the four dead hens, necks broken and floppy, beady eyes staring up empty.

"Captain, sir!" Steward shouted up the hull, hands to his mouth and hollering over the roar and splash of the churning sea, for the water surged in the shallower depths, rumbling against the ocean floor. "You've got to send her down!" Then, "Missus! Jump! You must! There is no time to lose!"

"Make haste!" the Captain yelled, cupping a hand to his mouth and leaning far over the rail. "Push for land!"

"But, Captain, sir!"

"She's coming with me! Hayward? What are you standing about for, looking the king's fool? The fore and aft! Unfurl and give her press! Sargent! See a rock, split your tongue! Full wind and we'll drive her into the ground! Johnny, take Steward's post! Emily! Go up to the poop and hang on!"

Sargent held the wheel, knuckles white, face grim. They were going to ride straight into the beach. Emily could hear the menacing rumble of the distant boomers. Which way would they tip, she wondered, when they struck? Starboard? Port? Would they roll right off the deck? Or hang themselves on the railing? Or, she wondered in renewed panic, would the fiery flames claim them yet?

Smoke and steam, black oozing oil, flames licking up through the hatches and the galley door, everything black and oozing. Water began to boil in the well, to spout steam. She turned to the sea, to Steward, a hundred feet clear of the ship now, just a shadow, a dark blotch atop the plunder, rowing for life. Waves tossed the boat carelessly, sideways and down. Harris, with a second set of oars, smacked the water with fearful blows, dip-swing, dip-swing, from the bow. Lawson bailed.

"Square the yards for the final drive!" shouted Richard. He stood at the helm, hand upheld, fingers and wrist signaling Sargent beside him at the wheel. Muscles flexed in both his throat and jaw. "Helm hard aweather!" His arm swung down. "Let the lee braces go!"

The ship answered obediently, veering southeast under command of rudder and squared canvas.

"*Stand by to strike!*"

"Missus! Don't touch the main boom!"

She let go, both hands up, palms out.

"If the mast goes when we hit," Oates hollered, "the shock will throw ye off yur feet!"

She grabbed the rail. She could hear the roar of the boomers more distinctly now. The first gentle bump. Her feet curled in her boots. Her fingers clamped tight the wet rail. *Oh, the poor little ship!* she thought in the splintering shudder. An inrush of the next comber and they hurtled forward, light and wobbly, striking suddenly with a terrific force against the hardened sand of the ocean floor. Emily took the blow to her stomach, thrown round the railing as the *Maid* heeled, seas breaking over them all with a vengeance. Directly the ship struck again—port, shuddered back—starboard, and she was thrown backward onto the deck, skirts flying.

A harsher wave, tearing up over the poop, raised the *Maid* up off the sea floor again and Emily rolled, skidding for the binnacle post. Her arms swung out. Midair, they all teetered on the crest of the surge, then impelled forward and downward, and with the speed of death the ship plowed on, keel biting deep into the sodden sand— then hung. The masts and rigging swayed, yet held fast. The ship rocked and stuck, dead but upright.

"Abandon ship!" Smoke sizzled from the deck holes, leaking between every break, every rift, shoots of fire sucking air. All around the air turned thick with smoke. Emily found her feet even as Richard's hand closed round hers, and they scrambled, slipping and leaping from the leaning poop, helm wheel spinning round and round forlornly in a dizzy gesture of farewell, and with

Sargent, Oates, Hayward, and Johnny they leaped, hopping over the main deck while the seawater streamed in puddles off the low slant of the floor and sizzled against the sucking flames. "Hayward, loosen the boat!" Richard commanded, stomping flames where they stood by the rail and the suspended, swinging longboat. He looked dazed. Sweat poured from his face.

"I can't, Old Man! Ropes got wet! These knots are all swollen up!"

"Johnny! Stop up these bloody holes. Over here! Hayward! Get those knots loose even if you have to tear them apart with your teeth!"

"The oars!" shouted Fielding in panic. "Where are they?"

"The other men have them!" shouted Emily above the roar of the plunging surf. "Harris has them!"

"But there's got to be another pair!" thundered the Captain. "Hayward! Keep at those knots! Oates! Help me!" And leaning off the rail he started tossing through the assortment of plunder in the swinging boat: saws, hatches, a broadaxe, hammers, pots and pans, the big cooking boiler, flour, and tins of meat. But no oars.

"Ropes are loose, Captain, sir!"

"*Oh, where are the oars?*" moaned Fielding. "*We can't go no place without oars!*"

"Give me the maul! The *maul!*" the Captain screamed, leaping back onto the deck and grabbing it himself. He swung at the deck. Flames leaped up to blister his hands. Another swing and he pried loose two boards. He threw them in. "They'll have to do!" he cried. "Emily! Get in!"

"Aren't you going to lower the boat?"

"*After* you're in!"

Johnny was over even as she was getting her skirts off the rail and they tangled in each other's arms and legs. Sargent, Oates, and Fielding followed. The small boat, still suspended, collided into the ship rail.

"Richard!" she cried, reaching for him just as Hayward sprung the tackle and the boat lowered, separating them. Ropes unwound hand over hand. Lower and lower they descended. She saw the wave just as the boat touched down, icy water smacking them backward and down. Drenched, she sat gasping and shivering, gripping the gunwale as the boat came back up under the sea's fury and she looked up, ship looming high above, looking oddly unfamiliar. Yet there was her name, *The Maid of Athens*, painted on the counter.

Hayward jumped, careening downward without balance. Those below only had time to tuck in their legs and he was in their midst, sprawled and groaning, blood gushing from his chin.

"Ma'am! Ma'am!" The orphan tugged in panic on Emily's hand. "Another wave!"

They could only watch. It grew as it came, higher and higher until it paused, hesitating at its height as if to take aim.

"Push off!" the Captain bawled, seeing it. "Or it'll dash you against the hull. *Push off!*"

Emily screamed in agony and he, hearing it, changed his mind and swung a leg over the rail to join them, lowering himself rapidly down the davit rope. Halfway down, the davit turned around his leg. The wave grew and accelerated. Still the wave came on. Oates tried to pull the rope straight.

The wave struck, lifting Emily off her seat. She hung fast, fingers frozen round the gunwales, letting the surge of the numbing sea throw them all up against the ship's hull—and Richard. But he was still there, hanging by what could only be the strength of God. Oates, with one final snap of the rope, pulled it straight and Richard was beside her. His pants had torn, his flesh was bruised. But he was alive. He took her seat, breathing hard, blowing out his cheeks, and put her between his legs so she sat on the floorboards, frigid water up round her waist to stop her heart. He brought his arms round tight. "Now row!" he cried, even as Oates and Fielding, deck boards for oars, tore up the sea, waves crashing on behind them, battering their boat with fury. "Row for shore," he cried, holding fast to Emily. "Row for heaven or this hell of water will claim us all! Row, and be done!"

"Captain!" screamed the boy, and he dove for Richard's lap as yet another wave, leaping toward their destruction, rolled higher and faster upon them.

"Oh God, we are gone!" said Richard, and he bent over the boy and held Emily close. They would die sharing the same breath.

But the boat lifted, catching the crest of the wave, and they were skimming the sea at a dead run, foam gushing over the gunwales. Emily pulled up, water to her neck, gagging and spitting, the smell of the slimy sea bottom in her nose, salty sand grating between her teeth.

"One!" shouted Oates. "Two!"

"One! Two!" answered Fielding, flailing.

"One, two! One, two!"

Both men grunted in unison to each jerk of their clumsy, makeshift paddles. Mad waves gave chase; wave after wave, spinning them closer and closer to the craggy rocks alive with barnacles as sharp as knives. Crosswaves, bouncing off the rocks, spun them back.

"One, two! One, two!"

Another wave, another, driving them ever into the rocks.

"One, two!"

The boat spun free, riding the spent energy of the wave, and they washed ashore, grinding against pebbles, boards falling from their blistered hands. Steward, Harris, and Lawson splashed in after them, dragging them up clear of the surf. Richard, lifting Emily out, carried her to dry ground, water pouring from their clothes with each step, and set her on her feet. She staggered, sea heavy in legs too numb, too cumbersome to know what to do. Again she tried to walk, again she tripped, petticoats and skirts tangling. Steward leaped to catch her.

"Take it easy," he muttered. "Your legs don't know how to relax, been at sea so long, Missus," and he half-led, half-carried her over to some large stones and set her on a high, flat, startlingly hot rock. He shoved a bottle of brandy under her nose.

"Drink," he commanded. "It'll warm the gizzard."

But she couldn't get her lips round the bottle, teeth chattering too hard against the glass. A taste of blood and she burst into tears. *Oh, what was to happen to them now?* and she held back a scream, pushing it back in her throat with both hands. *Oh, dear God, what have You done? What will we do?* Her hands tightened on her throat and she swept her eyes in a panic across the sea, begging God for any break in the distant horizon of surging bleakness. Nothing. Only blue water surging and swirling, locking them forever on this island of desolation. *Oh God, oh please, what have You done?* Johnny was set up next to her and she put out an arm, finding strength to hold his body, so thin and so icy, close to her own.

"Drink," said the Captain beside her, and she swallowed quick, blinking back the tears.

"I'll see to a fire, Captain, sir," said Steward. "We'll all catch a witch's death if I don't. Come, lad. There you go, let go of the Missus. That's a lad."

Emily watched the ship burn, for she could not bring herself to look on anything else. Not yet. She could not bear to see what lay behind: the hard, granite rock, the thick skirt of woods, the high, snowy mountains. No, she would not look. There was only their ship, a hundred yards ahead—flames dancing about her deck, the sea, roar after roar, washing over her hull and bow, the smoke, black as tar, billowing from her hold. She buried her head to shut the thing out.

"Emily, don't," said the Captain. "Don't cry. Please." He tried to bring her into his arms but she pushed him away. "Please," he tried again. "Darling, we have much to thank God for. He has spared us our lives."

God, in His providence, could have done something a little kinder than shipwreck them at the end of the world. *Shipwreck!* She rolled the word in her mind, tried it on her tongue. But the terrible word stuck in her heart. Only brave men like Alexander Selkirk shipwrecked and lived to tell. Never a woman. No, never a woman! Never *her!* Oh, what, she wondered in fresh agony of mind, were they to do with the lives that God had spared them? How did He expect them to live?

The Captain popped on the brandy cork. "Better save some for the heathen," he said, and clambered off the rock.

She let him go. There were times when his eternal optimism, rather than bringing comfort, made him a stranger to her, and she wept into her knees, alone.

PART 2

Marooned!

13

~~~~~~~~~~

The land was the island of Staten Island . . . a more desolate-looking spot I never wish to set eyes upon—bare, broken, and girt with rocks and ice. . . . It was a place well suited to stand at the junction of the two oceans, beyond the reach of human cultivation. . . .

—Richard Henry Dana, Jr.
Two Years Before the Mast

Staten Island is a far-flung spot of land 100 miles due east of the southern tip of Cape Horn. A hundred miles long, east to west, it is but 12 miles wide—at its broadest point. From the charts this narrow eruption looks more like the backbone of some prehistoric monster, riddled as it is with so many bays and inlets all twisting to the core, creating a curious curvature of what appears to be historic bone and vertebrae. Even from the sea it appears to be an ancient spine, humping out of the horizon, barren mountains rising straight up, right off the beaches, two and three thousand feet high, craggy faces bleached clean by wind and jagged heads capped by eternal snow. The lower slopes, in contrast, wear a dense skirt of towering trees and rain-forest undergrowth, but this growth is only a narrow ruffle, a flounce. Tree and underbrush, climbing the cliffs, thin quickly to nothing; altitude and rock supreme. Penguins live here, and wild geese beyond reach on the ocean-swept reefs, but nothing else. For on this place, Staten Island since 1616, there is only fish to feed on, and freezing temperatures ten months out of twelve.

Few who pass even see this frozen, rocky shore, for hurricanes and gales often sweep through. Any lull— brief and only during the summer months of February and March—is not invitation enough. White, surfbound reefs pose a hostile barrier, so ships tack far out. Any glimpse they might see is just that—a glimpse, a quick peek through cloud break, peek enough to warn the wise to steer clear.

Yet it was to this rocky, frozen island that the *Maid* had flown seeking refuge, and it was this rocky, frozen island that took the crew in—without loss of life or limb. And the Captain, knowing more clearly their fortuitous landing (considering the odds), was more easily encouraged at their prospects than either his wife or the men.

The men, wretched and so exhausted they could hardly stand on their feet, faced with despair due west and a turbulent bay of rolling surf which dumped in from the Strait of Lemaire to break at their weary feet in thunderous fury.

The bay was shaped like a J tipped back, the hook a rocky barrier of jagged granite invasive of the sea, wild in every respect. Ivory barnacles covered the jetty in treacherous lace. White geese honked from its distant crest, 200 yards out. Petrels, small black birds and cousin to the albatross, swooped and circled in spindrift, caw- ing in answer, and where Emily had been left, sitting on the high hot rocks, was where the rugged reef anchored itself to the island: a knot of rock left open to the after- noon sun, rock forged and welded to the grotesque outline of high granite cliffs, bald and pockmarked by wind and hail, towering straight up 200 feet.

The other reef, the stem of the J, met the sea more kindly, angling off to the north and disappearing with- out argument into the sea, a zigzag shoreline with its own inlets and bays and narrow crevices. Between these two jetties of granite rock the tide beat its path, a half-mile wide, hurtling in from the Strait and on past the burning ship to crash, Pacific and Atlantic, two seas mingled, in unrelenting rolls, throwing up pebbles in a spit of passion, only to draw back in ravenous hunger and spit again.

The beach itself consisted of white sand riddled with whiter stone, which even now was being swallowed by the rising tide, then white glittering shingle running 50 feet back to a steep embankment thick with the flounce of forest growth: giant evergreen trees, sword fern and devil's club, vines of moss, fungus and decay and fallen logs wrapped in more moss, sprinkled with lichen.

This forest hedged the bank to the north, where it thinned as the land dropped and jutted into the sea. To the south the woods detoured up and behind the high cliffs, thick and wild until they too thinned and disappeared as rock and altitude gained.

But back at the beach a struggling fire spit, hissing and threatening to go out, for it choked on the wet wood it was fed, and all around this fitful fire the shivering sailors huddled, slapping at themselves with blackened and blistered hands to keep warm. The Captain, a short distance off, pursed his lips, eyes reluctantly reading the shoreline, trying to gauge the secrets of the embankment and the high, bald, granite cliffs. Advantages and disadvantages lined up in his brain like debit and credit in a ledger.

No wild animals, *advantage*. Frigid, Antarctic temperatures, unable to sustain life, *disadvantage*. Belt of woods, *advantage*. Hopelessly damp, *disadvantage*. Salvaged supplies, *advantage*. Very few supplies, *disadvantage*. One thing was clear: They could not survive here long; it was up to him to get them all home again, and to keep them alive while he did it.

"Aye, Old Man," said Steward, seeing him wince. The cook sat on a wet log laced with seaweed, rubbing warmth into the boy's bare feet. "And what do you think?"

"We can't stay on the beach. We have to climb, find a sheltered spot. Find drinking water."

The men all nodded.

"But first the boats. Haul to. Let's get them past the high-tide line. Can't have everything wash away," he added, attempting a smile to encourage them.

"Ain't much to worry about," said Hayward with a woeful eye. He picked up a dead chicken and let it drop with a flop.

"Never mind," said Richard just as Emily approached, heavy skirts dragging in the sand. "We are not without at least one meal. Now heave to and let's get the job done."

Job done, they headed north, pacing the edge of the wooded embankment. At 300 paces, they arrived at a cut in the trees and moved off the beach and into a jungle that crawled straight up. One and all they shuddered, head to toe and back up, wet clothes wetter in the dark undergrowth, and with wary eyes they measured their sudden surroundings. What looked to be fir trees, thick in both girth and bough, filtered little sunlight or sky through their crisscross of limbs. Ferns and moss-covered logs littered the ground. Shrubs tangled amongst the litter. For a moment they waited, listening to a deep and eerie silence. The Captain was the first to move in, squeezing between two trees and climbing.

Whenever he had a go at fallen limbs with his hatchet, they all paused for needed breath, using the time to search further with their eyes the deep shadows. Suddenly a bird battered a tree; a woodpecker? Their anxiety scaled an octave in the lonely sound, yet they continued on—for what else was there to do?—penetrating further and higher. Where the Captain led no one knew, or asked.

"Listen!" said Oates suddenly, head tipped, ears trained. "Dae ye hear anything?"

"Only the surf," answered Fielding miserably, resting heavily upon Hayward's shoulder.

"Tis a watterfall!" Oates argued.

"Steady on then, Jack," replied Lawson with a shake of his curls and giving Fielding a prod. They plunged on, Captain in the lead. Emily, midline and seeing only slices of his familiar body passing in and out of vision, was struck by his seeming assurance. A pause, listening, then moving to the left, now right, moving forever and unerringly toward a destination yet unnamed.

"Dae ye hear it noo?" demanded Oates, insistent, pulling up again.

"Aye!" cried Harris with surprise. "I do at that!"

In two minutes they broke free of the brush and woods and came upon a thundering cascade, a high, plunging fall of water that nosedived, spilling over itself from a high, lofty pinnacle. A shimmering lace veil, it came crashing into a wide pool, where it eddied in a swirl before gathering its forces to run, tumbling over rocks and moss-covered stones, down a riverbed that cut a narrow, gurgling swath through the woods and out to sea. The Captain chuckled, and they descended upon the pool, scooping up the sweet, clear water by the handful, thirst from swallowed seawater suddenly afire. Johnny almost plunged into the bubbling pool, so eager was he to quench his thirst. Steward gave him his toque, full of water, which the boy took eagerly, and from the stiff wool cap he drank noisily.

They clambered on, following the Captain across chaotic piles of driftwood that had crashed down the cascade and been tossed. A burst of low bush further up the hill suggested a plateau, and it was toward this invitation they pressed, zigzagging up and up until they came at last through a gate of trees to a grassy swale— sheltered by further overhang of evergreen trees that grew out of a gully, trees that were much stouter and certainly much taller than any they had ever seen in England.

The men scattered, poking about. From where Emily stood, she guessed the beach to be perhaps 300 yards almost straight down—not a long walk, yet far enough up, she noticed, to be free of the worst of the pounding surf, an incessant roar in the ears. Too, from the higher vantage point she could see the endlessness of the ocean— the desolate, watery waste . . . and the *Maid of Athens* still aflame.

Camp was declared. The men returned to the shore, following the tumbling stream this time, hacking out a more direct trail down the steep incline, and Emily went in search of sticks to light a new fire, careful not to leave sight of the swale or the men, who one by one and sometimes in pairs slowly hauled up their goods from the beach.

The work was frustrating, for everything was damp: twigs, leaves, broken branches, rotting bark off the trees— everything moldy with mildew and fungus. Emily was hard-pressed to dismiss thoughts of home and hearth, but she forced her thoughts instead on the urgent need to keep moving, the need to keep from freezing. The sky darkened, furthering her frustration. To top it off, when it came time to strike her match, she found them all wet, phosphorus soaked right off.

"Naw, Missus," said Oates, shaking his head in the last light of day. "Ye didna gi'e me any matches."

"But I did! I put them in your pouch pocket!"

He held out his oilskin pouch. "Well, blaw me doon . . ."

She struck one thin matchstick gratefully. Suddenly, "You daft woman! You gone and let it go out!" One stride and Harris broke the ridge into "camp" and snatched from her hand the precious matches. One after another the wind snuffed them out, though, until at last he, with a groan, slapped the box back into her open hand and strode away.

Carefully, and fighting tears, she rebuilt the fire. A handful of grass, leaves, dry moss. Finally, after much blowing and careful shielding with her hands, she got a flame, and finally a fire.

Shadows leaped back, for dark had fallen. The men sat about on what crates and bags they'd been able to bring up, all breathing hard and falling asleep even as they sat. The Captain ordered the wet canvas and tarpaulin spread round the fire. Emily, fearful and silent, thrust one muddy boot toward the crackling flames, shuddering in the flicker of blessed heat. Her skirts, pulled up out of the way, revealed a filthy petticoat and too much pretty leg, pretty even through a pair of the Captain's baggy red longjohns. Suddenly she stamped her feet, both of them, and catching sight of an oar, used it like a roasting stick to dangle one cashmere boot over the flames like a slab of meat, standing on one foot and rubbing her stinging toes against an opposite calf.

"You're going to lose your boot, darling."

"No I shan't."

"Please, Emily, come to bed. Such as it is," Richard admitted. "Please. Now?" Then a whisper, "I need you beside me."

She crawled in, sharing his oilskin coat and snuggling in close the way he liked, filling the empty space on the other side of his heart. He laid his sou'ester over her face, covering them both with her wet rose and blue rug; wishing, no, *needing*, to kiss her. A strange wind moaned in the unnamed trees. The surf rolled over the shingles, a distant drumming. Rain fell. She kissed his hands and he fell asleep, her cheek resting softly, softly in his blistered, stinging palm while the *Maid of Athens* yet burned in the bay below.

⚓

At midnight the rainclouds passed on. The Southern stars glittered in crisp patterns, patterns different from anything seen north of the Line: a cloud of starburst on the horizon, the Magellan Clouds; at the zenith, Antares in the Scorpion, Centaurus too. As the crater opened, the Southern Triangle. And dropping right out of the crown the Southern Cross, the brightest of all constellations in the whole of heaven, and it was under the Cross that the Captain and his crew slept. Fitfully so, in fragmented dreams, turning in mud and cold.

At five o'clock in the morning, Thursday, February 17, 1870, the foreign sky began to lighten, the strange stars to dim, and daybreak to rise with a thick mist from the sea to greet new rain. Emily woke in the gentle fall. She saw first her husband's arm stretched beneath her head and beyond, then his hand. Palm up, the rain fell through his muddy fingers and into a puddle. The sound of pounding surf came to her ears and then she remembered. *Staten Island. Marooned at the end of the world.*

Softly she stole from her wet cocoon, easing out from under the yellow oilslicker and heavy, wet rug. Morning dripped, with dull, gloomy rain dropping off the trees, and she shivered in the cutting dampness and began, with numb fingers, to coax the low embers of the sorry fire. One by one the men, hearing her about, came to, until all stood in a circle about the sputtering, smoking flames, stomping their feet, mumbling, dull-witted and foggy, helpless to do anything but rub their arms and stare at the distant, still-burning ship. "Woman, this is a fine fix," muttered Harris with a glower, shivering into his wet jacket and hunching it up round his neck, joining the circle to stare with the rest of them, hands squeezed into his pockets.

They looked dreadful: hair matted, faces grizzly and blistered, eyes swollen, lips thin and colorless. She wondered what she looked like, grateful no mirror could tell the tale. Johnny put on his dirty, soaked clothes, crying at the icy cold. "At least your joints ain't screaming fire," Hayward told him, nursing his rheumatic shoulder. "But ye got yer boots!" cried Johnny, nursing his bare toes. Emily handed him the extra stockings in her pocket and with his child's smile he pulled them on.

The Captain, the last to join, ran his hands through bleached and salty hair, hopelessly tangled. "She'll burn for days," he said. Even as he spoke, even as he reached for Emily's hand, the ship's foremast toppled, careening downward in a shriek of tangled shrouds, mainmast cracking. Everything came down in a crash—halyards, sheets, guys, downhauls—everything washing in a tangle back and forth, knotting in the sea. The Captain turned away, sick. "Come," he said, and rumpled Johnny's head, "let's build up that fire and get the toast started."

But there could be no "toast" until all plunder was sorted and inventory taken. The food was quickly ascertained: three crates of tinned bully beef, one sack of wet flour, five large cheeses, tea drenched in saltwater, some hardtack, two bottles of gin, two of brandy, a cask of rum, one rusty tin of sugar (the sugar all but dissolved and thick with salt syrup in the seams), and several smaller tins of soup. The equipment wasn't much more encouraging: two rugs, two pillows, two buckets, a few knives, two small saucepans, a few tin measuring spoons, the galley boiler, two frying pans. Also there was the sextant, a couple of spyglasses (one soaking wet and gritty with sand), two charts, one compass, the Captain's hatchet, the carpenter's box, the sailors' five sheath knives, the box of ship's papers, Maurey's chart book and some rope. "Where's the chronometer?" the Captain asked. Cleverly salvaged through the skylight, it was nonetheless soaked through with seawater and ruined. Worthless. "Never mind," he said. "Steward has a watch." He tossed the chronometer into the gully. A flick of his wrist and it was gone, and Emily wondered if she had ever heard, metal snapping, glass breaking, a more lonely sound.

"Steward, put the chickens on the fire," said the Captain. "How many have we got—four? Men, there's bound to be something washed in by the tide. We best see what it is, then over breakfast figure out what we're to do." Without a word among themselves they followed him downhill, shoulders hunched into a wind that whipped up the cliff.

Emily headed for the Cascade—the name she'd already assigned the waterfall—to bathe her eyes, weepy and thick from the torment of the woodsmoke, and the held-back tears. The trail was precipitously steep. She slipped several times into muck and mud that wouldn't even shake off.

There was only a small handkerchief, absently tucked one day into the skirt pocket of her dress, to do the job. Over and over she dipped the hankie into the rush of water so cold it froze her fingers, and bathed her troubled eyes. Washing was a fine thing, wonderful even, with the icy cold cutting through her exhaustion to sharpen her senses. But it was quite another thing, she discovered, when it came to dabbing herself dry.

Sniffing, she thought of her cabin aboard ship—hot water brought down from the galley, her tin tub, the thick towels hanging off the dowels of her mother's marble washstand. Quite a contrast, she thought miserably, to this running stream, stooping stone, and sopping wet hankie.

But, she told herself, there is much to be grateful for. I must remind myself of this. She paused, teeth grinding. I must. We have fresh water. We have wood. We have the Captain. There be no natives to fear. She hesitated, suddenly unsure, and scrambled to her feet breathless and wary, trying hard not to remember the horrible stories of the Fuegian cannibals of Cape Horn. With great difficulty she lingered, slipping off her blue woolen dress with the high collar to lay over a rock under the icy Cascade. The pounding of the falling water would take out the soot of the fire and salty muck that had drenched her on landing. She would come back after breakfast and hang it to dry by the fire. By nightfall she could take off her amber gown and petticoats, and have something warm to wear to bed.

Back at the camp juice dripped from the roasting chickens, spitting and hissing. The smell made her stomach cramp. "Where be Steward?" she asked the boy, sitting beside him on a low log, dampness immediately soaking through to her skin.

"'E went doon to 'elp the men."

Resolved to endure the cold to her backside, but not her feet, she once again pulled off her boots and wrung her stockings, water squeezing out like a lemon. She reached for the oar she'd used the night before and showed the boy how to keep her boot from dropping into the flames. Soon, using both oars, they had both boots bobbing alongside the roasting breakfast—leather and suet, a curious blend of odors that did nothing for the ache in her gut.

"Tell me all ten commandments," she instructed the orphan, eyes scanning the empty loneliness of the thick, dark woods all around. Tell me anything, she thought, tell me anything to keep me from thinking. But no sooner had the boy started his recitation than the Captain appeared, catching Emily's eye with a wane smile. "Camphor," he told her, and tossed a piece, partly burnt, up under a tree with a satisfied grunt.

"Aye, and whut be camphor?" asked Johnny.

"A volitable, gummy stuff, lad. And," said the Captain, "it'll feed any fire we might make. No need to worry about freezing to death." But his cheerful assurances rang hollow to Emily's ears.

They all ate their breakfast hungrily, seated on logs and stumps hauled up to the warmth of the fire, leaning over their knees and wolfing down the last fresh meat they would taste in awhile. No one spoke until the meat was gone, until the bones were gnawed, broken, the marrow sucked, until at last they reluctantly dropped what was left into Steward's bucket for supper's soup.

The Captain dropped his drumstick in last, a muffled clatter of bone to bone, and he sat straight, hands to his knees, dimly aware of his torn trousers and the throb of the rope burn on his thigh. The time to speak had come; they waited. "Our first and primary task," he said, voice deliberate camouflage to his uncertainty, "is to see to our immediate survival—food, clothing, shelter. You all got your duds out of the ship, I hope?"

"Aye, bit whit aboot gettin' oota here?" put in Oates.

"We'll get out of here in due time. We have the boats, we're not helpless. But right now I'm more worried about the cold and our meager food supply. We're going to have to build tents somehow . . . it's bound to rain again—"

"Captain," interrupted Hayward. Worry haunted his fatigued eyes. He rubbed his brow. "I think, sir, we best get out of here—now. We can't sit around building tents while our food runs out. It'll be winter in a few weeks. And our clothes? Just look at your boots, Old Man . . . the soles are nearly burnt through. A week climbing the barnacles down there and you'll be walking in your stockings." He held up his own boot, badly burnt and worn thin.

"Things do look grim," said Richard compassionately, feeling a stirring of affection for his men and a resolve to do his best by them. "But we can only move one step at a time. We can't take the boats out the way they are. You saw how the water came up." Glum looks agreed with him. "We'd drown within five miles. No, first things first. We build tents. We search for food. We scrounge the tide for anything and everything the *Maid* may yield. Once we're warm and dry, once we figure a way to keep ourselves healthy, *then* we worry about making our escape."

"The Falkland Islands are 500 miles away," said Harris. "Even if we do get the boats patched, we can't row that far. And with the chronometer gone—"

"Steward has a watch."

"A *watch*? But Captain, sir, thirty seconds off and we'd be out to sea!"

"Who says we have to row to the Falklands?" put in Sargent, as if bored with the discussion.

"You aim to row across the *Strait*? Take your chances with those cannibals?" yelped Harris, punching the Bosun on the upper arm with a burst of helpless frustration. "You crazy, Jack? Those cannibals smoke their own *grandmothers* before they're dead and make steaks of them!"

"Who says we have to go anywhere?" insisted Sargent, shrugging Harris off, directing his question right to the Captain. "We sit tight. It's a trade route. Keep a fire going and someone's bound to see us and come fetch us home."

"You sit around waiting," said Richard carefully, sensing Sargent's animosity simmering again, ready perhaps to bubble openly, "and you freeze to death. You heard Hayward. In a few weeks it'll be winter—"

"*Winter*? We won't *be* here come winter! Whalers pass through all the time! This very afternoon one may come!"

To argue was insolence, to resist mutiny. Richard, hearing in Sargent's voice the threat of one and the dare of another, knew he must dash both without production and do it quickly. "Ah, you're right," he agreed with an exaggerated show of scanning the thickening fog. "*Ten* whalers could come through today."

Someone snickered, point taken.

"So 'ow we goin' to get 'ome?" cried Johnny, begging the Captain. "We all jist die? Like Stowaway an' Polly?

An' rot 'ere? An' nobudy to find our bones an' bery them?"

"You quit that howling," said Steward, turning on him before the Captain could answer, shaking a finger across the fire. "It isn't going to do you, or anybody else for that matter, a lick of good."

"There, there," said Emily quickly, everyone's nerves rubbing so raw they would be at each other's throats in a minute. "Johnny, do you suppose Robinson Crusoe howled like that on *his* island?"

"But 'e wuz jist a bloke whut someone said!"

"So you think Defoe made him up, do you? You forget the real story? Alexander Selkirk? No one found his bones, did they?"

"Nobody goin' to let us rot? We niver be jist bones on the beach then?" he begged.

"No one's going to find your bones," said the Captain, putting a stop to the entire discussion. He pulled to his feet, ponderously, stretching tired shoulder muscles. "Now. First things first. We haul up the broken cask staves that washed ashore. We'll use them to make ourselves beds of some kind. No sense sleeping on wet ground, not when there's something we can put between ourselves and the mud. And when the tide goes out? We'll go out to the *Maid* and see what we can find." If they were lucky they would find canvas to build tents. He hoped so, even prayed so. And not just canvas—they needed tar, white lead, chains, food . . .

They worked well into the afternoon, hauling up the staves, even a few charred deckboards that had washed loose. There was, however, no level ground in the swale, and they had to lay the boards on a slant. Harris suggested wedging the boards with moss, which helped a little. At three o'clock, tide out, the *Maid* was left stranded high and dry on hard white sand 100 yards offshore, looking like the smoldering skeleton of a beached whale.

The men, ropes thrown over their shoulders, headed downhill and across the sand.

Flames and fumes rose from her bow. Richard ordered the ropes thrown up over her stern and they clambered aboard, stepping around the gaping deck, leaping daringly from beam to beam over the steaming hull. They found rice, tea, and tobacco. With no small effort they brought out what they could—gunny sack, box, and tin. Lawson found a tin of preserved potatoes, Fielding several bolts of calico—which would do in lieu of canvas, thought Richard with a relieved smile. He ordered everything up to the encampment.

"We'll come again when the fire burns out," he said to Steward. He took a last look about the ruins of his smoking ship with a sorry sigh. The salvaging had only begun—of the stores, of the cargo, of their very lives. "What's that?" he asked, hearing an odd, familiar chirp. Steward, catching the sound too, headed fore, and in the low smoldering ashes of the galley they found Polly-wants-a-cracker, blue feathers ruffled, clinging tenaciously to the roost still swinging over the ship's stove.

"The story ain't over yet, Old Man," said Steward with a satisfied sigh, collecting his bird and putting her in the warm hollow of his toque. "No sir, the story ain't over yet."

⚓

Their second morning marooned, Emily determined to somehow get her blue woolen dress dry—and her bedding. The damp air yesterday had disallowed the dress to dry, as close as she'd hung it to the fire. And last night's rain? There be only one way, she realized, to dry such wet things: spread-eagled *over* the fire. And so her rug hung atop the crackling flames like a hammock, five feet off the ground, corners stretched taut between four distant trees. In the very center lay her dress—dress and rug drying simultaneously.

Except for Polly-wants-a-cracker, Emily was quite alone. The Captain had gone, hatchet in hand, uphill into the woods with Oates. A few of the men had gone down to the beach to see what new cargo might have washed in, to sort and store and stack. The others, taking Johnny with them, had gone to scout for food—berries, roots, shellfish, anything. What stores they had managed to salvage had proven so fire-damaged and tainted by smoke, and so steeped in salty seawater, that it was most unpalatable, barely edible. Even the bully beef, canned in tin, tasted foul.

"Emily! Emily!" The morning had gone, and she was just pulling on her clean dress, dry at last, when she heard the happy call of her husband. *"Emily!"* Taking her hand, and with a pleased smile on his face, he led her up a short incline. There, in a grassy swale just 50 yards uphill from the encampment, was a calico tent built in the trees.

"Oh, darling! It be lovely!" Surprised and cheered, she stepped inside. A long pole, stretched between high limbs of two tall evergreen trees, formed a six-foot peak over her head. Four shorter stakes, driven into the ground, marked the corners and framed a floor space of about 12 feet by 15. Young saplings, stripped of their boughs and set into the ground side by side, formed three of the four walls. The fourth wall, left open, faced onto a hedge and the sea. Over everything hung the calico Fielding had found. Calico draped off the peak to make the roof. Calico hung down the three walls to keep out the wind. Calico, tied back along the open wall, made a curtain that could easily be let down to give privacy, the whole arrangement a bright blue, a most cheery place indeed. Emily turned a slow circle, sunlight dappling the calico overhead. So cheery a haven in so dreary a spot! "Oh, darling," she whispered, grateful, "it be so pretty..."

She hung her red coat and the Captain's blue pea-jacket on two convenient knobs off the center beam, and while the Captain and Oates made a bed of sorts, using large pieces of driftwood brought up from the beach as a frame, and smaller pieces as fill, she made herself a shelf by rolling into the tent, hand over hand and prodded by her boot, two large boulders. Across the top of the two stones she lay a long piece of deckboard. "An' whit," Oates wanted to know, "will ye be pootin' on yer sideboard?"

There wasn't much. Her battered Bible. A baby bottle— with a broken candle Steward had found—propped inside. The tin box full of the ship's papers. And her sewing box with its picture of Buckingham Palace on the lid and the changing of the guard on the sides. The bright red offered a cheery spot of color.

"Only one thing's missing," said the Captain, winking at Oates.

"And what be that?" she asked.

"The sampler, *Home Sweet Home.*"

The next few days passed in a surreal swirl of activity, all of them salvaging what they could from the smoldering ship until a small pocket of civilization sprang out of the desolate patch of godforsaken tundra. Cargo piled the beach, up against the embankment and under the overhang of trees. Stores and provisions filled the two camps. Surprises and lucky finds often buoyed their spirits, and the need to know their fate eased in the collective realization that they would not immediately freeze or starve. Often wild shouts of glee occasioned the work. More candles . . . molasses to sweeten the ghastly tea . . . acres of canvas for the men to build a tent . . . another sack of flour.

On Friday Oates found a pair of men's boots for Emily, which she immediately tied on over her flimsy cashmere ones—a clumsy but remarkable improvement, for now her feet could stay dry. Saturday Fielding found the boy's boots. Someone found Emily a comb. Another cask of rum was found and a wild cheer went up, and very quickly out of chaos and fear, order and confidence emerged.

Sunday the Captain sent Oates and Fielding out to scout the surrounding terrain, to determine the wildlife, if any, and food, if any. And to see if they could find a vantage point high enough to scan the Strait, fog permitting. Steward handed the two men a sack with tins of bully beef. "Make it last," he told them. Grimly Emily wrote down their addresses on a paper that Lawson had given her from his duffel bag, in the event they did not return or should any accident befall them. More grimly the pair headed uphill from the Cascade, following the left bank of the river away from the camps while the rest bid Godspeed and watched in fearful silence as the shadows took them from view.

"Sargent," said the Captain, breaking the heavy quiet, "I know it's the Sabbath, but we have to keep busy. We'll use the day to build a ladder up the worst of this hill. Pick two men. Use the cask staves off the beach; there's plenty."

"What'll we use for nails?"

Harris laughed, grinning with humor. "Cask staves come with nails, you lucky mate."

"Very funny," said Sargent. "Just for that, I suppose *you* can pry the nails loose."

"*Me?*"

"Aye, and Lawson," commanded Sargent. "Get the saws and a hammer."

"The rest of us," said the Captain, "will haul up the deckboards. If we're going to save our boots..." He pulled up one foot. Water gurgled into the impression, the ground a veritable sponge. "Lay the boards end to end, make a sidewalk. We'll save useless wear and tear on our feet."

All day they kept busy, sawing, hammering, hauling, ladder and sidewalk progressing until by late afternoon and teatime their little pocket of civilization invited almost a homey appearance, starting at the beach, where the growing pile of plunder and supplies fenced the embankment. Sargent's ladder, crude but functional, formed a gate, ascending the steepest part of the trail to the Cascade, a good 50 yards up the incline. The deck-boards, charred and splintery, zigzagged the rest of the way to the "Encampment," the men's camp, and from there they took a turn up and around the short incline to the "Mount," the Captain's camp—and Emily's pretty tent.

For their Sunday afternoon tea Steward served a mess of scouse: moldy biscuits pounded fine, with salt beef cut into small pieces, a few potatoes boiled and mixed in, without the pepper. They sat about the fire, in front of the men's tent, a rather haphazard affair of calico and canvas hung off suspended oars and low-slung tree boughs.

"I ain't eatin' this slop," said Harris, grimacing.

"Get used to it," Steward told him. "It's going to get worse. Tea?"

"Get away from me."

"Captain," said Lawson, "can we have a swallow of rum to choke this down?"

"Tonight," he answered, "after hauling the firewood, as usual." He had, the past few days, insisted on dupli-cating ship life, adhering to strict routine. A cup of grog before turning in had been the usual fair; on the island it would be no different.

"Captain, where can Oates have gotten to?" Steward asked, worried. "You don't suppose they got lost, do you, Old Man?"

Richard had just been asking himself the same ques-tion, hoping the compass hadn't proven broken, when the two men staggered over the ridge and into camp, startling everyone. Their clothes hung in shreds from shoulders and hips. Scratches lacerated their faces and hands. Blood dripped off their bared arms, and angry welts festered.

"Them woods is nothing but brambles," panted Fielding, dropping to a stump, hardly able to project his voice. "Coming in wuz worse 'an goin' out." He dropped his head between his knees. "The whole island is nothing but brambles—and mountains," he added, wheezing.

"The trees stope aboot hawf a mile oop," said Oates, dropping beside the Captain and pulling off his tam, mopping his forehead and scratching a welt. "Funny thing. Ye walk right oot 'a the forest, A'm glad o' that—" He looked down at himself and the wretched condition of his clothes. "—directly into rock an' mountain that chust go on forever, Auld Man. Ye climb one mountain, an' there's the next one chust the same. Like the waves 'o the sea, sur. Och naw, there nuthin' or naebody on this bloody island but us, sur."

"You saw no animals?" Richard demanded. "No birds?"

"Chust a wee rat 'o some kind. That's whit is makin' a' the yammering we keep hearin' an' it no' a woodpecker. There's nae burds at a' on this island . . . 'cept Polly."

"You saw no sign of people? No ships out there?"

"Nane, sur."

Richard motioned to Emily and together they headed down the trail to the beach, where he stood a long, long while staring out to the sea and setting sun. "How can it be she still burns?" he asked absently, focusing on the *Maid*.

Emily counted on her fingers. Tuesday night the fire had broken out. Sunday night now. Five days? He took her hand, tucked it into the crook of his arm, and, tide out, they walked side by side to their ship, white shingle crunching underfoot, ankles twisting in the swath of barnacle-covered stones, now the stretch of hard, white sand beneath their feet.

The poor ship—she looked so sad, so beaten. She faced them at an angle, bow plowed deep into the ocean floor and holding despite the assault of waves that slapped her stern. Gutted, plundered, pillaged by the sea, yet there was the figurehead with her wooden smile. Black flames of charred wood scarred her Maiden's throat, her jaw, yet still she smiled, smiling and smiling as ever she'd done.

Emily and the Captain passed under her, straight through the charred hull and into the hold. A mournful sight. The cement, soaked solid in burlap sacks, would forever be marooned in this watery grave. Most of the coal, instigator of their trouble, still hissed on the wash of waves, smoking, smoking, a flick of fire. The hay, the wool, this was all gone. There remained the large boilers and much of the miscellaneous cargo. Without word they moved aft, to their old quarters below the poop.

A dismal thing, thought Emily, to kick aside the memories, sooty and charred and wet. Here was the marble of her mother's washstand, the tarnished brass of the fancy footlocker. Here their iron bedstead, twisted into odd shapes. Her bathtub, beaten and distorted and utterly useless. But here was a galvanized tin bowl, useful for washing. And a tray of knives. A bright color caught her eye. She bent to pick up the pretty shell. Only it wasn't a shell, it was a piece of her china—with glass melted to it. How fearful the fire, she thought with a shiver.

"Never mind," said the Captain gently, taking the fragment from her hand. "I shall get you more china. Oh, Emily!"

How long they stood she didn't know, holding each other in the ruin of their dreams while the Maid, visible through the crossbeams of steal and burned hull, resolutely smiled. The aggravation was more than Emily could bear, and she hid her face in her dear husband's shoulder.

"Don't, darling, don't cry." He took her face in his icy hands, blue eyes searching. "Darling, I have a plan," he whispered gently.

"Aye?"

"It's Sunday. When we go back I shall read to the men of St. Paul's shipwreck. I shall then commission them to begin at once on the boats. We'll caulk them, Emily. We'll make each a mast. We'll make sails with the canvas we have, and we'll make *sailboats*!" A happy smile in his eyes. "We shall *sail*, my dear girl! *Sail* to the Falklands!"

"*Sail*? Oh, but Richard, darling, it be 500 miles—"

"Don't you see, Emily?" and he grabbed her face tighter, as if to pass from his soul to hers his faith. "God has given us everything we need. Everything! Canvas, tools, charts, instruments, tar, rope, white lead—"

"But there be no chronometer, no way to measure—"

"There is cold current which flows between the Cape and the Falklands and—"

"Oh, yes, Richard!" she cried, reaching up to lay her hands over his, still on her face, believing in her husband's words, believing in his determination, wondering how she could ever have thought otherwise. They would sail, he had said, and thus it would be . . . for that's just the way it was with a determined man, her Captain Richard Gurney Wooldridge.

14

As an offshoot of the great Southern Ocean current, which flows east . . . past Cape Horn, the Falkland Current bears a cold stream northward to the islands.

—Ian J. Strange
The Falklands: South Atlantic Islands

Monday morning the sun rose with warmth, as if to bless the Captain's plan, spilling her light through eastern trees in dappled dance. *"Come all you young fellows who follow the sea, to me way, hey, blow the man down! Now, please pay attention and listen to me, Give me some time to blow the man down!"* Song, sweat, smiles. They would sail. Of course! Were they not sailors? *"I'm a deep-water sailor just come from Hong Kong, To me way, hey, blow the man down."*

"We'll start with the small boat," the Captain explained over breakfast. "Sargent, you're in charge. I want the seams caulked first with oakum; there's plenty of rope down there to get started. Oates? I've already picked a tree for the mast. Get the hatchet and we'll have a go at it. Any questions? Steward, a word with you, if I may."

"You want me to what?" Steward asked, men gone, just he and the Captain left by the fire. "You want me to haul all the foodstuffs up to *your* tent? Bully beef, salt pork, soup, flour, gin, claret, brandy, rum, potatoes, tea? *Everything?*"

"Aye. Cheese too. Put everything inside the tent to keep dry. Well, to keep from getting drenched," he amended. Nothing would stay dry in this miserable dampness.

"I don't understand. I'm to cook there as well?"

"Nay. You'll cook at the Encampment, as you're doing."

"*Sir?*"

The Captain looked into the face of his cook and steward, glad to have with him at least one man he could trust explicitly. "The men," he said, "are bound to get unbearably hungry before too long."

Steward sucked on his cheek, understanding.

"Can't have temptation sitting right under their noses, can we?"

"We're in for a hard time, aren't we, sir?"

"Aye, I'm afraid so, Steward."

Emily and the boy helped Steward arrange the stores, tucking the sacks, boxes, bottles, and tins up against one wall, away from her bed and the "sideboard." When everything was at last in order they went down to the beach, where they found the Captain and Oates stripping the limbs and bark off a fallen tree, the two men whistling a lively Scottish tune. "Aye, Missus!" cried Oates, seeing her. "Ye're lookin' bonny the day!"

"Why, thank you, Oates!" she exclaimed, giving him a quick curtsy, pleased that someone had noticed. With her "new" comb she'd managed to get the tangles out of her hair, and with a thread of burlap had tied it at the nape of her neck, just behind her right ear. Not a fancy coiffure, to be sure, but tidy, and certainly an improvement over the last few days. "Captain?" she asked, smiling at him, "be there anything I can do?"

"You want to teach her how to pick oakum, Steward?"

"If that's what we're doing."

"Aye, it is. And Sargent's going to need a ton, if we're to seal both boats. You too, Johnny."

All afternoon she and Steward and the boy picked oakum from the tarry ropes, plucking at the fuzz while sitting on the hot, flat rock they had first perched on after landing. A sticky but happy task, for up and down the beach the men whistled and sang, rhythm in their work as they bent over the small boat, chiseling out woodrot, cleaning the crevices for the oakum. *"Way, hey, blow the man down."* Yes, they were doing something; they had a plan, it was only a matter of time. Too, the day was sunny and bright, and while the unrelenting rollers tore up the beach as usual in a roar, throwing pebbles that scattered and ricocheted like a hundred guns going off (making it hard to hear themselves think, let alone talk), the sea beyond the surf was placid and smooth. A day like this and it was easy to believe that with a little effort they could sail anywhere in the world!

How familiar these men have become to me, thought Emily, watching Harris, Lawson, and Sargent, the tide gone out, head for the ship. There be Harris in the lead, bold and cocky as always. And Lawson, eager to follow. Sargent, distant and removed, bringing up the rear. Little Johnny dashing here, dashing there, the first to reach the bowsprit, and the Maid smiling at them all.

They brought back a ham and the rest of the men stormed the sandflats to greet them, eager to unburden Lawson of the ten-pound pork rump. "Nay, nay!" cried Steward with good humor, staking claim. "It'll be mine to tend, or I'll be sizing up the measure of your own rumps!"

"Ha!" roared Hayward in an uncharacteristic burst of laughter, slapping Harris on his derriere. Harris retaliated with a pig snort and glower, and everyone guffawed.

"Dinna a body care fer me own treasure me found?" cried Johnny, holding up the ship's bell as the men, still guffawing, tried again to grab the ham from Steward's hands. "It be a wee bent!" Johnny hollered above the ruckus, "but she still 'ave a ring! See?"

Oh, such a merry sound! thought Emily from her rock, where she watched the antics with amusement, pick-picking her oakum, thumb and fingers busy. Oh, such a merry sound, bringing memory of home, of school bells, of church on a Sunday morning, of weddings and sleigh rides! Ah, well, they should be home soon enough!

"Captain, sir?"

"Aye, Harris!" said the Captain, sauntering across the barnacles to join the group of men.

"Me and Lawson and Sargent," said the sailor, "don't think this is such a good idea to head out to sea like you're planning. Five hundred miles is a long way, even if you are sailing, sir—"

Like a cloud off a clear horizon, like wind out of nowhere, the sweep of such words touched off a quick chill, and Emily shivered in the scent of trouble hanging ominously in the air. The Captain held out a silencing hand. "What are you saying, Harris? Say it and be quick."

"We'd like to stay, sir. Take our chances on the island rather than the open sea."

"Sargent!" snapped the Captain, no secret amongst any of them whose idea this was.

"Sir?" the Bosun queried, wind whipping his hair, hips slung forward to hold his weight.

"*No* one stays on this island. We will *all* sail for the Falklands, whether it suits you or not."

"I only thought," said Sargent, smiling and holding up his hands in an innocent gesture, "that if we split ranks, we split odds. But it was only an idea. You're the Captain. Sir," he added.

Curse his insolent hide, thought Richard. Aloud he said, "Yes, I am the Captain. And as such, I am the one who will do the thinking. Not you."

"We only meant to ask," said Lawson quietly, heading off. "No harm intended, sir."

"No ye weren't!" screamed Johnny suddenly, clutching

his bell. "Ye an' Sargent be only thinkin' 'a yerself! I 'eard you! I 'eard you an' 'Arris an' Sargent!"

"Shut up, you runt," snapped Harris, giving the boy a knock upside the head so that he yelped and jumped sideways.

"I 'eard whut ye said on the ship!" cried Johnny, real tears this time, nursing his ear and hanging tight with the one hand to the battered bell. "Ye said if the rest 'a us go to sye ye dinna 'ave to face the danger! That's whut ye said! Ye said the Cap'n could send back 'elp—"

"You lie," hissed Lawson. "Where'd you get that fool notion anyway? Captain," he said, appealing, "it's like Sargent said, we only thought it might be smart to split the odds. If you make it to the Falklands you could send back help, but when a whaler comes through, why, we'd—"

"You were only thinking of your own neck!" roared the Captain, grabbing hold of Lawson's shirt front and bringing him up off his feet. Just as quickly he threw the man back, a fish too small, and went for Sargent. "Three would let seven take the risk?" he thundered. "Three would let seven take the risk, is that it? You miserable coward! You dirty, yellow *coward!*" and he flung him, suddenly disgusted, as he'd flung Lawson, driving him backward so forcibly that the man couldn't get his footing and he slammed, backside first, into the muck and barnacles with a yelp and whimper. There he left him, disgraced and exposed for the coward he was, and returned to his mast. He picked up his planer and tore into the bark, bark and wood chips flying, sorry and sick that the good humor of the day, gained by decision and direction, was so irrevocably dispensed. *Oh God*, he prayed, lips trembling, *I am only one man to see the job through . . . and there's an enemy on the beach.*

One by one the men went back to work, picking up where they'd left off. No one looked at anyone else, and Emily, hot and sick on her rock, felt the hammering of her heart in the very ends of her tarry thumbs as the truth of the Captain's words hit them all. Three would let seven take the risk. Oh how, she wondered, would they do this, thus betrayed?

⚓

The good weather held into the next day, the sun warm, the wind low, but song did not mingle as it had the day before with the roar of the sea, the occasional shriek of distant petrels and honk of geese as they roamed the reef end. Emily hummed to fill the gap, the sound low and tuneless, and unconscious.

"Emily?" called the Captain, having watched out the corner of his eye long enough her circle the stove which the men had hauled out of the ship and abandoned on the wrong side of the high-tide line. There was something heroic about the resolve in her pace, the determination on her pretty face as she summoned strength for a man's task. "Emily!" he insisted, setting aside his planer, and balancing it atop the nearly finished mast, for she'd dropped to her hands and knees and was now raking the sand from the stove. "Emily! What are you doing?"

"If we wait another day we'll never get it unburied!"

"But you're going to need help if you're thinking of bringing that stove up here!" he insisted. "It's a man's job!"

She didn't answer.

"Johnny?" The boy gave one last tug on a large piece of driftwood, swinging one end into the crackling beach fire. "Run tell Steward to come down and help the Missus. She's bound and determined to do something with that stove. Oates, another ten minutes on this mast and I think we'll be done!"

Sand had banked the stove several inches, and Steward, after giving it a quick study, whistled and blinked.

But a pretty smile from Emily and he dug in with both will and a whistle. Sleeves up, they dug together, digging and scooping, coarse grit flying. "It be even in the oven, Steward!" she declared, looking up, hair cutting eyes and face. She plucked at the calico and rope that had washed in and tangled.

"Your hands, Missus, are bleeding."

She held them out. "Look at yours, Steward."

"It's like glass," and he wiggled his fingers, feeling the pain.

The Captain, eye still on Emily, grunted. "Oates, go get the carving knife before she rips her fingers off."

Both Emily and Steward welcomed the Scot, for he made short work of the tangled debris in the oven. "The hard bit noo," he said with happy glee, "is gettin' it oop to the cliff. Is that no' where ye want it, Missus?"

"Aye. By the ladder, where it be handy."

"Handy," muttered Steward. "Ten minutes up the hill, ten minutes down . . ." He grabbed a cask stave and used it like a lever; edging one end under the heavy stove, he butted his shoulder up against the monstrous weight. "You going to watch, Oates?" he breathed out, wheezing, bracing his legs, "while I do all the work?"

"Aye, that is it!" shouted Oates, knees bent, tam off and eyeballing the stove, "Keep her goin'! Tip her end to end and gi'e her a heave. Save yer back a beatin'!"

"Steward! Steward!"

"*Johnny?*" Steward dropped the stove and it fell back with a thud to the sand. "JOHNNY!"

"A penguin, Steward!"

Down went everyone's tools—plane, chisel, hammer, and knives, echoing thuds in the sand as all the men on the beach eased up. The Captain forgot his mast and Harris the stubborn crevice just under the fourth thwart in the nose of the small boat. Emily eased up too, brushing sand and blood from fingers to skirt and lifting her hands to shield her eyes from the sun and glare off the

south rock. Johnny crested the reef with a penguin—
nearly as tall as he!—dodging first left, then right, ducking the gentle blows of the lad's stick and marching with
an unhurried, kingly gait down the rock.

"A penguin!" yelped Harris with electrified energy.
"Aye, Johnny! Run him down here!"

"Ah-ha! Unlucky bird!" cried Steward, spreading his
arms quick, back bent low and parallel to the ground,
moving in after the king in black and white. Away ran
the Captain, away ran Harris, away ran Oates and Lawson and Emily too, away ran Johnny with everyone else,
giving chase.

"Hayward! Over there! Get between it and the sea!"
shouted the Captain.

Lawson, Emily, Johnny, and Sargent cut off its escape,
splashing through the water.

"That's it!" shouted Sargent. "Ease him back up!"

"Fe, fi, fo, fum!" shouted Steward, edging in trium-
phantly, spread arms winging. "I smell the blood of a—I
smell the blood of a *peng-a-one!*"

Oates closed in. Harris held opposite. "Boo!" he
yelled. The penguin turned, eyes rolled in panic. Oates
sprang, carving knife across the throat in one quick,
merciful stroke, and if ever God worked in mysterious
ways, thought Emily, he certainly had done so this time.
A penguin. A penguin to pull them together. One penguin, one triumphant chase to help the men forget their
differences. A whoop and a holler, ten instead of seven
and three, betrayal forgiven and to God be the credit, she
decided. "Be ye dead or be ye live!" sang Steward, throwing an arm around Harris.

"I'll grind your bones," sang Harris back, "to make
my bread!"

"You pluck and I'll stew!"

"Nay," disagreed Harris with a gallant smile, "you
pluck *and* stew. We *eat*, eh, boys?"

But it was nine against one the moment the penguin was cooked, the moment the first taste of the foul meat met her mouth. Emily spit it out with a gagging "bah!" while the men, containing their laughter at her convulsions, choked it down in manly boast, even Johnny, even the Captain. Nine against one, men and a woman, a tolerable division. "Suit yourselves," she said, unwounded, and, to make them laugh again (for she enjoyed their restored gaiety), she waddled like a penguin up the slope to her tent. But she had to pass Sargent, who wasn't laughing, and what she saw in his eyes made her blood run cold. A red spark, like a spark from an anvil, a quick fierce light in the dark of his eyes that pulsed, and while she couldn't name such fire she knew well enough the danger of it.

As for Sargent, such involuntary disclosures of the fiery monomania within, generally covered by a disciplined demeanor, could not be quenched forever. The subterranean fire was eating its way deeper and deeper within and, like a smoldering volcano, something decisive would come of it.

15

Which way to London?
A poke full of plumes.

—Thomas Drake
Bibleotheca

If a pocket of civilization had sprung off Staten Island's dreary patch of desolation beneath the world's globe, this same pocket within a week fairly bristled with purpose. Three fires burned day in and night out—beach, Encampment, and Mount—lest through the come and go of fickle fog a whaler might yet sail and might yet catch sight of flame that bespoke a remnant's existence. No man among the remnant was fool enough to discredit the merest of chances simply because one amongst them held the view this was their *only* hope. There was also the ring of bells, not the chime of steeple spires as on land, and not the single ring of each half-past as upon a ship at sea, nor even at the top of every hour, but only every four, eight bells to rotate each day through . . . breakfast to dinner to tea. For the Captain, in keeping the fires and regular hours, and regular chores within those hours, hoped to hold the structure of civilization in the minds of his men, and not just in their dreams.

Thus the fires and the ring of the bell brought purpose to their days, and although the men did not know it—not even Sargent, who fought it—this gave them reason to rise and reason even to sing.

"I am the wind the seamen love—I am steady and strong and true. . . ." If a man worked the boats from breakfast to dinner, from dinner to tea he worked the sails, everyone taking a break at the turn in the tide, salvaging, salvaging, always salvaging the ship whenever they could. *"Through daylight and dark I follow the bark, I keep like a hound on her trail."* Cables, hawser, anchor, and beams. Another pot, a skillet, a mug, and yesterday a packet of raisins. From tea until dusk they gathered fuel and tossed up wreckage debris, from river and shore and wood. *"I am strongest at noon, yet under the moon I stiffen the bunt of her sail."* Under this regimen, clear-cut and defined, they prospered.

The Encampment took on a tidy look, earth tramped down hard and clean and as smooth as the face of a pocket watch. The men's tent, haphazard as it was, sat at the "five o'clock" hour of the pocket watch, canvas and calico draped over the limbs of trees butted against a rocky, ten-foot cliff. In front of the tent and to the south, right where the trail from the Mount let out at "ten," Steward had made his kitchen. Pots and pans were strung from a stout crossbeam tied to the crook of two upright, wooden tripods. Upturned stumps and a mossy log served as stools and a bench. The fire, circled with stones, sat five feet in front of the open wall of the tent so that it might warm and light the interior, edging the north brink of the swale, where a gully fell off at the "three," dropping several hundred feet into a dark ravine. Trees grew out of the ravine so tall that they shot past the camp, tumbling bough and limb over tent and fire alike, and the constant come and go of the fluctuating woodpile. "Twelve o'clock straight up," downhill and due west, was the precipitously steep trail leading past the Cascade and to the beach.

Up the other way, deckboards circled from the pocket watch "ten" to lead up a narrow trail cut back through the shrub, backing past "nine," "eight," and "seven," curving up and around the ten-foot cliff to the higher and smaller swale belonging to the Captain and his wife. Midway, this trail let out to a ridge which overlooked the Encampment directly below and the beach far below, and here one could sit and feel like a monarch, owning a bird's-eye view of all that happened. And so here Steward and Emily often sat, at this brow in the hill between the two camps, sifting sorry flour atop a soapbox tipped upside down between them, watching the comings and goings, and arguing Dickens versus Johnson.

Today, if they ever got the flour sifted and sorted, they would bake bread. Steward would make breadloaves, for he was resolved to try the stove squared away at the bottom of the cliff, right where Sargent's ladder gated the trail up. Emily would make little breadcakes of preserved potatoes and flour, for the trip ahead of them. "Steward!" she suddenly cried. "The Captain paces the beach! Aye, and Oates!"

"Did Harris and Lawson—"

"Oh, that's it! They've not come back with the small boat! They be out there still!" she exclaimed in a panic, jumping so quickly that dough and cakes tumbled off her lap and rolled. What had once been smooth water beyond the bay was now spiked with high combers and spindrift, and the rollers within the bay were washing ashore in stupendous fury, sweeping round the *Maid* and onto the beach aboil, the surf a four-foot wall of green spilling foam.

"Look!" she shouted, already running, "There they be!"

"Look! There they arr!"

Richard followed Oates' pointed finger and let out a slow sigh of relief as the prow of the small boat came into view, rounding the ragged reef. It had been foolish to let

Harris and Lawson take the small boat out untried, but he'd succumbed, bribed. They had claimed to have gotten the caulking done, and wanted to test their job; but what was the clincher was Lawson's fishhooks, discovered the day before aboard the ship. "Fresh fish," Harris had said with his bold and cocky grin, "might slide down the gullet a bit easier than that leftover penguin, Old Man." Well, they were back, and no harm done. He felt the constriction around his heart ease. And apparently the boat was tight, or they'd have drowned by now.

But almost immediately, just as the boat cleared the point, she spun and nosedived into the rocks to the south, and he nearly choked on the quick suck of his intaking breath.

"They're no' gawn to make it, Auld Man," said Oates.

But the next wave caught them square in the stern. Forward and free they flew, riding the crest, paddling frenetically, steering away from the rocks and in toward shore, their frenetic, whitened faces coming into focus. A second wave caught them crossbow and they twisted back into the reef; before they could catch their bearing another wave sent the boat crashing into rock and ruin, the splintering of the bow splitting the air with a painful crack above the roar of the waves. Richard plunged into the surf, Oates hot behind, both leaping through the rolling wall just as Emily and Steward arrived. Harris, knocked backward into the boat, scrambled up and pushed off the reef with his oar. A fourth wave threw them forward, flying the low tide like a duck and spitting them up onto the shore, plowing down the Captain in a blink. Harris and Lawson tumbled out, the Captain surfaced, blood on his head, and the four men hauled her up, Steward rushing in to guide.

She was a wreck, bow staved in with a hole as big as a man's boot. They would have to begin again. "Bail her out, tie her up, and come for dinner," was all Richard could say, and he took Emily's hand, glad she was there to soften the edge of his frustration and even anger. Yet he could not blame Harris for the miserable unrest of the tumultuous bay, or the unwieldiness of the boat.

"Did ye catch any fish?" asked Oates.

"Aye," said Lawson, "but it looks like we lost 'em."

Richard gently slapped Emily's hand, still clasped in his, against his thigh, and without more said, they all headed for camp. He went to inspect the work Hayward and Sargent had done while Steward dished out the dinner. He tested the seams and tugged on the grosgrain. "Who cut the canvas?" he demanded, anger again leaping into his breast. "Who," he repeated, "cut the canvas?"

No one answered. Finally, "Sargent, sir," from Hayward.

"You've cut it the wrong way! You're Bosun! You should know better! And it's not like we've got canvas to spare—"

Sargent leaped to his feet, and before Richard could blink Sargent lunged with his knife. Richard dodged the wide swing, and in the sound of Emily's scream he sent Sargent hurtling backward with a quick left hook to the jaw, snapping the Bosun's neck and throwing him back with a crash into the woodpile. Driftwood cracked and rolled. The knife spun from his hand.

"Don't hit him! Don't hit him! He ain't worth it!" screamed Hayward. Sargent, on his back, scrambled elbows and heels up the woodpile, and Richard, panting hard and watching him, and hearing in his ears yet another of his men cry "Don't hit him!" debated the full scope of the law at his hand and the ramifications should he not meet it. To pull a knife was mutiny. To actually lunge? To attack? A court of law exacted death, and to ignore such law would be to flinch, to invite the view that he was weak. But one look at his men and he knew they did not think him weak. To the contrary, in their eyes and upon their faces, drained of color and already blistered with pimpled sores, he saw a plea for life, all of their lives. To take a life down here at the end of the world would demoralize them all. They fought for life, with every limpet pulled off the rocks, with every mouthful downed of the awful penguin, and this fight for life would only grow more grim as the days unwound. Nay, there must be, there had to be, other ways to deal with mutiny. All this passed through his mind in an instant.

He advanced, pinning Sargent to the ground with his boot. "So help me God," he hissed down, "do that again and I will hang you from the nearest tree!"

"No, no," cried Sargent. "No, I didn't mean to, no, I didn't. As God is my witness, I didn't." He covered his face with both hands, weeping and crying. "Please," he begged, "I didn't mean to."

Richard pushed his boot further into the man's chest so that he gasped for breath. "No? Yet there is always method to your madness—I have seen it in your eye. Now before your madness takes over, listen here to me this day. I am the Captain, not you. I am responsible for getting everyone off this island, not you. If I say we go, we go. And all your sabotage of the sails isn't going to amount to a hill of beans. Even if you were man enough to kill me, Mr. Sargent, you will never be Captain. For that is what you want, isn't it? But know this: After me there is no you . . . there is God."

Emily followed her husband up to the Mount, where she found him standing by the fire, shuddering in the blast of heat that chilled his wet backside.

"You're bleeding," she said, still so badly shaken she could hardly stand on her feet.

"I am?" He pulled up an arm and looked down at himself.

"No, darling. Your head."

"Ah, yes, my head." And he touched his forehead gingerly, pulling back bloodied fingers.

The blood had dripped down his temple and was congealing in his beard. She pulled over the upside-down potato tin he used as a chair and told him to sit, then set a pan of water onto the fire to boil.

The wound was a clean one; it would heal. Given time, the bump would go down. She only hoped her heart would settle back into an even beat. "Do you think," she asked, wringing out her hankie and setting the saucepan of hot water back onto her fire, "he meant to harm you? He swung so far, I wonder if he changed his mind mid-leap." The fire hissed.

"Your water is too hot."

"It needs to be.

"Richard, please . . ."

Their eyes caught. "Emily, don't worry about it." He took the hankie and dabbed his head a few times. "No, I don't think the man meant to kill me, or even to wound me. He's a coward. He only *wishes* he could kill me."

"This be no comfort, darling."

He stripped off his wet clothes and ducked into the tent. "Emily? Someday soon we need to rip moss off the trees and try to make a softer mattress."

She gathered his wet clothes and hung them to dry, draping his shirt and torn trousers next to the hankie over an old davit rope all full of tar. "Shoo," she said to Polly-wants-a-cracker. "Don't be pooping on my wet things."

"Darling?"

"Aye?" She went to the tent door, heart aching with the confusion of this frightening men's world.

"Come lie with me," he said, eyes closed, "and help me think."

Muscles leaped, moving beneath satiny skin to welcome her, and she slid gratefully into his familiar embrace. "I'm sorry," he whispered, kissing her. "I didn't mean to make light of this."

"I don't trust the man...." The salt from her tears stung her chapped face.

"I miss Yates at times like these," he said, brushing away her tears very tenderly with the backs of his fingers. "Darling, I don't mind figuring a way out of here, but I really don't like riding herd on that brute. That's Yates' job. But he's gone. So now I have to do it, when I have so much else to do. And no telling what else he might pull. Whatever it is, it'll be on the sly." He turned, sniffing the air. "Emily? What's that dreadful smell?"

She lifted her own head, scanning the shadowed corners of the tent. "Oh! The penguin skin! Steward gave it to me. I be scraping the fat off so I can make a bonnet."

"A bonnet?" he cried, horrified. "Ugh!" And he fell back, holding his nose. "The thing stinks!"

"But the wind hurts my ears! My hair be always wet!"

"Darling, you come near me with that bonnet and I shall have to snuggle up with the men!"

"Richard!"

"Emily!"

Suddenly they were both laughing. He rolled over and gave her a peck on the nose so that she giggled in the light of his blue eyes. "We need a privacy curtain the other side of that fire," he said, blue eyes centering on hers mischievously. "I'll do it tomorrow, but right now..."

"Richard? You be right. The thing does stink like the dickens." And she laughed again. The bump on the head hadn't slowed him down at all, and one more time, as always, he made her forget her fear. Which meant she had nothing to fear.

16

Even the able seaman, deeming his
Days nearly o'er, might be disposed to riot,
As upon such occasions tars will ask
For grog, and sometimes drink rum from the cask.

—Lord Byron

Thursday morning, one week marooned, Steward helped Harris and Lawson mend the hole in the bow of the small boat while Sargent recut his sail, on the grain this time, and while Emily made and baked the bread herself, struggling gallantly up and down the hill between the stove at the bottom of the hill and the Encampment at the top. But because the hill was so steep and so slick, she, with just the one hand free, very nearly tore her wedding ring from her finger several times while trying to catch hold of the branches to keep from falling. And with each step? A pool of water to fill it, until her feet ached with the cold.

"We have to start rationing the food," she told the men the moment the Captain said amen and they dived into their noon meal, preserved potatoes and bully beef, tea and molasses. "It won't last," she hastened to say, "if we keep eating like this. The rice is all but gone—"

"Thank goodness," joked Lawson, elbowing Harris and holding his nose.

"Steward has already used half the flour. And I need to make dozens more of those breadcakes."

160

"Woman, I don't know why you bother," Harris announced. "They're just going to get wet out there, and spoil."

"But she's right," said Richard quickly. "We have to ration what we have—more than we have. It's taking time to put these boats in order. Especially," he couldn't help but add, "if we keep putting holes in them."

"I'll take complete inventory, this very afternoon," said Steward. "And divvy out."

"I kin catch a goose," put in Johnny, bewildered when the men all laughed.

"Ha!" Lawson slapped the boy's cap into his face. "You can forget it, mate. That ain't nothin' but a wild goose chase! Better off goin' after the limpets, boy."

"But I 'ate limpets, Lawson!"

"Now, what I want—" Harris poked a finger at the boy, "—is roast *duck*! With a sprinkle of basil just the way me mum . . . Hey! Where'd those clouds come from?"

Off the sea they rolled, gathering speed. With no more warning than that, the screaming fury of an Antarctic wind tore up the hill so swiftly and so savagely that it sent them all flying in a panic for shelter, white lines of hail streaking into their faces, bouncing off the ground, cutting their scalps and skin. "Run for the tent!" Richard called to Emily. "Oates! The tools! We have to get the tools off the beach!"

Emily tripped over a burlap sack on her way up and instinctively threw it over her red coat, covering head and face even as she dove for cover. When she peeked out, the flapping and billowing canvas of her tent cracking like a whip all round and tearing up at the corners, it was to skies hidden from her eyes that she stared, slashes of white ribbon out of heaven, perpetual streams, Staten Island a world instantaneously reduced to a bit of wild rock cast loose from the world. "Richard?" she whispered, peering again into the white violence. "Richard? RICHARD!"

He crashed through headfirst, clawing at the earth as he came, bubbles of blood on his hands and face. He threw off his boots, soles all but gone, and embraced his feet, hunching over them in agony. "We had to crawl on our hands and knees," he panted, grunting in pain, "it's so slippery. And I missed the trail coming up from the Encampment—ran right into thornbushes. Oh, my feet," he moaned. "I think my boots are gone." She struck a match, but her hands were shaking so badly with cold that she dropped the candle all the way into the baby bottle. She tried again and burned herself. Finally a feeble flicker and she picked up the shambles of his boots, burnt and shredded. Suddenly he started to laugh and she dropped the useless boots with a clatter.

"I don't see what be so funny," she said carefully. *Had he bumped his head again?*

"You look like Little Red Riding Hood! Inside out! With all that burlap and red coat!"

"Well, *you* look like the wolf just got you. You be covered in blood."

He wiped his face with his coatsleeve. "Blasted brambles." Another gust of wind shrieked through the tent. The candle blinked out. "Plummy!" he exclaimed, exasperated. "There goes the light!"

In the dark she wrapped his feet in the burlap he'd mocked, instantly regretting it: Her ears throbbed in the whistle of the wind.

"There must be another sack around here somewhere," he insisted. He found one among the supplies, and tearing out a seam, draped it over her head like a cape. "Do you have anything to hold it shut under your chin?" he asked tenderly, tucking her wet hair back up under the harsh burlap. "You can't always be holding your new bonnet."

"My Scotch pebble broach!"

He had bought it for her for a wedding present. It was one of the few pieces of jewelry she'd brought along, and when she pulled it out of her sewing box and held it on her palm for him to see, the pretty broach seemed strangely out of place, winking in the cold light of the storm.

"Can you pin it on for me?" she asked.

"Aye." But his fingers were so swollen and sore from working on the mast with the dulled tools that they were hard-pressed to perform the more delicate job. He scratched her throat clumsily, and winced for her.

"It's gone," she said.

"What?"

"The storm."

As suddenly as it had come, the squall had passed. And when they looked out their tattered tent they were back again upon a mountain island, anchored still. "My bread!" she said, sloshing down the running trail to beach and stove and her morning's work. Well . . . they would just have to eat heavy bread at teatime.

The bread was hard to get down. Hayward asked for some of the gin to help it along.

"No, the usual rum after hauling wood, that's all," said Richard.

"But what about all that gin?" Hayward whined. "What's a bloke supposed to do on a godforsaken island if he can't have a little gin now and then, especially after a storm like that? And my rheumatism? I can't hardly lift my arms and all my pills got left on the ship—"

"Did you and Sargent finish the sail?" Richard asked.

"Aye, sir. But the gin—"

"Good. Because Oates cut the jib. In the morning you and Sargent can get started on the jibsail. But for now," and he rose, kicking the cold damp cramps out of his legs, burlap around his feet stiff with the cold, "*everyone* shake a leg. We haul until it gets dark."

"Some rum then when we come in," said Lawson.

"A swallow, as always," he said, irritated. "Aye."

"But we don't want just a swallow," Lawson persisted.

"And we want some of that *gin!*" Hayward insisted.

"None of us," said Fielding with rare argument, "kin see what yer hoardin' it fer. Sir," he added, apologetic for his resistance.

So, thought Richard, they'd all sat out the storm wishing for a warm-up. He said firmly, "No gin. We have two bottles, and we have to save them for emergencies. As for the rum, you'll get your usual swallow, no more."

"But what about the brandy? The claret?"

"The matter is closed, Hayward."

By nightfall they'd foraged the entire riverbed for driftwood, finding several of the burlap gunnysacks—which they welcomed, for they were good for hauling and carrying, and for blankets, and for wrapping their feet—while they cleaned out the last log and sack right down to the river mouth and beach. And, unable to resist the chase, they caught and killed three more penguins.

"Which means we have to eat them," grumbled Harris to Lawson coming into camp.

"I heard that," said Emily, teasing them. She was scrubbing the last pan with sand in light of the men's fire. "And you both tried to make me think you *liked* it!" she accused with a smile.

Harris shrugged. Steward poured him his rum. "I'll make soup this time, Harris. I'll cut the meat into pieces so tiny you'll never taste it—"

"Steward," interrupted Sargent sourly, throwing back his own round of rum and ducking into the tent, "no matter what you do to the bloody birds—" he shouted through the canvas—"we'll still taste it!"

"Bloody fish rubber," muttered Harris, following him.

⚓

Steward and Emily decided to rotate the days between flour and potatoes. On flour days the men would each be allowed two tablespoons, the collective amount to be made into bread so long as the starter held. Should the starter fail, they would fry the flour in penguin oil and eat it that way. On potato days they could each have two tablespoons of preserved flakes, which Steward mixed with boiling water and set by the fire to reach the right consistency. The men could each have a slice of ham or bully beef a day, a tablespoon of cod-liver oil, and all the mildewed tea, with molasses, they wanted. Always there was the penguin. There was yet some rice, tinned soups, and snacks of cheese. And until it was gone, the cup of grog before turning in.

"So what'll we do with all this penguin fat?" It was Friday morning, eight whole days on the island, routine established—and with it, boredom. The men had dispersed, busy with their unvarying tasks—caulking boats, picking oakum, working on the mast. Sargent had fresh canvas spread on the ground just outside the men's tent, circling, circling again. Emily surreptitiously watched, waiting to see that he cut the jib right. Steward sent Johnny down to light the fire in the stove. "No runnin' off now!" he warned. "You leave those geese be! You'll never catch one and you'll only wear out your boots trying!"

"Well?" said Emily. "What are we going to do with it?"

"What's that? Oh, the penguin fat! I don't know. Try and make soap," and he laughed. Didn't he wish! She poked at the fat, then inspected the calico where it lay stacked in molding bolts under the trees. He gave the soup another swirl. "Why?" he asked, squinting suddenly. "You have an idea?"

"What if we made bags out of this calico? And then melted your fat over the fire? We could dip the bags into it. Wouldn't the oil, when it hardened, waterproof everything? Steward, we could put my breadcakes in a bag for the trip, and keep them that way. And wrap the matches too. I fear the dampness will spoil them sooner or later, and then where will we be?"

"You're a rare wonder. Of course, the very thing. But do you have any sewing needles? What about scissors?"

She brought down her sewing box and excitedly dumped the contents onto the soapbox. *Four* needles! But only *two* pins . . . and no scissors. Glum looks passed between them.

"Try these," said Hayward. He sat cross-legged on the canvas sea, adjoining two cuttings, scooting himself backward while his hands gathered, paired, lapped, and stitched the seam. He jabbed his scruffy chin to the left, to where the canvas shears lay in a canvas wrinkle. "Might pucker the calico, I don't know."

She sat with the men against the woodpile, closer to Hayward than Sargent. Morning sun fell in soft light and some warmth, and by dinner she had two bags sewn, dipped and drying on Steward's clothesline. "Not shabby," said Harris with a begrudging nod of approval, "for a woman."

"Missus?" said Fielding, thinking very carefully and eyeing the burlap pinned over her head. "If ye oiled yer new hat, could ye make a slicker fer yerself, eh?"

"He is not as slow-witted as he appears," said Emily that night, hanging her sack hat, stiff with three layers of oil, on a sapling knob next to the spirits. "Darling?" she said, looking closer, "A bottle of gin is missing."

"Are you sure?" he asked, damp shirt, more rag than garment, in his hand.

"Do *you* see it anywhere?"

Their only light, the candle in the baby bottle, didn't help, and Richard stuck out his bottom lip, the flickering shadow of his chin splashed across on his chest. "Sargent," he whispered, looking about the dim tent, "is the bad apple in this barrel."

"But it was Hayward who kept whining for it."

"Aye, Hayward whines, but he'd not do something like this—not on his own. No, if Hayward is in fact the thief, it had to have been Sargent who put him up to it. Sargent put *someone* up to it. Which only means the apple rot is spreading."

"What are you going to do?"

He draped his shirt across a harness cask, blew out the candle and climbed into the bed next to her.

"What are you going to do?" she asked again. "We can't have them stealing the spirits."

"Hard to do anything when you don't catch them red-handed."

The night was cold and so quiet she could hear him breathing. A full moon hung just outside; she could see his profile, strong arms crossed over his chest, nose and brow dark against moon and fire. "I don't envy you, darling," she said, and kissed his arm.

"We'll be fine. Just let me think about this."

A second storm swept in during the night—and held all Saturday morning, imprisoning them in their tents even as it tore them apart, the men's tent completely. "After you mend the damage," the Captain told them during dinner, wind at last gone but rain drizzling down, fires smoking without flame, "you can use the new sails for sheeting."

"Aye," joked Lawson to Fielding, "them sails will be good for one thing then, eh?"

"That's not funny," Fielding answered.

The Captain turned to Steward. "When they're finished straightening up, send them after us."

"Where will you be, sir?"

"The Missus and I are going to comb the beach for any wreckage that might have blown in."

"Best let me wrap your feet with more burlap then, Old Man. The barnacles are apt to tear apart what you got."

They headed north past the bare rock by the water, where they had to edge between the incoming waves and woods, out to rolling cliffs, sometimes scaling them with hands as well as feet. Sometimes the cliffs let them out to the edge of the shore again, where they clambered wave-wet rocks, leaping across little pools left by the tide. Here they stripped the pools of the limpets, putting them into Emily's coat pockets for Steward. Deckboards were the dominant debris, with the occasional gunny-sack snagged between the rocky crevices. These they pulled loose, gathering everything they could into piles to be picked up on the way back. Presently they came to a gully that split the shore, seemingly without bottom, and they peered awestruck into the gloomy crack, hearing water gurgle far below. "This is far enough," said Richard, taking her hand and backing away. "We'll go back, picking up the boards as we go. The men should be coming out soon to help."

"Wait! Look! A ham!"

"Where?"

She started to scramble across the rocks but he pulled her away. "Don't be a king's fool," he muttered, and eased out to where the ham was pinned in the crack.

She carried the ham back, he the boards and sacks—and an old sail—pile growing in his arms as they went. Slippery devils! The planks kept sliding out from under his arm and kept stabbing him in the chest. The sacks and sail kept dragging, tripping him.

"Look, darling! Steward be coming to meet us!"

"Coming on a might fast for Steward," he commented slowly. "I wonder where the men are."

"Steward!" she called, running to meet him. "Look what we found! A ham! A big one!" And she held it up to his face with both hands. "Steward? Whatever be the matter?"

"The men are all drunk, Captain, sir. Rip-roaring drunk. They got the lad in a real pickle too."

"What do you mean, drunk!" exclaimed Emily.

"Come on," chuckled the Captain, "don't be pulling my leg. On the one bottle of gin?"

"Gin?" said Steward, puzzled.

"Someone stole a bottle last night, yes."

"Well, sir, it wasn't gin they got drunk on. Try eau de cologne, sir."

"Eau de cologne?" both Emily and the Captain chorused.

"Aye. They got into the cargo."

Emily dropped the ham at the stove and tore up the hill, heels smacking the muck, toes digging in, hands reaching instinctively for memorized branches to pull her along. Up she plunged, past the Cascade and pool.

"Whiskey is the life of man, whiskey, Johnny! Yes, whiskey made me sell my coat—"

"They *are* drunk!" she cried, stunned and angry, yet still disbelieving. And there was Johnny in the middle, reeling, grubby hands over his ears, vomit down blue flannel shirt and ragged pants, spinning like a top between the men, all of them guffawing and chortling. *"Oh, whiskey's—"*

"You too, Oates?" she accused when he stumbled out of the bush, buttoning his pants. "You let Johnny—*What be the matter with your face!"*

"It's the eau de cologne," said Steward, pushing past the Scot with an armful of the deckboards. "See? They all have the look. Makes them swollen and stupid. Go on, get out 'a my way, Oates."

Emily dodged them both and raced up the trail to the Mount. She stopped quickly, unprepared for the sight. Her tattered tent, torn up by the roots from the storm but nevertheless straightened and swept by a fir bow before leaving, was now trampled, plunder scattered, bed torn apart. She whirled when Steward dropped the boards behind her in a clatter.

"They were after the spirits. I stopped them. That's when they went for the cologne down on the beach. I'm sorry," he said; "I should have cleaned up the mess before you got here. But I wanted the Captain to know—"

"It's all right," said Richard wearily, coming up with his deckboards. "Go fix some tea. I'll tend the boy. Emily, if you would go down and get the ham, please."

Behind their privacy curtain that night, the old sail installed between the two camps, Emily circled her fire. First one way, then the other. "Eau de cologne. Richard! *Why* must men *drink*?"

He sighed deeply and tossed another wood piece into the flames, the burst of blaze lighting his face. "This *is* the way they came to us. Drunk. Don't you remember?"

"It be pointless to get drunk! On anything, let alone eau de cologne! Eau de cologne, Richard? Pointless! Absolutely pointless! They've probably damaged their minds, to boot!"

"We shan't be able to leave the Mount together, ever again. Next time it'll be the spirits for sure, bottle by bottle, and we can't afford that."

"*Do* something then!"

"I am. We're not leaving the Mount untended."

She spun, hands on her hips, eyes flashing with anger. "This be not like you, Richard. For goodness sakes, they've been caught red-handed this time! Oh, that be just fine," she said when she saw he had nothing more to say. "That be just dandy. So I am to be made a prisoner? As well as marooned? And for what? For some stupid, idiotic drunkards?"

"We'll take turns."

She rolled her eyes and sat down hard on her bucket chair, nearly tipping it in her fury. Fine thing for the Captain to say, but how, *how!* could he be expected to sit around when there be so much work to do? Nay, it would be *she* who would be left, she knew that well enough.

Oh, this be just dandy. Suddenly she hated the men, every single one of them. She hated them all! Stupid, selfish, ugly men! She hated Steward for letting it happen. She hated the Captain too. And in helpless rage she threw herself over her knees, hating herself as well for crying.

17

A century ago, copper plates were nailed to the bottom of wooden ships to protect them against Toredo Novalis, *a large wood-burning worm.*

—Joe MacInnis
The Land that Devours

A third storm, the most vicious yet, rolled in that same Saturday night. Without mercy and throughout the long, dark hours the wind tore at the tents, driving freezing rain and sleet between every crack and every crevice, wherever canvas and calico gave way, until all shivered in abject misery, sober every one of them. At sea, iron boilers, five tons apiece, were wrenched loose of the *Maid's* hold and flung ashore. All along the bank trees toppled, ripped up by their roots. The second Sabbath on Staten Island dawned, chaos reclaiming order, and the sailors stumbled about, stunned.

The Captain issued his instructions: They face the chaos and conquer it lest in the chaos they lose heart and give up. *But what was the use?* was the question readable in everyone's eyes, and for awhile he moved amongst them gently chiding, quick with encouragement. Mid-morning, with Steward's kitchen righted, debris cleared, and bedding hung to dry, everyone working diligently and without complaint, he singled out Oates to help secure the boilers.

They hauled heavy chain, rusty but strong, through first one boiler, then a second, and a third, roping the three to stout trees growing out the embankment. The remaining two, thrown against the knot of rocks at the end of the beach, they weighted with rock and stone. The task, despite the arrival of Steward to help, took all afternoon, and the sun was low in the sky when, filthy and weary, they headed back to camp.

They found Emily perched on the ladder at the foot of the hill, beside the stove. "Emily!" exclaimed Richard, disturbed to see her there. "I thought we agreed one of us would stay at the Mount." Instantly he regretted the words. They sounded harsh, and she was so terribly weary. Skin stretched tight across her nose, tighter across her cheekbones. Her face was pale in the ugly burlap hood and cloak she called a hat, the pretty pebble broach glimmering out of place under her chin. "I'm sorry," he said hastily. "I'm sorry," and he kissed her cracked lips to cheer her.

"They be all sick, Richard. They found a crate of citrate of magnesia, blue bottles. And they discovered it effervescent in their mouths, and have eaten it by the handful. It's made them thirsty and now they've drunk so much water that their stomachs be swollen." She used her hands to demonstrate.

"You men," said Richard to Oates, discouraged himself by the news, "are not very bright."

"Me noo? Dae ye see me bloatit, sur?"

"Aye, I do. From yesterday's prank."

That night while the men huddled by the fire, moaning in their self-inflicted misery and sucking on homemade pipes, the tide swept in and swept out again, taking with it the boilers, snapping the chains as easily a child her bootlaces. "I don't know why we bother," said Fielding, picking at the sore on his knee. "I say, Captain, sir, what *is* the point?"

"The point," said Richard angrily, "is that we have, despite your idiotic flirtation with liquor and magnesia, accomplished a great deal in the past ten days! The point,

Fielding, is we've caulked the small boat! The point is we've readied the mast for the small boat! The point is we're ready to cut the sails for the longboat—"

"But Fielding's point," said Hayward, "is that we have a long way to go, sir. And it is getting colder. Daily."

"Hayward, we don't need any of your pessimism!"

"What if," drawled Sargent slowly, "it snows?"

"If it snows," said Richard, addressing the bad apple in his barrel, "we just wrap in burlap and keep on."

In the morning he couldn't find Harris and Lawson. Johnny he spotted easily enough, chasing geese on the reef instead of gathering wood for Steward's stove. The other men he could hear, hoots and hollers coming from somewhere aboard ship, where they were supposed to be—salvaging what might have loosened during the storms. But Harris and Lawson? The longboat sat quite deserted.

The boat measured 16 feet in length, 7 feet in beam, a big vessel, with extensive damage to be repaired. The entire boat needed overhauling, from caulking to patching, and their lives depended on it being done properly, and done quickly. How long could grown men live on two tablespoons of flour a day? And with three storms in as many days? Hayward was right—winter would not be long in coming. Even now, in the chill of dawn, their breath brought pockets of fog.

He ran a critical eye along the early work. What's this? His hand felt the seam. Putty? He squatted, eye sliding up and down each seam until he was breathing hard. Daylight! They had stuffed the seams with putty instead of oakum and tar! All up and down daylight leaked through! Daylight! *And when the putty shrank?*

"Harris! Lawson!" He yanked back from the longboat, trembling with fright. *What if he hadn't discovered the error?*

What if he had simply ordered the copper sheeting nailed on? "HARRIS!"

"They be gone," said Johnny, flying across the beach, hitching his pants, "to look fer limpets, fer tay."

Shingle and rock ground under his bound feet as he struck north. The putty would have shrunk, the water would have poured through. He would never have known. . . . This is what scared him the most. Did he have to check everything they did? But how could he? He was only one man.

Disobedient, lazy, irresponsible, incompetent—a whole string of adjectives to describe the two men bounced off the beach as he flung the words from his tongue and into the air, and when that didn't spend his fright-driven rage he picked up a rock and flung it as far as he could, frightening himself even further with evidence of failing strength: The rock missed its mark. He stood facing the hungry sea, trembling—both from spent energy and from sudden realization. *They had done it deliberately. Deliberately they had sabotaged the project.*

He turned back, sick with sorrow, knowing what he had to do.

He hardly noticed the others, hauling up the loosened plunder: the kedge anchor, tins of white lead, a cask of vinegar. Driven by a sense of urgency and rage that had not dwindled, and by his own dreadful resolve, he went over each seam carefully, and then with a pot of tar bubbling hot on the beach fire began the painstaking task of dipping canvas so he could seal the inside of his boat.

"If you want to know what the storms have done to the ship, Captain," said Steward, standing in the fall of thin sunlight, a charred crate caught on his shoulder and resting against his ear, "they stove in her stern. Nothing left of it."

"Found my rheumatism pills, Captain," said Hayward. "Only they're all disintegrated. They're ruined."

"Go up to the Encampment, Hayward. Get the flat-tened soup tins and any pieces of copper you can find. We'll start stripping the copper sheeting off the ship tomorrow, but we'll use what's handy for now. I want you and Fielding, if you're up to it, Fielding, to start nailing it on."

"Aye," said Fielding.

"You'll start at the keel. Steward," he said, the men moving off to do as they were bid, "put that crate down and come look at this."

Steward let out a long, low whistle, took off his toque, and rubbed his head. "What do you make of it, Old Man?"

"It turns my blood cold to say this, but Sargent's the shadow behind this fancy bit of work."

"That's a bit stiff, sir, if you don't mind."

"Think on it. Harris and Lawson are hardly bright enough to do such a thing. No, it took a more devious mind than they possess. Nay, it's Sargent's fancywork, all right. First the sails, now this. He's bound and deter-mined to stay on, and he'll stop at nothing—even if it means we have to *all* stay on the island."

"So what's there to do?" Steward asked quietly.

"Give them exactly what they want."

"You can't. You mustn't, sir."

"I can, and I will. I am going to leave those three here."

At dinner he announced his decision, almost off-handedly, keeping the secret of sabotage to himself. No point in pitting three against seven again. Nothing but evil could come of anyone knowing the truth. Best treat the split a sensible course. He used the boats to do it.

"I have bad news," he said, motioning them all to sit back down; and beginning carefully, and with a prayer on his lip, said, "The small boat is not going to make the open sea. We all saw that last week. Fact is, she needs more than just men at the oars to steer her straight."

"What are you saying?" asked Lawson, picking at a scab on his hand.

"I'm saying it'll take a hefty rudder to hold her steady in the crosswinds out there, and she isn't big enough to support one. Which leaves only the longboat, only there isn't room for all of us. We'll have to leave someone behind." Everyone stiffened. "Are you three," and here he directed his question right to Sargent, "still willing to stay on?"

"Och, we'll miss ye blokes like a rotten smell," said Oates, and the separation was struck. Harris and Lawson exchanged glances. Had they won? They suspected not. But Sargent knew. They most definitely had not.

As the week progressed the Captain complained of fatigue and a growing flame in his joints. At first Emily thought it due to the food rationing; they all complained of fatigue. But the increasing joint pain pointed more directly to the long hours he spent exposed to water and wind, wrestling off the copper sheeting from under the *Maid's* side so Hayward and Fielding could make patches that would mold to the longboat's surface.

Daily he grew worse, yet didn't they all? Not only their health, but their clothing too? Emily's hems had begun to fray, to even turn white from the salt of the sea. The men, boots shredded by barnacles and constant dampness, were now alternating between wrapping their feet in gunnysack and canvas strips or going barefoot, unable to decide which was worse—the wet or the cold. Only a fortnight marooned and they all walked about like ghosts—thin, worn out, bedraggled, hungry, and getting hungrier.

"Steward," said Emily one afternoon as they sat at the ridge, everyone else at the beach. She was watching Richard splash around out at the *Maid*—or at least the tiny dot she assumed was Richard. "I keep staring, Steward, thinking that if I stare hard enough maybe, maybe I can make sense of all this. Is this a trick? Are we being tested? Or is it just a joke we're victim of? Is God like the child who tears the wings off a butterfly for the pleasure of seeing it die?"

"Nay. We are never victims."

"Don't be daft."

"Would you say the Captain is a victim? Or would you say he's a man who, despite a twist of fate, chooses to rise above it?"

"You know," she said, lost in her own thoughts again, "maybe if the Lord's way were always plain there would be no cause to have faith, and faith is a gift we can lay before Him."

"That's one way of looking at it, I suppose."

"*I suppose*," she snorted, laughing just a little at him. "You only like your own answers, Steward."

"Missus, I'm worried about the Captain."

She set down her sewing, alarmed by the change in his voice.

"The men are at him all the time, whining about this, whining about that, complaining of all their aches and pains. It's enough to wear me out just watching. What if you and he took to eating your meals in your own camp? Away from everyone? He could relax, at least for a few minutes, and not have to keep his shoulders square."

But that night, no sooner had the Captain said amen to their first dinner alone, than the men, in a group, presented themselves.

"They want more bread," said Steward, rolling his eyes to warn of pending trouble.

"No," said the Captain, obliged to refuse.

Harris marched across camp and threw open the calico tent. "What do you mean *no*? Look at this! Just look at all this!"

"That's quite enough," said the Captain sternly, although he stayed put on his overturned potato tin, so tired and so sore he couldn't move. "Come away from the tent. That's off-limits to all but Steward, the Missus, and myself. Harris, away from the tent."

For an answer Harris arrogantly threw out tins of bully beef and soup, one after the other, until they were bouncing and rolling. "*She's* hoarding it all. The woman gets it! She gets everything!" He darted to where the remaining ham hung in a tree and smacked it with his palm. "I suppose because she found *this* ham, she thinks she can eat it all by herself—up here behind our backs!"

"Have you gone mad, boy? Look at the Missus' plate and tell me again she's gettin' it all!"

"*Her* gums ain't bleedin'!" Sargent hollered suddenly, jabbing a finger at Emily. "Guess that tells who's really getting all the food around here!"

The Captain rose to his feet to face them all. Haggard faces stared back and he read with little trouble the conflict of emotion in their eyes: belligerence, embarrassment, trust, despair. "Go back to your meal," he said gently, sorry for them all. "But," he added firmly, "be warned. Next man to ask for bread will eat my share."

The next afternoon Emily, sitting in her tent and keeping guard, was just tying off the last knot of the last buttonhole of a burlap shirt she had begun for the Captain when she heard some of the men yo-hoing up the trail.

"You saw a sea lion?" she wailed, ducking out to greet those who had come to tell her the news—their rudeness of last night apparently forgotten. "You saw a sea lion?" she fussed, grateful for the swing in their moods. "And you didn't come get me? Lawson, how could you?"

"Lawson, 'e 'ave the 'atchet!" panted Johnny, rain in his face, arms flapping, mimicking the fun, "an' he 'it 'im! Right on 'is nose—"

"Ye should 'a seen him, Miss," said Oates, "he galloped roit off to the saye. But 'afer he dove in, A swear he chuckled."

"Someone," she told the Captain at tea that night, still very much vexed that she'd missed all the fun, "should have been sent up to tell me!"

"We were too busy trying to catch it."

"I won't stay up here anymore, Richard—isolated like this. I won't. Let them steal the spirits, I don't care. I shall go mad, darling. I shall go stark raving mad if I must sit about all by myself. A *sea lion*, darling, and I *missed* it!"

She had expected him to smile, to let himself be amused by her. But blue eyes slid her way. His jaw hesitated on the potato he chewed.

"Darling. You don't look well."

He shrugged and hobbled into the tent. She watched him go, worried, and had only begun to tidy up when he called. "Emily? Some of the brandy is missing."

"But when, how, did they get in? *Who* got in?" she cried, ducking into the dank tent, musty from mold already growing on the damp calico. "I've been here all day! Except..." She paused, embarrassed. Someone must have waited in the woods for her to answer the call of nature. Her cheeks burned with the very shame.

"That takes the crown!" exploded Richard. He gathered up the bottles and, hobbling, carried everything up into the woods and buried it all.

Saturday morning he woke too ill to move.

18

What have you to do with the sea? You should have been content with land.

—Ovid
Amores

Emily built up the fire so Richard might see it and be cheered. When it was done she told him she would get Steward.

"No...don't leave me." He could hardly speak, the pain so tight in his jaw.

"But I must tell him."

Steward raced up the incline after her, out of breath, and the Captain, seeing him come through the door, whispered painfully, pushing the words off his tongue and shoving them between clenched teeth. "Keep the men busy. Keep an eye on the longboat. Don't let them cheat—"

"Aye, aye. Don't you worry a hair," said Steward, fighting alarm. "We'll get her caulked correctly—and made shipshape in no time." Outside the tent he stood biting his lip.

"What be wrong with him?" Emily pleaded.

He could hardly bring himself to speak. This was not the idle complaint of a lazy sailor, but a form of rheumatism that could, and sometimes did, kill—the body growing so weak with pain that it succumbed to deprivation less severe. He'd seen it a dozen times on other

181

journeys: men invincible to plague and pestilence none-theless struck down, rheumatism the red carpet for ailments of all kinds. And what chance did the Captain have for recovery, everything so damp and so wretch-edly cold? And with so little to eat to bring sustenance to starved muscle and ligament and bone? But sometimes it went away too, vanishing as mysteriously as it came on. He tried in vain to help Emily hold that hope.

She sat by his side all day in a numb state of grief, leaving only to feed the fire, to stir the potato he wouldn't eat. Excruciating pain in every joint, neck to toe, fatigue so pervasive that he lay weighted, pressed to his harsh, damp bed. Nothing to help him, and this was the worst—to watch him suffer. God had plucked the wings from the butterfly, and where was her faith—if indeed she ever had any?

Sunday he was worse: He couldn't reach even to touch her cheek when she peered into his pain-laced face; she had to help him. Even then the flame in his joints screamed fire and he moaned in the agony of the move-ment. "Don't leave me... please don't," he pleaded, "don't."

"Darling, I must," she said bravely, "but I be right back, I promise." And she fled the tent, fled the little clearing that had become home, fled the stinging tears. Oh please God, she prayed, twisting the torn skirt of her dress, pacing the trail between swale and ridge. Please, is there not anything I can do for him? Is there nothing to stop his pain? Nothing to help him sleep? "Oh, Stew-ard," she wept, for he had come to see how it was, "he be so ill, I be so afraid. I be so terribly afraid!"

He took her by the elbow and walked her up to the Mount. "Start heating some rocks. Get the rocks hot, tuck what you can in next to him. And try to get a shot of brandy down his throat, to kill the pain."

"Steward," she said, quite sick. "He buried it all Fri-day night."

"Dear Jesus," he moaned. "Well, nothing to be done about that then. The important thing is to keep him warm. Dry."

She followed him into the dank tent, where Richard feebly spoke. "How far... did they get on the boat yesterday?"

"Mast is in, Old Man. Jib is set."

"The rudder?"

"Not yet. She needs more caulking, more planking."

"It's Sunday. They mustn't work."

"I didn't mean today, Old Man. I sent them off on a wild goose chase. If," he said, forcing a smile, "you get my drift, mate."

The Captain smiled, instant pain slicing across his eyes. "They'll never... catch... one...."

"Ah, but if they do," said Steward, spirits picking up at the sight of his Captain's smile, brief though it was, "the two of us may have to eat our words."

"Not me."

"I'll bring you up the drumstick then. You can eat that."

Afternoon arrived, and with it one dead goose. Johnny had snared it. The men helped Steward pluck and gut the large fowl. He cooked it well and took the drumstick up to the Captain.

"Darling," said Emily, "please. Think of the trouble everyone's gone to."

But he shook his head.

"I'll chew it for you then," she said, nearly gagging on the first bite. So salty, so fishy, so oily. Like something rotten. Determined, she shivered back the nausea in her stomach and ground the tough meat into soft, tender flakes. "Please, darling," she begged. But he only turned away.

"He's got to have the nourishment," said Steward, desperate.

"What if you boil it, Steward? So? What do you mean, so? So we can *spoon* the broth into his mouth! That's better than nothing!"

But the Captain refused the broth, and that night, instead of Sabbath prayers and Bible reading, Emily wandered the woods alone. Please, she prayed, tell me where he put the brandy. Tell me! She parted bushes, she examined the ground for fresh signs of digging, she walked and rewalked the trails, she diverged off the path wherever she could. Just one small bottle, she begged. But no sign of the spirits, no voice from God, no flasks, no bottles of gin or brandy or rum, no glass stoppers sticking out of the mulch, and Steward found her tearing at the bushes, hands bleeding. "I can't find the spirits," she agonized.

"No, not in the dark. Come, you best go to bed, or *you'll* be sick, and then what will we do?"

Monday the Captain was delirious, gibbering unintelligent orders distorted by a jaw too tight to emit intelligent sound. All day, while Steward worked with the men, Emily fought to keep the rocks hot and under his covers, to feed him the warm goose broth, to wash his face with cool water. He would have none of it, fighting rock, broth, and cloth, and it broke her heart to see her beautiful husband so haggard, so gaunt, so grizzled. Grief turned to fear, then anger at her own helplessness, and back to fear; a terrible fear, fear that left her weak and cold and without hope, and she remembered her fear when Yates had died. *What if something were to happen to my dear husband?*

Desperate, she put a stick between his teeth and dribbled the goose soup, one spoon at a time, into his mouth. He choked and gagged and in the end swallowed, and with tears running down her face she kept on until a cup was gone. "Darling? Steward says to tell you the men have found a trail over to another bay. He says the bay is calm, that the water is like glass." Did he hear? Could he understand? "He says to tell you the men are behaving well, that they had their own prayer and Bible reading last night." Gently she replaced the moss beneath his head, tossing out what was wet. She combed his hair, his beard, then sang. And he slept. She stretched and ventured out, almost stumbling down the trail to the beach.

"How is he noo?" Oates asked when she drew alongside the longboat. He and the others had fastened a rudder to the stern, using the iron works from the *Maid*. Concern stood clearly in each familiar face. Concern and disquiet, Sargent excepted, which sharpened her fear, like a knife to the grinding stone. "Missus?" Oates asked again. "How is he?"

"He be fine," she lied, turning away from Sargent, squinting instead into the watery distance. Three days since she'd been to the beach. It seemed a foreign place to her, her world with the Captain something different than this, this a strange world of wood chips and iron bolts and quilted boats—and so much sea. "Where," she asked, even her voice strange and different, "be the Maid?"

"Ye canna see 'er?"

"I mean the figurehead, Oates. She be gone."

"Oh that," said Hayward, putting down his tools. "She washed ashore last night. If you want, Missus, I'll take a walk out with you, to yonder reef, where she lies."

"No, I hate that smiling face." Smiling, smiling, always smiling, mocking them all in their distress. Suddenly she started to cry, and she raced down the beach, away from the men, leaping the rocks and running still. She crested the reef to face the endless sea, and on she ran, blindly, weeping, ragged hems ripping and tearing on the boulders and barnacles, wind cutting her face and skin. With a start she all but fell over the Maid, and she screamed in fright. The head of the maiden, bare throat charred and splintered, lay in a clear pool of tidewater, staring up with blind, wooden eyes, smiling, smiling.

Emily rubbed her hands over her own face, salt and tears stinging her skin. "You smile!" she screamed. "You smile! You dare smile while my husband lies so ill? *You dare smile? Will you smile if he die?*" Sobbing, frantic with grief, she tore at her hair and stumbled backward. "Oh, and what if he *die*? Will you smile then? Oh God, oh God," she wailed, beating her chest and bending to her knees, "what if he die? I shall never be happy again. Oh God, I shall never see home, I shall never see England again!" With both hands she covered her ears, screaming, screaming, petrels whirling. "I shall be here forever with these men! Oh God, I cannot bear any more! *Do you hear me, God? I cannot bear it, I cannot bear it! I CANNOT BEAR IT!*"

There is a time that comes to all men when they must ask with Job of old this question to the wind: Who is God, and where is God, that I should live such pain?

19

It occurred to my mind that I poured so much upon my deliverance from the main affliction, that I disregarded the deliverance I had received.

—Robinson Crusoe
Robinson Crusoe, Daniel Defoe

Before the sun was up the Captain asked for Steward, and Emily hastened into her clothes, damp and gritty, fingers fumbling with both chill and excitement. He be better? He be better? Dare she believe?

In halting whispers the Captain gave Steward very clear, very concise orders for the day. He *was* better. He was thinking, fully conscious, and despite his pain, very aware of what was happening—and what needed to happen. The longboat was to be taken round to the quiet bay so the rudder and sails could be tested, and where the men could finish whatever planking and caulking still needed to be done. "Aye," said Steward to Emily, seeing her questioning glance. "His body may be crippled still, but his head? Sharp as a tack. He'll pull through, righto. Eh, Captain?"

"You will go with the men then, Steward?" she asked, delirious with relief over her dear husband's improvement, conscious though of the great work ahead if they were to flee this place which could yet claim them all. And the Captain, she knew, was *not* out of the woods yet.

"Someone must keep an eye on them, yes," said Steward. "But I'll leave you Fielding. And the boy."

Rain fell in sheets by the time the men were ready. Emily pinned her oiled burlap cloak tight beneath her chin, so tight it hurt to swallow, and, leaving Steward behind to fix another cup of tea for the Captain and to go over his instructions, she slithered and slid down the trail that she might report back to them both the progress.

Everything the men would need for the new camp was in the boat: calico for a tent, pannikins, knives, hatchet, some of the beef tins, the ham, a large bucket, the larger of the two small saucepans, the maul, canvas, nails, pitch pot. But the wind and tide, she saw, had turned in the preparations, the surf dangerously high, crashing over in six-foot breakers. Were they out of their minds? Would they ruin everything yet?

They had mounted the loaded longboat on a series of logs and were even now rolling her over them, pushing from the stern. As logs came free aft, they were laid at the bow, log after log, rotating stern to bow, until at last the boat eased down the shingle, the sea fairly flying over the bow to drench and upset everything. "*What* are you doing?" she demanded. "Men! The tide! It be turned! Can't you see? It be much too rough! *Men!*" she screamed, wind whistling through her hat. "You be out of your minds or king's fools! You can't go out! Not now! You'll capsize and all will be lost! STOP!" and, amazed at what had come over her, only knowing there be none to stop them but her, she flew at them—Harris, Fielding, Lawson—screaming "Stop! I say stop!"

They only looked at her stupidly.

Uphill at a run she flew, slipping and sliding, mud cold, hair tumbling out her hood and standing in her eyes. "Captain! Captain!" Arms up and running pell-mell through the trail between the camps, bushes bouncing back. "Captain!" She threw herself into the tent, onto the floor, shuddering with spent breath. "It be too stormy! Too rough! Everything will be for naught! Oh Richard, you should see it. Wind! Rain! The tide has turned! They'll *never* get past the surf! They'll destroy the boat!"

He struggled to sit, but gave up. "They are," he said, grinding his teeth on the words, "to come back. At once."

Back down the trail she flew, screaming "Stop!" as she went, both arms waving. "Stop!" she shouted, skidding onto the shingles, plowing on. "He says to stop!"

But Sargent kept pushing, boat bobbing and jumping in the crash of waves. "You're not!" screamed Emily at him, "going anywhere! Do you hear me? Sargent! Bring that boat up and bring it up at once! Or—"

"Or what?"

She stood trembling at the water's edge, enraged. "I don't have a *or what*! You just better do what I tell you!"

"Who are you to come into a man's world and tell a man what to do?" He gave the boat another shove and Emily swooped to pick up a rock, then aimed. In the pulling back of her arm something like a groan bled from every man's throat.

She dropped the rock, and without thought to feet or dress or raging sea stormed into the surf. "All right, Mr. Sargent," she hissed, water slapping up her thin body and chin, "I'll bring in the boat myself! *Get out 'a my way!*"

If there comes a time for every man to ask of God where He is and who He is to allow such pain, there is also a time when a man must come to God with the truth of his own error, and—if he be man—to admit the foolishness of his ways or forever be damned, in this world and the one beyond. *"Go tell the Wind and Fire where to stop, not me!"* Madame Defarge of Dickens' *Tale of Two Cities* cries when faced with the cruel evolution of her justice in revolutionary France. But "*No!*" protests Monsieur Defarge, facing his. "*I say, stop there!*"

And Sargent? Seeing his Captain's wife slapped against the patchworked longboat, cheek cracking with a thwack against the stern and blood sprouting forth, feet knocked out and seas washing into her ears and over the blood of her face, he was called to face the truth of his ways. Yet he felt not the tug of sanity or sorrow and regret but only the horrible enjoyment of a grim and deadly nature. Tell the Wind and Fire where to stop, he might well have cried with Madame Defarge if ever he had read Dickens. Tell the Wind and Fire where to stop, not me! So this was Sargent's choice, but Harris? Could he stand by and let his Captain's wife be battered by the sea? "Nay!" he cried, Monsieur Defarge come off the page and on his feet, plunging into the Antarctic sea. "I say, stop there!" And the man who'd once snarled now leaped to save, a heave and low groan, veins standing blue in his face.

"*Come all you young fellows who follow the sea, weigh, hey, blow the man down—*" and in the sound of his song the others were quick to follow. With a whoop and song the boat bounced out the boiling tide—but Emily was not done, not yet. Maiden from the sea she stomped free, swinging round the bow, grabbing hold with one hand, tangled skirts and wet petticoats with the other, and began with clumsy, thick boots to sweep aside shingle and stone to make a cleaner path. "Yo, Jack, clear the log fore! Lay it aft! Now heave to the port! Push!" And before any Jack knew it, the boat was back up at the bank.

"Now," she said, wiping carefully the filthy gravel from her bloodied hands, and wiping a sleeve across the wound beneath her eye which bled. "Leave what you can, men, in the boat for a fresh start tomorrow. Won't hurt the pans to get wet in the rain. But take the stores up to the Mount, and *not*," she warned, "the Encampment. Oh, and Sargent?" Steady and calm and deep breath drawn, she faced him. "You asked who I was to enter a man's world and tell a man what to do?"

His eyes narrowed, yet nearer to him she stepped, unafraid. "I did not enter this man's world yesterday, that I cower a woman before your eyes. I have lived in this man's world nigh onto four months, and I intend to live through this, to sail for the Falklands, *in that boat*! You will not get in my way. So until Captain Wooldridge is well, *I* be the Captain. And when he is better? I be the First Mate, a rank a sight higher than Bosun! That be who I am to tell you what to do!"

Harris yanked off his cap and saluted, one motion, and "aye aye Captain" echoed up the hill as she climbed, triumphant, in the pouring rain.

But triumph was not what she wanted. She wanted the Captain, and she started to weep again, and to pray, but not with the despair of yesterday. For yesterday she had faced her fears alone on the rock and come back, without answers, but with a calmness, unexplained, rooted way deep in the void of her soul.

Wednesday morning no one waited for breakfast. They loaded the longboat without waste, and one more time rolled her down to the water's edge. Lawson, Harris, Oates, Sargent, Hayward, and Steward waded in, arms up and grimacing on the frigid cold, sucking and whistling through their teeth. "Sargent! You steering, ain't you?" "I'm bailing!" "Shut up, you old wind bag. Lawson, yo! You in the bow!" "Who's pulling?"

They lost an oar in the scramble. It washed ashore in surges, rolling in with the waves, and Fielding picked it up and headed for camp.

Emily stayed on. The longboat, with her homemade mast rising out the fore, looked so tiny as it angled past the reef and out to the open sea, some of the men at the oars, some of them bailing, boat still leaking. How would they do this?

The day passed lonely and quiet, the loss of routine a disturbing, disorienting ordeal. The Captain slept while Fielding scoured the beaches. Only she and the boy were left, and together they sat at the fire, conscious of the quiet, with not even the bell to move them through the day, from breakfast to dinner to tea. Had time stopped?

Richard's ill-fated sweater, unraveling between her and the boy, was the only mark of passing time. She was knitting something new: stockings for everyone, beginning with the boy. Her own linen stockings, given to him when they had landed, were mere scraps now, and nice thick wool between bare feet and broken boots or gunnysack had to be, she figured, a better use of the yarn than the one sweater, and already (though it could only be early afternoon) she had turned her first heel and hoped to have enough inches behind to taper the toe. "Give me your foot," she told the boy, "and let me measure."

"Do ye miss Yates?" he asked, surprising her with the question.

"Aye, we all do."

"Did 'is ghost go to 'eaven or 'ell?"

She knit two together, trick enough with whittled sticks for needles. "I think he be in heaven, don't you?"

"But 'e dinna keep the Ten Commandments, ma'am. He—"

"But keeping the Ten Commandments is not what gets us to heaven!" she cried, startled that he had picked this up. "None of us, lad, can keep the commandments—not all of them, not all the time. We be bound to slip."

"Then 'ow does a bloke git to 'eaven?"

"By believing on the Lord Jesus Christ!"

"Why, ev'rybudy b'lieve that, ma'am! Dinna know a bloke whut don't!"

"Do you remember me telling you about the man who wrote 'Amazing Grace'?"

"Aye."

"His name be John Newton," she said, sliding the stitches down the rough sticks and beginning a new row, "and he be a very wicked man, just as wicked as Bully Hayes. He be a blackbird too. Only he sold his slaves to America, not Australia. But one day he believed in the Lord Jesus Christ—and it made him a new man. You have to believe enough, Johnny, to make you different."

"You mean good?"

"Aye."

"But, ma'am, ye jist tol' me, it ain't bein' good whut gits a bloke to 'eaven!"

"You do both, believe *and* be good," she said, knitting another two together, confused herself.

"Yo! Missus!"

"Harris!" she exclaimed, startled by the sound of his voice in the lonely stillness. "How did you get here? But goodness! Look at you!"

"Sargent and I came over the trail." He flopped exhausted onto a stump and held out his festering hands to the fire. Twigs had stuck in his scraggly beard. Evergreen needles and bits of bark fell out the length of his hair and down his back. "Wretched trail," he said, shivering. "Enough to take the stuffing out of a man."

"What of the longboat? Did you all arrive safely?" she asked eagerly, putting away her knitting and getting him a hot cup of tea—to warm his hands if nothing else.

"Aye. We did. Boat still leaks, but Oates says he can fix it. He has them building the tent, or he did when me and Sargent left. Steward's setting up camp."

"Captain in?" asked Sargent, arriving without greeting.

"Aye, I'll see if he be awake."

Over hot salty tea they huddled about the fire, Emily and the boy, Sargent, Harris, and the Captain—Fielding still gone. The Captain, sitting up for the first time in four days, and aching from head to toe, shivered with pain while the two men gave full report. The new bay was indeed calm enough to test the boat—calm enough, in fact, for even one of Her Majesty's men-of-war to weigh anchor. There was little or no surf; and a long, low sandy beach, sloping up into grass. "And *fish!*" said Harris, jabbing Johnny. "This big!" He held his fingers three feet apart.

"Go on!" said Johnny, laughing. "Ye be pullin' me leg, 'Arris!"

"People have been there," said Sargent abruptly and the laughter stopped. "We seen a campfire. And a stack of wood."

"Hey, where's the stocking? Go on, Jack, get that sock out 'a your pocket and show 'em. Now that, Captain, sir," said Harris, "proves white men have been here!"

Sargent lay the sock in the Captain's open palm. "This proves I'm right, Old Man. We only have to sit tight. We'll get picked up."

"I hope you *are* right," said the Captain, snuffing Sargent's boast while at the same time turning the dirty sock, hole in the heel, in his hands. "In the meantime, until they come for us, Sargent, does everyone have what they need over there?" *How*, he wondered—not for the first time since he had concocted this crazy scheme a day-and-a-half ago—*was he to watch the two camps? When he was still so ill?*

"Oates needs halyards and blocks."

"What's that?" he asked, losing track of his own questions.

"Oates needs halyards and blocks to get the running gear installed."

"Good for Oates," he said, taking heart. "Harris? How long does it take to hike that trail?"

Harris shrugged. "Twenty minutes?"

He debated. "Take what he needs over in the morning. This afternoon I want you two to haul wood for the Missus—and wash your clothes. You reek."

"Wash our clothes?" howled Harris, looking down at himself.

"Take a bath, too," said Emily.

"Steady on, no need to get personal," he shot back with an old snarl, and pulled to his feet. "Whoa!" he whistled, making way for Fielding.

"Captain! I found rice, Old Man!"

"My goodness!" Emily struggled quickly to her own feet, soggy hems ripping under her boot. "Rice! Oh, Captain! Look!" But the rice, when they got the bag open, was soaked through, kernels stuck together like paste. "Never mind," she said, "it'll fill our stomachs anyway. Men, fetch me wood to last a few days, then wash your clothes and take your bath. You can use the line at the Cascade to hang your clothes up. You do have another pair of pants? Then come for a proper tea."

"Emily," said the Captain when they were gone, all three shuffling off, grumbling oaths about bloody women and who bloody cares about smelling pretty. "Will you help me up, and before I lose my edge—for the pain is fair dancing behind my eyes—take me for a walk?"

"But you mustn't," she said softly, protesting. "It be enough you be up, and you be shivering with cold. Come to bed, darling, or I fear for you."

"Nay. While I'm up, we must hunt down that brandy."

Yes, yes, of course, and together they trudged back and forth through the trees, he leaning heavily upon her shoulders, poking wet leaves, shuffling aside wet grass. "That's odd," he complained; "they should be right here." But nothing. Only when he gave up and was about to return did he sight the neck of one bottle, almost stepping on it; the rest were easy to find.

That night a scream woke Emily. Another scream, a primal cry of pain, and it shot through her head—cannibals! The Captain pulled up. She could feel how white he was, without seeing him, and they rolled as one out the bed, as one raced out the tent.

"Oh, my God!" cried the Captain, stark naked in the night. "Fire! The men's tent is on fire!"

Fire?

She stood a moment, momentarily confused. No natives? No cannibals? *Fire?* Confused, she watched familiar flames of orange and yellow and red light a black sky, this time hissing and spitting on damp, mossy wood. "The tents are so close!" Richard bellowed, and he plunged into the black, crackling night. "If the Mount catches, there goes our provisions! Everything! Everything lost! We must save the Mount!"

Quickly she pulled on her boots, the big ones, threw on her coat and raced after him, bare toes stinging as they slammed against hollow hard leather.

He, arms out, spun when he came off the path, seeing the worst. The whole Encampment was afire! The tent, the trees, everything! Fielding, slapping at his face, was throwing his jacket at the flames leaping off the tent. "No!" cried Richard. "Pull down the branches between the tents! We must, we *must* save the Mount!"

The men began whacking at once the branches between the two camps, up under the cliff, quickly clearing a full circle all around their burning tent. Boughs cracked and fell, still burning. Emily worked alongside the men: As they chopped and hacked the flaming boughs, she and Johnny dragged the burning boughs to the very center of camp. Familiar smell, familiar fear, they all worked together, Emily mopping sweat from her brow, spitting hair from her mouth, until at last only hazy smoke curled up from the downed branches, everything suddenly and strangely quiet. The skeletal tent hissed and caved in, branches and oars giving way, final flames self-consuming and going out.

"How did this start?" Richard wheezed, flopping naked and trembling onto the ground, sick and heady, smoke still stinging his eyes. The others fell back, winded. Johnny collapsed in a heap.

"It was me, sir," said Harris, scared and dismayed, eyes darting across the ruins. "I hung my oilskin in front of the tent, to keep out the wind. I didn't mean—"

"Who bloody cares!" screamed Sargent, cutting him off with an explosive kick to a smoldering deckboard. "Who bloody cares *how* it started! We got nothing! Nothing! Our clothes! Our bedding!"

"Me shirt!" wailed Johnny suddenly, bird with more lives than a cat on his head. "Me shirt! Me blue shirt! Me blue shirt! Yates' shirt! Oh, me own blue flannel shirt!"

"Shut up!" screamed Sargent.

"You *do* have clothes!" protested Emily. "You have the ones down at the Cascade! You have at least one shirt, and your pants! And your longjohns!"

Harris, shivering in his nakedness and distress, stumbled about the smoking remains, out of his mind with the loss—jackets, slickers, what was left of their boots, burlap, tarp, all of it gone. He picked up a corner of the tent and dropped it fast, wincing and crying, leaping back, hopping sideways, cursing, bare feet burning on the scattered ash and rubble. Fielding, huddled by the water bucket, openly cried, and Emily, hearing him, eased across the camp, and nearly fainted when she saw his face.

"Oh, my God," she moaned, reaching out to grab something. She stared, sick, mind racing. "Oh, my God," she moaned again and dropped to a knee, tearing quickly at her muddied coat, fabric giving way with shocking ease, and plunged it into the water. "Was it you who screamed?"

"Aye. I felt the fire on my face."

"Here." She gave him the wet wool, afraid to touch him. The whole side of his face was raw, beard burned, left cheek scorched and blistering, eyelashes and eyebrows singed. The one eye was already almost swollen shut from the swelling.

"Did we lose the sails?" someone asked, and when she looked up Richard was stumbling in meaningless circles with Harris.

"You have your bloody sails," said Sargent, sitting, staring. "They went over in the boat this morning, yesterday, whatever!" he yelled. Harris, cursing again, threw a burnt oar against a scarred tree. The Captain teetered on his feet, trying to pick it up. "How many oars? How many oars did we lose?"

"I am taking the Captain to bed," Emily announced. "Harris, see to Fielding's face—Harris!" She marched to where he stood and shook him until he stared dully into her eyes. "I am taking the Captain to bed. He'll be sick again if I don't. You must tend Fielding. You must clean his wound. HARRIS!"

She had to leave them, the boy and the men, dazed and despairing, the imperative being to get the Captain out of the cold. Nothing that had happened, or could ever happen, would be worse than if the Captain got sick again.

Halfway up the trail he stumbled, tripping over a break in the boards. Teeth gritted, she staggered beneath his heavy arm, and half-carried him to their tent, where, candle flickering and campfire glimmering, she warmed water and bathed him clean, washing his blisters with the spirits they had dug up not a half dozen hours before.

"Darling," she whispered, kissing his closed eyes, "it be a miracle how quickly you rallied, how quickly you took charge. It be a wonder how well you were in an instant," and she chafed his arms and his hands, bringing warmth to cold skin.

"Aye," he mumbled, submissive to her administrations, "but I don't mind saying I am sore and tired again." Without opening his eyes he said, "Give me another swallow of the brandy. I am fair undone."

Outside, the burnt limbs of the trees stood stark against the glow of the men's meager campfire, and Emily, shivering in the wind, stood alone at the ridge, feeling the cold and hearing the men's cries below. She held what burlap she'd been able to gather, the remaining bottle of gin, a tarp, and a sheet of old, muddy canvas. Much passed through her mind and soul as she stood viewing the desolation below, so barren and bleak and flickering in and out of shadow to the pulse of feeble firelight. But (and she had to ask) had not their lives been spared again? And all their provisions saved? Had they not saved the Mount? And did the men, naked as the day they were born, not have some clean clothes hanging on the clothesline down at the Cascade? How had any of them forgotten this, this small blessing of clothes to be washed and hung to dry? Surely Providence did look after them still. And then the thought struck, as stark as the limbs before her and as frightening as Fielding's wounded cries coming off the wind—if they could not be thankful for these small deliverances of God, how in His name could they expect deliverance any greater?

She moved on down the rotting, wooden trail, the night moonless and dark, to tend the men, surprised to find them so helpless, and surprised to find herself so strong.

20

. . . I was a prisoner locked up with the eternal bars and bolts of the ocean, in an uninhabited wilderness, without redemption. In the midst of the greatest composures of my mind, this would break upon me like a storm, and make me wring my hands, and weep like a child.

—Robinson Crusoe
Robinson Crusoe, Daniel Defoe

Thursday, three weeks marooned, and the wind and rain, it seemed, had come to stay. The days passed in a dismal blur as the men traipsed the miserable trail back and forth between the two camps retrieving minor supplies, for it was all the trail allowed. First more rope, then buckets, then more tar until Emily got lost in the never-ending, muddy exchange. At night she hardly knew who was at the rebuilt Encampment, and who wasn't. All she knew was that Steward hadn't come back, not once, and that she missed his company.

"Nails," Harris kept insisting. "Old Man, Oates needs more nails!"

But the weather was so wet and so wild that they couldn't get out to the ship to retrieve more nails, nor could they get the small boat out to go around the reef with the nails they did have—and all the heavy supplies Oates needed. Richard, frustration compounded by his very slow return to health, thought he might go mad with anxiety. Were the men working? Were they doing it right? And what of the longboat? Did the rudder work?

Whatever had possessed him to split ranks like this? It had been a gamble, he knew that. Gambling that Oates and Hayward would carry out to the end. But would they? *Could they?* How? When they couldn't even get the small boat out with the needed supplies?

Penguins flocked the beach, so many now that they ceased to be a wonder, and seals and water rats too. Winter was coming on and time was running out, accelerating his anxiety, sand collecting in an hourglass. Daily he paced the beach, bundled against the icy wind and driving rain. They were prisoners of gray skies and sea and stone, and daily hope bled from his heart.

A bright spot was Steward's return. He came back Saturday to bake bread. Within an hour, bread begun, he and Emily were arguing Dickens versus Johnson, and Richard, coming upon them, interrupted, inquiring after the rudder. His voice broke when given the news that the tools were so dull that everything took three times longer than it should. "And the grinding stones are all cemented into the hold. Oh I wish," he said, making a fist and pushing his clenched fingers into his thigh, "I wish I could just get over there and see for myself. See if they are working. See if the tools—"

"You're not strong enough, sir," interrupted Steward. "The trail is an exacting one. But you needn't worry. They're coming along. They really are," he insisted. "Right now Oates is enclosing the boat's stern for the Missus, for privacy."

"We have to leave this place, Steward." He faced the gray, the sky and sea. "Everything in my body and soul says we must. Come April I dare not pilot us to the Falklands. It will be too late. And we shall never survive winter here. Look at us! Eczema, boils, open ulcers, infected cuts and scrapes. And Fielding's face—"

"Sir," said Steward gently, "we have a couple of weeks then. Don't torment yourself."

"But I must at least know how they're doing!"

"Captain?" Fielding, his blistered face covered with clean calico, stood hesitantly at the trailhead. "If you want, sir, I can help you, sir, get past the rough spots on the trail."

The next day, a Sunday, was a day of some sun, a welcome break from the bleak monotony that had set in. But the continual wind, the roar of the rolling waves, and the absence of the Captain all cast a gloomy spell of their own, and Emily, having gone out as far as the cliffs to say goodbye to her husband, reluctant to let him go, was meandering despondently back to camp, when she saw Steward come to meet her. Neither spoke, companionable in silence. She poked a toe at new markings in the sand.

"Seal," he said.

"We should try and catch it."

Suddenly from the woods Johnny cried, "Steward! Steward! The longboat! It be comin' in the bay an' the Captain be gone!" They saw both boat and boy at the same time, the boy leaping off the ladder, a streak of burlap running lickety-split straight toward them, arm jabbing out to the sea—and the boat? A glorious sight on the surging sea! A glorious, ugly white sail—the three-cornered "shoulder-of-mutton"! "Oh, glory, she *sails*!" screamed Emily, racing for the shore.

"Go back!" Steward hollered, racing too, hands cupped to his whiskered mouth. "Go back! Go back! The Captain is gone over!"

"They can't hear you!" Emily motioned retreat. This they saw, and with a quick tack they sailed back round the reef and out of sight. "Steward!" she gasped, spinning in sudden heady joy. "She sails! She really sails! Oh, Steward, we *shall* go home after all!" And suddenly she was in his arms, laughing, crying, choking on her breath. Could it be? Could it really be? "Oh, Steward, I have been so worried," and she pulled free to run, to spend her energy, to throw out her arms in wild elation, to lift her chin and cry out to the sky, to heaven, to God, to anyone who would listen, *"We be going home!"*

Up and off she ran, dancing away each time he overtook her. "The Captain has been so sick, the boats so leaky, everyone so hungry, Sargent so sneaky and mean, but oh Steward, Steward, we really are going home!" and again she leaped into his arms, laughing, laughing, tears streaming down her face. "Oh, Johnny!" she cried, pulling him into their embrace, "we be going home!"

A fine fix, Steward thought to himself, helping her up the trail, for he was unable anymore to take his eyes off his Captain's wife.

"Missus," said Steward a few hours later, "I've been thinking. A proper roof on your tent would make it snug. What do you say we have a go at it? We could prop tree limbs—"

She was knitting, and she put down her knitting. "Have you taken leave of your senses? Whatever for?"

"Keep out the rain, for starters."

"But we be going home! There be no point in making a fancy tent if we be just leaving it soon. Just think, down here under the globe it may be winter coming on, but in England? Spring, Steward. Daffodils, crocuses! Robins, Steward! Robins and sparrows and—What time is it?"

He pulled out his watch. "Half past eleven."

"That be all?" she wailed, throwing down her knitting altogether.

"Missus, the Captain won't be back for a long time yet."

"I'll go for a walk then. And I'm not," she said, shaking a finger at him, "coming back until I get to England!" Suddenly she laughed. "Or until I find something to eat."

She walked until her legs ached, walking still further and further still. Still further, spurred on by the large ham she found, stuck up under some brush, and it was a lucky stroke to have seen it at all. A glance at just the right time in passing, and there it was. More gunnysacks had washed up, wet and moldy and crusted with dried seaweed, but washed and sewn together they would make the blankets they desperately needed.

She was shaking out a particularly muddy sack, coughing and blinking grit from her eyes and throat, when she saw him: a dark figure wearily traversing the barnacle-laced rocks, stepping through the narrow, gurgling inlets and climbing low, flat rocks that humped out of the shore like bleached turtle backs. He disappeared, then reappeared, head and shoulders rising back into sight. Forgetting her sacks and the ham, she flew back from whence she'd come, regretting every step that had put distance between them. Sand, crushed barnacles, tiny stones, the very earth ground under her feet as she ran, thumping in her big men's boots, running until her burlap hood fell down over one eye, running until her breath came in ragged gulps, running until pain took root in her side. Still she ran, closing the gap, panting, stumbling, crashing with laughter into her dear, wonderful husband's most welcoming arms.

"Ah, sweet Emily!" Spinning her around, and laughing too, he said, "We'll not do this again, separate ourselves like this," and his arms tightened so fiercely she thought her ribs might crack. "Oh my girl, I have missed you. The day has been long," and he kissed her soundly. Standing back, he held her at arm's length to get a good look.

"What happened to you?" she demanded, horrified to see the state of his clothes. The new burlap shirt she'd made hung in shreds, torn to ribbons; his canvas pants, wet with filth, were all but worthless. And indecent. Bare thighs showed through and she bit her lips together, saying nothing more, the emaciated condition of his legs shocking, and further pronouncement of their deteriorating condition.

"It *is* a rough trail," he said.

"I reckon it be..."

"Look, I have something for you." A wild grin and out of his hat, six berries.

"Goodness, and what be these?"

"Berries."

"I know they be berries, darling! But what kind?"

"Raspberries, or very near like raspberries. No, no worry. I've tasted them." And he laughed to see her fright grow. "Come. I haven't died."

"It be hardly worth the risk," she said, memory of unspeakable fear coming to mind.

"Emily, the men have been eating them, when they can find them. So three for you, three for me."

"Then pop them back in your hat," she said, smiling bravely, "and help me with these smelly sacks and we'll go put on your pot of tea. No, wait! We must to go back for the ham!"

Camp was a startling surprise. A half-dozen short, thin trees, stripped of their limbs and spaced two feet apart—three and three each side of her tent—were propped *over* her tent like an upside down V. The root ends were grounded in narrow troughs dug parallel to, and five feet out from, opposite walls. The spar tips met at the tent peak. And between the spars? Deckboards nailed between the sparred tree trunks to form a rough roof. Steward, standing on a stump beside the tent, bent nails in his mouth, was busy banging away, for the thing was not done, but only begun. "Steward!" Emily exclaimed, "you must persist with your notions?"

"Aye, we may be going home at that, Missus," he said, mumbling around the nails, "but in the meantime we've got to keep the provisions dry. The rain..." It was in the mumbling she noticed the smaller changes. The actual walls of the tent had been straightened on their corners;

calico hung in graceful lines. The sidewalks, inside and out, were spotless. The fire roared and crackled. The whole camp glistened, the whole of it cheery and bright. "Steward! You've swept everything," she admonished, "you needn't have done that."

"Aye, but I was of a mind to pacify you for my meddling."

"Come, sit with us," she invited. "The Captain has brought us berries. Six of them, enough for two each."

"Sir?"

"Aye, sit, Steward, by all means."

Emily could not remember having tasted anything so divine, so sweet and so lovely. Were these the things they had once enjoyed in England? And taken for granted? Never having stopped to ponder the wonder of such a treat? She refused to drink her tea lest the mildew and brine spoil the wonderful fresh taste, and they all sat before the fire, the Captain on his tin, she on a low log rolled between his feet so she might sit between his legs, Steward perched nearby on a stump. The Captain had taken off her bonnet and was trying to straighten her tangled hair with his fingers. Idly she watched the dance of the warming flames, content to have him back, content to be sitting so listlessly, with nothing more pressing to do than listen to the comforting banter of the two men. She might even be seated in her own parlor, she was that content—and seated in her own parlor soon she would be. "I have bad news," said Richard suddenly, and the roaring fire of her parlor blinked out. "The men have done virtually nothing on the boat."

"But, Richard, I *saw* the boat! She looked *wonderful* to me!"

"Well, she's not wonderful—far from it. It's one thing to tack round the reef or fish in the bay, but quite another to sail under full press on the open sea, waves 12 feet high and higher sloshing over the bow."

"What's to be done then, Old Man?" asked Steward.

"I left them a list. I have little faith, though, that they'll carry it through."

"Oates is dependable," said Steward, taking his pipe out of his mouth, "and Hayward to a degree."

"Aye, but they have little influence over Lawson, certainly none over Sargent—and Harris? I don't know. He's a man on a yo-yo these days."

"Do you think it best if *you* go over?" Emily asked, tipping back her head so their eyes met upside down.

"Aye."

"Then you better go. But take me with you," she added, smiling. "Wither thou goest, I go."

"You'd never make the trail. There are places, darling, where you must scale a rope to climb the cliffs. And there's one point where you must crawl on your belly and wiggle under a fallen tree to get past. The brambles are so thick you can't go over."

"He tells the truth, Missus."

"We'll load the small boat, then, and go over that way."

"Emily," said the Captain. "We haven't been able to *get* the small boat out, remember? Besides, the ground over there is too swampy. It wouldn't make a good camp."

"How can anything be more swampy than here? Every step filling with water?"

"We're better off here," he insisted. "Over there the fresh water is too far away. It has to be carried over high rocks. Here we have the Cascade. Here we have the stove. Steward? That's another thing. They misuse the provisions. A whole day's worth of rations for one meal! They'll be back, I reckon, soon enough—even though they took enough yesterday to last four days."

"They've been back already, Old Man."

"When?" he demanded.

"Sargent followed you in. I gave him enough of that new rice to keep down a fistfight."

He let out a weary sigh, pulled off his hat, and scratched his head. "Is there something wrong with their brains, Steward? That they have no concept of tomorrow? What do they think we'll eat next week? Never mind. Emily will find them another ham, won't you, darling? It's why they're sailors and I'm the Captain, I suppose. Well," he said as he stood, wincing and dismissing his pain. "Who do we have in camp tonight? I expect it's time for Sunday services."

⚓

The rain came down in earnest on Monday, the incomplete roof at the Mount insufficient to meet the steady downpour. Rain found every tear and every seam in the calico, every hole in the boards, until the floor carved its own riverbed, running under the back wall and out the front. After three days Emily and the Captain's bed sat in puddles, their shelf dripped, and despair grew along with the thick mold. With the small boat still unable to get out, a mounting sense of claustrophobia encased them all.

But Thursday morning, four weeks marooned, Emily stood outside her tent, breathing for the first time in days the clear, early morning mist, and holding fast to the yellow cast of the sun with her eyes, listening to the pleasant drip of old rain off the trees. A glorious, pretty morning! One to make you glad you were alive.

"Fielding, how is your face this morning?" she asked. He had come to start her fire. It was he who'd wakened her.

"Mending, ma'am, thank you."

"The other men awake?" the Captain asked, stepping out and buttoning his ragged pants, eyes on the water below stretched smooth as glass.

"Aye, and ready to take the small boat out with the supplies, sir, just waiting for you to give word."

Right after breakfast, planks, tar, provisions, and nails all carefully stowed, Harris and Lawson were chosen to take the long-awaited load over. The boat, just a slip of wisp, slipped easily enough past the quiet surf and into the sea. The Captain let out a whoop. "Eh, Johnny, yo!" he yelled, catching up to the boy and giving him a toss, setting him back on his feet. *"There's a fire in the fore hold, fire down below!"* Motion again to his plans, he bound up the hill. *"To me weigh, hey, hey, ho!* Yo, Sargent, where are the charts?"

All morning up at the Mount he labored. Copying Emily's idea of spreading a blanket over the fire to act as hammock, he carefully set his charts, so damp they tore in his fingers, into the sling. *"There's a fire up aloft, there's fire down below. . . ."* He was just cutting apart the larger charts, taking out the sections he would need for the trip and getting ready to gum them together to make himself a smaller map, when Lawson and Harris made their appearance. "Something wrong at the other camp?" he asked, surprised and disturbed to see them.

Predictably, it was Harris who answered. "Oates says he needs white lead now. And he sent us back with all the tools. Can't do anything, he says, until they're sharpened."

"And he wants more provisions."

Lawson smiles like a fox, thought the Captain grimly, like a fox with chicken feathers still in his mouth. "That subject," he said, "is closed. I'm getting a little bored with this constant whining. But what about the tools? Where are they? In the boat?" He started gathering the crinkled chart pieces, mind racing as to how he might work loose a grindstone from the *Maid*, and who he would need to help him do it. Perhaps all of them.

"But, sir," persisted Lawson, "we were so hungry we ate everything you sent this morning. There ain't nothing left."

"We're *all* hungry!" exploded the Captain, "and if there isn't anything left—"

A scream, coming off the beach, cut him short and he jammed the chart pieces into his pocket, racing after Emily. He paused at the ridge to scan the shoreline, to catch again the direction of the cry. "My God!" he choked, slamming right into Steward. The two of them, stumbling over each other in haste to reach the beach, raced each other for the trail, the lad's scream clear in their ears.

"SHIP A-HOY! SHIP, SHIP A-HOY! OH MAN, OH MAN! SHIP, SHIP A-HOY!"

"Get some camphor!" yelled Richard on his way past the Encampment. Down the trail he plunged. Emily and Steward splashed right behind. Harris and Lawson followed, with Fielding, Sargent, everyone carrying camphor. Johnny, leaping rock and log on the beach below, raced in and they all scattered, looking for more wood, tar, anything to make the fire bigger, and to send up thick, black smoke.

The small boat, with the old, dull tools scattered on her floor, sat just high of the tide. Emily fanned the flaming fire while Richard and Steward and Johnny, now Harris and Lawson, now Fielding, now Sargent tossed out the tools, saws and chisels and axes flying, across the beach—and she threw on more driftwood when the boat bounced loose on the waves, she tossed in more camphor when the men leaped her bow. More logs, more camphor. The fire spit and roared, a towering inferno, climbing the sky in a spiral of smoke and flame, but when Emily looked out to sea the ship was moving away. "NO!" she cried, even as a wave, seemingly out of nowhere, dumped the small boat upside down. She dove in, gasping on the icy splash, plowing on through the surf, where the men floundered and came up spitting, water streaking off their chins and beards, helping them to right the boat. She swallowed water and choked, waves sloshing up over her chest. "No!" she cried to the retreating ship. "No! Come back!" She could hear the ship's yards go round, the blocks creak—so close she was! Men moved about on her deck; she could *see* them! "No! No! Come back! COME BACK!"

Richard pulled her out of the water still screaming. "Stop it!" he told her, "Stop it!" and he slapped her face with both hands, holding her tight so that she danced between his palms.

"Captain!" yelled Harris, hanging onto the bow of the small boat, pulling her in by the painter. "I can sprint over to the other camp! Get Hayward and Oates to go after her!"

"No! You'd never make it! She'll be gone before you're halfway there!"

"Maybe," said Sargent, face white and pacing the beach, eyes focused like everyone else's on the shrinking ship, "Oates will see her himself. Maybe Hayward will get his head out from under his armpit."

"Maybe," said the Captain quietly, without hope. Why, he asked himself, had the ship turned? Why? They had seen the fire, surely they had seen the fire. . . .

"What is the matter with Oates!" cried Sargent, tightening his hands into fists, feet splashing through the waves, his eyes blistering. "What is he doing that he doesn't see the bloody ship!"

"Captain!" Johnny came flying off the reef. "There she is—the longboat, sir!"

The longboat! Sailing like a blessed angel round the reef, wings aflutter and singing in the wind, Oates and Hayward pulling back on the oars so she soared! Emily, beside the Captain, gulped, hands to her mouth. Oh, please, dear God, oh please, please, please. . . . The barque slowed, tacking back. "YO!" screamed Sargent, throwing back his head in relief, fists up, "I told you this would happen! I told you, Captain! Didn't I tell you? *Didn't I tell you a ship would pick us up!"*

Emily threw herself into the Captain's wet arms. They were going home . . . they really were going home! Sargent was right. This very day they were at last going home!

21

The Bible is to a sailor a sacred book. . . . I never knew but one sailor who doubted its being the inspired word of God. . . .

—Richard Henry Dana, Jr.
Two Years Before the Mast

"Request permission to come alongside!" Hayward sang, bracing the yard. Oates turned the rudder and the longboat eased up alongside the black barque towering above them. "Yo! Crew of the shipwrecked *Maid* hail!" hollered Hayward. "Hail from London and in dire distress! Request permission to come aboard the—" his eyes flew to the counter, his voice cracked, "—*Leonora*?"

"Eh, an' look 'oo we got, mate," cried one of the pirates, grinning down at them. "If'n it ain't our old friends from the Line! Yo! Jack! Fetch Mr. 'Ayes from the saloon fer a sight fer bleary eyes!"

But there was no need to call Bully Hayes. The infamous pirate had already approached the lee rail and was leaning over, casually dangling his hands loosely from the wrists out over the water. A slow smile came to cruel lips, and a low laugh spilled between his gold teeth, a rumble from his jacketed chest, a villainous sound that bode no good for the two stupefied men in the frail longboat below. "And what can we do?" the pirate teased, "to repay the kindness of your Captain from the last time we met? Wooldridge was his name? I never forget names, or faces." Smiling again he quickly mumbled something to the Jack beside him. The man took off. "Speak up, my man!" he suddenly roared at Hayward, "or has the cat got yer black tongue?"

"Sir," squeaked Hayward, reaching for a davit rope to steady their craft, "we caught fire and—"

"HO!" crowed Bully, standing upright. "Ye caught fire now, did ye? And where be the scoundrel what said I'd cook in hell, the devil be the stoker?"

"He is drowned," said Oates evenly. "Washed owerboard in a pompero. An' I'd advise ye to speak kindly o' the deed!"

The news only made Bully laugh more. "Look like the ugly bloke got the thing backwards then, eh? Aye, but there might be a God after all! Yes, in the name of the Devil I should say so! And Yates, yes, that be the name, he knows it well enough now, I expect, for 'e cooks in 'ellfire below while 'e leaves his mates to freeze on the 'igh sea? And ye be asking me now, I suppose, to be yer savior?" Another roar, hair whipping out the collar of his pea-coat. "Tell me, is there anything left 'a yer ship?" He pointed to the wreck, a skeleton now of open crossbeams, charred and bludgeoned by the sea. "Nay, I expect not, ye plundered whut was left fer yerselves, no doubt." His wrinkled blue eyes scanned the beach, the roaring fire spewing black smoke to the sky, the figures on the beach. "Aye," he said suddenly, turning, "and here be my man. I thank ye, Jack!" he said to the man who came alongside him, laden down with a sack.

Suddenly Bully Hayes leaned over the rail. "An eye fer an eye, mate," he wheezed, breath foul, "a tooth fer a tooth, that's whut the good book declares! So ye tell that Captain Wooldridge a yer's that he be gettin' his just deserts! Yer gonna starve, Jack! Yer bones are gonna be left to rot on this godforsaken, frozen island, Jack! Ha! And the wind ain't come in yet, nor the ice, or hail, or snow from the witches' icy brew! No, ye ain't felt yer death yet, but ye will! Aye, but ye will an' mighty soon at that! But not without me generosity! And don't ye be thankin' me, I only be givin' ye back whut yer good Captain be willin' to share! Jack!" and up he wheeled. "Give the bloody beasts a taste 'a the good book!"

A Bible, pages flying, splattered at Hayward's feet, and when he looked up again, curious and stunned, down came another. And another, and another, men lining the rail and taking aim with distorted smiles until he and Oates could only duck, hands up to protect their heads, moaning when struck, their ears ringing with the malevolent howl and clamor of the men above.

"Board the main tack!" Hayward gasped, pushing off from the *Leonora* with his hand, fumbling for the lines, Bible glancing off his skull. "Man your oars, Oates!"

Those that stood on the beach heard none of the gloating and cheering cries, nor could they see what was transpiring, ship and longboat too far distant in the mist, and so happy smiles still played in various measures over their faces and hearts still beat wildly. "Sargent, you were right!" declared the Captain, and he reached for Emily, swung her up and around, feet skimming the water, toes throwing a circle of spray. "I'll be a monkey's uncle! A ship—"

"Wait! Put me down!" She glanced out to sea. "Wait, Richard—darling—put me down. Put me down!"

He lowered her slowly, and when she turned in his arms, and when they both looked up there was the barque, sails set and disappearing, scudding before the wind and sailing into the waiting fog, longboat going back the other way, back round the reef and out of sight.

For a moment no one moved. It couldn't be true. No, it couldn't be true. Who would leave them here like this? Who? *Who?* Who could abandon them? It *wasn't* true! But there was the horizon, the last of the sun hovering just above the unbroken line. The ship was gone.

Richard painfully maneuvered them all up the beach, out of the water, reaching for Johnny when he saw the blank, numbed expression in the boy's eyes, sick himself with a suffocating heat when he saw tears running down Fielding's wounded face, running down over the festering sore, down over a mouth sagging in utter defeat. "Do not take it hard," he told them all, putting away his own despair. "They, whoever they are, will meet their reward."

Up at the Encampment he tossed several logs onto the men's fire without bothering to go up and change his wet clothes. He didn't want to leave the men, not yet. They stumbled, wet, into their new tent, one that Sargent, Fielding and Harris had put together after the fire, and they stumbled out again, some of them in the dry burlap clothes Emily had made for them of sack and sail twine. He threw on yet another log so that the flames blazed with furious heat, beating back in vulgar shadows the approaching night.

"Do you think one of them will come over from the other camp?" Harris asked, "to tell us what happened?"

"Not tonight. It's too dark now to see the trail." He pulled Johnny, still shivering, into his arms and settled onto a log, leading out in a hymn. Johnny picked up the harmony. Emily joined, and soon all the men sang. Sargent lit his pipe from the fire and sank back into the dark shadows. "Men," said Richard after a third hymn, "I am sorry for what happened. But we are not without hope. We still have ourselves, and we have God. I don't wish to preach, we're all too tired and we're all terribly disappointed. I only wish to remind you, before going to bed, that we are not forgotten by the One who made the sky and sea—and this island of stone."

"Captain? Sir?"

"Aye, Fielding."

"I been thinking, sir. The sky and sea?" He spoke in his usual ponderous and simple way, mulling over each word and thinking as he spoke, the significance of his ideas startling, for he was the one among them who had, and did, suffer the most: first his near-death the day Yates had drowned, and now with his ugly, disfigured and painful face. "If God made both," he said, "and us too, there can't nothing happen whut He don't know. He must know us blokes is here. He tells the waves to come and go, can't figger no other reason they do, so—"

"So what do you say?" asked Lawson. "Come on, spit it out, Jack."

"I say," answered Fielding, "it might be whut God—fixed all of this to happen without us knowing. But now I get stuck, Captain, sir. Can't figger why."

"Poppycock!" snorted Sargent, invisible in his corner. "Is God a beast that He appoints this hell?"

"Perhaps," put in Steward, "this is not hell, but our appointed time that we might choose what manner of men we are. Are we beasts, or are we—"

"Someone shut him up! I've had enough of his bloody lip!"

"Remembering that things always look better in the morning," said Richard quickly, grateful to both Steward and Fielding but knowing also that theology and theory were useless to any man without hope, "we should go to bed. But perhaps we can recite the Lord's Prayer together before we do."

Sargent sprang to his feet. "Recite prayers! Is that what you do, Captain? Stranded on this bloody island, without a chance in the world of getting off, to perish and die like dogs and you sit around in burlap and breeches reciting mumbo jumbo? We're going to die! Die, do you hear me? We're all going to die on this bloody, godforsaken island of hell—" Johnny started to cry and the Captain, staring at Sargent, absently kissed the boy, softly, just his lips against the boy's hair, and pulled him close, smothering his cries. Sargent's black eyes blazed when he saw the gentle gesture. *"We're going to die!"* he screamed.

"Our Father..." Richard whispered, watching the Bosun go and wondering at the horrible change in the man. Despair had totally eclipsed his earlier belligerent assurance of easy salvation. But one by one the others joined him, reciting the words of the prayer, their heads bowed, their bruised and bloodied hands clasped, firelight flickering over their weary faces. "... hallowed be Thy name. Thy kingdom come, Thy will be done on earth as it is in heaven. Give us this day our daily bread. Forgive us our debts, as we forgive our debtors. And lead us not into temptation but deliver us from evil, for Thine is the kingdom, and the power, and the glory forever. Amen."

First thing in the morning Richard took everyone out to the ship to see what could be done about pulling loose a grindstone. "If Oates needs the tools sharpened," he said, splashing through the low tide, "we'd better get on with it." Time waited for no man, which was just as well today. Hard work would remind them all of their own strength.

Emily went with them, and was startled by the changes. The *Maid*, no longer familiar but strangely removed, was a mere ghost of her former self. The forecastle, which had been raised six feet, was now lying in sand. The stern, which had been broken in pieces, was now separated from the rest of the ship by the force of the sea and was tossed up on one side; the sand, thrown against her, lay so high that one had to descend into the hold rather than climb. It was too sad. She allowed Steward to give her a hand, and then, with the Captain, walked slowly through the ghostly chamber of grotesque oddities, astonished to see great casks of cement, anchors, chain and cables, grindstones, iron pieces, and numerous other things too heavy to move. The sea had left weeds and sand amongst it all—useless, rusting cargo. They trespassed a silent cemetery.

"They saw us and left us," she said, more to herself than anyone else, sorting through the forecastle while the men, using hammers and block and tackle, chiseled and pulled from the hold a likely grindstone. She had just pocketed a whole box of candles when there was a distant shout, and then the scramble of feet.

"Yo! Anyone home?" Hayward's voice rang down through the hold. "Bully Hayes! Bully Hayes! It was Bully Hayes!" *Bully Hayes! Bully Hayes! Bully Hayes!* The echo rang through the cemetery.

Richard, crawling swiftly aft and up to the open stern, wincing on the pain he could no longer ignore, wondered, Bully Hayes? What was *he* doing in this corner of the world? "You're telling us it was Bully Hayes in that barque?" he demanded, hauling himself onto a beam.

"Bully Hayes in his *Leonora*," spit Hayward, "sure as Victoria is the Queen!" and the story tumbled out while everyone clustered around him.

The Captain's face showed no emotion. "So where are all the Bibles?" he asked.

Hayward pulled his shirt out of his trousers. A dozen Bibles, different sizes, fell into the hold, and Emily picked one up, then another. French, Spanish, English.

"Wait a minute," said Sargent, swinging up beside Hayward, foot braced to a charred spar, "you mean to tell me it was Bully Hayes who left us? The same chap the Captain wouldn't feed on the Line?"

She dropped the Bible. Chap? Feed? What had come over the man that he should twist things so?

Sargent's eyes flashed from Hayward to the Captain. "*You* cooked us, Captain! If you'd have just given the bloody bloke what he'd wanted in the first place, we'd 'a been sailing out 'a here by now!"

"You bloody blackguard!" yelled Steward, jabbing a hammer across a cement cask into Sargent's face. "If that be the case, you lazy Jack, then what would we be eating right now?"

"Steward," said Richard, motioning the cook back.

Steward ignored him. "What are you blaming the Captain for, anyway?"

"Steward!" snapped Richard, and Steward, nostrils flared, pulled back.

"Men!" shouted Richard, arms out, fingers spread to hush the racket. "Whether I let Bully Hayes have our food or not is hardly the point. Think about it, all of you. Every British naval ship is on the lookout for the pirate. Every harbor of the civilized world holds a warrant for his arrest. How could he take us aboard? What would he do with us? He'd have killed us all." With a concerned look to Emily, who looked rather ill, he said, "No, but for the hand of Providence, we might already be food for the sharks. Our disappointment turns out to be God's blessing, and I for one," he said, smiling at each of them, "am grateful Bully left us be. Here we fight only time and the elements."

"And a bloody leaky boat," said Sargent.

"The leak!" argued Hayward, "is not that bad! Captain, he doesn't know what he's talking about! Oates says he'll get the leak fixed! And we're ready to put in the compass!"

"Hayward, come lend us a hand," said Richard, cheered and even encouraged by the news Hayward had brought. "God has not abandoned us at all, and we've got a grindstone loose. We can use another pair of hands, Hayward, to haul it ashore." He swung off the beam and back into the hold, men leaping and jumping after him. "We'll get your tools sharpened this afternoon, and in the morning I'll take them over myself and see just what this leak is all about."

"But you can't go," Emily wept in the privacy of their own tent that night.

"I must."

"Darling, I shall go mad—"

"Don't. Don't make it any harder. I have to go. That's all there is to it. I have to see for myself what this leak is."

"You don't have all the tools sharpened yet. Maybe you won't be able to go. Maybe the tide will—"

"Then I'll go on Sunday."

"Please," she whispered in the dark, familiar tent. "I can't stand it here by myself. It's so lonely. A lonely, godforsaken place and I worry you won't come back to me. That you'll be sick again. I've seen you wince, and hobble around. I've seen the pain in your eyes when you don't think anyone is watching. Oh, darling, I be so afraid. Don't go."

He held her the way she loved, warm and close, him beneath, her on top, their legs tangled together beneath the burlap bags. She could feel him breathing, gentle rise and fall beneath her breast.

"I'll only go see how things are," he whispered. "I'll deliver the tools and see to the leak and come right back to you."

"Maybe you won't get the tools sharpened," she said again, and fell asleep in his arms, crying, no longer strong but very, very weak, afraid not only for the Captain, but of the shadow that had come over Sargent.

22

Also there was a lust in him akin to madness, which had come with sight of the blood he had drawn. . . . The psychology of it is sadly tangled, and yet I could read the workings of his mind as clearly as though it were a written book.

—Humphrey Van Weyden
The Sea Wolf, Jack London

As Emily predicted, they did not finish sharpening the tools. The whole process was too agonizingly slow. The grindstone, set up by the stove, warbled and wobbled on its clumsy pivot; at times it completely gave way, collapsing into the shingle. Frustrated, the Captain finally sent Hayward back Saturday afternoon through the trail with a saw lashed to his back and a message for Oates: They were to proceed as best they could, given what they had. He would be over, with the rest of the tools, first thing in the morning.

"Richard?"

Something about her posture, bolt upright in the bed, woke Richard instantly Sunday morning.

"Look," she whispered, fright in her voice. "There be molasses all over the floor. Someone sneaked in here last night and stole—Richard!" She scrambled across the top of him and he bit back a cry, sharp pain fairly dancing joint to joint. "They've stolen some of the rice. And the last of the flour!" she wailed.

He moved quickly, rolling out of bed, throwing on his clothes almost simultaneously, and veered out the door.

Back quick for his Captain's jacket, he bounded down the trail to the Encampment, doing up his pants as he went, bellowing for full muster. The last to emerge and fall into line was Sargent.

"What's all this about?" asked Lawson, knuckling his eyes while Richard strode the line, his own eyes passing from one face to the other.

"Please," pleaded the boy, "please, sir, whut be wrong?"

"One of you, and maybe more than one," he said, coming to a full stop, head of the line and Sargent, "committed the gravest of crimes, a crime against every one of us. One of you, or maybe more than one, broke into the Missus' tent last night and stole some of the provisions."

Eyes shifted. He passed again down the line. "Whoever it was also stole the very last of the flour—"

"The very last of the flour?" screeched Lawson. "You took it *all*?" And he was out of the line, facing off with Sargent.

"I don't know what you're talking about." Sargent pushed him back.

"You pig! Pig! Pig! Pig! You said only molasses for us, and some rice! None that nobody would notice! But you had to go take all the bloody flour? How were we going to eat flour behind everyone's backs anyway, tell me that one, you pig! Now you got us all caught—" Lawson stopped short, realizing in a jolt that he had put the noose around his own neck.

"You weasel!" shouted Richard, springing for Sargent. One tumble and he had the Bosun pinned to the mud, whimpering, kicking his feet in frantic, futile jerks while Richard, knees in the mud, straddled Sargent's chest, sitting high and rigid and breathing hard, one fist embedded in burlap shirt, the other raised, just waiting for reason to send it crashing into the man's miserable flesh and beastly bone. "Steward," he panted, "shackle his feet before I'm forced to hit him again."

"No!" roared Sargent, "no chains!" and he arched his
back so quickly Richard pitched forward. Sargent strove
in vain to flee. Midleap the Captain caught his ankle. In
vain Sargent strove to gain the tent. He crawled toward
it, groveled toward it, fell toward it when knocked flat.
But blow after blow the Captain brought him down,
knocking him about like a shuttlecock until at last he lay
prostrate, bruised and bloodied, and the Captain drew
away, leaving the Bosun to whimper and whine like a
puppy. But when Steward approached with the chains,
Sargent was again on his feet. "We're all going to die!"
he erupted, hitting back blindly.

"Nay!" thundered Harris in a surprise move, and he
lunged, swinging a fist into the Bosun's face so fast and
so hard that Sargent was struck dumb by the speed and
the force, and flew back like a feather, slamming into a
stump and slumping, crack to his head . . . dizzy, world
fragmenting into a kaleidoscope of color and sound in
his eyes.

Richard stood over him, breathing hard, his chest
heaving, blood and sweat dripping off his face. "A ship
came and went and you lose hope?" he asked, panting.
"Is that it? And so you must thieve and rob—and corral
us into the grave? But we're not going to die, Sargent.
The grave is yours, not ours! We fight to live—"

"You'll die," snarled Sargent from where he lay, and
despite a face livid with fear for what might come of his
deed, there was more fierceness too in the demeanor of
it. A lust had come to border madness, a lust for more of
the blood that gushed from his Captain's nose.

"He said we'd all die," admitted Harris, his face grim
behind the mat of his now-mangy blond beard, "unless
we, me, Lawson, and him took enough food and found
another camp, and from there hoped another ship would
put through. But I told him no, that we had to let you try.
Sir, I didn't know he stole the food. I would have stopped
him."

Richard squatted beside his bloodied Bosun, wondering what drove a man to such hate and so selfish a scheme. How did he think he could even carry out such a plan? Where would he go, and how? But then, did desperate men always think? Or were they at times just jerked along by the chain of their contention? "Sargent, I have sworn to you before," he said, "and I will swear to you again, I will see us off this island, even you. Because I fight for my life and the lives of my men with a weapon you do not have: courage." Abruptly he stood, catching himself with a tree, for he had forgotten his pain. "Steward? Chain him. He won't argue with you now. Then take him down to the Cascade and have him wash. And when the tide comes in we'll take him with us to the other camp—and if he steals all the grub over there I personally won't stop Hayward and Oates from killing him.

"As for you, Lawson, I assume you knew of this? Yes, I thought so. You'll eat my food for the rest of the day. I warned every man of you—"

"No!" cried Emily in terrible anguish. "You mustn't! Captain, you'll be sick again!"

"Aye, I may," he agreed, narrowing his gaze on Sargent's back as the man stumbled away, tether tight, "but I'll *give* a man food before I'll let him steal it."

Emily, so upset she was nearly crying, begged him to eat her rice, fried in penguin fat. He wouldn't hear of it. And Lawson, sick with shame, plate of double rice on his knee, *couldn't* eat. The others choked down their breakfasts with silent, sorry eyes, and finally, with an awful cry, Lawson threw his plate off his lap with a sweep of an arm, plate and rice flying, and he ran from camp.

Several hours later the tide finally came in enough to let the men take the boat out. Emily's chestnut-colored eyes scanned the bay and sea beyond from the high vantage point of the Mount. The wind had picked up, but the bay had been worse. "The men look like they're ready," she said.

"Give me just two hours," Richard told her, hating to go, to leave her so distraught. But one look at her, seeing her bleeding gums and cracked lips, the ugly scab under her eye, and he knew he had to go; he had to get the tools over; he had to see about the boat. "Come," he said, and held out his hand.

"You're not to get wet," she reminded him. "Or do any of the work. See, you're already trembling."

Her hand felt so small in his. "I'm all right. I've just had no food, that's all."

"You'll do no work," she insisted. "Let the men get her launched."

"Aye, Captain," he teased, trying to make her smile. "Steward?" he hollered when they came off the trail, "you got everything loaded and ready?"

"Aye, almost!"

Reluctantly Emily let him go, reluctantly she smiled for him. She retreated to the ladder and reluctantly watched him help load the last of what was going over— white lead, planks, more of the nails, the compass, extra provisions, all of the sharpened tools. Sargent startled her, standing before her in his hobbled tether. "Yesterday you told the Captain to come back," he snarled, face twisted and ugly. " 'No, no, come back!' " he whined, exaggerating her words. " *'Come back!'* "

"In case you don't remember," she interrupted, heart hammering so hard it hurt, "the boat dumped upside down—"

"You had to call him back, tell him what to do, just like you always tell the Captain what to do!" he hissed, ignoring her, "just like you told him to take the Strait of Lemaire and not Magellan! And do you think we'd be in this mess if it weren't for you? No! We'd be sailing out the Magellan right now and into the Pacific—"

"Does it make you feel more like a man," interrupted Steward evenly, stepping between Emily and Sargent, "to treat a woman this way?"

"Oh ho, Steward!" cried Sargent with a malevolent smile. "If it isn't the lady's paramour! Hey hey, but I've been watchin' you two, and don't think I don't see what hanky-panky goes on behind the Captain's back!"

Steward's face drained of color, and for a moment he stared at Sargent, then, recovering himself, said slowly, "I think you owe the Missus an apology."

"Never mind, Steward," said Emily quietly, her own face white. "Sargent, the Captain be calling you."

When he was gone Steward tried to apologize. "I'm sorry, Missus. Take no heed of what he says."

"I won't."

They loaded the Bosun, still shackled, into the bow. Harris and Lawson, Fielding and Steward, two and two on either side of the boat, singing and swearing and pushing the boat out, they broke through the high surf with a shout. But just as they were bellyflopping over the gunwales and finding their spots at the oars a kicker rolled in, zipping them back through the surf and back onto shore. The Captain leaped out and took the stern. This time they made it. "He'll kill himself yet," whispered Emily.

She put the spyglass to her eye, training it on the boat. "Two hours, Johnny," she told him. "Two hours and they'll be back. You want a look?"

A grubby eye scrunched shut. " 'Oly smokes! I kin see Sargent pickin' 'is nose! Whut a charmin' bloke 'e turned out to be, eh, ma'am?"

Yes, a fine bloke, she thought, grateful he was gone— at least from this camp; grateful because she saw now that he, given the power and the intelligence, could soon be just like Bully Hayes. What had Steward once said? All brute and none of the gentleness of God in such a man?

Two hours later the boat indeed cleared the reef, and, spyglass to her eye, Emily counted the silhouettes: the Captain, Steward, Fielding, Harris. "Come, Johnny, let's go freshen the fires and put on the tea. The Captain will be wet and hungry. Wait!" She held out her hand, stopping the boy. The Captain sat braced over himself, and as the boat came on she saw the old pain undisguised in his eyes. The boat bounced, hung, then swung through the surf.

"Look out and stand by, Missus!" hollered Steward, leaping off the bow and pulling up the boat with a grind. "He's sick again and needs to be helped ashore!"

23

On every side the sky, on every side the sea.

—Virgil
Aeneid

You confound the sea and sky with your bellowing.

Juvenal
Satires

Throughout the long night Emily and Steward heated rocks and spooned brandy into the Captain's mouth, alternating watch: first one at the fire to keep the flames going, new rocks heating, the other huddled asleep over their knees. Now and then, sleep evasive, they worked together, and once, in a dark hour of the night, Steward broached again the subject of Sargent and his insinuations.

"Why speak of this now," Emily asked sadly, "when we have our greater worries?"

"I just want you to know, there is no dishonor in me."

"And you have to *tell* me this? Steward, go back to sleep."

"He's jealous. It's why he must make us look wicked."

"Aye, I know. He must destroy what he can't have; we've said it before. But please, go to sleep, Steward. And if you will," she asked, "pray for my husband?"

Ironically, it was one of Bully's Bibles that brought Emily her peace that night. While Steward slept, his dear lined face all wrinkled and shrunken over the bones of his skull and set in a heap atop his arms crossed atop bared knees, she opened one of the Bibles, surprisingly intact and certainly more complete than her own ragged, half-torn-apart Old Testament. Heart drawn to Job of old, she read in the flickering shadows of his familiar troubles, suddenly so much more real. Boils and sores and even sackcloth. Aye, even sackcloth. She turned back the crinkled pages to read of Elijah, lost and alone and hiding in his cave—abandoned, he thought, of God. She read, flipping to the New Testament, of Christ and His last words to the disciples. And all through the night she faced again her God, not in the frenzy as of before, out on the reef with the tearing of her hair—but here at her fire, gravely, her question, quietly, still the same. *Where are You and who are You, that I, that we, should live such pain?*

She thought of all they had been through. Storm and fire, wind and hail and fire again . . . without and within, and now the Captain? Again so ill? *Where are You and who are You, that I, that we, should live such pain?* And then out of the void of her inner soul—where no man can speak nor teacher explain but where knowledge reigns—a whisper, and to the sound of the pounding waves, a still small voice. *WHERE were you when I laid the foundations of the earth, and WHO did say to the sea, "This far you may come and no farther, here is where your proud waves halt?"* To the roar of the falling Cascade, the same small voice, *Stand on the mountain that I might pass by.* And one more time, in the moan of the wind, *I am with you even to the end of the world.* And hearing the voice, she was strong again.

⚓

The next day while the Captain slept, Steward and Fielding worked on the half-finished roof at the Mount, each hammer blow an intense irritation to Emily. Why must Steward persist with this idiotic notion of his? And why must he order Harris out to the ship to pry loose every nail from every remaining board and every beam? Why, when they would soon be leaving? For they would leave, even if she had to *carry* the Captain into the boat.

"Why?" she finally hollered at him.

He paused, leaning on the roof. "The leak in the boat? The Captain can't trace it. We're going nowhere in a hurry. Johnny!" he bellowed, "go fetch us some limpets, boy!"

And so to the sound of dismal hammer blows she kept the fire going, hot rocks always in the Captain's bed, where he lay watching her—when he wasn't sleeping—through the opened door, immobile with pain, yet following her every move with quiet eyes.

"Darling?" she whispered, sun at last closing its curtain on the weary day. "How do you feel?"

"I'm afraid," he whispered back, tongue slurring the words.

Yes, she could see it in his eyes. "Why?" she said simply, kissing him, putting her fingers in his hair, gritty and stringy, too tangled to smooth.

"Because Sargent was right."

"So this be what you've been thinking all day," she said lightheartedly, a little alarmed at the depression in his voice. "So what," she teased more boldly, "can the man be right about? I can't say, darling, as I can imagine."

"Everything."

"Everything?"

"Taking Lemaire instead of Magellan, trying to fix these ridiculous boats. We're never going to make it out of here. I know that now. T'was a foolish scheme. I have just been too pigheaded to see it."

"Oh my darling," she said, kissing him, seeing his depression for what it was. "You're tired, that be all, and you're sick. Things will look different in the morning."

"The longboat leaks like a sieve . . ."

"Then Oates will fix it!"

"We can't find the leak. Maybe when Harris and Lawson put the putty—"

"Oates will fix it!"

"You will lie with me tonight, not keep hopping in and out of the tent?"

"Aye, I will, if you be dry enough, and warm enough. And if you be quiet."

Tuesday morning she woke to an empty bed. *"Richard?"*

He sat on his tin outside, eating Steward's breakfast, the two of them just sitting, watching the sun trying to burn off the fog. *"On every side the sky,"* quoted the Captain forlornly, *"on every side the sea . . ."*

"You confound the sea and sky with your bellowing," said Emily, coming to stand in relief behind him. He was up again. That's all that counted. Gently she rubbed his shoulders, and without mercy she said, "What *do* you bellow for? When you be on your feet again, and right quick at that? With a belt of brandy to kill the pain and a loving wife and loyal cook to tend to your every need?"

He smiled slightly, and absently reached up to pat her hand, taking her fingers when she gave them, his own swollen and enflamed. Suddenly he stiffened. "Steward! The spyglass! Quick!"

She squinted into the fog to see what it was that had arrested his attention. *A clipper? Weaving through the mist?*

"Harris still around?" the Captain asked, glass to his eye, sitting very still and speaking very low.

"Aye," said Steward.

"Send him over to the other camp. On the double. Tell him to hustle Oates after that ship, for they'll never see our fires in this fog. Emily, don't fret," he said the moment Steward was gone and as the clipper rounded the reef without slowing up, her four masts under full press of sail, top royals set. "Oates is bound to see her. He'll catch her."

"I'm not fretting. And if Oates can't catch the clipper, we still have the longboat."

"It leaks."

"You better stop talking like this or you'll frighten me."

Two hours later Harris' dragging steps up the trail, Lawson in his wake, heralded a disappointing story. Oates had made repeated tacks, but couldn't even get round the point. "Clipper's gone, and we're still here," said Harris morosely, collapsing onto a tree root, back against the tree. He plucked a twig off his shoulder and gave it a spin into the fire.

For a time no one spoke, memory of Bully Hayes and that disappointment still too fresh in their minds. And now this? A clipper? Within their grasp? Then Emily, mesmerized by the fire, found herself whispering. *"A great and strong wind split the mountains and broke in pieces the rocks . . . but the Lord was not in the wind. And after the wind an earthquake, but the Lord was not in the earthquake. And after the earthquake a fire, but the Lord was not in the fire And after the fire . . ."*

"And after the fire?" urged Harris.

"A still small voice."

"And what does the still small voice say, woman?" he asked, rolling his head against the tree trunk to look her way, and to focus very carefully on her face.

"Does not every man need to hear this for himself?" she asked.

"What does it say to you?"

"That God is not in the wind or earth or fire. But in the *after*. In the stillness . . . in the disappointment . . ."

"And in the wake of a passing clipper . . ." murmured Richard, catching up with his wife, amazed and ashamed. The past few days he had been listening to the voice of Sargent, pouting like old Elijah in his cave. But if God was not in the wind or earth and fire back then, He wasn't now. He *was*, as always and as Emily knew, in the silence and the invisible, and very much in the after. "Harris?" he asked suddenly. "What of the longboat? Is the compass in?"

"Aye, the compass is in, sir. Why?"

"Did she leak while you were out there chasing that clipper?"

Emily laughed when Harris said, "No."

"So our own boat is seaworthy then?" he persisted, just to hear Emily laugh again. "You drew no water?"

"Nay. Oates said he found the leak yesterday—after you left. He's got her all painted in the white lead already."

"Then that clipper," he exclaimed, confidence restored and faith unshakable, "that clipper came by that we might prove our *own* boat seaworthy! Harris, is there *anything* that needs to be done before she's ready to sail to the Falklands?"

"Nay," said Harris, smiling now, "Oates was to come over today to tell you."

"Then why," Richard exclaimed again, "do we all sit about like bumps on a log? We have done it! *You* have done it! And we sit like bumps when our *own* ship sits ready to sail? Come, we must pack! Today! We're leaving!" and he struggled to his feet that they might begin at once.

"Sir?" said Steward quietly, interrupting. "What of the small boat?"

"What of it?"

"Mast isn't in. We can't go anywhere until we get that done—for the boys staying on."

Depression threatened to come on again, for how could he get the mast in, as sick and as weak as he was? For he was sick, and he was weak. He held out a swollen, scabby hand. His fingers trembled noticeably.

"You can let Harris do it," said Emily, reading his mind, and he closed his eyes, remembering the putty in the longboat.

"Old Man?"

"Aye, Harris?"

"I'll do it right, I swear. I've been a real goat, I know. But give me a chance. Lawson too. We'll carry you down to the beach—and you can tell us exactly how it's done."

"Lawson?"

"Aye, if you would only let me. Sir."

Two hectic and frenetic days followed. The Captain did little of the actual work, convalescing carefully by the beach fire, quick with instruction, quicker with encouragement.

But could it be they were really leaving? The question dazzled them all, teasing them; they catered to the unreality in happy song. *"There's a fire in the fore hold, fire down below." "Come all you young fellows who follow the sea." "Haul away together, we'll either break or bend 'er . . ."*

On Wednesday the small boat tested like a cork. Harris and Lawson took her out with their fishhooks to give both boat and luck a whirl. The others sorted, packed, eliminated, changed their minds, and packed again.

Thursday morning, their fifth on Staten Island, Steward made flares of penguin oil and camphor. Johnny wrapped them in one of Emily's many calico bags, oiled and waterproofed. Candles were packed in the bags. The Captain's pasted chart was wrapped. The ship's papers were wrapped, and Steward wrapped his pocket watch in the oiled cloth and put it back in his pocket. Emily filled her own bag with more of the precious matches, a small compass, a lead pencil, note paper from Lawson, and what was left of her Bible.

Thursday afternoon the rum and brandy, what was left, was brought down to the beach. Bully beef tins, too, and the two small hams the boy had found only days before. Emily boiled fresh water, with tea and molasses, in the galley boiler, mildew rising to the top. Over and over and again and again she skimmed it off until at last, two hours later, the tea boiled clean. Steward helped her pour it steaming hot into an old rum cask. While it cooled she brought out the dozens of little breadcakes she'd made, looking them over for sign of spoiling. Finding none she put them back in their bag. Tea cool, Steward closed the cask.

"Too much plunder for the old longboat?" Steward asked during tea, dismayed at the growing pile on the beach: sextant and carpenter's tools, casks, bottles, blankets, and bags.

"Nay," said the Captain, determined, for he could think of nothing they dare leave behind. "Harris? Lawson? Run fetch Sargent at the other camp."

"Sargent, sir?" they both chorused, shocked as the rest of them.

"Aye. We'll need him in the morning to help launch the small boat with the supplies. It'll take two trips, and it'll take all hands."

"Why not fetch Hayward, or Oates?"

"And leave Sargent over there alone?"

⚓

Friday dawned a glorious day, clear and cold, with a small breeze out of the south. The surf was relatively calm, the waves a matching blue to the sky, and with a shout all hands were out of the tents and hustling down the trail to the small boat—just waiting to be loaded and carried round to the longboat.

"My rug! Don't forget my rug, or my blanket!" cried Emily, afraid her bedding would be left in the excitement.

"I won't, Missus," Steward assured her on the run, "but first things first," and he hoisted the rum cask, filled with the tea, up onto his shoulder, bouncing it into place alongside the thick of his neck before staggering across the shingle to the boat.

"Steward, Lawson, Fielding, you three on the oars," directed the Captain, first load ready to go. "Sargent, you'll steer and run up the sail when she clears the reef."

But the Bosun made no move into the water.

"Sargent, you'll steer," said the Captain again.

"Surf's too high. Don't want to get myself killed."

"What do ye mean, ye ain't goin' out!" bellowed Steward, swinging around in the water so quickly he nearly lost his grip on the bouncing boat. "Never mind! We'll do it ourselves, we don't beg! Ready, boys? In we go . . . one!"

Richard advanced toward the Bosun who so clearly hated him. "Sargent, have I wronged you," he asked quietly, "that you should despise me? What have I done? Have I treated you any less than the others—"

"You have done nothing to me!" snarled Sargent, cutting him off with a vengeful cry, the toxin of his envy erupting like acid. "It's you and your whole kind! Born with a silver spoon in your mouth, never doing an honest day's work in your life, climbing up behind the mast like I've had to, groveling for a pannikin 'a cold tea and a kid of stale bread! Whipped at the whim of men more stupid than you but a bloody sight luckier in life!"

"But I hold no station to a man. I have let you eat at the Captain's table."

"You let!" screamed Sargent, bouncing back on his feet, fists up. "Listen to yourself, you bloody aristocrat! What makes you a better man that you let me do anything! You were born under the right stars is all! Everything given to you on a silver platter and you think you're so bloody noble as to let me eat off your bloody table? You, who would be scrubbing decks if you weren't given your bloody ship! You with your bloody wife at your side, boasting your bloody superiority over us all because you got a woman? Rubbin' our noses—"

"Sargent," interrupted Richard. If a man was envious, let him make something more of himself, not less.

"There's something you'd be wise to learn. Nobility is not a birthright. You have to work for it. Now into the water before I give the others liberty to keel haul you thrice!"

The boat cleared easily with Sargent's silent help, and Richard, holding Emily's hand, watched it round the reef. "He better not give them any lip on the other side," he whispered. Then, more happily, and to the boy, rumpling his knot of ragged hair, "Do you want to go with us for a last look at the camp?"

"Now whut would a bloke wanna' do that fer? Polly, come back! You sceered 'er, sir."

"She'll come back. Will you give a shout, boy, when you see the men return?"

"Aye, aye, Captain, sir!"

And so tugging on Emily's hand he backtracked to see the Mount one more time.

24

The day came for our departure. There was no longer anything to detain us on Endeavor Island. The Ghost's *stumpy masts were in place, her crazy sails bent.*

—Humphrey Van Weyden
The Sea Wolf, Jack London

The Mount was a desolate place. The wind had already made itself at home, blowing softly through the empty calico of the tent to make the corners flap forlornly and sporadically beneath the heavy tree and plank roof that Steward had only begun. Emily and the Captain wordlessly crossed the clearing, stepping over the cold fire to peer inside. Dark and dank, shadows hid the frame of their bed, the pine boughs of their mattress, the damp shelf—with only the empty baby bottle left, candle gone. In a back corner hulked the provisions for the three staying on, to divvy and devour as they dared. "I wonder how long our tent will stand," whispered Emily.

"Not long, darling."

One final sweep of their eyes and they backed out, and without further word or a backward glance they descended for the last time the steep, slick trail, water sucking at their heels. Today they would move to the new camp. Tomorrow they would leave for good.

"Yo, Missus, you in the bow," said Lawson, helping her into the boat only moments after it had beached. But with one foot over she couldn't do it.

"No!" she cried. "No, not yet! Not yet!" And she pulled back her foot, as much stunned by her reaction as any of the men.

"Emily!" the Captain asked, concern in his face, "whatever is the matter?"

"I don't know!" But she did know. The waves, the awful waves. How could she not have thought of the surf, thought that *she* should have to face the angry, tumultuous roll? *And the 500 miles of open sea?* My dear God, she thought in sudden terror, I am afraid!

Over the rocks she flew, down to the cliffs and up the high rocks that had taken her in. Oh my God, this be all there is! she cried to herself. The sea and yet more sea! She plunged down a hollow in the wide, wide reef, leaping flat stones and tidepools, scraping her worn boots on the barnacles, scattering penguins and geese and one mighty sea lion, who took one look at her lumbering chaotically from stone to stone and lumbered off himself, slapping into the water with a flop. Two boulders rose up sharp off a ledge and she ran panting to lean over them, sick and weak, for she had no strength to run. Weak and trembling, faint in the head, she clasped the one boulder and leaned in.

Steward was the first to reach her, and then the Captain. "She'll be all right," she heard Steward say, and she was.

"I'm sorry." She straightened what was left of her skirts. Coat and dress hems had either been torn off or rotted off; only muslin and petticoats covered her from the knee down. "I don't know what got into me. But I be fine now."

"Missus, you can't be doing this," said Steward. "You can't let the men know you're afraid. It unnerves them."

"I'm not afraid."

"Steward, let me," said the Captain. "Emily, we're all afraid, the men are afraid. But if they see you..." He started over. "In the past five weeks the men have all come to rely on you. You've been their strength, you've kept them going. And so now you *must* be brave and strong—they haven't got it in themselves." He pulled her into his arms, resting his chin on her head, crushing the stiff, smelly burlap of her cap into her skull. "The men know they can do anything, if you, a woman, can. And you can, darling."

"Well of course I can," she said out loud, but inside she thought, so we are back to Steward and his *ezer*. She thought of many things, quickly and in an instant, and she turned her face from the Captain's chest to see Steward who stood close. "Aye, dear Steward," she said, and reached out her hand for him, "it has just come to me. On this wretched island I have been forced to find what it means to really be a woman, the *ezer* of your ancient Hebrew, the helpmeet." She looked into her husband's face, and Steward's again. "And now I must draw upon that strength to bring the men through?"

Steward nodded, biting his bottom lip with a returned smile. "The beastly lot of a woman, Missus."

⚓

They passed the Maid on their way back, wedged between two high stones and still smiling. Well, let her smile, thought Emily, fully recovered from her unfortunate moment, if it brings her comfort to pretend. A small white stone lay nearby. She stooped to pick it up. "It be for Catherine," she explained, "should I ever see her again."

"And you think you won't?" asked the Captain.

"I think," she said, feeling the hardness of the stone in her hand, and seeing too her home in London, "there will come a time when I won't remember being here. I mean *really* remember." She pocketed her stone and moved on. "Like the smell of the air, the absolute gray of the water, the barrenness of this rock. It will all seem a dream."

The men were clearly relieved to see her, and she let Lawson help her once again into the bow. But no sooner had she sat than the little boat was swept out, floating, and her breath came in hard, quick gasps. The men, keeping their eye on her, swarmed out alongside, hands to the gunwales, splashing through the low waves: Harris and Lawson, port, Steward and the Captain, starboard, sullen Sargent astern.

"Where's Fielding and Johnny?" she asked, alarmed.

"They'll walk over in the morning," Steward assured her, maneuvering the boat out.

"Can't overload the boat," Richard explained. "Ready, men?"

She gripped the seat thwart and sat absolutely still, staring straight ahead.

"We jump on the next wave!" her husband hollered. "Here it comes, men! One! Two!" She closed her eyes, feeling the growing swell of the wave crescendo beneath her. "THREE!"

The boat rocked and tipped. The men bellied up like seals, teetering on the gunwales, feet kicking—and then they were in, noses down and scrambling quick for their seats amongst the crowded plunder. She clung fast to her own seat as they pulled back with all their might on the oars. Two minutes, waves spilling over the bow and onto her feet. Two minutes, breath held and heart hammering. Two minutes and they were clear, out in the sea and she was alive. This was not so bad!

Behind her the mountains she had remembered from the burning deck of the *Maid* rose up tall and frowning, the face of Staten Island as stern as ever. They rounded the reef, a pleasant sensation of steady, even surges through the gray water. Ahead were the high rocks of the new bay, the welcoming flicker of a fire, now the longboat at anchor.

Closer they drew, surge after surge, until she could see two figures on the beach. The gap closed, the figures took shape and form, and Oates and Hayward were plunging into the water to guide them in. There was the familiar scrape of rock and wood as the boat came to a stop. Oates jammed his pipe into his pocket and held out his hand.

"Oh, Oates, it be so good to see you!" she exclaimed, taking his hand and stepping ashore.

"Ye git yerself oop to the fire, Missus! An' warm yer wet toes!"

"Hello, Hayward! How are you?" she asked, delighted to see them both, delighted even more to find they seemed to have missed her. She let Hayward hurry her along a plank spread over swampy grass while Oates, with another smile for her, hurried back to help the others with the boat and supplies.

"Goodness!" She had to stop, stunned by the immensity of the fire. A whole tree trunk, lying atop two or three others, blazed and crackled. You couldn't get near it for the heat.

And the camp? She was unprepared for the beauty; it almost took her breath. High, steep mountains rose up on every side, a shelter from the wind. Dense trees encircled the camp, a large level space of land with a low, sloping beach that reached back to the trees, and large tent.

"Have you eaten?" Hayward asked. "Hey, where's Johnny?"

"He'll be over in the morning, with Fielding. No, no, we haven't eaten."

All afternoon while she explored, looking for the sweet berries the Captain had brought over that one time, the men worked on a lantern of some kind. They would need light to measure the stars and chart their position, and to read the compass at night. Candles would be useless, snuffing out before they could even be lit.

It was Oates who finally figured one out, using a soup tin. By using a piece of wire at the bottom of the tin he was able to hold the candle upright. "Make another one," said the Captain, "and figure out how to hang it from the rigging."

But by this time it was dark, and Emily was cold and tired. Her rug and blanket had already been taken to the tent. "Let me show you the way," said Steward, "so I can see if this lantern of Oates' really works." And he laughed. Oates waved him on, laughing too, everyone's spirits bright. This was their last night marooned.

The tent was divided down the middle into two even halves, sacks hanging as the wall. Her rug was in the very back, atop dry leaves. "Oates says you and the Captain are to have the one side to yourselves. Do you need anything else?" Steward asked, holding up the quaint little lantern. "Before I go?"

"I be fine. Thank you, Steward." She yawned and sat carefully onto the rustling mattress, glad to feel her familiar blanket.

"Goodnight, Missus."

"Goodnight, Steward."

She hardly heard Richard scoot in beside her and pull her into his arms. She was asleep, asleep with the blissful vision of home at last.

The scent of fried fish woke her with a start. She'd been dreaming—no, it *was* fish she smelled. Sitting up, just a little disoriented, she found the tent empty and the air strangely quiet without the roar of the surf or Cascade in her ears. The men's voices were startling, strangely sharp and clear, and it all came back: the new camp. And, she thought with a leap, they were leaving! Today!

She ducked out the door.

"Emily!" called the Captain from the fire. "Fresh fish! Hurry up or they'll be gone!"

"Fish? And you be eating them without waking me?"

"We were going to save you one," said Hayward.

"The little one!" said Harris, laughing.

She could hardly believe the sight: fish the color of silver, flecked in red, five to six inches long, simmering in fat over the fire.

"Who caught them?"

"The Captain and Lawson," said Harris. "They went out this morning, before any of us got up."

There were 20 of them, and they ate them all.

"So," said Hayward, "when do we leave?"

"Soon as we can get packed," the Captain mumbled, his mouth full. "And as soon as Fielding and the boy arrive."

"The wind isn't fair." Steward's eyes darted back and forth along the horizon and up the mountains.

"Do you know when it will be?" the Captain asked, putting down his plate. "Lawson, take good care of those fishhooks and you won't starve. Up, up. Yo! Here's Fielding and the boy!" And Polly-wants-a-cracker, riding the boy's head. Suddenly, and all at once, they realized no one had thought to tell the boy he couldn't take Polly on the boat.

"But he be mine!" he whimpered, reaching up a finger, bringing Polly down beak to nose, going cross-eyed. "Me canna leave the only thing whut ever b'longed to just me! Me canna do it!"

"Harris!" called Emily. "Promise the boy you'll take care of his bird. There, see? Harris will watch out for her, and bring her along when the Captain comes back to fetch them all."

"That I will, Jack," promised Harris. "Tell her to come to me—I have just the roost for her in the tent."

In less than an hour they were ready and aboard "ship"—the Captain, Johnny, Emily, Steward, Hayward, Oates, and Fielding all but sitting in each other's laps, legs squeezed between boxes and bags. The small enclosure that Oates had built into the stern of the boat for Emily offered a sitting space, and Johnny, seeing it, elbowed his way aft, bumping into the compass, tripping clumsily over toes and rigging.

"Goodbye and Godspeed!" hollered Harris from the small boat bobbing in the water 10, 15, 20 feet away. "Don't forget to come back, sir!"

"By the grace of God," shouted Richard from where he stood at the mast, "I shall come for you!" And he sniffed the wind, a sailor again, and for a moment he forgot where he was, or what had to be done, the thrill of the sea taking full possession of his soul. A quick glance to Emily, her wane face smiling up at him, and the moment passed. He held their lives, her life, in his hands. And for an instant panic pounded in his breast. Had he made the right decision? Should they stay behind? *Was* Sargent right? But nay, surely an attempt, any attempt, was better than the agony of sitting day after day with desperate eyes on the horizon, despair sharpening each time a ship passed on. Aye, let God go with them. The time had come.

"Up anchor and away!" he hollered and men scrambled to the port. Up came the kedge anchor hand over hand. "To your posts!" Men scrambled back to their oars. They were moving out, gliding through the smooth surface of the sea. A nod to Oates and up ran the sail. "Up on the tiller! And stand by to come about!" The jib boom slid clear, the boat swung northeast. Wind caught her sail, a whistle and pop, and the bow cut clean. In her wake Harris and Lawson in the small boat hollered and waved and grew tiny. Goodbyes and farewells grew faint, distance driving her wedge.

"They are gone," said Hayward, twisting to see.

But I'll be back, thought Richard, narrowing his eyes and taking the familiar sway of the sea in his knees. The ugly lines of his patchwork boat stood clear in his peripheral vision. What a boat she is, he thought with pride. She isn't beautiful, but she's strong. All panic subsided; he felt himself a man of power just to see her, to feel her forge ahead, to hear her creak and groan and sail on.

"Yo! There be the old camp!" shouted Johnny, hanging over the gunwale, fingers playing with the icy water. Steward saluted the wreckage. It too faded.

Within an hour the wind shifted, and began to blow. The sea ran high, and Emily, struck by sudden seasickness, crawled over the rigging and into her waterproof hole in the stern, dragging her bedding with her. To her horror, the space was too small to sit up and too short to lie down. How would she make it a day in this space? Five days? A week? And what if I be sick? she wondered in agony, holding her queasy stomach.

The sea grew rougher still, and she, now on her back, with knees up and holding her stomach, listened to the men complain as the conditions grew worse. At last she crawled out to get a whiff of air, and the tilting horizon drew her into a kaleidoscope of sea and sky, boat tossing. Wind and seaspray whipped the bow. Waves sloshed the gunwales, splashing plunder and men alike. Their feet, and the stockings she'd knit them and the burlap sacks and canvas strips they'd wrapped their feet in, were hopelessly wet, their toes bitterly cold. The men sat huddled, backs to the wind, biting their lips on the pain. Johnny began to cry and wouldn't stop, not even when Oates threatened to keelhaul him. She crawled back into her hole, wretched in her own way.

"We're going back!"

"Captain! You can't! We can't!"

They all objected, loath to return despite their misery.

"But we'll never make it this way," she heard him explain, his voice firm and comfortably nearby; he sat with Johnny atop her "cabin" at the tiller. "We'll freeze if we do! We'll go back and tomorrow we'll make stanchions! And stretch a canvas screen around her like a bulwark! That should ward off the worst of this!"

When the Captain called her to come out it was quite dark and they were sailing into the new camp.

"This is not the way to begin," said Hayward with a frown.

"We haven't begun," said the Captain, angling in alongside a reef.

The new camp was deserted, the three men left behind apparently having gone back to the old one. "Probably went to see what we left," said Steward, poking about the provisions. "Hope Lawson and Harris can keep Sargent out of the grub."

"Have they left *us* anything?" the Captain asked.

"Not much, but enough. But we can't dillydally, Old Man."

The delay cost them two nights and a day, and a great deal of anxiety. Frost appeared their first morning back. But mussels for breakfast first thing Monday morning, a clear day of open sky, and they were ready to try again.

They left without having seen hide nor hair of the other three. Without the small boat they loaded in from the reef, stepping carefully into the longboat lest they clip the canvas bulwark or get their feet wet. But come Johnny's turn he overestimated and catapulted into the drink, tearing the bulwark on his way down, grabbing at it in his panicked fall.

"You idiot!" raged Hayward. "You stupid idiot!"

"Leave him alone," said Fielding, holding out a hand.

"You never pay attention, you know that, boy? Look at you! Dripping wet and shivering and we haven't even started! A water rat, you are, and getting everything and everyone else wet!"

"We're all gonna be wet soon enough, Jack," insisted Fielding, making room for the child, who said nothing, but watched Emily with anxious eyes.

"Hayward, leave him alone," echoed Emily, looking at Fielding's face thick with scab while Steward pulled out a hammer and started banging the wet canvas back into place.

"Next time," Steward said, mouth full of bent nails, "don't grab, lad, let yourself go. We'll fish you out. Ain't none of us going to leave you to drown."

"I will," said Hayward, but he relented. "Here, take off your rags and put on my shirt or you'll freeze. Ow, you're stepping on my foot, Steward. Mind how you go!"

"Man your oars!" shouted the Captain at the tiller.

The four men scrambled for their posts, and the boat, canvas nailed back on, surged stroke by strong stroke back to the sea. Once again the wind came up. Once again Oates raised the sail. Once again it bellied, a whistle and pop, and once again they were on their way.

For a long time they sailed the north coast, closer to the island this time to save themselves the fierce winds, and the closer proximity provided an interesting panorama that captured their attention. Dozens of ravines and inlets invaded the island, harbor to hundreds of petrels and penguins, some inlets so thickly populated with the oily bird that the rock was fairly carpeted with black and white. A heavy stink of penguin droppings laced the air currents and Emily laughed, plugging her nose.

At noon the wind picked up, driving on the stench, and it wasn't so funny anymore. The boat jumped about, the sea rippling in strange sounds around the boat. "I don't think we're making headway!" hollered Steward, fore. "We're caught, I think, in a disagreeable riptide!"

"Take out the oars then!" the Captain shouted, aft.

The men pulled a half-hour or more until they were out and the rippling whisper was gone. Emily opened a tin of bully beef and passed it around. Everyone dipped in with their fingers. The wind settled and on they sailed, a pleasant journey into the afternoon. At four o'clock and teatime they passed St. John's Point, the easternmost bluff of the bony back of Staten Island. No sooner had they passed, though, when two schooners came into view, sailing past with a fair wind, down and around St. John's Point and to the south.

"Och," begged Oates, hand on the boom and ready to give chase. "Can we no' try to take them?"

"They are going back the way we came," cautioned the Captain, "*downside* the island."

"But if we can *catch* them!" argued Hayward.

"They're ten miles off! Under full press of sail!" But he couldn't argue the look in their eyes.

"Stand by to come about!" shouted Hayward with a wild, exultant shout, leaping into action. Emily and Johnny ducked, boom whistling over their heads. Back they sailed, everyone at the oars to make her fly.

But the schooners were too fast, and the men could see in short order that they were only exhausting themselves to no purpose. The Captain was right. So they pulled in their oars and returned to course. They were on their own, with none to help them out. They would have to do this themselves.

And so, setting sail, they moved forward and onward, toward whatever might come.

PART 3

The Open Sea

25

They were faced with three killers: the sea, the sun, and the wind. . . . The sea came first.

—Alexander McKee
H.M.S. Bounty

A sloshing splash, subtle and distant, whispered in the black of night, an odd sound. Emily woke from her cramped hole, ears tuned to identify the unremitting noise. Nothing in her experience could name it, yet all senses told her the meaning was something to be feared. Twisting, then curving her back, she was able to poke her face out the door. Gentle moonlight picked out the silhouette of the men. Five were asleep: Oates, Hayward, Fielding, and the boy side by side like spoons in the bottom of the boat, a tarpaulin spread over them, ship rigging laced over their heads; the Captain sitting up, back against the wall of her hole, chin in his chest. Only Steward was awake, sitting on the smooth top of her hole, hand on the tiller.

"What is it, Emily?" he whispered.

"That noise. There be something wrong. Can't you hear it?"

"We had some porpoises awhile back. Maybe it was—"

"No, I hear it still!"

He waited, but finally shook his chin. "Nay, I hear nothing. You're imagining things. Easy to do," he said kindly, "on a night like this."

She tried to sleep, but couldn't. Splash, slosh, splash. *Splash, slosh, splash.* "Steward!" she whispered again, "Can you not hear it?"

"No."

"Something be wrong. I can feel the short hairs on the back of my neck. Please, wake the Captain."

"He ain't going to like it."

"Hang the Captain. I must know!"

Only five seconds after he was roused and his ear picked up the crash of surf, Richard was waking the men. "Yo," he said, gently shaking their shoulders. "Yo. We are too near some island. Another five minutes and we shall be in a surf we'll never come out of. Quick. Up and man your oars. No lollygagging till we're gone."

They obeyed, clumsily finding their posts on the two seats that crossed the boat, mumbling and wincing over stubbed toes and wet rigging in their faces, fumbling for the oars and sliding them into the oarlocks on the gunwales beside them.

"Hark!" whispered Hayward, for the night was eerie, everything as black as pitch but for the light of the wane moon and thin stars, and the pinholes of light coming from Oates' tin lamp hung over the compass. "A fire, I think," said Hayward, "on shore!"

"Aye," confirmed Oates with a whisper, "someither body shipwrecked on a godforsaken isle?"

"Shall we head in?" Hayward asked the Captain.

"No. They'll be no better off than us. Steward, the sextant. Emily, the notepaper—and Steward's watch and the tables. We'll let the folks at Stanley Harbor on the Falklands know where they are."

"You'll never pinpoint it," said Hayward. "There's too many variables, you haven't got—"

The Captain's head snapped up and Hayward shrank back.

"Cap'ain?" Johnny whispered, jaw bouncing with the

cold. "There be water o'er the bottom. Do ye want me to bail out afer we lay doon again?"

Soon the quiet of the night swallowed their stirring, everything hushed, everyone asleep. Emily, back in her hole, wondered how her husband managed, sitting up, the night so bitterly cold. The other men had each other to keep warm, but he? Soon all her wondering, though, was lost to alarm and then horror when she felt the boat come alive, jumping about in the most frightful manner, creaking and groaning and tearing at her seams as wave after wave piled over from every side.

Someone pulled the canvas covering across her door, sealing her in perfect blackness, and in her blackness she took repeated blows to her head, slamming against the sheer. No amount of rearranging her bedding helped, first bunched at her ears, now wrapped round her skull. At last she gave up and just submitted to the violent dashing. A mad wave mashed the stern and like a rag doll she rocked sideways. When she fell back dead center water was trickling in and she stuffed back a startled cry.

"Is there any water coming in?" *Hayward.*

"Are you all right, Missus?" *Fielding.*

"Yes!" she lied. "Please, do we have a head wind?"

"Aye!" *Steward.*

Their voices were quiet after that, nothing heard but the repeated dash of waves and the grunt of men hard at the oars, the scrape of a saucepan against the bottom of the boat, an occasional, quick "Hard up! Hard up!" from the Captain just outside the door, his voice so laced with tension and the sharp edge of worry that it told more of their peril than any mad thump of waves washing over her head. Her head began to burn, and in her fever she remembered Oates' worry, *Should we take too many seas over her stern, it'll go hard for us.* Pulling up her knees and tucking in her head to protect herself as best she could, she began to pray quietly, to commend their souls into the almighty hand of Providence.

Three hours later the Captain moved away from the door and told her to come out for some air, and to stretch. Daylight had come, and with it a balmy calm. The men sat without strength. Drenched to the bone, they shivered, exhaustion thick in their eyes, and Emily bit her lips, sick with alarm. They were men pushed to the limit. They needed dry clothes, they needed sleep. She squeezed out and sat with a long breath beside her husband on the bottom of the wet boat, pressing her aching back up against the short wall of her hole, and stared at them. Hayward was the first to smile, fresh blood from his gums staining his teeth.

"I figure we made it," he said, as if he didn't quite believe it.

They were quite alone on the wide, wide sea, a water-color world where horizon blended sea and sky. Emily broke open another tin of beef, this time giving the men some rum to go with it, to warm their bodies, and one by one they began to unwrap the canvas and wool stockings from their feet and to spread the wrappings to dry. She gave Johnny new sacks to cover himself. Oates cut him holes in each, for arms and legs. The sun came out, and although it was cold and they shivered still, the yellow of the sun picked up their spirits and they all began to look more cheerfully on the day. At noon the Captain took measurements by the sun, played with some numbers, told which way to steer, and they sailed on.

Night fell again, and once more they lay down, leaving one man at the tiller. They rotated every two hours in the light of stars and moon, and the feeble flicker of Oates' lamp. Emily, back in her hole, slept and woke, slept and woke, once coming to long enough to hear the Captain complain of an odd sensation in the soles of his feet, like water running up and down. "Are you wet?" she called through the canvas door.

"My coat is damp, but my feet, I think, are dry."

In the morning they found Johnny, again, to be the wettest. Emily pulled off her boots, unwrapped the flannel that she had swaddled her feet in, and gave them to him, for all the good it did. He simply huddled in the bottom of the boat and was wet again. Only 48 hours into their journey and he was already getting stupid, dull-eyed, and listless, stupefied with cold, hunger, and fatigue.

The Captain ordered the oars out and for the men to pull, to move them along quicker and to warm them, and when they found the advantage, they put Johnny on the job as well.

In the afternoon a drenching rain beat down on their heads, cutting into their faces and swollen hands, running down their backs between coat collar and neck. And in the downpour Emily opened another tin of meat and passed it around, with a breadcake each, and water to drink. "We must save the rum. You be drinking too much." But she had to add when their faces fell, "a tablespoon each, then, before you go to bed."

She did not sleep well that night, head too hot and pounding with each beat of her heart. The poor men, the poor boy, she kept thinking while passing in and out of consciousness. "Missus, the candle snuffed out." Oates, at the tiller, beckoned, and with great force of will she eased up from her cramped position and thrust her face into the dark, salty wind.

"Captain telt me to gi'e ye a shout. We've lost the matches. Do ye ha'e ony in yer bag? I canna see the compass."

"You be sure they be lost?" she asked, alarmed. "I have only packed a few!"

"We'll ha'e to make them last then, Missus," said the Scot, handing in his lamp for her to light.

She would have to keep a candle burning night and day then, to save what matches they had. She began cutting the candles in short pieces; they were too long to fit inside the tin lamp. It be a lucky thing the Captain had Oates make two, she thought, handing the one lantern back to him and hanging the second from her low roof. Then she fell back into a fitful, feverish sleep, trusting Providence to wake her in time to light a new candle before this one blinked out.

Thursday dawned clear, with little or no wind, and so brittle with cold that the men's breath froze in their beards. When Emily crept out she was alarmed to see their deterioration. Open, irritated sores festered, draining pus. The sores itched and the men clawed their arms and legs until blood ran, so that scarlet threads and knots laced skin almost white with salt. And they were so tired they kept falling asleep sitting up, toppling over and waking in a start. She pleaded with the Captain, nodding off and jerking up, to go into the hole to rest. "Wake me at noon," he said, giving no argument and backing in, pulling up his bare feet, rags unwrapped and set to dry. "So I can take the altitude of the sun."

The men had only their stories to amuse themselves, and one pipe, and so as the morning dragged on they passed both back and forth, the privileged one getting to smoke and regale the others with exaggerated exploits while the others pulled on the oars, thinking of their own tales to fame. Driftwood washed slowly past. Thousands of whalebirds came round. Porpoises swam by, one school skirting the boat before they were gone. At noon the Captain was wakened, and after he figured their whereabouts by chart and sun he announced them to be halfway. "What's today?" he asked. "Thursday? By Saturday, just a couple more days, men, and we should see land—or earlier if we can get some wind." Johnny rocked, feet curled up. "Me canna feel a thing in 'em," he whimpered. "Pray to God for wind, sir."

"Aye," said the Captain, "I have."

They had another dinner of tinned meat and breadcakes. "I think but whut I want is shepherd's pie," said

Fielding, swallowing with difficulty the salty beef. "And duff pudding with raisins."

"Aw, shut up," said Hayward, "or you'll have my boot in your mouth for supper."

"Ye ain't got no boot."

The little wind they had fell off and the men opted once more to pull out their oars, the Captain steering. The little boat surged forward in steady strokes and time lost all meaning as they rowed on. Johnny gave out, asleep over his oar, feet wrapped in Emily's damp skirts. The sun slid low, and then, just as she winked out, the sails ruffled. A breeze? In came the oars. Emily disentangled herself from the boy, heart wrenching to hear him cry, to give each weary man a tablespoon of rum. They passed around the pipe one more time, and then baling out the boat bottom, lay down to get what sleep they could, Johnny tucked between them, while the sails did the work, a fourth night.

"Who's crowdin' the tarp?"

"I ain't got even a corner."

"Wake me when it's me turn at the till."

Emily couldn't sleep. The tiny candles needed constant attention. Her head burned. She found that her husband didn't sleep either, but sat in his place at the stern, talking nonstop to the man at the tiller to keep him awake. As night wore on it became a dismal test of endurance as she lay in silent misery, measuring its passing only by the shift of men at the tiller, lurching to the stern.

Friday morning the Captain tried over and over to rouse the men, but they were unwilling to move. All groaned and hunched in. Johnny cried. The Captain tried to crawl over them, concerned particularly with the boy in the bow, and when he had the child up he found the boy couldn't make sense of where he was. "Oates, be up," urged Richard. "Hayward. Fielding. Here, Johnny, you are to fold the tarpaulin, and when you have it done, a biscuit. Fielding, stand on the seat. See if you can't spot any ships or land."

This roused some degree of interest. Hand to the mast, spy-glass to his eye, Fielding stretched his neck. But nothing. He sat back dejected, looking quite freakish with his scarred face, and Emily hastened to pour some tea to cheer them all.

All day the Captain called on Fielding to take a look. Each time the gangly youth sat back looking more dejected and more wretched: nothing in sight but sea and sky. Emily strained her eyes to see what he missed; a ship on the horizon? The endless ocean, mixed with the sun's bright rays, presented to her view a yellow gloom where every cloud bespoke a sail. But then from her tired eyes the object would blink from view and leave her as dejected and wretched as Fielding.

Oates and Steward were the more lively, haggling turns on the pipe. The tobacco was so wet that no sooner would Emily give Steward the candle to light it than he would have two comfortable puffs and it would go out again, with Oates in the bow arguing with jealous eyes for his turn.

"Gi'e it to me!" he would declare, able to bear no more. "Ye always get the best 'o it, Jack!"

Steward would slowly pull it from his mouth and slowly hand it over, but before giving it up, snatch it back quick for another whiff.

"Blarney," Oates would fuss the moment he would get it, "ye let it go oot," and he would have to crawl over everyone to Emily to have it lit again—Steward, of course, following with watchful eyes the whole way, ready to move in the moment it was done.

By night Johnny was delirious with cold, and could only moan. "You better put him in with me," said Emily, "if someone can stay awake with the candles."

But she could only bear an hour or two; he was so brutally cold and the space so crowded that they couldn't twist to restore circulation to their deadened limbs. She tried leaving him inside, wrapped in her blanket and rug while she sat outside with the men, curled between her husband's legs, head on his knee, but the boy cried behind the wall. At last the Captain pulled the boy out and laid him between Hayward and Fielding on the wet floor of the boat. "Keep him between you," he said. He's like to freeze if you don't."

"Richard, my blanket and rug. See if they help the poor child," Emily whispered, handing them out, and when they were gone from her she curled up as best she could on the bare thwarts to endure the rest of the icy night, chin shivering into her chest without stop.

Saturday's mist did not burn off until noon, the day colder, if possible, and the wind nothing more than short gusts of icy air to send them miserably forward in short bursts. It wasn't until noon and the sun out that the men expressed any interest in trying to better their condition. Even then they were listless, hardly able to do more than haphazardly stretch out their jackets to dry, shivering wretchedly with a wild, wolfish look in their eyes, and a fevered glimmer. Johnny lay down as if dead on his stomach across a boat seat, arms and legs dangling loose, not even drawing them up when bumped.

"Would you like water?" Emily asked him.

"It's all gone," said Steward.

"Tea then, Johnny?"

Only his eyes answered, following her every movement between his fingers. "Captain," she said, "we must make him drink. Johnny, you have a little tea and I'll hold your feet for you." But he screamed when she touched them. In desperation she started tearing off her own boots.

Hayward stopped her. "No, Missus, your boots will only fill with water. He'll be no better off."

"He's right," said the Captain. "Johnny? Sit here, that's a boy. Now put your feet in my lap."

Sunday morning the men refused to move out from under the mud-caked tarpaulin. "Hayward," the Captain argued over and over, himself so weak there was little punch in his voice. "Hayward, you must come out and relieve Fielding. He has fallen asleep and we are way off course. You must rouse yourself and let him have your place. Hayward? Hayward!"

Finally they all pulled up and the boat was set back on course, and Emily served the men tea and some meager bread, mildewed now. Being Sunday, the Captain, his voice oddly weak and tremorous, read from Emily's ragged Bible. *"The Lord is my shepherd, I shall not want—"*

"Read somethin' else," Oates pleaded. "Ye only read that when a' body is deein.'"

"We are dying," said Hayward glumly. "Didn't the Captain tell us we'd see land by Saturday? Maybe we shot past it."

"Emily," said Richard, turning the Bible's pages, "you're missing half the Psalms. Never mind," he said weakly. "Here is what I want. Hayward, a little patience, and steady on. Listen. *Hungry and thirsty, their soul fainted in them. Then they cried unto the Lord in their trouble, and he delivered them out of their distresses. He led them forth by the right way, that they might go to a city of habitation. . . . He maketh the storm a calm, so that the waves thereof are still. Then are they glad. . . . He bringeth them unto their desired haven."*

He led in prayer and each man was quick to say amen.

At noon Richard took out the quadrant. Everyone held quiet while he squinted at the sun and studied his chart, then made his figures. "Fielding, another look. We should come to land soon." But there was no sighting of land.

They had dinner, more moldy breadcakes and more beef. A stiff wind picked up, and they were relieved to cut swiftly through the water, but presently the sea began to churn so disagreeably that the boat began to bounce and to jump. "Sail's hauling too close to the wind," said Steward anxiously.

"Mainsheet is chafed," said the Captain, inspecting where it passed through the block. "Hayward, see if you can't splice it. Fielding? Another look. Nothing you say?"

A half-hour later he asked again. "Fielding. Stretch your neck and give us a report." But Fielding sat down more despondent than ever. The Captain kept his hand on the tiller, his voice steady. "I am *sure* we are nearing land. Oates, take the tiller."

He crawled up to the bow and stood into the wind, knees braced against the short seat. They *had* to be near land, they just *had* to be. Or had he totally miscalculated? The thought was too dreadful to bear and he discarded it immediately, leaning into the wind. And then he smelled it, not the salt, not the seaweed, but something sweet. Another full breath and he was sure—the tussock grass! The Falklands *were* just ahead! They were nearing the south coast of the east island! He had done it! He had brought them in! He took the tiller again, saying nothing, his faith and resolve, aye, and his expertise, validated. "Hayward," he said in half an hour. "Tell me, what lies ahead?"

Hayward put up the spyglass. "Aye, it's land!"

"LAND!"

"But it's a far piece off," qualified Hayward.

Before dusk they all saw the land, a rise of gray unfolding into a formidable array of cliff faces cut through with beaches made of blinding white sand. Beyond the beaches a band of rich, green tussock grass, six feet high, blew into the wind, feeding off the salt spray. And beyond the band of grass were sweeping hills of deeper greens, and then reds and ochers and grays of all shade. Inlets beckoned as they passed, evoking mystery and intrigue and wonder, and all through the evening they sailed alongside the comforting bluffs, and as dark came on hope again beat in their hearts, wildly so. Seven days on open sea, and they had come through. They only had to hang on until they came to the far end of the land, to Stanley's Harbor—and then home.

At daylight on Monday morning, their eighth day, they passed Beuchene Island, one of the many offshore islands, breathtaking in its pastoral breadth and its contrasting jagged rocks, layers of stones smashed together and yet rising high and sharp along beaches aclutter with penguins and albatrosses and seals. Emily pulled out the bread bag for breakfast, rummaging thoroughly now about the bottom. Empty. "Never mind," she said, and dumped the last of the crumbs over the side. "We still have meat and tea. And tonight we shall have bread and milk!" A smile from everyone but Johnny.

"Steward," said the Captain. "Get some meat into the boy. Then wrap him *with* you in your coat. Mine is too wet to do the lad any good."

All morning they sailed on, Steward bouncing the boy on his knee, shaking warmth into his bones, rubbing his feet despite his cries. "See here?" he would say, and point from the Captain's small navigational chart to the land alongside them. "*Rincon de los Indios?* Do you see it, boy? No? Then Cape Bougainville? And here, Black Point!" Wineglass Hill, Macbride Head, Eagle Hill. One by one they passed the various points, spirits picking up. Every hour brought them closer to their journey's end.

At noon Fielding sighted the Stanley lighthouse through the spyglass. How grand it is! thought Emily, taking her turn. Such broad bands of white and black! And to think! They only had to round the ragged reef and move up the wide inlet of Port William, and then drop into Stanley Harbor! Could it be? Could it be they were nearly home? "Look, Johnny," she cried, trying to stir the lethargic boy. "Look! There be the lighthouse! We be nearly there!"

But the wind altered, and the long day passed before reaching it, a flashing beacon of three paraffin lamps powered by a revolving clockwork system, drawing them steadily onward and through the coming dusk. They edged closer in for a better look: The lone stone pillar sat atop the high point of a sand-dune-covered cape.

"Plummy," exclaimed Oates, "but it looke like o' lamp to guard o' Scottish sea loch!"

The strong light flashed across face and boat and sail, and Emily poked her head out the door of her damp hole. A blot on the beach arrested her attention. "A cow! Or is it a house?"

Steward laughed. "Make up your mind, Missus!"

"A *man*! There be a man coming down the beach!" The boat nearly tipped in their ache to see.

"Lower the sail!" shouted the Captain. "Perhaps we can put in here instead of going around the Point! Hail!" he called to the figure. "Crew of the *Maid* in dire distress!"

The man waved from shore a hundred yards distant, voice muffled by the pounding surf.

"Hail! Crew of the *Maid*—"

"He can't hear you, Old Man!" shouted Steward.

"CREW OF THE *MAID* OF LONDON IN DIRE DISTRESS!"

"He motions for us to come in!" cried Hayward, oar in the sea.

"To your posts then, men, we're going in!"

"No!" wailed Emily, seeing the dreadful rush of black waves, far worse than any they'd had at Staten Island. "We'll never make it! Please, no! We shall all be dashed to pieces! The boy! He cannot do it! And you be all too weary! Please, Captain, please, go around and into the Harbor as we planned!"

"But it's night," he argued, not knowing what other

choice they had, "we cannot live another night out here. The boy—"

"Old Man," interrupted Steward, "we won't be out here all night. We're nearly there, only a little while more. And the Missus is right. We have no strength. We'll not make that surf."

Richard wearily sighed. "Aye, you're right. I was just anxious to put in. Very well, men," he said, "pull hard up, men. We're going round the Point."

The sea grew choppy as they put back to sea—to skirt the treacherous rocks that laced the Point and of which the lighthouse warned to steer clear. Emily scrunched in beside her husband, eyes transfixed on the flashing glare of the mighty lighthouse as they rounded the throne of ragged rocks. Up went the sail, in came the oars. Oh how long, she wondered with an ache, before reaching the Harbor? Surely, surely, the man at the lighthouse would send word around to Stanley Harbor that a ship-wrecked crew was coming in. *Surely* he would, and in just a few moments they would be safe. Suddenly the flashing beacon was gone. Just a few flashes of light blinked on the water behind them, and then that too was gone, and they were left in night as black as pitch, moon hidden by cloudbank. Only feeble starlight and the pinpricks of light flickering from their lamp gave them any sense of space. They could hardly see beyond the reach of their hands.

"Look out for Wolf Rock," warned the Captain. "It should be coming up soon. Steward, best light your flares, for we won't see a thing in this witch's stew!"

The flare blazed, a wild start of light, and in a gasp they saw the rock, and even as the Captain screamed "Hard up the tiller! Reef the sail!" he was leaping, plunging up over everyone to get to the bow, to push off, to ward off the collision.

"Nay!" cried Steward, leaping too, yanking the Captain back by a jerk on his coat collar, knocking him backward and plunging fore himself. "An oar!" he screamed, standing and bracing himself in the Captain's place, reaching back for the oar. "Give me an oar! An oar!"

"Hard up! Hard up!" cried Richard, scrambling to pull on the halyards. Oates threw round the tiller, the boat veered starboard.

Steward teetered, caught his balance. *An oar!* But it was too late. The keel nudged hidden granite, the boat tipped. Steward spun backwards. In slow motion Emily saw it all. His foot caught behind a crate, crashing down, canvas bulwark splintered, head against the gunwale, back arching up, feet flying, fast twist. In an instant Steward was gone.

26

Steward came up in a dead man's float. "Aye, I got him!" cried Hayward, reaching through the break in the bulwark. He grabbed Steward's coat collar and pulled up with a groan. Fielding and Oates rushed to get hold of arms and legs as the flare burned itself out. Emily lit another blinding flare, and quickly, shivering, everyone hauled Steward in, dead weight that flopped out of grasp.

"Oates! Man the tiller! Fielding, unfurl and make sail for the opening to Stanley!"

"I don't know where it is! I can't see a bloody thing!"

Richard rolled Steward over and pushed on his back. Water gushed out. Another push, another. Steward choked. " He's breathing! Quick, make room! Steward? Steward? Can you hear me?" the Captain raged, bent over the still form, his own face white with shock. "Oh, Steward, you shouldn't have done it. . . ." But the man was unconscious, and blood drained out nose and mouth and ears.

"Sir, the wind is gone."

Steward's breathing quickly became belabored, painful to hear, low rattles of blood gurgling in his throat. Emily crawled forward, moaning. He had deliberately put himself in front of the Captain. Why? Why had he done it?

"Old Man." Again Hayward, trying to tell there was no wind.

"*Keep* tacking!" shouted Richard. "And get out the oars! The man at the beach will have sent word we're coming in! We'll soon have help! Johnny? Help us, lad. We must get him warm and dry. Emily, feel for broken bones."

"Will he die?" Johnny asked, his dulled wits brutally sharpened by fright. "Will he die?"

"Emily, your blankets." She already had them, but they were too damp to be much good, and the Captain, seeing them, began stripping off his own clothes. "Oates!" he cried, handing over shirt and pants, "get Steward into these! Quick! Emily? Cover him with my coat! Row, Fielding! *Row!*"

Emily put her husband's coat over the man who had deliberately put himself between boat and rock, deliberately laying down his life for the Captain. Why? Why had he done it?

"Will he die?" Johnny asked again.

"I pray to God not," said Richard, teeth chattering and struggling to pull on Steward's icy trousers.

Fifteen minutes separated them from Wolf Rock and the harbor, but they couldn't bridge the gap. The wind was too weak to sail, the men too weak to row, and the tide was sweeping out. Not that they didn't try. "Stand by to come about!" Again and again, spurred by the sight of Steward's unconscious body, they tried; to port, to starboard, tacking back and forth in search of even a pocket of wind, oars splashing the water clumsily. Then seaweed tangled in their rudder. The rudder lifted off. They rowed in circles. The shoreline, dimly etched in starlight, taunted, wavering close and then slipping away. *Where was the opening to Stanley Harbor?* They put Johnny whimpering in beside Steward, that they might warm each other. Emily sat with them, rubbing their limbs, rotating arm for leg. Exhausted, hardly able to even focus on the shadowed faces around her, she kept at it until she would fall forward, asleep herself, waking mid-descent. A deep breath and she would begin again, fevered head pounding.

Hours passed as they rowed in useless circles, the night growing colder and darker, shoreline gone from sight, yet hauntingly near.

"Why don't someone come?" Fielding despaired.

"Kin a body," said Oates, begging, "have a wee dram?"

"The rum be gone," Emily whispered sadly. "But I can give you some brandy."

"Have the brandy," said the Captain from the tiller, "and then we'll bring out the oars again."

But the men had no strength. They couldn't pull and to Emily it seemed that time truly had at last stopped. Why had not the man from the lighthouse sent word? Why did they slip back and forth so close to land, so close to help? A bitter, cruel twist to their fate.

"I canna do no more," said Oates. The others silently agreed: Their oars rested on the gunwales, water dripping off the blades. Waves slapped the bow. On the sea they rocked.

"Have a rest, then," said the Captain gently, "and then we'll carry on. Don't give up yet. We must keep trying."

"No," moaned Fielding. "I am bitter cold, sir."

"We will sing, then, to keep warm," said the Captain. But the men had no breath. And their teeth chattered uncontrollably, ice thick in their beards. Hayward, bent over himself, mumbled something about his mother, and then clearly, "We'll be dead by morning. Steward first, then us."

"Perhaps, Captain," whispered Emily in the dark, reaching for him, "we should have put in at the lighthouse, when we had the chance? Sargent, I think, be right—I always be telling you what to do."

"*Sargent?* Even here the miserable man follows us? Nay, if we put in at the lighthouse we could all be dead right now."

"Oh, Captain," whispered Emily, "if we are to die, I be glad to die *with* you."

"*The Lord is my Shepherd*," Oates began to recite, "*A canna want—*"

"We are not dead yet, Oates," snapped Richard suddenly, done with their sorry misery and his own. Corralling what strength he had left, he said, "God would not bring us this far just to leave us. A little faith, men. Put in your oars." He had just dropped in a blade when a shot rang, an explosive bullet in the sky. Shivers ripped up their spines and their heads swiveled to meet the sky as a spray of fire whistled, and as the whole of heaven lit! Light poured and flashed again, crimson, golden, white, red!

"A rocket!" cried Oates, disbelief popping from his eyes. Another, and another! Shoreline leaped into view. Whizz! Whistle-whizz! Another and another, and to the west, lit in bursts, the narrow opening between two low hills, entrance to Port Stanley!

"Dear God, we have been saved!" cried the Captain. "They are showing us the way in! The man at the lighthouse *did* send word! Quick men, quick! Make all haste while we may yet see our way!"

Their oars *sliced* the water! Dip, pull, surge! Dip, pull, surge! Another rocket! Dip, pull, surge! Another and another, over and over the rockets flared, bursting in the air, red light bleeding to white, white streaking the sky, illuminating the narrow channel, closer, closer: and they were passing through!

Emily bent over Steward. His eyes were open, focused on her face in a glassy stare. "Oh, Steward!" she breathed, smiling, taking his hand in hers. So cold, so icy cold. "We be here at last! And you be awake to see it now!"

He tried to speak, but choked on the blood. She lifted his head to clear the passage. All around the rockets whistled. " *'It was the best of times,'* " he murmured, " *'it was the worst of times. . . .'* "

"Oh, Steward," she moaned, "I didn't think you liked Dickens."

"Yo! What is *that*?" whistled Fielding, taking off his cap, agog at the dark rise of a ship's hull just inside the harbor's entrance. Another rocket and he read out loud from the counter, "*Pleiades*. Yo, ho! One of Her Majesty's men-of-war!"

"Shall we put in for the ship then?" asked Hayward, "or shoot for shore?"

"Oh, Steward, look! We be home! Home!" Emily cried.

" *'It is a far, far better thing that I do, than I have ever done. It is a far, far better rest that I go to—'* "

"No, Steward! No! You are not going to die! Do you hear me? You are not going to die! Not for me! Not for the Captain! Steward! *You are not Sydney Carton that you must die for either of us!* Oh, Steward! We be nearly there! Hang on, they have—"

" *'. . . a far better rest that I go to . . .'* " His voice sank to a whisper and Emily herself could have finished the last line of the *Tale of Two Cities*. " *'. . . a far better rest that I go to than I have ever known.'* "

"Sir!" cried Hayward again. "Sir! I say, shall we put in to the ship? Or shoot for shore?"

Steward? She threw her hand to his chest. "Steward!" she screamed. "Oh, Steward, oh my dear Steward," she cried and pulled him into her arms, rocking him cumbersomely, arms around his neck, head bent low over his. "Oh, Steward, we be here, we be here, we have made it. We be in the shadow of an English man-of-war. It be over. Do you hear them? Do you hear them sing aboard ship? They be singing the anthem! Listen! No?" and she started to sing brokenly for him "God Save the Queen."

"*Sir! Ship* or *shore?*" badgered Hayward, then saw the arrested gaze of the Captain and fell silent.

"Is he dead?" the Captain asked in the eerie sound of majestic song wafting through the night from the man-of-war.

"Nay, darling, he be hanging on. But, darling, we must hurry."

"We'll go into shore," said Hayward softly, and the men fell to, praying each one of them for strength they didn't have. Slowly, slowly, out of the clinging, murderous sea they rowed, slowly, slowly they skirted past the man-of-war and into the arms of an all-but-land-locked bay. Slowly, slowly and now silently they slid toward a distant, beckoning light. Slowly a stone jetty emerged from the dark. More slowly still the dark frame of a hulk loomed into view. Without strength they floated, without strength they butted the stone, a scraping, a crash and a bounce, and without strength they lost the oars from their hands, a quiet, clear splash.

27

Walking along Ross Road we observe a public house on the left. . . . The church, on a raised space by itself, comes next. Beyond the church are a few wooden houses, then comes the private house of Mr. Dean, the storekeeper, banker, agent, etc., then his store; next another wooden house. . . .

—Parker Snow, Captain
of *Allen Gardner*, circa 1880

"Yo! Who goes there?" Lanterns swung over the rails of the hulk tied to the jetty, and shouts of surprise shot across the stone, and more questions. Figures leaped off the open boat. Lanterns bobbed in their hands and light swung over the stunned and disbelieving group in the patchwork boat. Emily and the others could only blink in dismay. Uniformed soldiers running to greet them could only fall back, struck dumb by what they saw.

"Captain Wooldridge," mumbled Richard finally, at the mast, unable to pull himself out of the boat or to even cordially offer his frozen hand to a tall and imposing figure in the flickering shadows who introduced himself as Lieutenant Robinson of the Her Majesty's Imperial Navy. "We have a sick man," Richard mumbled, desperate suddenly that all should be lost even now; he could not believe this illusion of extended hands and anxious faces, the thick scent of kerosene heavy in the air. "And a boy," he whispered, "and a woman too."

For a moment complete and painful confusion reigned. Then orders were barked in crisp British staccato. Boots pounded in the night, receding and approaching, and the next thing Emily knew men in uniform were gently lifting Steward onto a stretcher, giving her no time to adjust to the swiftness of sudden time, carrying him off at a run into the night. Someone took hold of Johnny: He could not put weight on his feet. The Captain, mumbling shipwreck and 500 miles and three left, allowed two men to ease him onto the jetty, where he staggered, reeling down the stone parapet. He came back for Emily, but could not lift her from the boat. Nor could she lift herself. Two rushed to help, yet even with their support, one on either side, she too reeled and staggered, legs too weak, too wobbly to support any weight. *I be a puppet, whose strings have tangled!* Helplessly she tripped over her own wooden limbs.

Where be the Captain? The others? she wondered in her wooden daze, suddenly very disoriented and quite frightened by the lanterns and polka dots of light dancing dizzily on the ground as men swarmed busy as bees, and as noisy. Aye, there be the Captain! Just ahead and leaning on the arm of a soldier, and looking back to see that she followed. Hayward and Oates and Fielding came alongside, each submissive as well to supporting arms. She took a small step, and another, held by the strangers at her side. *Nay, I not be a puppet*, she thought, pain ricocheting through her body as blood began to move, and so gritting her teeth to face the pain, and tucking her chin to hide the pain, she too allowed herself to be led along, slowly passing off the jetty and onto a cobbled path, circling up and around to a low, open road.

The road stretched straight ahead, water on one side, buildings on the other. A house or two, with dark empty windows, stood to the right. More buildings, to the right, in the distant darkness. Suddenly, to the right, short white picket fences like those from home, making tiny, separate yards along the front of a long, low stone building, and when she looked up, mystified, as if in a dream (for nothing seemed real), she saw a sign, EAGLE HOTEL, stuck up off a roof eave—directly over a peaked, tiny foyer which poked from the front wall to shelter a front door.

"Eagle Hotel," she whispered, voice catching as she stared, then stumbled, still staring, through a picket gate to gather with everyone else before a heavy, oak door. *They had made it?*

Torches and lamps lit the facade of the hotel, etching stone and glass in shimmering shadow. Someone knocked.

"Where is everyone?" another asked, perhaps Hayward.

"Mr. Goss, the keeper, is no doubt still at the ball," said one of the soldiers in the yard with them, eyes shifting in light of the lanterns to another man in uniform. "The whole town is at the ball in honor," he explained, "of the new Governor. Did you see our rockets? We just put the incumbent governor on the *Pleiades*. Set off 30 rockets and sang a song to bid him fond farewell. His man-of-war will set sail for London in a couple of hours. But here I'm gabbing and you need hot soup and a bed." He lifted his hand to knock again but the Captain restrained him.

"Those rockets? You mean to say . . . they weren't for us? To show us the way? A man from your lighthouse? He didn't let you know we were coming in?"

"There's been a change in governors," the soldier explained again. Suddenly, and with a dark glance to the bay and back to the Captain, he said, "My God, you're lucky, sir. You could still be out there."

The Captain sank against the doorpost. In the stark light Emily saw his drooping, leaning posture, his clothes in shreds, his voice so low and so weak, and suddenly, with realization, she too felt faint. The rockets had not been for them? Their death had been snatched from them by luck? "Oh, please," she said, giddy, "where have they taken Steward?" The ground came up even as she thought, *we'd all be dead but for hand of Providence,* and she gave way to the rising ground, falling into its silent, soft embrace.

The Falkland Islands in 1870 were a strategic outpost of British rule, the headquarters of the great whaling and sealing trade that dominated the South Atlantic Sea. Port Stanley, with its small, almost landlocked bay at the east tip of the east island, was the capital. On the one end of the harbor, the west shore, was the Government House and stone jetty. The east end housed the Falkland Islands Company Store and Fleet. The only street in town, Ross Road, stretched east to west for two miles along the elongated south shore, running a connection between the two places, and all along this one and only road, and all lined up to face the sea, on just the one side, the far side, were white clapboard and stone houses with brightly painted tin roofs—and Mr. Dean's store, Dr. Hamblin's flower garden, and Eagle Hotel, Surgery in the back. Midway, and focal point of the town from any direction, was a rise in the ground upon which rested the large stone and red brick Holy Trinity Church—without steeple but with its own shiny red tin roof. And scattered across the only road, up and down the shore itself, were docks and wharfs, public and private, stone and wood.

The people of this tiny and picturesque port were of sturdy stock, homespun whalers and sealers and company workers, as well as government employees, pensioners, and navymen. What united them all, a hundred souls, was a curious combination of adventure, an unexplained challenge to recreate merrie olde England so far from home, and an avowed dedication to the survival of many a shipwreck victim. Together they made Port Stanley a haven from hell, particularly for an Englishman, and of this, at least, Emily knew the moment she woke, for the fall flowers of England rested by her head, a burst of orange and red and russet and yellow, a brilliant bouquet of dahlias.

I am with Englishmen, she thought with slow awareness and sudden relief, focusing on the bright color of the flowers. I am safe. I am alive. Her eyes wandered to the ceiling. White. Four corners. Yellow walls. Sunlight filtered through gauze curtains, a soft and airy light, and when she turned her head there be her husband, asleep in the bed beside her, one arm thrown up under his head, the other resting, as always, across her chest. She felt the weight of it now, her body strangely light and without substance atop a soft mattress, his arm the only thing that seemed real and to be a part of her. She closed her eyes again, to sleep again, and was just drifting off when she smelled the dampness and felt the biting wind whip through the tent. She started up, heart hammering. Nay, there be no tent. She be in a room, a pretty yellow bed chamber. And she sat dumbfounded. *How did I get here?*

Much she remembered, much seemed uncertain. She remembered Steward certainly, being rushed away. *Was he alive?* Instantly the anguish of their ordeal rushed in, anguish that belied reality—and she sat dazed, batted between fantasy, fear, and what was. Did she trust this bed? The clean sheets and this strange gown she wore? The soft sunlight? The pretty yellow walls? But there be the flowers, sweet with scent.

Very carefully, so not as to disturb her husband, she slipped from the bed, suddenly aware of the pain in her feet as they sank into thick, soft carpet. Could this be? To know such pain and such comfort at once?

An oak washstand stood near the bed, with a pitcher of water and bowl, and mirror. She could not reach it for the trembling that had taken hold of her limbs, and she had to first take hold of the bed table where the flowers

sat, and then the wall. She nearly fell when she stood
before the mirror, the image staring back giving her such
a start. But it wasn't her—it couldn't be—and she leaned
in again for closer inspection.

So who be this . . . person? Was it even human? This
wolfish apparition that stared with great, wild eyes from
a bony, tight face. Who was this "thing" with brown,
sunken skin? Whose tangled hair hung like strings of fur
and twine? Slowly she raised her hand to touch her own
face, shocked to see echoing movement in the glass
before her, and tenderly, oh so tenderly, she ran her
shaking fingers over the thin, fresh scar beneath her eye,
weeping to see tears, her tears, run off the face that was
not her own.

"Emily?" The Captain's voice, weak and hoarse, brought
her back to herself. "Come back to bed, for a few minutes," he said, almost weeping. "Until I can move."

They lay side by side, hand in hand, listening to unusual sounds: a door shutting, a cat meowing, somewhere a clock bonging. "I have to go back," he said at
last, staring with her at the flat white ceiling with the
four squared corners.

"Who brought us here? Where are we?" she answered,
unwilling to think of him going back out. Not now, not
ever.

"Emily?" he asked suddenly, still staring at the ceiling. "Did Steward do what he did . . . for me? Or for
you?"

She turned to face him, to lay her hand on his chest.
"Do you remember *A Tale of Two Cities*? How Sydney
Carton chose to die at the guillotine for Darnay? Because
he loved Lucie?"

"He *loves* you?"

"Steward did what he did for us both."

"He loves you?"

"He loves us both."

They bathed, carefully, for they both trembled, using the towels and soap put out for them, and while dressing, donning the clothes laid for them on the hassock, he explained to her where they were and how they'd gotten there and where everyone else was. The men and the boy were at a Boarding House. Steward was at the Surgery, behind the Inn.

"If this Mr. Dean carried me to his house, who took my clothes? *Where be my stone for Catherine?*" she asked in sudden panic.

"It's right here, darling."

"Did Mrs. Dean put me in this nightdress?"

"I did."

"Thank you."

There were two new suits for Richard, and a pair of boots, government issue, he explained, for all "distressed British subjects." For Emily there was a royal rose silk dress, with long sleeves and high collar, with stays and bustle and a short line of pearl buttons from chin to chest. "But wherever did this come from?" she exclaimed in sudden happiness.

"Mr. Dean owns the town mercantile. I told him last night to pick out his finest. He has, I see, very good taste. You look beautiful, darling."

"No I don't." She dropped the dress. "I look worse than an animal."

He gave her a tremorous kiss. "I'll go down now. While I'm gone you can tend your hair. See here, here is a pretty brush and comb. Emily, don't cry. I'll come back and get you. But right now I must find Steward and see how he is."

She was just buttoning her dress and straightening the handsome bustle when there was a quiet knock on the door. "Aye," she said, and the door opened to reveal a pleasant, portly woman.

"I am Mrs. Dean. Oh my dear, excuse me," she said, for Emily stared. "Are you all right?"

"Yes, yes. Aye, but it's been months since I've seen a woman. I'm sorry for staring."

Mrs. Dean smiled kindly. "I just came to see if you have everything you need, and to ask if you'd like your egg boiled or poached."

"Poached. Please," said Emily, almost too stunned to speak. Eggs? There be eggs here? To eat?

"Is there anything I can do for you?" Mrs. Dean asked again, eyes tender and full of concern.

"Yes, yes," said Emily, starting to cry. "Will you, will you help me wash my hair?"

Downstairs in Mrs. Dean's bright and cheery kitchen, her hair washed and brushed, her face bathed and softened with cream, Emily asked where her husband was.

"To the Government House, with Mr. Dean, to see the new Governor and Lieutenant Robinson about taking out the *Foam* and going after the rest of your crew. And to stop at the Surgery, to see your Steward."

"And do you know how Steward be?"

"Dr. Hamblin says he'll live. Mrs. Wooldridge, would you like a spot of tea?"

Emily held the china teacup in both hands and couldn't drink, overwhelmed by the very ordinariness of English life so startlingly sudden back in her life. China, real china. Tea without salt. Without mildew, without brine. English breakfast tea. And pretty silver and carrot cake on the sideboard and a brown betty teapot with a chipped spout sitting atop the icebox. The linen tablecloth? And pastries cooking? Sausage meat? Eggs? Her mouth watered to taste it all, but her stomach cramped to think of putting such rich food in so long an empty stomach. "If you please," she said, "just a piece of toast. I don't think I can eat anything else. No, no marmalade. Thank you."

She watched in silence as the kind woman she only knew as Mrs. Dean bustled about her bright, cheery kitchen, rubbing flour from her hands to a real linen apron. Outside, a low sloping hill of little vegetation, a tundra landscape, appeared to be quite the contrast to the little bit of England inside. Goodness, was that snow?

"More toast?" Mrs. Dean asked.

"Yes, yes, please. We've been living off flour fried in penguin oil," she said, going back to Staten Island too quickly.

"Well, you can eat all the bread you want, and butter. I have my own cow and make my own." Suddenly Mrs. Dean sat down across the table from her. "I'm sorry," she whispered. "I'm sorry you've been through so much. You and your husband are quite remarkable to have come through. An uncommon feat, I'm told."

"My husband is a determined man, Mrs. Dean."

"Another cup of tea?"

The men came in, Mr. Dean blowing off the light dusting of snow from his cap and whistling on the cold, the Captain wincing with pain. He fell weakly into the chair beside her, happy to see her. "Steward is conscious. He's asking for you," he said, and then made the introductions to Mr. Dean, who took her hand, a very dashing and very British gentleman in tweed.

⚓

For Emily the Captain's absence was endless bittersweet days. Sweet because Steward regained strength daily, coming back to her no worse for the wear except for the same trembling weakness that plagued them all—and a few fainting spells and a numbness in his left leg. Sweet too because the Stanley ladies took turns inviting her to tea each afternoon and to spend the night in their homes. But bitter because the Captain was gone.

He'd left against Dr. Hamblin's advice. Weak, trembling, with feet so badly frostbitten that Dr. Hamblin worried about gangrene, what further suffering, she wondered, did he endure in the growing cold? Did his rheumatism, her real fear, return? And Lieutenant Robinson? And this Captain Smyley whom the islanders swore could find anything and anyone in these seas? Would they find Harris and the others all right? *Would they bring the Captain back to her?*

The long, lonely nights preyed on her nerves. The hollow darkness of unfamiliar rooms, closeted with strange smells and shadows, and an empty bed. She imagined the worst, and these nights became something to dread. She would wake, frightened, and with a start jump straight up in a foreign bed in a foreign room, trembling in every limb and wet with sweat. Back she would have to lie, alone, frostbitten feet giving her sharp pains, sharp enough to make her cry into the pillow and to feel despair, for she could never remember what had frightened her—except that the Captain was gone.

Thus the bittersweet days passed: Thursday, Friday, Saturday. On Sunday the Stanley ladies invited her to church. Dr. Hamblin and his wife greeted her in the foyer, carrying Johnny, for he still couldn't put weight on his badly frostbitten feet. Hayward was there with Steward, stronger than even last night. Oates and Fielding arrived. They all stood uncertain, eyeing one another, so strange was this hallowed surrounding compared to what they had been through. Mrs. Dean rescued them from themselves and herded them down a wooden aisle, chin indicating pews to fold into.

So Sunday passed, and then Monday, days more bitter than sweet as they passed. "Come for a walk, Steward," Emily said late Tuesday afternoon. They had just finished tea in the Surgery—not that Steward still required the doctor's attention, but he stayed on to be with Johnny, whose toes daily deteriorated. "The boy," said Steward. "He sleeps, but what if he wakes and we're gone?"

"He has the toy soldiers the Captain bought him."

"Are you up to this? It's blowing hard, and there's ice in the wind."

"We can bundle up, and we need not go far. And we can, I suppose, help each other along."

"I expect we can."

They took the road west, into the wind and past all the cottages, waving to Mrs. Hover at her clothesline, clothes snapping, waving again to the children playing outside the school wing of the church, and then to Widow Martha coming out of Mr. Dean's store, all of it so very ordinary and therefore extraordinary.

"Were we ever shipwrecked, Steward?" Emily asked. "How is it we be here, and not there? Time and place be such an odd thing."

"You be coomin' to my house tonight, will ye?" called Widow Martha, and when Emily nodded, the old woman pointed to the clapboard cottage which was hers. They passed Mr. Murray in the back of his Boarding House at the muddy end of the long road.

"Where you headed?" he asked, looking up from his tub, where he boiled clean the sheets, the strong smell of lye thick in the icy air. "Ain't nuthin' up there but the cemetery. Mostly a shipwrecked sailor up there," he added, "who managed to make it in, only to die."

They had to pass through a stand of tussock grass, entering a different world: outside blustery and cold, inside calm and warm. "We better not get lost," said Steward, pushing aside the tall, thick, rattling weed that clapped overhead.

They didn't. Coming out the other side was a weather-beaten plank swinging in the wind between two iron pillars, announcing with a bony clatter where they were. CEMETERY CHAPEL.

Maybe 30 wooden crosses and stone pillars marked the high bluff of land. The bluff itself was riddled with dwarf diddle-dee and teaberry shrubs. The sound of surf smashing stone far below and out of sight bled the fence of diddle-dee to thrum their eardrums, or was it the wind, redoubling in caverns and caves along the cliff, now tossing tussock grass in rattled rhythms behind them?

The crosses and tombstones, many of them, were broken and toppling, weatherworn and rotting. Some, strangely, were burnt, as if someone irreverently had used them to back a fire. The largest cross was Emily's height, tipped to the north, and was once painted white but was now blistered and crawling with ants. She watched them awhile before moving on, trying to read the faded names of unknown sailors who had made it into harbor only to die. "It could be our names we look for," she said quite solemnly, struck by the truth. And then facing Steward, she said, "Steward. I didn't know you loved me."

His gray eyes regarded her quietly. "I didn't know you knew."

"You don't remember the accident? Wolf Rock? And Dickens?" she asked to each shake of his head. "You don't remember pulling back the Captain, and taking his place at the bow?"

"Aye, I remember that." They stood on the crest of the hill, wind in their hair, in Emily's rose skirts and new woolen cape, in his brand-new corduroys, government issue. Crosses leaned between them.

"You deliberately put yourself in way of danger for the Captain. And when you were dying you whispered the first and last lines of A Tale of Two Cities."

"A poet, then, when I'm hit upside the head?" he said with a slow smile in his eyes.

She turned her back, not sure what to say, or how to thank him, or how to understand any of this.

"There is no need to talk of this, Emily. You'd never have known. Let's leave it that way."

"Steward? Why did you do it?"

"Do you have to ask? For him, for you. Let's go back. I'm tired." He led her back into through the tussock, leaving behind the tombstones.

"You would die, Steward, for the Captain?"

"Aye, but I would live, too, for the woman who called me back."

"And I called you back, did I, Steward?"

"You don't remember?"

A sea gull flew over and she lifted her chin to watch the flight. Yes, she remembered. She said, "He loves you, Steward."

"And you?" he asked, drawing on his breath.

"Aye, and I too," she admitted, wondering at these things, love and death. The sea gull was gone; there was only Steward, standing in the tussock.

"Then we will carry on," he said, taking her hand and moving them on. "We'll go back to London. Lloyd's will cash the Captain out, and he'll get himself another ship. And we'll sail again."

"I haven't been to Peru yet, Steward, or Ecuador."

"We'll take you. There are so many places to see."

"I wonder, though, if I want to see them anymore."

They came into the open. He dropped her hand. And wind to their backs this time and hands in their coat pockets, they passed again down the long row of houses on the one side of the singular road. They had just passed the doctor's house and his rose gardens when they heard a frightful wail. Only yards to the Surgery and the wail came again. "Stew'rd! Stew'rd! Oh save me! Stew'rd! They be gonna cut off me toes!"

Emily heard the child's cries simultaneous with the slap of the rising flag down at the jetty. A ship! Raise the flag to greet the ships! And there be the furled sails of the *Foam* slipping through the two hills of the harbor's entrance, and she, forgetting Steward and the boy and both their lonely cries, chased the wind to the jetty, collapsing dizzy and trembling and hardly able to draw breath in the shadow of the hulk, to wait. Richard, dear Richard, had come back.

28

Foam *rescued remainder of crew of* Maid of Athens, *London to Valparaiso, and took to Stanley.*

—Lloyd's List, 21/6/70

The Captain had to be carried to shore perfectly helpless and in pain so acute he couldn't find strength to even smile when Emily, with an anxious face, raced and bobbed alongside his stretcher, with Robinson and Smyley jogging him over the rough tundra. He saw the diamond-latticed windows of the Surgery and was unconscious before they could even roll him into a bed, and he did not rise from his stupor for three days.

He and the boy recovered together, the boy minus two toes, the Captain with his surprisingly intact. But he was weak and slow to pull out of the rheumatism. He had time, though. Not all ships putting into Port Stanley were bound for London.

One by one his crew found passage on other ships, shipping out to other destinations, signing on as deckhands whenever opportunity arose. First Lawson with his fair, and no longer sly, smile, then Fielding, face on the mend. Hayward and Oates went together. Only Sargent and Harris hung back, waiting for what yet may come—a sailor's life, with only memory now to hold them together.

April passed, the weather turned winter, and the Navy returned—without Bully Hayes. "He must be back in the South Pacific," Lieutenant Robinson sighed, and filed his report. Stanley fell into endless routine—endless monotony of agonizing time. Home was all Emily wanted, yet home remained as elusive as ever. April turned May, winter turned bitter, and just when Emily thought they might never get home, but live in Stanley forever, an English four-masted clipper bound for London put in.

The *Mary Catherine* cast anchor May 6, 1870, a Friday, on a pearly gray noon with a high, icy wind out of the south, sleet in her teeth, and she cast off with Steward aboard as assistant cook, Johnny—with his parakeet—as second cabin boy, Harris as foremast hand, and Emily and the Captain as passengers. Sargent they left behind, distant and removed but eyes filling with thwarted envy and hatred whenever the Captain and his wife passed by.

"Take good care of the Captain, ma'am," said Dr. Hamblin, standing on the jetty with Johnny's hand in his. "He's a good bloke. And this chap too." He handed off Johnny, Polly-wants-a-cracker faithfully perched atop his capped head. "Be a good man," he warned, heart obviously attached to his young patient. "You obey your Missus, and say your prayers."

"Better to sail on a Friday," hissed Harris with a grin, coming alongside to help her board the hulk, which would take them out to the ship, "than to sail with a woman."

"Mind a minute, Harris," she said, giving another hug to Mrs. Dean, one more teary embrace, and then she was standing in the hulk's stern next to Richard, leaning over the taffrail of the open boat, waving goodbye to the cluster of good people on the jetty, everyone, everything shrinking and blurring in the driving drizzle.

The wind turned southwest, blowing into a gale before they could even leave Port William, driving the majestic clipper into a tossing, foaming Atlantic Ocean. But the *Mary Catherine* took to the seas like a stallion to the open plains, shaking her mane and sails. Hands were ordered aloft to shake loose a reef in the snapping topsails. Hands at the halyards stood by, ready to masthead the topsail yards. *"Come all you young fellows who follow the sea—"*

For two days the gale winds blew. They made eight degrees of latitude, Cape Horn and the Falkland Islands falling well over the taffrail. Still the *Mary Catherine* ran gloriously on until at last the gale blew herself out, leaving the sun to rise high and quieter days to reign. Into this fine weather they galloped straight, sail after sail added until, a week out of the islands, the long topgallant masts were got up, topgallant and royal yards crossed, nothing between ship and shore but God's wind.

God's wind drove them on. The sun arched higher and the nights grew shorter. The Magellan Clouds and Southern Cross tipped in the horizon; constellations dropped right off to make room for the Northern stars, and then came the eve when the Northern Star twinkled—a joyous, pulsing beacon that told Emily as nothing else that they were closing in, every heave of the sea leaving behind them the end of the world, every hour bringing them to the center, to Greenwich Meridian, to London and home.

The Captain saw her joy; he had been watching her growing excitement juxtaposed to his growing depression. In the weeks since Smyley had carried him ashore into Stanley more dead than alive, the two of them had been careful not to discuss sailing again. He had assumed she would never consider leaving London once he got her home. Now he was sure. Hours she spent leaning over the rails, eyes focused beneath her pretty new bonnet to England ahead. Hours she spent, too, with Steward in the galley—wrangling their old debate of Dickens versus Johnson and more of Steward's odd ideas. She hungered to be home, where such things as intellectual discussion went on; theatre, too, and dance and dinner parties (preferable, he had to admit, to filling one's time stewing penguin over an open fire).

But Staten Island was not what sailing was all about, and he longed to interrupt her thoughts and dreams, to remind her of the adventure, of foreign ports still ahead . . . of new places to see, new people to meet, new customs and ideas to explore. But he couldn't, for thinking of her own waiting pleasures had put the sparkle back into her eyes, and each passing day she grew prettier and happier. Her lips had healed and the resiliency was even now coming back to her skin. She glowed, and he could not, he knew now, ever ask that she give up London again—not for adventure, and not for him.

They approached the Line at a clip, weather sizzling, alternating between scorching sun and sudden squalls, a routine easily predictable. First the clear sky, with a burning, vertical sun, men going lazily about their work in duck trousers, checked shirts, and straw hats. Men at the helm leaning over the wheel, hats over their eyes, the Captain below, snoozing through a nap, Emily and Richard leaning over the taffrail to watch a dolphin follow the wake and an albatross circle. Suddenly a cloud rises to windward.

The Captain moseys out the companion hatch to give eye to the growing cloud. The tub of yarns, the sail, the carpenter's tools—all are thrown below. The skylight and hatches are battened down. Royals are clewed up, fore and aft. Topgallant yards are clewed down and flying-jib hauled down, and in a minute drenching rain comes.

The squalls strike hard, but no one puts on jacket or cap. There isn't time. Besides, it's warm enough, and it's a bath.

"Keep her up to her course again!" the Mate will holler when no eye can yet see the calm but the force of the squall is gone.

"Keep her up, sir!"

"Hoist away the topgallant yards! Run up the flying jib! Lay aloft, you boys, and loose the royals!"

All sail is on again before they're out of the squall, racing on and on as if nothing has happened.

In these fair winds they crossed the Line, meeting the trade winds steady and strong. A week to ten days they cantered, the trades freshening the sea and giving them as much as they could carry in her royals, so that *Mary Catherine* sliced the seas and dashed up spray far ahead and to leeward, straining, straining, galloping now past latitude 22 N only to suddenly rein in, quivering, trade winds gone.

Abandoned. Only a light wind blew in from the south. By midnight it too was gone and the ship rocked in a dead calm under a heavy black cloud which shrouded the entire sky.

Emily awoke in the eerie stillness. "Richard, something be wrong." They both dressed and went on deck.

"Black as a pocket," he mumbled, squinting through black cloud to find any hint of moon or stars. Studdingsails were in, the royals furled. Other sails hung heavy, motionless from their yards. No one spoke, yet all hands were up, shadows, forms on the deck, everyone waiting, waiting for what? Not a breath stirred, stillness and darkness almost palpable. Past lantern light Emily could not see her fingers lifted in front of her face, and the blackness reminded her of another night. She grew afraid, and unconsciously flared her nostrils to sniff for smoke and flame. There was only empty, hollow air.

The mate eased past, moving aft and in a low tone, almost a whisper, calling the jib hauled down. The fore and mizzen-topgallant sails were taken in with uneasy expectation. Captain Brownlee walked the deck, boot thumps hollow in the dark. Emily took her husband's arm, the long suspense becoming painful.

"What, what is it?"

He pulled her into his arms. "A storm debates."

The mate came by again, ordering in low tone to clew up the main topgallant sail. The stealthy whisper of clewlines and buntlines whispered as men silently felt their way up the rigging and into the canvas.

"*Hoy!*"

Emily whirled. Aloft and alow everyone gasped, eyes riveted suddenly skyward to the top of the main topgallant masthead to gaze in awed silence at a giant, shimmering ball of light, pulsating with energy to stop the heart. Emily shrank back into her husband's arms.

"A corposant," he whispered, almost reverently; this was the first he'd seen of the rare phenomenon. "If it rises in the rigging," he said, explaining what all sailors understood, "it means we are to have fair weather. But if it sinks, there will be a dandy of a storm."

"It sinks," she whispered as men scrambled off the topgallant yardarm in haste—for if the sinking forewarned, resting light on your face was fatal.

"Where has it gone?" she wondered, blinking, seeing spots in black velvet. There, there it be, again on the fore topgallant yard. No, now it was on the flying-jib boomend. Only gradually did she become aware of falling rain, of a new shade of blackness being added to the night. Low thunder rattled off the horizon. Lightning flashed from the southwest, and the corposant, its warning delivered, vanished.

Rain, thunder, lightning, yet still no wind; only a few puffs to tease the remaining canvas, everything as still as death, and as dark. Suddenly a roar, a thunderous, ripping cry of fire, and the cloud overhead tore open without wind, dropping a wall of water, in one body, a falling ocean, and everyone stood motionless, stupefied, blinking in the running sea. Richard, drenched and coughing for breath, seized Emily and steered her back to the companion hatch, blindly groping for the door winking in and out of vision. But before he reached it the rain had ceased, leaving as quickly as it had come, leaving only the lightning to bear down in speedy gleams, the whole ocean a mirror of light—and they the only object on the whole of the ocean for a thousand miles: fixed, a mark to be shot at.

"A man is no sailor if he cannot sleep when he turns in," whispered Richard, pulling up the cold sheets.

"Then I be no sailor."

She spoke the truth. She was no sailor, and so for her he stayed awake, stroking her hair and rubbing her neck, humming quiet songs, until at last he had to whisper, "I told you I would get you home, Emily. As God is my witness, I shall." And he was sad, for her mind, if ever she debated, he knew was now resolved. They would never sail together again.

"All the starboard watch, ahoy!"

Dawn broke under sunny skies and fine breeze, and *Mary Catherine* was loping home, all sails set.

During the last weeks of June seaweed appeared. Every hour now meant they were pulling closer to land. Soon the stink of seaweed intoxicated the air, and the sailors were drunk from breathing it in, as ready as any to see land, and all hands on deck at dogwatch discussed nothing but getting in.

"Who'll go to church with me a week from today?"

"I will."

"Go away, saltwater, you ain't seen the insides of a church since you was in knickerbockers."

Laughter broke all around and there were quick puffs on the pipes.

"Nay, nay, nay! Soon as I get me legs I'm going to shoe me heels and button me ears! And start straight into the bush and not stop till I'm out of the sight a saltwater forever!"

"Belay that! You get moored stem and stern in old Jack's grogshop, with a coal fire ahead and bar under lee, and you won't never see daylight!"

A moderate breeze came up and fog came in. Suddenly from the bow, "Hard up on the helm!" A ship loomed out of the thick soup, bearing directly down on them. Emily, fixing herself a cup of tea in the galley, saw both ships luff, and skim past each other so close that the *Mary Catherine's* spanker boom grazed the other ship's quarter. The officer on deck only had time to hail. Back came the call of Bristol. *Bristol?*

"Oh, darling!" she cried, racing down deck. "I think we be nearly to the Channel! Come, come up top! Tell me what you see!"

But the fog continued on through the night, and the Captain could make no sense of their bearings. All the while Captain Brownlee crept them carefully and cautiously, but nonetheless easterly, sails furled and reefed, feeling their way.

When morning broke Emily and Richard went in for breakfast. They were just finishing when the fog thinned and a shout and a cry, and a rousing round of "Cheerily Men," broke from aloft. Emily and Richard tumbled hastily out the hatch, straining to see through the gauze. Plymouth! The Eddystone Light! Emily, stumbling over the lip, could hardly believe her eyes. *England?*

29

My fond heart beats quick, and my dim eyes run o'er,
When I muse on the last glance I gave to thy shore . . .

No home to which memory so fondly would turn,
No thought that within me so madly would burn . . .

Bless'd Isle of the Free! I must view thee no more;
My fortunes are cast on [a] distant shore . . .

In dreams, lovely England! my spirit still hails
Thy soft waving woodlands, thy green, daisied vales.

—Susanna Moody, circa 1850

They put into the Thames Mouth three days later, rounding the ridge of North Foreland just as the morning's sun pushed up the horizon in a bubble of gold. Emily, almost beside herself with anxiety to see Catherine, paced the deck, white stone in her pocket. The Captain sat in a chair out of the wind, going through his mind what papers were needed at Lloyds. Gravesend was sighted and Captain Brownlee ran up his flag.

The telegraph station picked up the signal. A tug put out. All crew hands scampered aloft to strip off the chafing gear in dawn's thin chill—battens, parcelings, roundings, hoops, mats, and leathers, all flying aloft and alow until nothing was left but the rigging, neat and clean. The tug came alongside, the hawser was hooked and the clipper eased up the Thames in the tug's wake. A small craft carrying three men sidled in.

"Where do you hail?" hollered up a hardboiled bloke, dressed in tweed, derby launched to one side of his head. *Dirty shark,* thought Emily, knowing he was a boarding-house runner sent to lure sailors into debt.

"In from Calcutta!" hollered a Jack, throwing down a line from the crowded rail.

"How long you been on this hooker?" the man asked, tying up his launch.

"Three years!"

"A lime-juicer, ain't she?" hollered up another of the three below. "Jump ship! We got a boarding house, good food! Jobs what don't have no night watches! And we got newspapers! Cards, anyone?"

Newspapers! Emily leaned over the rail with the rest, grabbing, tipping too far over and nearly going into the drink. "No! A newspaper!" and she threw off the tin of cards.

"Here ye go, ma'am," volunteered a sailor, snatching one for her.

"Oh, thank you!" she cried, breathless and exultant, hardly able to believe the touch of damp newspaper in her hand. *The London Daily Times?* Oh, they *had* to be home! And she started to cry, the black print blurring in her tears.

"I want a message! Telegraphed to London! Can you do it?"

Richard?

He swung off the rail, handing down a leather pouch.

"And who are you?" the man in tweed demanded. "Aye, it don't matter, not with the pounds in yer fist, sir! And what be the message?"

"Mrs. George Wainwright. Home tonight. Open Kensington house and put on fire. Bring all haste another copy of Dickens."

"Dickens, sir? And which one'll—?"

"She'll know."

Richard landed with both feet in the waist, startled to see, through the press of men, Emily weeping.

"Dickens be dead. He died! He be dead! Oh, Richard! See?" She held up a newspaper, snapping it stiff. He read quickly—something to do with the estate, some sort of confusion over the first wife's settlement. "June 9th!" Emily cried, tears streaming down her face. "He died just three days after we left the Falklands!"

He pulled her into his arms, alarmed and amazed. "I don't understand," he whispered, hugging her close. "After all you've survived, darling, why do you weep for Charles Dickens?"

"I don't know, I don't know. But he be dead and it makes me sad, and—"

"Oh, darling, darling, we're home! I've brought you home!"

It took the day to sail up the Thames, pulling against the wind. Nine o'clock in the evening they at last slid beneath Tower Bridge and eased past Execution Dock. Ahead London Bridge beckoned. They slipped beneath the moss-covered stone, sun dropping to greet them in a shower of royal colors, spilling flames of firelight over the river and inflaming the city spread before them.

Emily stood at the rail, sunset and tears obscuring familiar dear landmarks. St. Paul's Cathedral. The distant spires of Westminster Abbey. London's Tower. Center of the world, and she had sailed 10,000 miles from off the map to come back! Oh, but here, in London, Dickens had died. What did it matter then *where* one lived? Suddenly the clangor of church bells, wild and sweet, ringing, singing through London's cobblestone streets, and she was swept back to Staten Island and the chime of the dented ship's bell, last struck the day they'd split camps. But these were ringing, singing, clamoring bells, calling men to sea, to church, to school, to weddings . . . and finally, for them all, on land or on sea, to their end. What mattered then was not *where* one lived, but *how*?

"None of this is quite like we planned, is it, darling?" Richard took her hand, staring somberly out to the bustle of the approaching wharf as one by one the St. Paul Cathedral bells now rang out the hour in deep and hollow knells—wild, sweet music mingling with one thought for Emily: It mattered not *where* one lived, but *how*.

"No. It be not quite like we planned," she said, thinking clearly again. "But darling? We can try again."

"To sail again? Together? Do you mean it?" he asked, and he took her face in his calloused hands, searching for the truth. Yes, there, in the dark oval pools of chestnut eyes, where he could always find all that mattered in the world, was her answer, and a reflection of his own grateful smile.

"Can we do it, though?" she asked anxiously. "Can you get another ship? Do we have money—"

"Insurance, darling. Lloyds of London will send for the salvaged cargo, and they'll outfit another ship, aye."

She smiled her sweet, pretty smile and the last bell rang. A whistle wheezed. *Mary Catherine* rounded off the end of the wharf.

"Heave ho! And tie off!"

"I love you, Emily."

The gangway opened, the decks filled, people swarmed aboard ship. *"Get out of my way!"* Catherine stood on the midship capstan three feet off the deck, shoulders thrown back, voice clear and shrill above the babble, and Emily tore herself loose from her husband's arms, hands to her skirts, leaping the coiled-up buntlines, dodging the cleats and henhouses, ducking between a boarding-house runner and a wary sailor.

"You be late," said Catherine all too saucily from her lofty height, cocky and pretty and red cape thrown back.

"Aye, but I be here." Breathless, laughing, looking up.

"Aye, that you be!" and Catherine, leaping nimbly to the deck and with an exultant whoop, pulled Emily into her arms, now laughing, now crying. "I've brought you a new Dickens!" she whispered, pulling her close.

Aye, Emily thought with a triumphant smile, smelling the sweet scent of her sister's skin and seeing a peek of the Captain press his way through the crowd, it *had* been the best of times, and the worst. And seeing Steward, Harris, and Johnny in the Captain's tow she knew too that none of them were ready yet to find their better rest. Oh, someday they would. But not today, not tomorrow.

"Emily, there be a new author, one of Dickens' protegees. You're going to have to read her," said Catherine, steering them off the ship and up onto the dock and waiting carriage that would take her home to her own fire and grate and cozy bedchamber with paneled walls. "I would have brought it with me, with Dickens— Elizabeth Gaskell is her name, she's a minister's wife and all of England is talking about her, but Effie—"

"Catherine? I have brought you something."

"Aye, and what can it be?"

And in the surge of the bustling crowd, coming and going, shouts colliding with the cry of the gulls, Emily lay in her dear sister's hand a small and single white stone, beacon of distant shores.

People Making A Difference

Family Bookshelf offers the finest in good wholesome Christian literature, written by best-selling authors. All books are recommended by an Advisory Board of distinguished writers and editors.

We are also a vital part of a compassionate outreach called **Bowery Mission Ministries**. Our evangelical mission is devoted to helping the destitute of the inner city.

Our ministries date back more than a century and began by aiding homeless men lost in alcoholism. Now we also offer hope and Gospel strength to homeless, inner-city women and children. Our goal, in fact, is to end homelessness by teaching these deprived people how to be independent with the Lord by their side.

Downtrodden, homeless men are fed and clothed and may enter a discipleship program of one-on-one professional counseling, nutrition therapy and Bible study. This same Christian care is provided at our women and children's shelter.

We also welcome nearly 1,000 underprivileged children each summer at our Mont Lawn Camp located in Pennsylvania's beautiful Poconos. Here, impoverished youngsters enjoy the serenity of nature and an opportunity to receive the teachings of Jesus Christ. We also provide year-round assistance through teen activities, tutoring in reading and writing, Bible study, family counseling, college scholarships and vocational training.

During the spring, fall and winter months, our children's camp becomes a lovely retreat for religious gatherings of up to 200. Excellent accommodations include heated cabins, chapel, country-style meals and recreational facilities. Write to Paradise Lake Retreat Center, Box 252, Bushkill, PA 18324 or call: (717) 588-6067.

Still another vital part of our ministry is **Christian Herald magazine**. Our dynamic, bimonthly publication focuses on the true personal stories of men and women who, as "doers of the Word," are making a difference in their lives and the lives of others.

Bowery Mission Ministries are supported by voluntary contributions of individuals and bequests. Contributions are tax deductible. Checks should be made payable to Bowery Mission.

 Fully accredited Member of the Evangelical Council for Financial Accountability

Every Monday morning, our ministries staff joins together in prayer. If you have a prayer request for yourself or a loved one, simply write to us.

 Administrative Office: 40 Overlook Drive, Chappaqua, New York 10514 Telephone: (914) 769-9000